Praise for *Daughter of Calabria*
Previously published as *Echoes of War*

'Blanchard at her breathtaking best.
Rich in every sight, taste and smell.'
Australian Women's Weekly

'Richly imagined, heartbreaking and utterly captivating . . .
yet another outstanding piece of historical fiction from
Blanchard, cementing her place at the top of this genre.'
Better Reading

'This is emotional reading for anyone born of immigrant
stock as it explores the pain of leaving your homeland
and your family to find opportunity elsewhere . . .
an entertaining tale of fiction that will make your
heart melt and sing and shatter.'
Glam Adelaide

'A powerful novel about powerful women . . . a powerful
evocation of a time, a place and a cultural vision which
provided a significant boost to Australia's population and
its development as a multi-cultural destination of choice
for refugees – both voluntary and choiceless.'
Carpe Librum

Also by Tania Blanchard

The Girl from Munich
Suitcase of Dreams
Letters from Berlin

DAUGHTER
OF
CALABRIA

TANIA BLANCHARD

SIMON &
SCHUSTER

London · New York · Sydney · Toronto · New Delhi

DAUGHTER OF CALABRIA
First published in Australia in 2021 by
Simon & Schuster (Australia) Pty Limited
Level 4, 32 York Street, Sydney, NSW 2000

10 9 8 7 6 5 4 3 2

New York Amsterdam Antwerp London Toronto Sydney New Delhi
Visit our website at www.simonandschuster.com.au

A catalogue record for this
book is available from the
National Library of Australia

ISBN: 9781761104749

Cover design: Christa Moffitt
Cover images: Ildiko Neer/Trevillion Images
Typeset by Midland Typesetters, Australia
Printed and bound in Australia by Griffin Press

The paper this book is printed on is certified against the Forest
Stewardship Council® Standards. Griffin Press – a member of the
Opus Group holds chain of custody certification SCS-COC-001185.
FSC® promotes environmentally responsible, socially beneficial and
economically viable management of the world's forests.

For the amazing women of my family. Their strength, tenacity and perseverance are a continual source of inspiration.

Love is the crowning grace of humanity, the holiest right of the soul, the golden link which binds us to duty and truth, the redeeming principle that chiefly reconciles the heart to life, and is prophetic of eternal good.

Francesco Petrarch

1

February, 1936
Calabria, Southern Italy

I followed the nun in a haze of exhaustion. I had been trying to memorise the turns along the corridors of the monastery, but when we finally stopped, I realised that I was utterly lost.

'Here we are,' said the nun, opening the door to my cell. 'You'll find it has everything you need.' She smiled encouragingly. 'It will feel like home before you know it.'

'Grazie, sorella,' I said in a small voice.

'One of the sisters will take you to see Mother Superior in the morning. Buona notte,' she said, before turning back down the long corridor.

I raised my lantern and surveyed the tiny room. A wave of loneliness overcame me and I burst into tears. I'd never been away from home before and I already missed my family.

The single bed against the whitewashed wall was covered with a sheepskin spread, with another sheepskin on the stone floor under the narrow window. The plain cell was more than I was used to. I'd never had the luxury of privacy and freedom of my own space before – but it wasn't home. How would I ever sleep without the comfort of my sister Paola's warm body next to me and the soft sleepy noises of my oldest sister Teresa in the bed beside us?

I sat heavily on the bed. I was so far from everyone I loved and it was my own fault. My family would be celebrating the last night before Teresa's wedding, enjoying a specially cooked meal. I could picture them laughing, singing and dancing to the music of fiddles and accordions, as our neighbours and friends joined in. The view of the village from our hillside farm, about a fifteen-minute walk from our home, flashed through my mind: the tumble of red terracotta roofs and white lime-washed walls on the river flats. Bruzzano was a small village situated on the very tip of the toe of Italy, just a stone's throw from the island of Sicily. The Bruzzano River ran right alongside the town, moving slowly towards the east coast, while the Aspromonte Mountains towered around it, stretching to the very edges of Calabria's coastline like guardians. A wave of fresh tears turned into gasping sobs as I collapsed into the comfort of the sheepskin.

Two days earlier, Papà had summoned me to the dining table, his face like thunder. At forty-two, he was fit and strong from all the work on the land and, despite the long hours and constant worry over whether we'd have enough food to keep us going for another year, he didn't look his age; his hair was still thick with only a few strands of grey that glinted

2

against the black curls. He often told us that his grey hairs had sprouted because he had to provide for five children, and when I looked at Mamma, who did the most for us, three years younger than Papà but her hair streaked with grey, I thought maybe he was right. Vincenzo was the oldest of us at twenty-one, then Teresa a year younger. Paola, eighteen, was nearly two years older than me and then there was Antonio, who was fourteen. But I was the one who gave him the most grief.

'Did you look after the sheep yesterday for Vincenzo?' he asked as he finished off his café e latte.

'No, Papà,' I whispered, standing before him in bare feet on the tiles. But I had covered for Vincenzo, who was supposed to look after the sheep on our thirty-acre farm. As shepherd, it was his job to keep them safe from wild animals, especially wolves, but he'd wanted to visit a girl, his latest *amore*, in the village, before he left for Africa with the army. He had taken his best friends, Stefano and Angelo Modaferi, cousins who lived in the next village, with him to act as lookout. Although the cousins were just like brothers to us, spending as much time at our home while we were growing up as Vincenzo did at theirs, sometimes I wasn't sure I liked them, despite their jokes and clowning around. They could be dismissive, arrogant and annoying: pulling our hair, taking our biscotti and refusing to let us play football because we were girls.

But I didn't mind helping Vincenzo because, when I did, I felt like I was a part of a world that was carefree and wild. I longed for the freedoms the boys had.

Papà stared at me, his dark eyes, usually filled with kindness for his daughters, hard as obsidian. 'Don't lie to me, Giulia.'

'I'm not.' I knew how much trouble Vincenzo would be in if Papà found out he was sneaking away rather than doing his work. Papà had caught me telling lies more than a few times, but there was no way he could know the truth this time. I'd been so careful and even though one of the boys from the adjoining farm had come across to play cards and offered me my first cigarette, I'd only taken one puff before giving it back.

'Mamma mia!' He slammed the table. 'Then who did? Because he was seen in the village when he was supposed to be with the sheep. If anything had happened to even one of them . . .'

I flinched and swallowed hard. 'Whoever thinks they saw him must be mistaken,' I lied. I was in too deep now to come clean.

'Testa dura!' Papà rumbled, his hands pressed together as if asking for God's help. 'You told your mother you were going to help Zia Francesca at the trattoria but I was talking to Signora Lipari at the post office this morning and she said she saw you walking in the opposite direction, towards the farm and worse still, that her nephew saw you in the field.' He shook his head. 'I don't know where to begin. It's bad enough that you were smoking cigarettes but you were alone with a boy and you're still lying to me? You know how much I hate lying! I'm so very disappointed in you.' My heart fell.

'But Papà—'

He put his hand up to stop me. 'Basta! Enough, Giulia! You will go nowhere until I'm satisfied that you've learnt your lesson. For a girl your age, you should know better. I thought you'd learnt after the incident with the bicycle.'

I dropped my gaze. I'd taken the bicycle without asking, to borrow a white blouse I was supposed to wear as part of my uniform for the weekly Fascist parade. I'd hidden my blouse, which had a large mud stain and a tear from chasing Antonio after the last parade. The only problem was that I'd got a flat tyre on the way home. Mamma found out about the blouse and the tyre cost a lot for Papà to have fixed.

'I've indulged you and tolerated your impetuous ways for far too long. You have to learn obedience and your place in this village, because this is where you belong.'

I saw red. 'I'll never belong here!' I shouted. 'And why do I have to do what I'm told when the boys do whatever they want?'

'Because it's the way things are done. If you don't learn some respect and you keep on like this, nobody will want you.'

'I don't care! Damn the way things are done. Why would I want to be stuck here in a dead-end village with people who can't see beyond their own noses?'

Papà got up so quickly his chair crashed to the ground. 'I've a good mind to find you a husband who'll tame your wild ways and teach you respect.'

'I'd rather die than marry anyone you want me to.' We were nose to nose.

'Go to your room!' bellowed Papà. 'And don't come out until you're ready to see sense.'

'Well, that would be never!' I screamed, turning on my heel and rushing to my bedroom, slamming the door behind me.

The memory of that fight still made my blood boil. Sobbing, I buried my face in the sheepskin and pounded my pillow with fury until I was spent.

I took a shuddering breath and stared at the shadows the lantern made on the cell wall. I was here now and had to make the best of it. Somehow, the Madonna had heard my prayers and given me an opportunity to do what I'd always dreamed of.

I'd finished school nearly two years earlier, at the age of fourteen. At first, I helped Papà on the farm with Paola. As well as tending our flock of sheep, we planted wheat and had an olive grove, a small orchard of citrus trees and some grape vines for wine. We raised pigs, chickens and goats, and had our milking cow Bella and our donkey Benito, named after Il Duce, Prime Minister Mussolini. I helped milk the sheep and prepared the milk for cheesemaking, threshed wheat at harvest time to separate the grain to be milled into bread and pasta flour and picked olives to be crushed for oil, grapes for wine, and the citrus fruits. I never seemed to do my chores as well as Paola and I usually disappeared as soon as I could to spend time with my Nonna Mariana, Mamma's mother, who was a maga, a traditional folk healer.

I'd always been interested in healing and I loved walking with her as she picked wild herbs from the surrounding hills and explained how to find them and what they were good for. I enjoyed watching her in her busy clinic, which she ran from the front room of her house, choosing herbs to treat someone's illness. But spending time with Nonna was another thing that Papà had forbidden, after his younger sister had died following treatment from a woman who called herself a maga but was really a strega, who practised witchcraft. He never went as far as stopping Nonna from visiting us at home because he knew it would break Mamma's heart. He reluctantly accepted her place in our family, on the condition that she never treat any of us.

Even though Papà yelled at me time after time and punished me for disobeying him, I continued to sneak away to Nonna's whenever I could. Finally, he decided that I'd be better off working in his sister's trattoria, where I could be kept busy helping Zia Francesca prepare and cook meals. Whenever I wasn't needed at the restaurant, I was helping Paola on the farm.

Papà didn't realise Zia Francesca gave me freedoms he would never allow. After her customers were gone, she often let me look through glamorous magazines that came from the big cities of the north, like Milano. The women in these magazines were dressed so differently from me, in clothes that looked like they were designed for lives of purpose and independence. There had even been an advertisement for women to join the Red Cross as volunteer nurses. Could women become more than wives and mothers, forever controlled by their husbands and fathers, despite the Catholic Church's rules and the Fascist teachings we had drummed into us at school? If the women in these magazines could choose how they lived, perhaps I could find a way to do the same. I wasn't going to live my life like a prisoner.

After my fight with Papà, I decided to run away. I would join the Red Cross in Reggio and become a nurse rather than marry the husband Papà would choose for me, trapping me in the village. Reggio, the biggest city in Calabria and the capital of our province, was over forty miles away on the opposite, west coast.

I'd packed my few belongings and was walking the road to the coast, where I'd meet the bus to Reggio, when Zia Francesca caught up with me. She begged me to come back before anyone saw me, telling me she had an idea to get me what I wanted.

Back at the trattoria, I waited in the kitchen making the sugo for the evening's menu while Zia Francesca, Mamma and Nonna Mariana talked in hushed whispers.

'What are we going to do?' Mamma whispered in a panic. 'Mannaggia! I know she's strong-willed but I never thought she'd do something like this. If Andrea finds out . . .'

'She's safe now, Gabriella,' said Nonna soothingly.

'But she can't stay here and I'm worried that if she comes home, she'll do something stupid or try to run away again the next time she and Andrea fight.'

Hearing Mamma's deep sigh, I hunched over the pot, ashamed I'd disappointed her. She was right, I couldn't go back home. If Papà found out I'd tried to run away, my life was as good as over. Family honour meant everything and my actions would only bring shame on my family. And even if he didn't find out what I'd done, I couldn't forgive him for what he'd said. The memory of that morning flared my anger, hot and explosive, once more. I took a breath to calm myself.

'Allora, so, I have an idea,' said Zia Francesca. 'Maybe we can solve this problem and at the same time get the education that Giulia needs to fulfil her desire to become the type of healer that Andrea would approve of.'

'Basta!' said Mamma abruptly. 'We've been through this before. Andrea won't hear of it.'

I crept to the door to hear better and peered at the three women, their dark and grey heads together. It was reassuring to see Nonna Mariana, her long hair plaited into braids and twisted onto the back of her head. She was always a steadfast and calming presence.

'Mariana, didn't you once tell me that you know the renowned herbalist Fra Fortunato?' asked Zia Francesca. She was immaculate as always in a tailored skirt and blouse that Teresa had no doubt made for her from fabric sourced in Milano. Her long hair was parted in the middle and swept up in a fashionable knot at the back of her head, no strand out of place. I touched my own hair briefly. Like hers, it was thick and black, but unruly and hastily tied into a braid, loose pieces snaking down my back and around my face.

'Si,' said Nonna, her eyebrows raised in surprise.

'And that he now resides at the Monastery of the Madonna where you know the abbess?' Zia continued. 'With your connections, Giulia could go and study herbalism under the tutelage of the monks.'

I was taken aback by this new revelation. Perhaps there was more to Nonna than I knew.

'What do you think?' Zia asked, looking from my grandmother to my mother. I felt sure she was holding her breath, just as I was.

Mamma shook her head. 'Do you really think it's possible?' she asked. Her curly brown hair spread around her head like a halo. As least I knew where I got my unmanageable locks from.

Nonna squeezed Mamma's hand, her luminous green eyes beseeching. I had inherited Nonna's eyes, less common in this part of Calabria. 'Giulia has a gift from God and it would be an affront to Jesus and the Madonna if she was not allowed to develop her talents.' She shrugged an apology. 'Fra

9

Fortunato's knowledge of herbal medicine is second to none, not just of our local plants, but of other Italian and European remedies too. And if Giulia's half as good as I think she'll be, she'll make a decent living. People will come from all over the region to see her once her reputation spreads.'

Butterflies fluttered in my stomach at her words. I'd often wondered about the strong connection I had with her and how we just knew what was wrong with somebody when they weren't feeling well.

Calabria was an ancient place and its history of healing dated back thousands of years. Many rituals and traditions were passed down generation to generation, mother to daughter, and most maghe used 'the old ways', a combination of herbal treatments, common-sense remedies, superstition and the power of faith in God, Jesus, the Madonna and all of the saints of the Catholic Church, to help people to feel better. Nonna carried on the traditions that many locals expected her to use. As she had explained to me, there were many ways to treat illness, but if a patient didn't believe in what you were doing, it was much harder – if not impossible – to heal them.

'But what about Andrea?' said Mamma, pulling her hand away in frustration. 'He'll never allow it.' Mamma had happily given up any thought of being a healer to marry Papà; her passion didn't run as deep as mine and Nonna's, even though she had talent. Nonna's world was the realm of women and magic, unfathomable and uncontrollable, something Papà didn't understand. But what upset Papà the most was Nonna's treatment of people affected by il malocchio, the evil eye. He believed she resorted to witchcraft to treat such cases.

Zia Francesca nodded. 'I've thought about that . . .' She put her head close to Mamma and Nonna, even though they were alone. 'Andrea doesn't have to know that she's studying, only that she's learning how to behave from the nuns.'

Mamma shook her head, eyes wide with alarm.

'Think about it, Gabriella,' said Nonna firmly. 'This could be a good opportunity to give Giulia and Andrea time apart, give them a chance to calm down, and for Giulia to think about her future with a level head without the worry that she'll run away again. Andrea gets what he wants too – a disciplined daughter.'

I wasn't sure how I felt about the idea of going to the monastery. It was an isolated place high in the mountains not too far from here. The thought of joining the Red Cross had been filled with adventure; spending my days with monks and nuns sounded dull in comparison. But I knew I'd go anywhere to learn any form of healing. And if it took me away from Papà and his anger, even better.

'But what happens when she comes home?' Mamma said.

'Since she's not yet ready for marriage, once she's gained skills in a reputable manner, she can bring in a proper income for the family. Surely Andrea can't object to that?' If Nonna thought this was a good idea, then maybe it was a way to get what I wanted: a purpose for my life besides marriage and children.

'I want Giulia to be happy too, but it's just not possible,' said Mamma, her voice rising in desperation. She dropped her head into her hands and my heart dropped too. Of course it was too good to be true.

'This is the perfect opportunity to help her do the work she was born to do,' Zia Francesca said. 'If somebody saw her on the road and my brother finds out, especially after he caught her lying again, the monastery's far enough away to keep her safe and they'll both have time to come to their senses.' She hesitated. 'I know it means deceiving Andrea, but this is Giulia's future. All that matters to my brother is taming Giulia's wild ways and if she learns a craft in the process, then surely he'll be happy she's bringing in an income, just like Teresa.' Zia looked pleased with herself and I had to admit that I couldn't see a single hole in her argument. My sister Teresa always did what was expected of her and Papà had supported her wish to become a dressmaker. I wasn't sure about being tamed by the nuns but if it meant Papà would let me work as a healer . . .

Mamma sighed. 'I want Giulia to have a chance. But we'd have to make a plan to convince him.'

'Then it's settled,' said Nonna Mariana, smiling broadly and sagging back into her chair with relief. 'We'll arrange for her to go as soon as possible, otherwise who knows what she might do next.'

'What about Giulia?' asked Mamma. 'We should make sure she's happy about this.'

'Oh, she knows,' said Zia Francesca with a smirk. 'She's been listening at the door this whole time and hasn't been stirring my sugo.'

Papà had agreed to send me to the monastery after Mamma and Zia Francesca spoke to him about an opportunity to work there that had become available. Hard work and discipline were all I needed, they reminded him, not the threat of a husband.

The night air seeping through the stone walls of the cell was enough to force me from my stupor. I changed out of my dress and into my nightgown, slipping between the coarse sheets on the small bed, desperate to get warm. If only I was still in the kitchen at the trattoria, surrounded by the rich aromas, talking and laughing with Zia Francesca, warm, happy and content. My stomach grumbled loudly. I knew I should be grateful for being here but I was finding it hard to be thankful. I missed my mother, brothers and sisters, Nonna, and Zia Francesca's cheerful disposition and optimism. I still couldn't believe I wasn't at Teresa's wedding. Had it been only this morning that Zia drove me to the village at the bottom of the mountain pass where Fra Giacomo, a monk from the monastery, waited for me with his cart loaded with supplies?

'Forza! Take this opportunity with both hands,' Mamma had said as we parted. 'Make us proud. Study hard and do what the nuns and monks ask of you. When you come home, what happened between you and your father will be forgotten.'

Papà had barely looked at me as he'd muttered a gruff goodbye before he'd left for the farm that morning, which made me even more angry.

'He might forget, but I won't.'

Mamma touched my cheek. 'He loves you and wants the best for you but he doesn't understand what it's like to be a young woman with her life just beginning. You're passion-ate and stubborn like he is. Just remember: if we're smart, we can get what we want, even in a man's world. But you have to be sensible. We rarely get second chances.'

My father might think that this was a way to subdue my wild ways, to remind me of my responsibilities as a young woman, but I saw this as an opportunity to improve my life.

But only with my first sight of the monastery as the sun began to fall behind the mountain peaks had the enormity of what I'd done hit me.

'Home – there's no better sight,' Fra Giacomo had said with a sigh.

Home . . . I had never been so far from my home before. How was I going to manage among strangers without the love and support of my family for seven months?

Tears fell down my cheeks as I huddled under the covers. Tomorrow I would meet Mother Superior and I needed to make a good impression to prove that I deserved to be here. Without her support, I'd never last long enough to learn all I needed to become a herbalist – and change my path.

2

I woke to the sound of bells ringing in the pre-dawn light and a knock on the door of my cell.

'Buongiorno, signorina,' said the nun, placing a jug of water and a basin on the table. 'I'm Sister Agata and I'll take you to see Mother Superior.'

I nodded, shivering with excitement and nervousness, then she was gone again, to wait outside while I dressed. After a good night's sleep I was feeling much better, more optimistic. I was surprised that I'd slept so well despite being all alone in a strange place, but yesterday had been long and draining. My mind raced with the possibilities ahead of me. I was finally free of Papà's controlling ways and about to learn from one of the best herbalists in Calabria. I was anxious too, worried that I wouldn't be good enough. But I was determined to do my best.

After a quick wash, I plaited my hair into a thick braid and dressed in a fresh dress and woollen tights, then followed the nun down the deserted corridor.

'Where is everybody?' I whispered.

'At morning prayers,' she said. 'Nervous?' I nodded and she smiled in encouragement. 'Don't be. Mother Superior Maria won't bite.'

Before I knew it, I was being ushered into Mother Superior's study and a gust of warmth from the crackling fire enveloped me. The abbess sat behind a massive desk neatly stacked with books and papers. The walls were covered in shelves filled with more books. My reading was rusty and I wondered what it might be like to be able to read any book from cover to cover.

Mother Superior Maria's alert blue eyes, nestled in the wrinkled skin of her pale, round face, regarded me with interest. Her face was the only part of her uncovered besides her hands: she wore a white wimple over a long black habit and there was a black veil on her head. She also wore the pectoral cross as a sign of her authority.

'Buongiorno, Signorina Tallariti,' she said, standing. 'Please, sit.' She gestured to the chair on the opposite side of the desk.

'Grazie, Mother Superior,' I murmured, sitting carefully.

'You've arrived at a very unusual time, right in the dead of winter, but perhaps it's God's will that you come among us now,' she began. Her eyes narrowed, fixing me with a razor sharp gaze and her keen intelligence. I shrank back in the chair, sure that she'd worked out why I was here, but she only sat again and sighed. 'Because by spring, when the roads open to pilgrims, Fra Fortunato will be too busy with the Festival of the Madonna to begin your studies. You'll stay with us until after the festa. I know that living in a convent will feel very strange, but if you follow our rules and routines, you'll find that we're a nurturing community who can support you and your vocation. Now, Sister Agata will take you to breakfast, then show you around and take you to your first lesson with Fra Fortunato. She'll explain life here at the convent and make sure you have everything you need.'

I was dismissed.

According to Sister Agata, Fra Fortunato had been well known and respected right across the south of Italy for over thirty years. Pilgrims often travelled from afar, visiting him during the festival of the Madonna of the Mountain where he sold his tonics and teas. With my father's bias against traditional medicine and only the little snatches of time I'd spent with Nonna Mariana, I'd never heard of him.

I had expected Fra Fortunato to be a tall, imperious man who might be impatient with a village girl's basic education. It was a surprise to find that he was ordinary and rather short, wearing plain black robes. I was struck by his kindly face. I could tell immediately that there was something special about him and after spending only a little time with him, I knew that everything that was said about him was true.

'The most commonly found herbs are often the most useful,' he said to me not long after I'd started my lessons. We were in his work room, poring over the drawings and descriptions of herbs and their uses in the massive books he pulled from the shelves that lined one wall. Glass jars of dried herbs were organised along shelves on the opposite wall and drying racks lay to one side of the room, bare until fresh herbs could be gathered in the spring. A long bench with a collection of mortars and pestles ran underneath a large window that looked out over the mountains and the snow-covered landscape. 'Take chamomile, for example. It grows almost anywhere but prefers a sunny location. Do you know what part of the plant is used?'

'The flower,' I said, pleased I'd taken notice when my mother made us chamomile tea when we were upset or restless at night.

'Very good. The whole flower can be used but the centre of the flower is most effective.'

We spent the mornings going over the theory, learning the names and uses of herbs and plants, learning to recognise what they looked like fresh and dry and what parts were useful for different ailments. In the afternoons I learnt about the herbs' practical applications while we tended to Fra Fortunato's garden, kept in a special glass house, or while he pounded the dry herbs in his work room to make tinctures. Fra Fortunato was a patient teacher but he expected me to remember what he taught, moving quickly to the next plant or condition. The rows of books on his shelves made me realise that there was so much to know and I wondered if I would learn enough in the time I was here.

'And do you know what chamomile is good for?' He handed me the open bottle of dried chamomile and I breathed in the sweet grassy scent, a little like cut hay.

'To calm and relax. And for women's troubles,' I said, remembering how my mother would give us girls chamomile tea for our monthly pain, but feeling a little uncomfortable talking about such things.

He nodded. 'Yes, but not just women's cramps – cramps of all internal organs. It helps calm the stomach and is useful for digestive disorders, stomach cramps, indigestion, anxiety and overexcitement, especially in children. I've also used it as a soothing wash for skin irritations. It's one of my most-used herbs.' He reached across the bench and handed me a length of dried root. 'This grows all over Calabria. Do you know its medicinal uses?'

I rolled the root between my fingers, the distinctive smell unmistakable. Liquorice was harvested by the monks in the autumn and they spent winter making liqueur, while the nuns produced confectionery and lozenges by pressing the malleable black resin into shapes and moulds. Calabrese liquorice was famous for its natural sweetness, making it popular right across Italy.

'Liquorice!' I thought for a moment, recollecting why my mother had occasionally allowed us to suck on a small piece. 'It's for coughs and constipation.'

He nodded. 'It might not surprise you that it's also useful to improve energy levels in those who are constantly busy. Can you think of a particular type of person who would benefit from liquorice?'

'Yes,' I said, thinking of my sister Teresa.

'So, you see both these common plants have many uses and I'm sure most households are aware of some of them, but I will teach you how certain personalities have an affinity to certain plants and why each herb is used in particular conditions and how it can be used with other herbs.'

'I can't wait,' I said, smiling broadly.

It didn't take long for the routine of life at the monastery to feel like home, familiar and busy. I'd been assigned chores to fit in around my lessons with Fra Fortunato of two hours in the morning and two hours in the afternoon. I was up before dawn with the nuns to pray at Lauds, then helped in the convent kitchen to prepare a light breakfast to be served after the Prime prayers. After breakfast and before my morning lesson, I was put to work chopping vegetables for the main meal of the day, lunch. Most people in the countryside normally had dried beans, chickpeas or fresh vegetables and could only afford to eat meat occasionally. My family killed a pig once or twice a year for meat, making sausages and salami and soap from the rendered pork fat mixed with lye. The monastery was no different. The head cook was a nun who'd fed her flock for years, able to make a substantial meal from the simplest of ingredients. As soon as she discovered that I'd worked in Zia Francesca's kitchen, she gave me greater responsibility and began to share snippets of advice. I washed dishes, swept and mopped floors and helped in any way I was asked. I didn't mind. Unlike at home, where Papà expected me to obey no matter what, here I was always treated kindly and with respect and there was the added benefit of gaining an education.

Sister Agata had been designated my companion, reminding me of the routines and rules of the monastery and helping me to adjust to life in the convent, and I was grateful for all the thoughtful ways she made me feel more at ease. When I mentioned that I was struggling with my lessons, especially reading the Italian texts, she offered to help me. I'd had little chance to practise my formal Italian since I'd left school, using mostly the local Calabrese dialect in my day-to-day life. The process was painstaking, but we spent time following my afternoon lesson with Fra Fortunato each day, going over

Italian newspapers and progressing to harder books. I learnt that Agata was in her early twenties and had been with the nuns for about seven years.

'I was fifteen and refused to marry the man my father chose for me,' she said one afternoon as she sifted through the pile of books she'd picked out from the library for me to read. We were in our usual corner of the cloister where we sat each afternoon. 'He was an old man with grandchildren of his own, but had a good-sized farm and a respectable income. My parents thought they were providing for my future, but I didn't want to marry an old man. Already then I knew that I wanted to care for the sick and dying and I could never do that if I was married. But there was no money to send me away to become a nurse.'

'How did you come to be here?'

'The decision was taken out of my hands. I couldn't remain at home without contributing an income to the family and I had no skills. But God was watching over me and He knew my deepest desire. My parents insisted that I join the nuns if I was adamant I wasn't going to marry. That's when I realised that this was the only way I could care for the sick and so I agreed.

'I cared for tuberculosis sufferers at the sanatorium in Napoli for five years and it didn't take long to realise that my heart belonged to God and that my work was an expression of my love for Him. I met Mother Superior Maria there and joined her when she became abbess here. It's a far cry from the sanatorium, but I needed a rest.'

'It must have been tiring work, caring for the sick and dying.'

She smiled, hesitating before answering. 'I became infected with tuberculosis.'

I gasped. 'You have the disease?'

She shrugged. 'Maybe. All I know for sure is that I carry it, but I'm well enough and not contagious. I may never develop the active disease but Mother Superior recommended I join her here to rest while I'm under the care of Fra Fortunato. His herbal treatments will make me strong. One day I might return to nurse the sick or perhaps, like you, I'll learn from Fra Fortunato and become a herbalist too. For now, I do what's asked of me. I know that being in this place is part of God's plan and in time His purpose will become clear. Here on the highest peaks of the mountains, everyone seems closer to God.' She made the Sign of the Cross, her hand touching her forehead, heart and shoulders reverently.

'Neither of us expected to be here,' I whispered. 'Maybe we were meant to meet each other.'

She smiled. 'I'm sure of it.'

Despite my new friendship with Sister Agata and the busy but fulfilling routine at the monastery, I still missed my family and home, especially when I went to sleep at night. It was a constant ache in my chest. I knew how lost Mamma would be with only two children at home, and I missed my conversations with Zia Francesca and the bustle of working with her in the trattoria. I even wondered how Papà was coping on the farm without Vincenzo and me and whether he and Paola were able to carry the extra workload.

I missed my sisters most. We understood each other. Paola and I had a special connection. Like me, she wanted to live her life outside of what was expected of her. I especially missed her calm presence and practicality, her acceptance of who I was and the outrageous ideas I'd confided in her, her wisdom and the joy we shared in the simple pleasures of life, like the taste of a lemon plucked straight from the tree and the excitement of new life after the birth of the little lambs. I felt that a part of me was missing without her.

'You can't be so impetuous,' Paola had whispered as I slipped into bed next to her after my fate had been decided at the trattoria, the linen sheets rustling as she turned to face me. 'You hurt Mamma, Teresa and me, and involved Nonna Mariana and Zia Francesca. Papà would cut them off from us if he ever found out what they've done tonight. Your actions affect the lives of others, can't you see? We have to follow the rules.'

I'd shaken my head as a shot of white-hot anger flared through me, but she'd grabbed me by the shoulders.

'You have to be smart, be realistic, work within the boundaries to find a way to do what you want. Make Papà think that he's getting what he wants while you get what *you* want. That's what Mamma tells us all the time. Give him what he wants, be respectful of his wishes while you work towards what you want too.'

'It's never going to change around here,' I'd hissed.

She'd let go of me and sighed. 'Mamma mia! How do you think Teresa is getting to do exactly what she wants? And do you think that Papà really wants me to become a farmer? All I want is to stay on the farm. I have such big plans. We could improve productivity and the quality of our yields and the work would be so much more efficient if we used modern machinery and equipment for starters.' I could hear the rising excitement and the passion in her voice. Paola loved the farm more than ogling at the boys. 'And I'd enjoy nothing more than to refine the cheesemaking process and make cheese nobody else can. If I can become indispensable to Papà, if I can build up our farming business, producing and selling specialty products that everybody wants, then he'll never want me to leave his side and there's less chance he'll start looking for a husband for me.'

'You don't want to get married?'

'I want to dedicate my life to farming. You're not the only one who wants to live a life outside of what's expected of us. There are ways around the obstacles we face, we just have to find them.'

And she was right. I was determined now to make the most of this wonderful blessing that had been bestowed upon me, to make everyone who believed in me and loved me proud, even Papà.

I'd written to my parents and to Paola but I hadn't received anything from them yet. The longer the wait, the more I worried they were angry with me or, worse still, that something terrible had happened at home. But I knew that Paola would never abandon me, no matter what, and hers was the first letter that I received, two months after my arrival.

My dear sister,

We've received your letters. Mamma read hers out to us after dinner and she and Papà seem pleased that you've settled in so well, that you're being kept busy in the convent and your skill in the kitchen has been utilised. I've told Mamma about your lessons and she's happy that your healing talents are being nurtured. She's been writing little bits to you when she can but wants to wait until she has more to tell you. Antonio just wants to know if you're going to become a nun and is dying to see how they could possibly contain your hair under the veil!

Teresa is happy with Santoro and she's forgiven you for missing her wedding. She's made the schoolmaster's residence homely and Santoro's mother has been showing her how he likes things to be done. Teresa's more than capable but she's patiently taking her mother-in-law's advice. I thought of how you would have rolled your eyes and told her Santoro has two hands and feet and is just as able to look after himself. They both work all day, after all, but Teresa's determined to be a good wife and to save as much money as she can so that they can have a better future in America.

I still can't believe that she wants to go. I often think back to that special night before you left when Teresa showed us her wedding dress and told us of their plan.

I was relieved to know that Teresa was enjoying married life and that she'd forgiven me.

'All I want is to be married to Santoro and to have his babies,' Teresa had said dreamily that night, opening her trousseau at the end of her bed. At twenty, she was rather old to be a newlywed, but Santoro had not long returned from teacher's college in Reggio, coming home to take up the posting of schoolmaster in our small school. Our parents had arranged their engagement, impressed that Santoro was going to become a teacher. It looked like they had made a good match.

We each had a trousseau to begin our married life: boxes Mamma had helped us put together since we were young girls.

My trousseau was less extensive and my embroidery skills more basic than Teresa's, but the linen would still be useful. Teresa showed us hemp linen towels and bed sheets embroidered with her initials and fine embellishments of flowers and leaves. Her delicate nightgowns and bed covers were edged with lace made by her own hand.

Paola brushed her fingers lightly over the tiny, dainty stitches, shaking her head with amazement. 'So beautiful,' she murmured.

'Everyone from miles around would be devastated if you stopped producing such wonderful garments,' I said, admiring Teresa's exquisite workmanship. 'Please show me your wedding dress,' I added softly. 'I want to see you in it . . . At least I can imagine you at the church then.'

She'd stared at me a moment then nodded, tears in her eyes, and I had to swallow the lump in my throat.

She returned the items to her trousseau and then transformed into a vision in white. A white wedding dress had been almost unheard of in Calabria until recently. Most girls generally married in the dress they wore to Sunday Mass, although men earning good money in the United States sometimes sent white gowns home for their daughters to be married in. Santoro had insisted Teresa have a new dress and had saved the money to purchase the material.

'It's magnificent,' I whispered. 'You look beautiful.' The satin dress was simple but Teresa looked like a model in one of Milano's designer gowns.

'Beautiful,' echoed Paola, her eyes shimmering with pride and love.

Teresa's face was alight with pleasure. 'Here, help me with the buttons at the back.'

'You'll be the talk of the district with this dress,' I said as I did up the buttons.

'I wouldn't be a very good advertisement if I didn't make a dress that was difficult to master,' said Teresa smugly.

'Santoro's agreed that I should keep working,' she continued, then paused. 'We want to save as much money as we can to go to America,' she whispered. 'The government pay for a school teacher is steady and regular, but it's still not very much. One of Santoro's friends went to America and he earns good money there. They live in a house with electricity and hot water, have carpet on the floor, and can afford to eat well. Children can go to school long enough to have the chance of going to university. It's what Santoro wants for our children. It's what I want for them too: a future and a better life than what we can give them here.'

Paola and I had stared at her, incredulous. I'd never thought that Teresa would ever think about leaving Bruzzano and our parents, let alone Italy. Maybe she and I weren't so different after all. She wanted something more, something Santoro also wanted, and she had the courage to work towards that dream as surely as Paola and I did.

'First Giulia and now you,' said Paola, looking stricken. A shot of pain had stabbed me in the chest – guilt and heartbreak for my sister.

Teresa hugged her tight. 'It will be a long time before we save enough to even think of going.'

'I'll be home again soon and Teresa's only across the village.' I held out my hand to Paola, tears in my eyes. 'And we'll always be sisters, no matter where life takes us.'

That night was bittersweet, just like the sugared almonds we sneaked into the dining room to eat, a symbol of the ups and downs of married life.

I looked down to the letter once again.

Papà and I are managing on the farm without Vincenzo. Antonio helps after school and even Mamma joins us sometimes. Most of the ewes are close to lambing and Antonio's excited to see the new lambs but I'll be sad that you won't be here with us when they come. It won't be the same.

It sounds like you're learning lots and getting used to life at the convent. I'm so proud of you. You'll make a wonderful healer and maybe one day you'll even take your skills to the rest of Italy. But I miss you. It's so quiet and lonely in a room by myself. I miss the sound of your voice and I still can't get used to sleeping without you next to me.

Your loving sister,
Paola.
PS. Mamma's been waiting for a letter from Vincenzo but nothing yet from him, hopefully soon.

I blinked the tears away and breathed a sigh of relief. Although it was reassuring to hear from Paola and know that life continued at home as it always had – even with Teresa newly married and Vincenzo and I away – I missed them all even more. Unlike Santoro, who had been exempt because of his club foot, Vincenzo had been drafted to fight a war somewhere in Africa as soon as his pre-military training had ended. It was one of Il Duce's teachings that it was a man's duty to go to war, and Vincenzo was happy to go, exchanging the unforgiving toil of daily life on the land for adventure in exotic Africa and steady pay, but I worried about him, so far away.

I felt bad that I wasn't there to pull my weight but it would be months before I could go home. I was determined more than ever to learn all I could while I was here, to become someone of worth.

Not just for my family, but for myself too.

3

Fra Fortunato ensured my attention had no chance to wander. He pushed me further every day, demanding I do my very best, and there was always study to do between lessons. A few months after my arrival, Mother Superior had also requested that I come to her study each afternoon after my lesson with Fra Fortunato instead of studying with Agata, sometimes instructing me to read various passages from books, discussing them afterwards or stretching my knowledge. We explored science, botany and philosophy, and even sometimes history and geography, with an overview of the political systems across Europe. My education was broad and although I discovered a love of learning and I especially enjoyed history, I sometimes wondered whether it was relevant. Agata assured me that Mother Superior was giving me a good grounding for an intelligent, thinking person and for whatever life might throw at me. I couldn't imagine why she took such an interest in my education but Agata told me that it was because I had an enquiring mind and I was a quick learner. But I wondered if it also had something to do with her connection to Nonna Mariana.

'I understand that your father doesn't want you to learn from your Nonna Mariana,' Mother Superior Maria said one afternoon in June. 'It's a shame, because she's one of the best healers I've ever seen.'

I stared at her in amazement. Papà had always made Nonna out to be no better than a strega, even though I knew she wasn't. 'How do you know her?' I asked.

Mother Superior smiled fondly. 'Fra Fortunato and I have known her for years. She used to come here often and the three of us would discuss healing and some of our more interesting cases. It was a good way to learn from each other.'

I nodded, though I was confused. 'But how did you meet her?'

'She was a novice and I was in charge of the novices at that time.'

The book I was holding fell to the floor with a thump. 'Nonna Mariana was a nun?'

Mother Superior shook her head and laughed. 'Oh no, she never took her vows.'

She explained that Nonna, only sixteen and already a healer, had entered the convent distraught because she had been unable to save more people, especially her mother and first husband, who were killed in the earthquakes of 1894. She was my age, already widowed and suffering from such loss. I couldn't imagine how I'd cope if something like that happened to me. Nonna stayed at the convent for two years and was encouraged to practise her craft. She taught Mother Superior what she had learnt from her grandmother, how health came from the wellbeing of body, mind and spirit.

Ultimately, Nonna had decided to continue the family tradition rather than become a nun. My grandfather proposed to her not long after she left the convent but I'd never known him – he died before I was born. Nonna had lost not one but two husbands by the time she was Mamma's age.

'Mariana returned each year to help teach the nuns basic techniques as a way to show gratitude for what they had done for her. I joined her when I could and she continued to teach me and we became very good friends,' said Mother Superior, leaning back in her chair, a distant look in her eyes.

'And Fra Fortunato?' I asked, retrieving the biology book I'd dropped, unable to believe there was so much about Nonna I hadn't known.

'He received his classical training in herbalism in Germany and Rome and worked for some years across Italy before coming south. When he heard about Mariana and our meetings, he wrote to me. By then your nonna had a growing reputation as an exceptional healer. People came from all over the district to see her.'

My heart filled with pride. I'd always believed that Nonna was a good healer but to know that she was so well regarded was a huge thrill. I wondered if Papà realised that she was thought of so highly.

'It was only a matter of time before Fra Fortunato met with us both and decided to remain here at the monastery. The three of us have benefitted from talking and learning from one another ever since.'

'Thank you for telling me,' I said.

She nodded and waved her hand dismissively. 'Enough of that. You still have much to learn before you're as good as your grandmother. Now, Fra Fortunato can teach you about the properties of herbs and how to apply them but we have much we can teach you about caring for those who need our help.'

'In what way?' I asked, leaning forward, curious to know more and determined to live up to her expectation that I could ever be as good as Nonna.

'My sisters and I have nursed those who have lingered in their illness, many who were sick of heart and those who were very near death. Illness is not always a physical manifestation, but has much to do with strong emotion, the state of the mind and the circumstances that life has handed the afflicted. Illness can be a combination of mind, body and spirit.'

I nodded. 'I think I understand. I've seen it before when people who should have died weeks earlier have hung on until they've received a visit or news from a loved one. I know Nonna treats patients who believe they've been cursed with the "evil eye" with what they believe will make them better – the old ways.'

'Calabrese are a superstitious folk and the old traditions can be very useful in helping the patient feel confident about their recovery. Remember that the greatest healers are not too proud to learn from everything around them and all manner of healing techniques can provide inspiration.' Mother Superior smiled. 'Very good, Giulia. You're learning quickly. Your comprehension of the texts I've given you is improving and your reading is getting faster too. Make sure you keep up with the daily reading.' She handed me a book on philosophy. 'We'll discuss this when we next meet.'

I gazed at it with dismay.

Her brows knitted at my expression. 'Remember that learning is the foundation of knowledge and knowledge is power, the key to success and to an independent mind, especially for a woman.'

'I'm far from being learned like you.'

'But I can see you have a keen mind, even with your limited education. With a little broadening of your knowledge, you'll develop the confidence to learn further on your own. There's a whole world out there for you to explore if you only have the imagination and the resourcefulness to discover what's beyond your doorstep.'

'Do you really think so?'

'I know so. Even women should have the power to make informed decisions and considered choices. Our intelligence and how we use it is no different from men's, after all, although they'd often like us to think so.' Mother Superior smiled, the wealth of life experience expressed in the wrinkles on her face.

I wanted so much to be like her.

Mother Superior Maria announced the Italian victory in Abyssinia on 7th May, after the news came through on the radio.

'It's been a big success,' said Agata as we cleared the tables after lunch. 'Italians have taken this as a sign that our nation is finally on the rise again and they love Il Duce for it. Now that Abyssinia has joined the Italian colonies in East Africa, the rest of the world has to take Italy seriously as a major power player in Europe.'

'Il Duce promises that we'll become the new Roman Empire. Maybe this is the first step,' I said as I collected the leftover bread into one basket.

Mussolini and his Fascist government had been in power for fourteen years. My parents and most people in our village believed he was a good leader. He wanted to make Italy great again and that would be good for us in the south too. I'd heard Papà tell Mamma that Il Duce had drained the marshlands, promising more land to farmers and help for them to grow and sell wheat. He'd even heard that large portions of land in Abyssinia would become available to farm.

'But I still haven't heard from Vincenzo. I just hope that he's alright and comes home now the war is won.' Vincenzo and I had always been close, perhaps because he was less serious than Teresa and Paola and a bit wild like me. He felt sorry that Papà was so hard on me, especially the older I got, and did what he could to ease my pain. With his cheeky good humour, he was always the first one to joke and laugh, making me feel part of his group with Stefano and Angelo by asking me to do something daring for him. I was never afraid, only proud that he could trust me. I knew that he loved me even more for it.

Agata squeezed my hand. 'Africa's a long way away. It takes time for letters to get back to us and perhaps he hasn't had time to write.'

'Where exactly is Abyssinia?'

Agata thought for a moment. 'It's better if I show you on a map. Let's finish up here and I'll see if I can find one.'

Agata spread the map she'd found on one of the refectory tables. 'It's old, but it still shows us what we want. See here,' she said, pointing to the toe of Italy. 'This is where we are. It's not so far across the Mediterranean Sea to the top of Africa. If we could look out across the sea from the southernmost point of Calabria, we'd see Libya. But our soldiers have to sail east across the Mediterranean through the Suez Canal in Egypt and into the Red Sea to get to the coast of East Africa where Abyssinia and the Italian colonies lie,' she explained, tracing the route with her finger.

'Africa's so big compared to Italy.'

Agata nodded. 'So now you can see it would take time for the letters to travel to and from our colonies and to go overland to wherever Vincenzo is. Six weeks or more.'

'Vincenzo's only been gone a couple of months,' I said. At least now I had some idea where he was. 'Thank you for showing me.'

It wasn't until late May, when the forest was verdant with the fresh green leaves of beech and oak, that I finally received another letter from Mamma and Paola. One of the nuns handed it to me after lunch and it was only after my lesson in the herb garden, concentrating on the harvesting of *ruta graveolens*, commonly known as rue, that I was able to duck away for a few minutes to myself, passing the Stations of the Cross sculpted in bronze that were spread across the gardens and through the groves of chestnut trees at the bottom of the mountain path. Agata had shown me a secluded spot during our few expeditions into the forest where the waters from the melted snow high up on the mountain flowed along streams to gush down waterfalls too numerous to count. It was the same water that flowed into the Bruzzano River and out into the sea. At a smaller waterfall, where the water fell more gently, I sat on a fallen log surrounded by a green curtain of privacy to read Paola's letter.

Dear Giulia,

Mamma finally finished her letter to you and we've just received one from Vincenzo, so I thought I'd send you a little note with her letter to let you know what he said.

After a month or so of battling the Abyssinian army, Vincenzo's now in Addis Ababa, the capital of Abyssinia, after they arrived victorious in a convoy of trucks. His unit is keeping peace in the city and outlying areas and he says he's doing fine.

Listen to this! Apparently after seeing some soldiers injured in battle, Stefano wishes he'd done some medical training so he could work with the medics. Who knew that one of Vincenzo's friends would want to do medicine? And apparently Angelo's not sure he wants to continue to be a butcher when he comes home after what he's seen.

I shook my head in amazement. The Stefano I knew couldn't stand the sight of blood, which was why he never wanted to be a butcher with Angelo, and he'd never been interested in anything but having fun. Abyssinia had definitely changed him.

Anyway, Vincenzo says that you'd be fascinated by the exotic culture of the local people and he writes that it's a mix of many ancient influences across Africa and the Arabic nations. Just like Calabria, I suppose. He's even eaten a spicy stew called a wat, which he said was delicious. But the sight of women in their flowing robes carrying big amphorae of water on their heads from the rivers and wells like we do, made him homesick. He misses the smells, tastes and sights of home – bergamot and lemons, jasmine and basil, Papà's ricotta with honey and the hills and mountains that overlook the sea. But most of all he says he misses us – even Teresa! I think he secretly misses Rosa the most. She was the girl Vincenzo was meeting when you last covered for him with the sheep. I've heard that he's been writing to her and whenever I see her around the village, she smiles at me but I can see the worry in her eyes too.

Anyway, I hope you're learning lots. I can't wait to hear all about it when you come home in September after the Festa.

I'll write again soon.

I read Mamma's letter after Paola's, then sat for a long while, staring at the waterfall cascading over the rocks. I could only imagine Vincenzo's experience of war and how lonely he must be, so far away from Italy. The mention of injured soldiers struck a chord with me and I wondered how confronting it would be to see a brave man reduced to such a helpless state, so far from home and his loved ones.

I gazed up towards Montalto, the tallest mountain peak, and noticed a magnificent golden eagle gliding above it. How could anything as devastating as war touch the serenity of a pristine sanctuary like this? Yet I knew it could, if only because it had touched me through Vincenzo's letter. I made the Sign of the Cross and prayed.

'Please God, bring Vincenzo home safely and ease the torment and suffering of those touched by war. Madonna, mother of God, keep all my family safe, healthy and whole and may Papà give me some freedom to be myself and practise my healing when I return home. I promise to study hard at the monastery and do my very best to heal the sick and suffering with your guidance and for your glory and the glory of Jesus and God.'

When I was finished, I felt somehow blessed and light of heart, and I returned to the convent determined not to let the Madonna down.

4

It was August and although Mother Superior had agreed to Agata having lessons with Fra Fortunato, there was no chance of her beginning yet, because every set of hands was put to work as the Festa of the Madonna of the Mountain grew closer. The excitement in the air was palpable. Liquorice sweets and herbal teas were packaged and rosaries and cards depicting the Virgin Mary and her son were readied for sale. The gardens were tended with care and the church, monastery, convent and the visiting dignitaries' rooms were scrubbed until they gleamed. Fra Fortunato and I were busy looking after pilgrims and making sure we had enough herbal tinctures and tonics ready for the festa.

A couple of weeks before the main event, I was surprised to learn that we would host a group of pilgrims everyone was being very secretive about.

'What is going on?' I asked Agata when we were sent to the kitchen to make sweets and pastries for our mystery guests.

'They come every year for a few days just before the Festa,' she said evasively. 'We provide them with privacy, meals and clean rooms. I've heard whispers that they donate to the upkeep of the monastery.'

'Who are they?'

She shook her head, concentrating on kneading. 'I shouldn't say. The fewer who know, the better.'

'Come on, Agata. Who am I going to tell?'

She scanned the kitchen but the head cook and kitchen hands were down the other end, working on meal preparations. She leaned close. 'It's the 'Ndrangheta.'

'Mannaggia!' I gasped. 'The Calabrese mafia?'

'The bosses have their annual meeting here. But they stay in private meeting rooms, interacting with only a handful of monks. We won't see them for the whole three days.'

'*Here?*'

She shrugged. 'How can the Abbot refuse hospitality to these pilgrims when hundreds of others find respite and refuge here every year? These men pay for their meals and accommodation and who's to say that they haven't come to pray? Perhaps they'll feel closer to God's presence here. If the Church can guide these men towards God and our Lord Jesus, then how can we deny them?'

'When you put it like that . . .' When we were at school, we'd learnt how Mussolini had stamped out the corruption and standover tactics of the Sicilian Mafia, which had undermined the local community. I remembered telling my parents and Zia Francesca about it. My parents had nodded and said Il Duce had done a good thing and perhaps he'd start on the 'Ndrangheta next. But Zia Francesca had only shrugged and said, 'They'll be back.'

41

The 'Ndrangheta were more secretive and less well known than the Sicilian Mafia, but remained a part of the everyday fabric in Calabria. Everyone knew someone connected to the 'Ndrangheta, many with strong blood ties, as they provided 'protection' to businesses. Even Zia Francesca had to pay for the certainty of top produce and deliveries arriving when they should. Mamma said that Zia would never be free of them and that there was nothing she could do about it. I knew she had wanted to tell me more, but she changed the subject abruptly when Papà came into the room. The 'Ndrangheta's strict code of honour, loyalty and secrecy made them both a powerful ally and a vengeful enemy. They often gave assistance to communities in trouble. I'd heard from one of my school friends that their father was working on one of the new bridges in a neighbouring village funded by the local clan after destructive floods tore through.

But with every favour afforded, there was an obligation. My parents always told us to stay away from the 'Ndrangheta, no matter what they did for the community. Silence was golden.

With the monastery so busy preparing for the festa, I never expected to be treating patients with Fra Fortunato, let alone continuing our lessons. However, on the second day of the 'Ndrangheta's meeting, Fra Fortunato asked me to join him to attend one of the pilgrims, who had taken ill.

'He has excruciating abdominal pain. I want you to go through the diagnosis and treatment with me. It will be good practice. Correct diagnosis is crucial to a swift recovery,' he said as we walked towards the accommodation wing.

I frowned. I'd seen quite a few pilgrims by now but not someone of that reputation.

Fra Fortunato smiled reassuringly, picking up on my concern. 'There's nothing to fear. He's a man who needs our help, that's all.'

I nodded.

A fleshy middle-aged man was lying flat on his bed, wearing a singlet and pyjama pants. Another man, perhaps in his late forties and smartly dressed in a dark suit, rose from his chair by the patient's bed to greet us.

'Buongiorno, Fra Fortunato, thank you for coming so quickly,' he said. He looked pointedly at me, his intelligent light brown eyes appraising me. He was intimidating, his manner that of a powerful man. Regal, somehow, like a mountain wildcat, ferocity barely contained behind congeniality. 'And who is this?'

'My student, Giulia Tallariti. She's here to observe and learn.'

The man's eyes narrowed and then he nodded curtly and gestured to the man on the bed. 'Please, help him. He's been like this since rising this morning.'

The man on the bed groaned and writhed as a spasm of pain overcame him.

'Where does it hurt?' asked Fra Fortunato gently, his hand on the man's shoulder. I hung back a little, not wanting to get in the way.

The man in the suit indicated I should move closer with a flick of his hand. 'Don't worry, he won't bite,' he said. 'If you want to learn you have to be able to see.'

I nodded, moving next to the monk as requested.

'My right side,' the sick man whispered, his silver hair damp and plastered to his pale forehead. I reached for the towel on the end of the bed and gently wiped the man's brow, pushing the hair from his face. 'Grazie,' he whispered.

'Front or back?' asked Fra Fortunato.

'Front,' he muttered, pointing to his abdomen, 'and around to the back of my shoulder.'

Fra Fortunato nodded. 'Sore here?' He gently pressed the right abdomen and the man grunted, nearly lifting from the bed in agony. 'I'm sorry, but I have to know where the problem is.'

'Mannaggia! Do what you have to do,' he forced out between gritted teeth.

Fra Fortunato turned to me. 'Based on that assessment, what structures do you think could be involved?'

'The liver, gallbladder, appendix, maybe kidney or lung,' I said, thinking about the area of pain and the point of tenderness.

He nodded. 'How can you tell which?'

'I'm not sure.'

'Both the radiation of pain and the palpation can give you the clues you need but you also must question the patient.' Fra Fortunato smiled at the man on the bed. 'Are there any foods that upset you?'

'I don't think I can tolerate rich foods like I used to, I feel nauseous, and the pain often comes on after that.'

'Does your pain come on after other foods?'

The man nodded and grimaced. 'Red wine and olives. God is punishing me by taking away the pleasure of my favourite foods.'

'We had plenty of red wine last night with olives and cheese, as well as pasta with sausage ragú,' said the man in the suit, spreading his hands expansively and shaking his head. 'There were zippoli after.'

My mouth watered at the thought of the fried doughnuts.

Fra Fortunato nodded. 'That would do it.' He looked to me in anticipation. 'What do you think now?'

'It could be appendix, liver or gallbladder,' I said more confidently.

'Si, the symptoms fit all those. But the pain is specific. Pain under the shoulder blade often points to the gallbladder or blockage of the ducts by gallstones. We know olives and red wine often upset the gallbladder, and rich, heavy foods can cause nausea and a flare up of symptoms. Now, if you feel the area, it can give you a more definitive answer.'

'Let the girl have a feel if she's going to learn properly,' said the man in the suit. The man on the bed nodded and gestured for me to come closer. I looked at Fra Fortunato and he too nodded.

'Don't be shy,' said the sick man gruffly as I placed my fingertips gingerly on his abdomen. He grimaced as I pressed my hands over where his liver, gallbladder and right bowel were. I could sense the abnormal heat and firmness over the gallbladder.

'I think it's the gallbladder,' I said to Fra Fortunato as I straightened up. 'It's enlarged and tender.' The symptoms were all coming together like a jigsaw puzzle.

'What herbs might be useful?'

'Uva ursi, hydrangea, gentian . . . definitely dandelion and maybe fenugreek,' I said confidently.

'I agree,' he said, his brown eyes crinkling with a smile.

'Will he be alright?' asked the man in the suit anxiously. 'We have another busy day ahead of us.'

'He'll be back to normal soon,' said Fra Fortunato.

The man nodded, the worry lines around his eyes relaxing a little. 'Very good.' He stood tall, as though ready to face the next battle.

'Giulia and I will go and put together a herbal mix. It will soothe your gallbladder and help with the pain.'

'Grazie, Fra Fortunato,' said the man on the bed. 'I've been suffering from this for years but never this bad.'

'Stay away from rich foods or anything that aggravates you until you feel better. I'll give you a follow-up mixture to take home and I'll send more when you run low. You'll have to stay on treatment for some time. Come back to see me if you have another flare up, otherwise I expect to check on your condition when I see you next year.'

'I'll do as you say and I'll pray to the Madonna for a full cure.'

Fra Fortunato patted the man's shoulder. 'Rest for now. We'll be back shortly with your herbs.'

I was sent to visit the patient twice more to give him his herbs, instruct him on how and when to take them and to ensure that he was improving. On the last day of the man's stay, Fra Fortunato tended to him himself while I was busy with my chores at the convent. It wasn't until I was harvesting chamomile flowers in the herb garden a few hours later that I was approached by the man who had been by his bedside.

'Buongiorno, Signorina Tallariti,' he said, smiling broadly. 'We're leaving today and I was told I might find you here.'

'Buongiorno.' I straightened and wiped my hands on my apron. 'How's your companion?'

'He's my cousin and he's feeling much better already, well enough to travel. You have our gratitude.'

'Thank you, and I'm glad he's improved. Fra Fortunato's a skilled herbalist, one of the best.'

'We were very impressed with your knowledge and manner. You're a very compassionate young lady. Fra Fortunato thinks you'll make a fine healer, so I hope you continue your studies. We need more people like you out in the community.'

'That's very kind of you and, yes, I'll continue learning. I've always wanted to be a healer.'

'That's good to hear. Allora, we must be off. Thank you again and all the best for your future.' He turned to go but stopped and looked back at me. 'You're the niece of Signora Francesca Tallariti, who owns the trattoria in Bruzzano, aren't you?'

I nodded nervously. How did he know?

'Ahh! I've eaten the best swordfish at her restaurant. Her pasta with chickpeas and sugo is heavenly too.' His face transformed from controlled civility to pure joy and I could almost imagine him as a small boy.

I blushed, realising that I'd seen him there before. I wondered briefly if he was the man who collected Zia's protection money, but surely he was too powerful for such basic jobs. 'I worked there before I came here.'

'I know. At first, I couldn't remember where I'd seen you. I haven't been there for a while but when I heard your name, I knew. Well, it seems you're a woman of many talents.' He dipped his head and smiled and this time the smile touched his eyes. 'Arrivederci, signorina. We won't forget your assistance. Maybe I'll see you again. If there's ever anything I can do for you, leave a message with your zia.'

'Grazie e arrivederci,' I said, but I had no intention of ever seeking a favour.

As I watched him walk away, I thought about the 'Ndrangheta. These men had been respectful and considerate, but I knew their reputation and wasn't sure I wanted to cross paths with them again.

September brought the Festa of the Madonna of the Mountain. Pilgrims, some with caravans of heavily laden donkeys, had been arriving since early in the day and setting up camp along the riverbed and throughout the valley. We watched them from the windows of the convent. Girls and women danced as if in a trance, only to collapse with exhaustion once they reached the Monastery grounds.

'What are they doing?' I asked Agata, craning my neck to see beyond the trees. Agata was a good head taller than me. Most towns and villages had their own festival to honour the saints and the Madonna. Bruzzano had its own festa, but I'd never seen anything like this before.

'It's a form of religious ecstasy,' she said. 'Our festival has links to the ancient fertility rites associated with Persephone and Demetra that were first performed here about a thousand years before the birth of our Lord. Many women come here to ask the Madonna for her favour in matters of fertility, childbirth and marriage. She's been known to grant miracles.'

I looked at her in surprise. 'I never imagined we had a religious history that stretched back so far.' I remembered the Greek gods and goddesses from the books she'd read with me. Persephone was the Greek goddess of rebirth and Demetra, her mother, was goddess of agriculture, fertility, the seasons and the harvest. The association made sense. This festival of the Madonna, like ours in Bruzzano and Ferruzzano, came at the end of the summer harvest of grain. There was a profound connection between the people here, the land and divinity. It made my heart swell with pride to think that women had been practising their rites right here nearly three thousand years earlier and now we were following in their footsteps.

'They dance in thanks or in penance and to ask the Madonna's favour. Men sometimes carry heavy rocks or crawl on hands and knees some of the way. But just wait until the procession. The hysteria intensifies and often women and even men collapse with the emotion. Then the feasting begins and everyone celebrates. We'll be busy then, tending those who have overdone it.'

On the morning of the festa, hundreds gathered around the route of the procession. From my vantage point on the outside stairs of the second storey of the convent, I could feel the energy building, the press of bodies singing songs honouring the mother of God as they waited for the Madonna. I could see the crowd surge as the Madonna came into view, hands reaching desperately to touch her. Six men carried the statue, the poles holding her caravan thrust high above their heads as people swarmed them. She was magnificent, splendid in vibrant pink and blue robes, cradling the baby Jesus, both with majestic gold crowns on their heads. Her throne was surrounded by flowers.

The excitement was palpable, like a ripple across water, as she arrived in the piazza. Women began chanting, some screaming, 'Viva Maria!' and sobbing with emotion. Men and women beat their chests, and grain and flowers were thrown over the sacred form of the Madonna. The bishop, abbot, Mother Superior and a line of priests, monks and nuns followed the Madonna and, behind them, men playing tambourines, guitars, piano accordions and pipes. The firing of guns in triumph echoed across the valley. Not even when the Madonna had entered the seventh-century Byzantine church for a Mass in her honour did the noise abate.

Finally, when the formal religious rituals were over, the crowd began to dissipate. The smell of goat meat roasting on large outdoor spits wafted across the piazza as I made my way back to the convent kitchen where I was helping prepare and serve lunch and dinner to the visiting dignitaries.

Fra Fortunato and I were busier the last evening of the festival and the following morning than we had been in the previous week. There were many who were overcome with the intensity of emotion evoked by the Madonna's procession and required calmative herbs. Some had suffered from sunstroke and exhaustion from dancing the tarantella right through the afternoon. The evening's feasting had caught up with others. The feast was more like a tribute to Dionysus, the Greek god of wine, and I wasn't surprised to learn that even the ritual roasting and eating of goat was symbolic of the satyrs associated with him. I only wished I'd had time to wander among the pilgrims to enjoy a sense of community. It was a time to forget about day-to-day worries, bathed in the blessings bestowed by the Madonna, Jesus and God. It was a time to believe in better times ahead.

*

It wasn't long after that Mother Superior Maria asked me to see her. We sat at the small table by the window in her study and drank coffee.

'Allora, Giulia, your time with us is coming to an end.'

'Si, I know, Mother Superior,' I said, my heart sinking at the thought of leaving this place, and losing the stimulating lessons of Fra Fortunato and Mother Superior and my friendship with Agata. But part of me soared at the thought of returning to Bruzzano. Although I'd always dreamed of leaving home, I'd missed my family so much, especially Paola. I even missed Papà, although I wasn't sure what reception I'd receive from him or how he'd react when he found out what I'd been learning.

'Don't worry,' said Mother Superior at the look of consternation on my face. 'It's time for you to practise what you've learnt from Fra Fortunato under the guidance of Mariana. I expect to see you both here again next summer.'

I bowed my head, my face burning with embarrassment. 'My father. He doesn't know what I've been studying.'

She grasped my hand across the table. 'I won't lie for you, but Fra Fortunato and I will send letters home with you, explaining that your talent for healing is a gift given by God and, consequently, you've been instructed in the art of herbalism, which now requires practical application under supervision. Since you can no longer remain here, we believe that Mariana would be the best one to undertake your further training. Our endorsement of her skills should bring her the respectability your father demands. I see no impediment to you becoming apprenticed to her.'

'You'd do this for me?' I stared at her in shock.

'You have a bright future ahead of you, Giulia. We need more talented healers like you. Surely you know how busy Mariana is and you can see how Fra Fortunato's services are in demand right across Calabria and beyond?'

Maybe the Madonna had been listening to my prayers all this time. My decision to run away and join the Red Cross had sparked this remarkable chapter in my life and the women in my life had made it all possible. I was surrounded by strong, incredible women and I was enormously grateful for their belief in me. I would not let them down.

'Grazie, Mother Superior. I promise that when Nonna and I return, I'll have something useful to share with you.'

'I know you will,' she said, patting my hand. 'We look forward to seeing you again next summer.'

I had a few days before Fra Giacomo would take me down to the village where Zia Francesca would pick me up in her red Fiat. I spent the time with Fra Fortunato, reviewing the most important skills I had learnt and I helped him select and package a collection of dried herbs, tinctures and ointments.

'Think of this as your starting kit,' he said as he presented the package to me. 'Mariana will know them all but you may have some different uses that you can discuss with her. We all learn from one another. A good practitioner must remain humble and be ready to re-evaluate and revise their approach when new information or results arise, no matter the source. It's what makes us better at what we do. It's what may give a patient improved comfort or healing.'

'Grazie, Fra Fortunato,' I said, tears in my eyes. 'I'll do everything to make you proud. I've been blessed to have the best teacher . . .' I wiped my cheeks hastily with my sleeve.

'I'm going to miss you and your lessons but I look forward to seeing you in the summer and telling you everything I've learnt.'

'It's been my pleasure to teach you, Giulia,' he said solemnly. 'You're just like your grandmother, a quick learner, gifted and intuitive. I shall look forward to seeing you both again.' He began blinking furiously and I stood up on my toes to kiss him on his smooth cheek.

As my thoughts turned to my future, I made one final visit to the church and the Madonna. The church was silent and empty as I slipped through the heavy brass door, tucking the corner of my headscarf securely in place so my head was covered in this sacred place. Candles and lanterns had been lit at Vespers and the vestibule glowed with a soft golden light, illuminating the figure of the Madonna on her throne. She seemed almost real in the half-light, her dark eyes looking through to my soul. I had nothing to give her except a posy of flowers I had picked from the meadow, which I lay at her feet.

Sinking to my knees, I gazed up at her serene face. 'Mother of God,' I prayed silently, 'you know what's in my heart. I'm grateful for your intervention in bringing me here to learn. I now realise that I can do so much more than I knew. If Papà refuses to let me train with Nonna Mariana, it will be all for nothing. Help him to see my dedication, that my healing is important and poses no threat to anyone. I know I caused a lot of trouble and brought my family a lot of heartache before I came but I've learnt so much since then. I was lost, trying to find my path in this life, and now I have. Healing is my purpose, the way I choose to live my life – not just for me, but for the benefit of my family and my village too. I ask that you guide me in my work and help me be the very best I can be.

'Thank you for giving me this time at the monastery and the sense of clarity, purpose and strength I now feel. Bless Mother Superior Maria, Fra Fortunato and all who reside here at your monastery. Watch over my family and keep them safe from harm . . .'

My goodbyes were more difficult than I imagined, especially to Agata. She had become like a sister to me and we clung to each other before Fra Giacomo called me impatiently to join him on the cart.

'I'll write to you,' I said as we pulled away.

'See you next summer,' she cried, waving until the chestnut and larch trees obscured her from view.

The glorious vistas of green-clad mountains, the warm sunshine on my skin and the relief of the shady copses as we travelled brought lightness to my heart. It was a far cry from the oppressive and never-ending white of deep winter that I had experienced on the journey to the monastery seven months earlier.

But Fra Giacomo was now an old acquaintance and we chatted amiably for a time about life at the monastery and the gardens that required new plantings. Then my thoughts turned to home and the new life I was about to embark upon. My hand strayed to the deep pockets of my skirt where I felt the crinkle of the monastery letters. I only hoped that my father would forgive that I'd studied without his knowledge and permission, accept what was written on those pages and allow me to work with Nonna Mariana.

5

Mamma, Paola and Teresa were waiting when Zia Francesca and I arrived home late in the afternoon. I rushed into my mother's arms and held her tight. She smelt of fresh bread. Unlike Zia's modern stove, Mamma still cooked the old-fashioned way, on an open fire using heavy iron pots, pans and griddles. She said she preferred it but I was sure that she'd love a wood-fired stove if we could afford one.

'We missed you,' whispered Mamma. 'Was it everything you hoped for?'

'It was wonderful. I have you to thank for making it possible.' I kissed her on the cheek.

'What's a mother for if not to promote her daughter's future? I always knew that this was your path.'

A burst of happiness rushed through me like a ray of sunshine. 'I'm so glad to be home.' Before I went to the monastery, I'd thought that I'd be pleased to finally be free of home and the village. But being away somehow brought me a new appreciation for my family. I looked around the dining room with its fading paint and worn tiles. It was *home*, comfortable as a well-worn shoe, and there was nothing better.

Mamma, Teresa and Paola wanted to hear about my time at the monastery and we sat around the table outside, shelling the last of the summer peas. The afternoon breeze that came off the sea, gently teasing the hair at the nape of my neck, was a welcome relief from the heat while I shared my experiences up in the mountains.

Soon, the light began to fade, the pink blush in the sky heralding the end of the day. It was time for Teresa to return home to her husband and she hugged me tight before making me promise to visit her the following day. Mamma filled her arms with a pot of zucchini and eggplant stew and a loaf of freshly baked bread. The scent of fresh bread made my mouth water but the rich aroma of the stew made my stomach grumble. I couldn't wait until my own dinner. There was nothing like Mamma's cooking.

Papà arrived soon after from a meeting with the government officials in the village and went straight to his room to change. I was helping Paola set the table and my stomach clenched with worry while I waited for him to wash his hands and face.

'You're home,' said Papà, walking into the dining room behind me.

Paola squeezed my hand before I spun around to face him. The lines on his face seemed etched more deeply than I remembered and his hair was beginning to recede. It had clearly been another difficult year on the farm.

56

'Ciao, Papà,' I said softly. 'It's good to be back.'

He gazed at me a moment, his dark eyes holding mine, his expression unreadable, and then he nodded. 'It's good to have you back.' He opened his arms. 'Do I get a hug?'

I fell into Papà's arms and he held me tight against his chest.

'I've missed you,' he whispered.

Tears welled in my eyes. 'I've missed you too, Papà.' It seemed that all was forgiven but I wondered how long that would last once I gave him the letters.

Papà was more animated than usual at dinner. 'Paola,' he said, 'tell Giulia about the new lambs we have. Mamma Mia! They're bigger and fatter than last year's lambs already.' He grinned as he mopped up the sauce on his plate with a chunk of bread.

Paola met my gaze and smiled. I knew she would tell me everything that had been happening when we retired to our room.

'Antonio jumped on the ram's back and rode him across the hill while you were away,' said our next-door neighbour Pietro with a mischievous look on his face. Pietro was often at our place because his mother was ill and Mamma felt sorry for him. Antonio elbowed Pietro in the ribs and shot a panicked glance at our father.

'Mannaggia! You better not have,' growled Papà, his brows lowered threateningly. 'If that ram gets hurt because of your antics . . .'

'No, Papà,' said Antonio quickly. 'I didn't. Pietro's just joking.'

Pietro nodded vigorously, looking ashamed.

'It looks like I need to find you more chores after school if you have time to think up silly pranks,' said Papà, taking a swallow of his homemade wine. He wasn't really angry at Antonio. He would have been up and whipping his backside with his belt if any damage had been done.

'How did you go speaking to the government officials about our wheat quotas?' asked Paola.

Papà shook his head. 'I haven't yet. I want to talk with some of the other farmers first. I've heard that grain is being stockpiled by the local officials.' He shook his head. 'They want to control and regulate supplies and fix a price suitable to them but it only drives us further into the ground. We can't supply grain at such a low price. Something has to change.'

'Maybe you should run for mayor,' said Antonio fiercely. 'Someone has to stand up to the officials.' Everyone knew that the local Fascist officials were corrupt.

'No,' said Papà. 'I have enough to do here and it wouldn't make any difference anyway.' Papà often helped others in the community deal with the government officials or explain the new and changing regulations that Il Duce had introduced. 'The government in Roma doesn't want to listen to us. We're expected to support them even though it's the powerful industrialists in the north who influence government policy.'

Antonio only shrugged but I could see that he wanted to say more. I was too nervous about what I had to tell Papà to say much myself. I'd already shown Mamma the letters and she agreed that I had to be the one to discuss their contents with him.

'I learnt lots of interesting things at the monastery,' I told Papà across the table.

'Off you go, boys,' said Papà, dismissing them from the table with a flick of his wrist. 'Go and put the ricotta away. It should have drained by now.'

Both boys happily obliged, scraping their chairs against the floor as they left, Antonio glad to be off the hook and away from Papà's scathing gaze.

Paola stood. 'I'll clear the table, Mamma, and keep an eye on the boys. You stay and talk to Giulia and Papà.'

'It was just what you needed,' said my father. 'Hard work and discipline . . . I hope you've learnt your lesson, to respect your elders and do as you're told.'

I swallowed hard. 'Si, Papà.'

He nodded with satisfaction.

'I want to make you proud,' I whispered, my stomach churning. 'I learnt some valuable skills from the monks and nuns. Mother Superior took me under her wing when she realised I had talents.'

Papà frowned, waving his hand. 'Your mother already told me that they put you in the kitchen.'

'Si . . . I learnt from the cook, but also from one of the most celebrated herbalists in Italy, Fra Fortunato.'

'Meaning what?'

I swallowed the lump that was still in my throat. 'I've been training to be a herbalist.'

'A herbalist?'

I nodded. 'Healing with herbs, under Fra Fortunato and Mother Superior.'

Papà banged the table hard with his hand, making me jump. 'I know what a herbalist is!' he shouted. 'But who told you you could study up in the mountains? You were there to

59

be disciplined, not to indulge in grand dreams of independence.' He leaned forward, his face beetroot red with fury and only inches away from mine. 'And you know how I feel about you having anything to do with becoming a maga.'

'But you let Teresa become a dressmaker,' said Mamma, coming to my defence. She rested her hand on his arm, trying to soothe and reason with him at the same time.

He pulled his arm away roughly. 'Teresa earned my trust and my support. She's always been a good girl. You, on the other hand,' he said, glaring at me, 'have only caused me trouble with your disrespect and still you think you deserve to have what you want and learn a craft.'

'Please, Papà! I have learnt my lesson. I promise I'll listen to you and do what I'm told. Mother Superior and Fra Fortunato think that I have a gift for healing. Fra Fortunato studied in Germany and Roma. He taught me about healing with herbs, nothing to do with the old ways. It's approved by the Church!' I was desperate for him to understand, desperate to have the chance to prove myself to him. Papà had always had the greatest respect for the Church and I hoped it would make him consider forgiving me and allowing me to further my training.

'How could she pass up such an opportunity?' pleaded Mamma. 'To train under God's roof with one of Italy's leading herbalists? It's the highest honour, Andrea. She has a gift from God and it would be a sin to ignore it.'

'A sin?' Papà growled, seething with anger. 'Mannaggia! I'm still the head of this house and what I say goes.'

Remembering the advice Mamma and Paola had given me about getting what I wanted, I sat quietly, feeling the anger swelling inside me, but I was determined not to make matters worse by erupting. Instead, I sent a swift prayer to the Madonna, reminding her of my need for her help.

'At least look at the letters they've written,' Mamma said. 'They have only the highest praise for Giulia's talent and for how hard she applied herself to her studies. It seems a waste to let all that hard work go to waste—'

'Letters? What letters?'

'Letters of recommendation. Giulia needs to continue her training with a healer, an apprenticeship, until she's ready to work on her own.'

His eyes narrowed. 'What healer?'

I took a deep breath. 'Nonna Mariana.'

Papà stood abruptly, scraping his chair against the tiles, and I noticed Mamma flinch. 'You think I'd let you learn the witchcraft she performs? Not on my life!'

I shook my head, tears in my eyes. 'I wouldn't do any of that. Please, Papà, read what they've written.' I pulled the letters from my skirt pocket and passed them to him with a trembling hand.

But he threw them onto the table with disgust. 'How do I know that you didn't plan this from the very beginning?'

I returned his gaze, determined to remain calm. If either Mamma or I told the truth now, he'd never let me become a healer and my time at the monastery would all have been for nothing.

'Don't be ridiculous, Andrea,' said Mamma with a wave of her hand. 'It so happens that Mother Superior Maria and Fra Fortunato have both worked with my mother and they know that she's not a witch but a skilled and well-respected healer.

She's the perfect person to train Giulia . . . But of course, it's your decision.'

'That's right. It's my decision,' he said, glaring at us.

I bit my tongue hard. I had to keep quiet if I wanted a chance. Mamma squeezed my hand beneath the table.

'Just remember that Giulia has spent the last seven months leading a disciplined life, she's been obedient and worked hard, just as you wanted,' Mamma said. 'Surely she's earned the right to further her training? And spending her time doing something she's passionate about means she'll have no time or reason to cause you any headaches.'

'Basta!' bellowed Papà. 'I'll make my decision when I'm good and ready.' With that, he stormed out of the room.

Mamma wiped the tears from my cheeks. 'It will be alright,' she whispered, before picking up the letters and following Papà to the bedroom.

I couldn't stop worrying. Paola and I still slept in the same bed even though there was a spare one now Teresa had left. We'd always shared our day with each other – after our prayers and before we slept – drawing comfort from each other's nearness and sleeping soundly in the knowledge that we always had each other. But the night I returned home, I barely heard anything Paola told me about what had happened on the farm and in the village while I was away. My stomach was tied in knots and I was restless.

'Worried about Papà's decision?' she asked gently.

I sighed. 'I don't know what I'll do if he says no. Now that I've started my training, I can't ever imagine not being allowed to do the one thing I've always wanted to do. I love it, Paola.'

Paola hugged me tight. 'You'll find a way. All the women of our family are behind you and we'll help you.'

She stroked my hair, brushing the stray strands off my face, and I relaxed in her arms. I'd find a way, no matter the obstacles I encountered.

Papà left me waiting for two days in the agony of not knowing. Each morning I was up early before he and Paola went to the farm, desperate for his decision. I couldn't even drink my café e latte while I waited for him – just looking at the film of scalded milk on top turned my stomach. But both mornings he said nothing, giving me the cold shoulder until he closed the door behind him. The evenings were no better. Although Mamma reassured me, telling me to be patient, and her nimble fingers moved swiftly over the rosary beads in silent prayer, I went to bed crying my eyes out, Paola consoling me. I was powerless.

On the third morning, Papà joined me at the table and a spike of anxiety shot through me.

'I don't approve of what you did, studying without my permission.'

'I'm sorry, Papà,' I murmured.

'But what's done is done. The monks and nuns saw fit to teach you and maybe it's God's will.' He dunked his biscotti into his coffee and I held my breath while he ate the soggy biscuit. 'Their letters explain that you have a rare gift and that you've been taught according to the Church's teachings ... Perhaps you deserve a chance to prove to me that you've changed.'

But Papà didn't know the truth, that my lessons had been planned. I glanced at my mother, now sitting beside him and she smiled.

'I-I promise to make you proud,' I stammered, choked up with tears.

'I know Nonna Mariana's a good woman,' he said gruffly. 'You can continue your studies with her until you've finished your apprenticeship and you're old enough to work on your own. But promise me that you'll stay away from superstitious charms and chants or anything associated with magic and witchcraft, otherwise it's finished.' He held my gaze to make sure I understood his conditions.

'Yes, Papà,' I said, wiping my eyes, containing the excitement that threatened to burst from me. Finally, I understood about working within boundaries, and the power of women united in a common cause. 'I promise.'

A small smile played across the corners of his mouth. 'Then you can visit your nonna this morning and tell her we want you to further your training with her.'

Overjoyed, I jumped up and rushed over to Papà's chair and hugged him tightly. He smelt of the faint tang of sheep's milk. 'Grazie, Papà. I'll work hard and become the best healer in the district.'

'I know you will,' he said, putting his arm around me. 'It's good to have you back.'

It came as a bit of a surprise to realise how much Papà had missed me. Maybe his forgiveness proved that the rift between us was finally healed.

*

I began working with Nonna Mariana that morning.

'I'm so happy your father allowed you to continue your studies,' said Nonna. She pulled me to her and kissed my cheek. 'I never believed this day would happen.'

'Neither did I.'

We were in her workroom next to the kitchen at the back of her house, overlooking the river below. She had two long wooden tables against the walls lined with cork-stoppered glass bottles and jars, some filled with seeds and berries, tinctures, herbal oils and ointments, some empty. There were paper packages of herbs in timber boxes and drying racks erected to one side filled with a variety of herbs such as comfrey, nettle and rue. Down the tiny hallway at the front of her house where the light was always the best was her treatment room, only big enough for a plinth and a table with a few chairs around it. Although Nonna regularly visited other towns in the district, most of her clients came here to see her. She was easily accessible, living on the edge of the village on the main road to the coast.

'Allora, tell me about your time at the monastery,' she said, passing the mortar and pestle to me to crush herbs. We were making a tincture for the patient we'd just seen, a middle-aged woman who complained of feeling constantly hot and bothered and retaining fluid, with terribly swollen legs. I inhaled the mixture – the heady pine of juniper berry and the herbaceous spiciness of celery seeds. I talked while we worked and Nonna asked questions from time to time.

Suddenly the ground beneath us began shaking, the glass bottles on the table tinkling. Nonna and I stopped what we were doing until the tremor passed. We were used to small tremors in

Calabria and thankfully we hadn't experienced anything bigger since the quake in 1908, which destroyed much of Messina, Reggio and many Calabrese villages including Bruzzano Vecchio. But I saw the shadow cross Nonna's face, her eyes wide and unseeing for just a moment. Now that I knew how much she'd lost in the 1894 quake, her mother and first husband, I understood how every tremor reminded her of her loss and filled her with fear of that calamity repeating itself again.

'I'm so happy that Mother Superior, Fra Fortunato and Sister Agata pushed you in your studies and instilled a thirst for learning. Now you finally have the skills and the confidence to do what you were born to do,' said Nonna, placing the herbs in a glass jar and covering them with grappa. The alcohol would extract the medicinal qualities from the plants. 'And I'm so happy that you're here with me. There's so much I can teach you.' She patted my hand before putting the lid on the jar and making sure it was airtight.

'I just want to learn everything. That feeling of curiosity and excitement I felt as a child was pushed down inside of me for so long.'

Nonna nodded, smiling sadly. 'Any natural exuberance is looked on with disapproval once you become a young woman for fear that you might step outside the conventional expectations. It's no wonder you've been wild and reckless.'

I followed her gaze out the window towards the silver-grey ribbon created by the gravel riverbed of the Bruzzano River and the green mountains that loomed in the distance behind it and kissed her soft cheek.

She handed me the jar to label. 'Is your father still insistent on finding you a husband?'

I shook my head. 'He hasn't said anything. I think he's glad I'm home and he's forgiven me. Besides, I can't imagine living the traditional life everyone expects me to.' I wanted to be like Nonna and Zia Francesca, living life on my own terms without a husband to control me. 'I want something more. I want to make a difference to the world somehow ... Mother Superior's lessons have helped me realise that Italy's changing, becoming a modern nation.'

'Change is coming but I fear it will be a long while before it reaches us here in the south. I worry that you'll be beating your head against a stone wall, trying to break down traditions that have been the very fabric of this society for hundreds of years.' She put the labelled jar on the shelf. 'You're right, you don't need anyone else to give you a sense of worth, to tell you who you are. But please think carefully about the choices you make. Remember that you live in a community that isn't as forward thinking as you yet, and your father still has the say over what you can and can't do.'

6

Teresa invited me to join her and Santoro on an outing after the October rains, showing a relative of Santoro's the sights of the district. We'd ended up at Bruzzano Vecchio, the old village abandoned in the earthquake at the turn of the century, nearly a mile further into the mountains.

Teresa took my arm and we allowed the others to walk ahead as we climbed the stone steps towards the ruins on Rocca Armenia. 'I'm pregnant,' she whispered.

I stopped and looked into her face, bright with joy, and hugged her tight.

'It's early days. Only Santoro knows for now but I couldn't wait any longer to share my news.'

'Congratulations,' I said. 'I know how much you've wanted to start a family.' I kissed her on the cheek. 'You'll make a wonderful mother.'

She smiled brilliantly, and I'd never seen her so happy.

Paola had told her about what had happened with Papà and the real reason I had gone to the monastery. When I came home, I'd waited for her judgement and disappointment but it never came. It was good to spend time with her.

I put my arm around Teresa's waist like I used to do when we were younger. We glanced across to the hills gently undulating towards the coast where the Ionian Sea met the Mediterranean. The vista from the top of the cliff was magnificent. Behind the hills, the blue silhouette of the Aspromonte Mountains curved around the valley like a parent protecting its precious child. Nothing seemed to have changed since I last looked out over the valley the day I agreed to watch the sheep for Vincenzo, yet my world had changed in ways I could never have imagined. Teresa's world had changed too: she was married and would soon have a baby.

Santoro played guide as we walked among the derelict buildings. 'This castle was the residence of the Carafa dynasty,' he began.

Trailing my hand across the thousand-year-old walls as I listened to his narrative, I wondered how these buildings had survived for so long, despite the harsh conditions of this land, and the invasions, wars and the jealous embrace of Mother Nature, who wreaked devastation with floods, droughts, earthquakes and tidal waves, purging the country-side of any who thought they could tame this wild land. These walls had finally succumbed to time and nature but they had seen so much.

'Do you know anything about who lived here before the Carafas?' I asked.

Santoro nodded. 'I have a few books on the history of this area if you're interested in learning more? Teresa tells me that you learnt to read fluently up at the monastery.'

'I've discovered that I love history and I want to know more about Calabria's past, and Italy's too.'

'Well, come to the schoolhouse after class one afternoon and I'll give you some books to read.'

'I'll come tomorrow,' I said, hugging him quickly, unable to contain my delight.

The following afternoon I arrived at the schoolhouse to find the classrooms empty. It was strange to be back here as a grown-up, the room silent, no impatient movement or noisy children. I walked around but not much had changed, there were still the same wooden desks and chairs, banged up, dented and chipped after years of use.

Hanging at the front of the room was a large map, much larger than the one Agata had shown me. I moved closer to see what the children were studying. I recognised the outline of Italy, our unified nation, with each region shaded in a different colour. I read the names: Lombardy and Emilia-Romagna in the north; Umbria and Lazio in the centre around Roma; and Campagna and Calabria in the south. It was a very long way to the northern border in the Alps. As I inspected the map, I realised that I knew little about the countries outside of our own.

I thought back to Vincenzo's latest letter. *Addis Ababa is a fascinating place. After months of being stationed here, I know the city like the back of my hand. The locals are slowly getting used to our presence although I'm not sure they'll ever accept us being here. There's talk of us coming home and I hope it's before Christmas . . .*

Looking at the continent of Africa, I still couldn't believe how tiny Italy was in comparison. I searched for Addis Ababa.

'Here,' I whispered, placing my finger on the centre of the country next to the easternmost point of Africa. I shook my head in amazement. My brother and his friends Stefano and Angelo were so far away. If the cultural differences were so noticeable from one Italian region to another, how different they must be between the Italian and Abyssinian peoples. I could only begin to imagine how alien Vincenzo must feel.

'There you are,' said Santoro, carrying a stack of books to the desk at the front. 'I have plenty for you to read, as long as you're interested. Where do you want to start?'

'How about with Calabria's history?' I said tentatively. 'I want to understand why the Mezzogiorno is so different to the north. I've been studying old newspapers to keep up with my reading and learn more about the issues that affect our community.' I was too embarrassed to tell him that I usually found them in the piazza, discarded on benches outside our local church.

'Eccellente! It's a good place to start.' He sorted through the books, taking a selection from the pile. 'I'm very pleased to help you continue your learning. God knows I don't get enthusiastic students like you every day.' We shared a smile. It seemed we were both excited by this opportunity. 'Teresa says you were always the brightest one in your class. Such a shame you couldn't continue your schooling.'

I blushed at the compliment, especially from Teresa, and wondered what might have happened if Santoro had been my teacher.

'But you know that girls don't get the same opportunities as boys,' I said.

'In my classroom they do,' said Santoro emphatically. 'I value intelligence, curiosity and dedication, girl or boy. Pushing the mind is just as important as maintaining a healthy body.' He pulled one of the books towards him and placed it in front of me, opening it to a map of Calabria. 'This book is perfect to give you an overview of Calabria's past. When you're reading, you'll find that dynasties colonising this part of Calabria, like the Carafas, came and went: Norman, Swabian, Spanish, Austrian and French. But the Calabrese people have always endured. This region was part of "Magna Graecia", which the ancient Greeks colonised nearly three thousand years ago, long before the Romans and Ottomans.'

'Is that why lots of villages and towns still speak Griko?'

Santoro's face lit up. 'That's right. It's an ancient Greek dialect.'

This was part of the reason we were so different from the north. Our people were ancient, with ancient traditions, but the sophisticated northerners only saw us as backward and primitive. I told him about the ancient Greek ties to the festa at the monastery. He was intrigued and I was glad to have something to share with him, someone I could explore ideas with and talk to about subjects that interested me. But most of all, I appreciated the respect that Santoro gave me. It was empowering to know that I was valued for whatever I had to say – and for just being me.

One night in late November, Papà asked Paola and I to stay at the table after dinner.

'What is it, Papà?' asked Paola, sinking into the chair next to him. He seemed more serious than usual, his arms resting on the table, a look of determination on his face.

As I pulled out the chair next to her, I wondered briefly if I'd done something wrong and then dismissed the thought. I'd listened to Mamma's and Paola's advice and I'd done everything right: I'd studied hard to make my family proud, was respectful of Papà's wishes and I didn't rock the boat. Perhaps something had happened on the farm.

'I know, Paola, that you're happy to work the farm – and God knows you're a help and a comfort to me – but I'd be selfish to keep you here at home and wouldn't be doing what's right for you if I didn't look to your future.' He put up his hand to stop Paola from speaking and the disquiet that had been swirling in my belly erupted as waves of alarm. 'Now that your sister Teresa is well settled into married life, it's high time your mother and I found you a husband.'

Paola turned the colour of milk and I clutched her hand tightly under the table.

'Papà, please! I don't need or want a husband. I'll stay here, work the farm with you and look after you and Mamma in your old age.'

Papà shook his head sadly.

'Truly, Papà, this is the life that I want. It's what makes me happiest.'

'I know, Paola, but what happens when we die? You'll be alone with no one to care for you. No husband and no children. Who will want you when you're too old to bear children?' His brown eyes were tortured, his handsome features haggard. Of the three girls, Paola was closest to him. Maybe this was why

73

Papà had asked me to stay? To support Paola in this? My eyes brimmed with tears. Paola didn't have to marry to have a good life. She had no interest in marriage. She already had what she wanted.

'I have my brothers and sisters. They'll always help and support me.'

'Paola can do anything a man can do,' I said defensively. 'She can run the farm and live her life without a husband. We'll always be here for her.'

'A simple life, that's all I want,' Paola said beseechingly, her hands folded as though in prayer.

Papà shook his head. 'What don't you understand?' he asked, pinching his fingers together, a sign of his growing frustration. 'It's not possible. I'd be failing in my duty as a father if I don't see you settled in marriage like Teresa.'

'I won't do it, Papà,' said Paola, sitting tall and resolute.

'Don't make her do it, Papà,' I said. Paola was a gentle and compassionate soul and I worried about what an unwanted marriage would do to her.

'Mannaggia! You will do as I say!' yelled Papà, banging on the table with his fist, but I could see the hurt in his face. He didn't want to see Paola go any more than she wanted to leave. 'And you,' he said, turning his attention to me, 'I should never have allowed you to become apprenticed to your nonna against my better judgement. I was too soft on you, like I have always been, but now you have what you wanted, I expect you to do as you're told.'

Like a slap across the face, I suddenly realised that Papà hadn't forgotten anything. Fear crawled up my spine like a scorpion. I stared at the jar of pickled green chillies sitting on the table, trying to make sense of what was happening.

'It's time you were married too. I should have done that instead of sending you to the monastery. A husband and children will settle your fiery temperament and you'll soon see that your family comes first.'

The blood drained from my face. 'What do you mean? I've done everything you've asked of me. I've changed my ways.' I felt faint, as though I was far away, but Paola squeezed my hand and brought me back to the moment. 'What about my training with Nonna?'

'You think I don't know why you were sent away? It wasn't until Signora Polenti told me how surprised she was that you were back home and apprenticed after you'd been seen on the road to the coast that I learnt what you'd done. At first, I couldn't believe the old busybody, but I made sure I got to the bottom of it. How could you? How could you put your own selfish desires above your family? You put your family's reputation in danger, your *own* reputation on the line. You missed Teresa's special day and upset your mother and sisters. And then you were rewarded by being allowed to study what you wanted. You've caused me so much shame and embarrassment.'

'Papà, I'm sorry,' I muttered, mortified.

'I didn't ask you to speak!' he roared. 'You jeopardise this family's honour. I can't take back your time at the monastery but I'll make sure you remain an honest woman. You will marry who I say you will to regain my trust and this family's honour.'

My mind worked furiously, thinking of the best way to pacify my father. 'Papà . . . I want to make something of my life, not just become a wife and mother,' I pleaded desperately.

'You want to make something of your life?' His eyebrows lifted in contempt. 'Your mother and I work to the bone to give you the best life we can and you want more. Well, you have what you wanted. Now you marry who I say.'

I doubled over as though I'd been kicked in the stomach. I had to swallow hard to prevent the scream bursting from my lips, but I couldn't stop the tears running down my face.

I thought of Agata and the old man her family had chosen for her. She had only escaped when she entered the convent. Papà would never give me that choice. Not now.

Papà looked away from my distress and took a deep breath as if to calm down. 'I'm sorry, Giulia. I know you're upset but I'm doing this for your own good and for our family's honour. It will be for the best in the long run.'

Desolate, I covered my face with my hands and began to sob. After everything I'd been through, control of my destiny was being ripped from me.

7

Papà kept to his word, despite the entreaties of Mamma and even Zia Francesca, who he was furious with for their part in my deception. He found suitors for both me and Paola and began making arrangements between the families with regard to dowries and announcements. Paola and I wrote desperate letters to Vincenzo, telling him of our plight, begging him to find a way to come home as soon as possible to save us. I wrote to Agata too, pouring out my heart to her. I knew she'd understand, after what she'd been through.

'I won't do it,' said Paola resolutely one night in early December as we huddled under the blankets to keep warm. It wasn't as cold as winter in the mountains, but with the stiff sea breeze whistling through the village, it was still cold enough to wish we were lying beside the kitchen hearth.

'I know, but at least this one's young and Mamma's insisted that he comes from a farming background,' I said, shifting onto my side to face her, the thin, worn sheet soft against my skin. Her potential husband was a man in his early twenties from a nearby village who had inherited his father's small farm after his death from malaria.

'I can't believe the man Papà has chosen for you,' Paola whispered in horror.

Although not as old as the grandfather Agata had been matched with, Massimo was a widower in his early forties, old enough to be my father. His wife had died in childbirth a year earlier, along with their baby. Their two surviving sons, similar in age to Paola and me, were in Reggio. Massimo was a fisherman who lived not far from Brancaleone, near the marina where he kept a fleet of fishing boats.

'I won't do it either,' I said defiantly. 'Nobody can make us.' But in my heart, I knew that Papà could indeed make us, and I was terrified. A prosperous man of Papà's generation might be against his wife having independent work and could refuse to let me continue my apprenticeship with Nonna. I hoped against hope that the small distance from the marina to the clinic would persuade him to let me continue. If not, any part of the real me that remained would be consumed by caring for a large family. The thought made me feel hollow, empty with despair.

'We'll have a fight on our hands, but we have to find a way to stop these weddings. Mamma knows I belong here with them and Papà knows it too, deep down. It's his stubborn refusal to allow anything outside tradition that's forcing this.'

'That and his bloody honour,' I said darkly. I flung myself onto my back.

'If we can delay the announcement of the engagements until Vincenzo comes home, maybe he can think of a way to persuade Papà that marriage isn't right for either of us . . .'

It was an idea born of desperation. Even though we were girls, Vincenzo felt bad that Papà was always so strict with us when he had so many more freedoms. He'd understand our horror at being forced into marriage and our hope was that he'd somehow find a way to get us out of Papà's arrangements. And as the oldest son and now a seasoned soldier returning from war, maybe he'd finally have some sway over Papà's decision.

'I'm not sure how long we can delay things, if he's not home soon,' I said.

'Then we have to rely on each other as we always have,' said Paola, hugging me tight.

'I'll go and see Zia Francesca,' I said. She'd always found a way to help me before, and I was sure she would think of something this time.

'I'm so sorry, Giulia. Your father refuses to talk to me and I don't think there's anything anyone can say to dissuade him,' Zia Francesca said as she prepared to open the restaurant.

I blinked away tears of disappointment. She was my role model – strong, smart, independent – but for the first time in my life she didn't have a solution to my problem. 'Please, Zia, there has to be a way! Papà can't do this to us.'

'I'll continue to try and I know your mother will too.'

I left the pot I'd been stirring and walked into her arms. 'Grazie.' At least she wasn't going to give up. Paola and I weren't alone, despite feeling adrift.

She kissed the top of my head. 'Come now, we'd better open the doors and serve these hungry customers.'

Sometime later, after everyone had been served and seemed content, Zia Francesca came into the kitchen with a strange expression on her face. 'Don Silvio would like to see you.'

I frowned. 'Who?'

'He said he met you while on pilgrimage at the monastery and that you helped his cousin, Don Giovanni, who was unwell.'

The man in the suit. I glanced at her, my eyes wide with surprise. 'He did say that he'd been here before and would seek me out when he next came this way,' I said. 'Do you know him?'

She nodded. 'Quite well. He's my late husband's godson. He used to come here quite regularly . . . You know what he is?' she asked quietly. I nodded. 'Alright then, as long as you know. He's at the table in the back corner.'

Don Silvio was on his own, dressed in an expensive suit with his dark hair slicked back. His brown eyes sparkled and he smiled as I approached. 'Buona sera, Signorina Tallariti, do you remember me?'

'Of course, from your pilgrimage.'

He nodded, pleased at my discretion, and gestured for me to sit.

'How is your cousin? Is he recovering?'

'He's much better now, thanks to Fra Fortunato and you. He takes his medicine every day.'

'That's good.'

'It is an unexpected pleasure to find you here. I thought you were training to become a healer.' He reached across to the next table to pick up another glass and poured me some red wine. He wore a gold signet ring with a large red stone on his finger and an expensive watch circled his wrist.

'Grazie,' I said, sipping the wine. It was a bottle from a local vineyard and much smoother than the homemade wine my father made. 'I am. I'm working with my nonna but from time to time I help Zia Francesca in the kitchen.'

'The pasta and ragú are perfect as usual,' he said.

'Zia Francesca's a wonderful cook.'

'Even still. It seems that you are a young lady of many talents. I'll let Don Giovanni know that you're doing well, learning with Signora Palamara.'

I didn't even flinch. Of course he would have known who my nonna was. He probably already knew that I'd be here at the trattoria and even perhaps that I'd soon be engaged.

'I wanted to give you something as a token of our appreciation.'

'I don't need anything,' I mumbled shyly. 'It really was my pleasure and I'm glad that Don Giovanni's better.'

'No, don't be silly. I insist,' he said, sliding a slim box across the table. 'Open it.'

What could I do? I opened the box – and gasped. Nestled inside was the most gorgeous gold fountain pen. I picked it up and it balanced perfectly in my hand. 'It's beautiful, but this is too much,' I whispered. 'I can't take it.'

'But it has your name on it,' he said, grinning at my reaction. 'You have to take it now.'

'Grazie. It's more than generous.'

Don Silvio beamed with pleasure. 'Use it in your work and remember my cousin as one of the first patients you ever helped.'

'Thank you, I will,' I murmured. But my smile wobbled as I wondered if I'd be able to use it once I was married.

'Allora, I should let you return to help your zia, but we will see each other again sometime.'

'Buon Natale,' I said, rising from the chair. *Merry Christmas.*

'Buon Natale to you and your family too, signorina.'

Zia Francesca said nothing when I told her what had happened, only to keep the pen safe and not tell my parents who had given it to me. She didn't want them to worry, but somehow this kind gesture had warmed my heart and made me more determined than ever to continue learning.

Two weeks later, Paola and I were helping Mamma make festive biscuits – nacatole, a delicate, ladder-shaped biscuit that represents the good will of the season, and petrali, traditional biscuits shaped in a half-moon and stuffed with fruit and nuts – when we heard the front door open.

'Mamma!' called a voice.

We looked up from our rolling and pinching of pastry.

'It's Vincenzo,' said Mamma, her face alight with joy as she wiped her floury hands on her apron.

Paola and I looked at each other in surprise. We'd not heard about his return from Abyssinia.

Mamma was in his arms in an instant. 'My beautiful boy,' she whispered, holding him tight. 'You're finally home.'

'Buon Natale, Mamma,' Vincenzo said. Dark circles were under his eyes but he was beaming with pleasure. 'I travelled for two days straight to get home to you before Christmas.'

'Let me look at you,' she said, wiping the tears from her cheeks. She held him at arm's length and scrutinised him. 'Are you still all in one piece?' Vincenzo had grown taller and his olive skin was dark from countless days under the African sun, but the biggest change was not physical. He seemed somehow older, more mature, perhaps even wiser. I could see it in his eyes and wondered what he'd seen and done to create such a change. My heart went out to him. I wished I could wash away whatever had happened and bring back the mischievous, carefree, laughing boy he had been before he'd left.

'I'm fine, Mamma,' said Vincenzo. 'Just tired and happy to be home.' He glanced at Paola and me, our fingers caked in dough, and at the large bowl filled with the sweet marinating-fruit mixture: figs, raisins, tangerine and orange peels, walnuts, almonds, honey, cooked wine, cinnamon, cloves and coffee. 'Are you making petrali? My favourite.' He groaned and closed his eyes in bliss. 'I've waited so long for your cooking, Mamma . . . I've missed you all so much.'

Paola rushed into his arms and I was close behind, the three of us in a tight embrace.

It wasn't until after dinner that evening, where Mamma placed the choicest morsels on his plate, that Paola and I got a chance to talk with him. Vincenzo joined us in our bedroom, the three of us sitting on the bed.

'I haven't the heart to tell Mamma that I'm only home for two weeks. I leave again to join a new regiment that's going to Spain. Stefano and Angelo too.'

'What?' I said. As I gazed at him, I saw an assuredness that hadn't been so noticeable before, a confidence in himself and his abilities.

Vincenzo shrugged. 'We had no choice, were only told to pack up and that we were returning to Italy before going to Spain to help General Franco in the civil war there.'

Paola's face fell. 'So you're going to another war?'

He took Paola's hand and kissed it. 'Don't worry, I'll be fine. I'm a seasoned soldier now. I know how to look out for myself.'

'How was it?' I asked him gently.

He shook his head. 'It was war but . . .' He stared at the worn sheepskin rug on the floor. 'It was brutal. I can barely come to terms with the carnage I witnessed.'

Paola covered his hand with hers, as though to lend him her strength.

'We had more advanced weapons than the Abyssinians – their forces were decimated.' He shook his head, closing his eyes at the memory. 'We entered Addis Ababa victorious, in a convoy of trucks with General Badoglio at its head, but we found scenes of chaos, citizens fleeing and the Abyssinian forces in retreat. I know that territory is won or lost by wars such as these and God knows we need more farming land for our southern farmers, but what happened in Abyssinia was wrong. To force a people from their home and land.' There was so much more to war than winning or losing.

'I can't imagine what it's been like for you,' whispered Paola, squeezing Vincenzo's hand. I could only sit stunned and rigid by his side, my heart aching with the knowledge that my innocent, carefree brother was gone.

'We had to focus on what we had to do and do that well,' Vincenzo continued, 'because our own survival and that of the men around us counted on it. Angelo, Stefano and I left for Africa proud to serve our country and excited for a grand adventure in a strange new land but we're changed men now. Our innocence is lost. We've seen things nobody should ever see and . . . we'll never be the same again.'

With a shuddering breath, I took his face in my hands and kissed his dark head. 'You're home now and if Mamma has her way, she'll smother you with love until you forget you ever left.'

'I can't forget. The images are there when I close my eyes, in my dreams. But we're the lucky ones . . . there are those who died on the battlefield, others who were maimed. We all felt so helpless . . . But Stefano still wants to become a doctor.' He shook his head, eyebrows raised in wonder. 'They'll need all the help they can get, even from someone like him.'

I wrapped my arms around him. 'Oh, Vincenzo, I'm so sorry you had to go through this.'

He patted me on the shoulder and drew back. 'I'm home now. Not a word to Mamma of any of this,' he said, frowning ferociously, although his eyes were bright with tears. 'Now, tell me what's been happening here.'

Paola and I shared a look.

'Didn't you get our letters?' I asked. Agata had replied, shocked and sympathetic at my predicament, but she couldn't think of any useful escape. Instead, she tried to lift my spirits with news that she'd started her own training with Fra Fortunato.

He shrugged. 'Last I heard was that you'd come home from the monastery.'

'You must have left before they arrived,' whispered Paola. 'Papà wants us to marry suitors of his choosing and he's close to announcing the engagements. We have to find a way to stop that from happening.' Papà was finalising the engagements and would make them public knowledge in the New Year.

We launched into the tale of the events that had unfolded since my return.

Vincenzo frowned in consternation. 'I'll try to talk Papà around ... I don't know that he'll listen to me but I'll see what I can do. Otherwise, maybe we can somehow upset the negotiations. You both deserve to be happy.'

Paola and I sighed with relief. Vincenzo was all we had. But I hoped that Papà would listen to him and respect his opinion, because although I had faith in Vincenzo doing all he could, I wasn't sure how we would get out of the arrangements otherwise.

The following evening after dinner, we sat around the table drinking coffee and chatting like nothing had changed. Angelo and Stefano had called in after they'd finished running errands for their grandfather.

'How's your grandfather?' asked Papà while I poured the coffee. 'I haven't seen much of him lately.'

'He's fine but busy,' said Stefano, nodding as I handed him his cup. 'He's been helping Papà manage the farm while we've been away, much like you I suppose, except my sister's not as interested in farming and cheesemaking as Paola, and my brother's too young to be much help.'

I sat down, my eyebrows raised in surprise at such a compliment to my sister. I glanced at Paola, who had blushed beetroot red. But it was true. She was becoming a good farmer and indispensable to Papà. Paola understood what had to be done without Papà having to tell her and she had some good ideas on how to improve the farm, like moving from bullock-drawn plough to tractor-driven implements. Her cheeses were as good as Papà's, if not better, and he was beginning to let her do a large portion of the cheesemaking. Which was why her imminent engagement baffled us even more.

Papà nodded. 'I'm sure he missed you while you were away. But you're both back now, older and wiser.'

Angelo nodded thoughtfully, sipping the hot coffee. 'After everything the three of us have seen and done, we're as close as brothers could be.'

'I wouldn't have got through the war without them,' said Vincenzo quietly. His eyes were filled with regret and sorrow.

I remembered the days that the three of them had gone on hunting trips with Papà into the mountains, tumbling into the house at the end of the day, shouting and yelling, pushing and shoving to be the first to show Mamma the hare they'd caught, only to collapse onto the floor in a tangle of gangly arms and legs and dissolve into uncontrollable fits of laughter. Their innocence was gone and despite the resentment I felt towards their freedoms, I felt sorry for them.

'I have no doubt you all experienced things you never imagined,' said Papà softly. 'War will do that to you. Nobody can understand what you've been through. All the public sees is the result of the war, the bitter defeats or the glorious victories.'

Mamma and I shared a glance. Papà rarely talked about his experiences in the Great War. The only evidence we saw of his time with the Bersaglieri was when we watched him shoot quail in the straw-coloured grass or hares that pushed under our fences.

'The oppression against the local people was one of the hardest things to witness,' Stefano said, dragging a hand through his dark curly hair, much like Angelo's and Vincenzo's. It had been some time since any of them had had a haircut. 'It's one thing to take land to help our own poor, especially here in the south, and bolster the Italian economy and patriotism, but it's another to witness the massacre of a suppressed people.'

'No one I know will settle in Abyssinia,' said Angelo.

I offered the plate of nacatole and petrali to him. He took one eagerly and smiled. Antonio was still at the table with us, staring at the boys with fascination. I shivered, suddenly glad that he was too young to be drafted.

'Mussolini has created a nation of restless nationalists looking beyond Italy's borders to recreate the glory of Roma, rather than looking inward at the terrible conditions us farmers in the south have to endure,' said Papà. 'I know he's done many good things to try to unite north and south, but without understanding the needs of the Mezzogiorno, he'll never truly bring us together.' He gulped his coffee, then gestured for a refill. Paola filled his cup and passed it back to him.

'Most Italians will never know the cost of the Abyssinian war.' Stefano tipped his cup with a flick of his wrist, finishing his espresso in one swallow.

'I'm just glad we're home,' said Vincenzo abruptly.

'And sitting around the table, drinking coffee and just talking like this is something we've both missed,' said Stefano. 'It's what we leave behind here that makes us take what we do so seriously. Because there's no place like home and the love of family and friends.'

I stared at him, my mouth agape. I never imagined hearing such passionate and wise words come out of my brother's or any of his friends' mouths.

Noticing my expression, Stefano grinned at me. 'Catching flies, Giulia, or are you just astounded by my wisdom?'

'Don't be silly, Stefano,' I shot back, embarrassed. 'I was just looking at that mop of hair on your head. It makes you look like a scarecrow. When did you last get a haircut?'

I noticed Angelo and Vincenzo smirk. Stefano raised his eyebrows at my quick reply, challenge in his eyes. It was almost reassuring to see that the old Stefano was still there.

'Well, Topolina, I'll make sure my hair is in an acceptable condition before I next visit,' he said, pushing a hand through his unruly locks.

I stared at him, not sure whether to laugh or be mad. Topolina was the pet name the boys had called me when I was younger. It had made me feel special until I decided that I had outgrown it and wasn't a 'little mouse' anymore. Then the boys used it just to annoy me.

'Allora, we'd better get home,' Stefano said, rising from the table. 'Mamma will be waiting up and Papà has a long list of chores for me in the morning.'

Once the cousins had left, Vincenzo and Mamma remained sitting with Papà while Paola and I cleared the table.

'I hear that you've found suitors for the girls,' Vincenzo said conversationally. Paola and I shared a look of trepidation. My heart began racing and I grasped her clammy hand as we hovered at the end of the table.

'That's right,' said Papà, leaning back in his chair.

'You know that neither of them wants to get married yet.'

'Both of them are already promised,' said Papà bluntly.

'I know, but I'm asking you to consider not going ahead with the engagements. Paola only wants to work with you on the farm and from what I hear, her reputation as a cheese-maker is beginning to grow. Giulia's only just starting out in her new profession and won't be qualified for a while yet. Wouldn't it be better to wait until they're both more established and can offer their husbands a more solid income?'

'And why would I do that? I've found them both good matches. Paola's suitor has a farm she can become involved with and Giulia's man is mature and experienced, and can provide for her. They'll have good lives.' Papà gazed at Vincenzo, implacable, and fear welled up within me like the water from an underground spring. I wanted to yell, but Paola squeezed my hand tight and I remained silent, quivering with anger.

'Andrea, give them a chance,' said Mamma. 'Can't you see that they don't want to marry yet? Paola wants to stay with us and Giulia has finally grown up and has her head screwed on right.'

'Giulia might be seventeen now but she's still a child in many ways and needs a strong man who can guide her,' Papà said.

'She needs to be with the one she loves to make her happy,' said Mamma, grasping Papà's hand across the table. 'Just like us. Wait until she's found him. She doesn't need to marry until then. She's under your watchful eye. She's learnt her lesson . . .'

The tension thrummed through the air, thick as honey. I could barely stand it.

'That's right, they're young and don't know what's best for them. I'm their father and I know what's best. One day they'll thank me.'

'But!' said Vincenzo, trying again.

'Basta!' said Papà. 'Don't push me, Vincenzo. I won't change my mind.'

Vincenzo slumped in his chair, dejected. Papà could be stubborn and completely immovable when he wanted.

I glanced at Mamma beseechingly but she smiled sadly and shook her head. Papà would not be swayed. The anger and fear within me boiled over. I pulled away from Paola.

'Why, Papà?' I yelled. 'You wouldn't do this to the boys! I don't see you looking for a wife for Vincenzo or reprimanding Antonio for doing something you don't agree with. Paola's the perfect daughter and you want to inflict misery and suffering on her when all she wants to do is run the farm with you! And me, I've studied hard, settled down, learnt to be respectful and I'm trying to make something of myself!'

My family stared at me in shock.

Papà stood, his chair falling to the floor. 'Go to your room.'

I was too furious to heed caution. 'No, Papà, not until you listen to reason. You can't force us to marry against our will. We're not livestock that you can pen up in enclosures and control our every move, we're your daughters and no different to your sons. We can do anything they can do and I know that I cause you trouble but Paola—' my voice caught as I glanced at her pale face and terrified expression, '—she's never caused you grief, not one single day of her life.'

Papà slashed his hands through the air. *Enough!* 'You'll marry who I say and that's final,' he roared, his face scarlet with rage.

I flicked my fingers from under my chin. *I don't give a damn.* 'Well, I'm telling you that I won't! I'll run away if I have to, your family honour be damned!'

Out of the corner of my eye I could see Mamma flinch at my gesture and words. Paola and Vincenzo stared at me like I'd gone crazy, but Papà's eyes bulged with fury and suddenly I was afraid.

'Mannaggia! I'll disown you and you'll never see your mother and your brothers and sisters again!'

'Giulia,' cried Paola frantically. 'Don't. Not like this.'

'I'll make sure you both marry as soon as is permissible,' Papà said. 'After the marriage banns have been read.'

I shook my head in disbelief. Once the engagement was official, marriage banns were read at Sunday Mass for three consecutive weeks before the wedding could take place. This meant that Papà intended us to wed in as soon as a month.

'No, none of this is Paola's fault! Don't make her go through with it.' I looked at my sister's stunned face as panic blossomed in my chest. I felt faint. I couldn't be the cause of making matters worse for her.

'Andrea,' said Mamma, coming to my side and placing a protective arm around me and Paola. 'Don't you see that all you're doing is hurting them? Do you really want to push them away like this?'

Papà stared at her as though she'd gone mad. 'My mind's made up, Gabriella.'

'You're a logical man, Andrea. Don't make a decision you later regret because your daughter pushed you beyond reason.'

'It's enough that you knew what she did and you hid it from me. All you do is coddle her, make excuses for her and

give her what she wants, but this time she'll do as she's told.'
He stood over me, glowering. 'I'll lock her in her room until
the wedding day if I have to.'

'No,' I sobbed. Tears were streaming down my cheeks. 'I'll
behave and do what I'm told, but you can't make Paola marry.
She's never wanted marriage. It will destroy her soul. The farm
is her passion. She belongs here. Don't punish her because
of me.'

Papà stared at me, saying nothing, before striding out into
the night, slamming the door behind him.

8

It was the most miserable Christmas of my life. The sound of yelling had punctuated the silence of the nights since my outburst. My parents' arguing was something I'd heard only a few times in my life. I'd never seen my father so angry and resolute that even my mother couldn't sway him. He blamed Mamma for not stopping me from studying at the monastery but if he ever found out that it had been planned . . .

But Vincenzo hadn't given up and early in the new year, he discovered that Paola's suitor suffered from malaria. Between Mamma's anger and Teresa's and Vincenzo's persuasive and persistent comments to Papà, he finally relented and ended the negotiations with the boy's family. It was the excuse Papà needed to back down from one wedding without losing face. Paola was his right-hand woman on the farm and we all knew that he'd be lost without her. Everyone was relieved that Paola was free to remain at home and even Papà was beginning to realise the benefits of having her help and insisted she accompany him on farm business.

Vincenzo also finally announced that he was going to ask for Rosa's hand in marriage. Nineteen thirty-seven suddenly seemed a brighter year, at least for Paola, Vincenzo and Rosa.

I was not so lucky. Papà went ahead and announced my engagement to Massimo and there was nothing any of us could do.

'I'm sorry I couldn't do more to help,' Vincenzo murmured as I hugged him tight. He was leaving again to meet his regiment. He and Rosa didn't plan on getting married until he returned home – but I'd be married in a matter of weeks.

I nodded, tears in my eyes. 'Papà's determined to make me do what he expects of me, marry for the sake of family honour and have plenty of babies, but I'll make him regret his decision. I never want to speak to him again.' I'd written to Agata to tell her what had happened. I'd never had a friend like her before, someone I could confide in and tell anything to without judgement or worrying about family dynamics.

Paola lay beside me that night, smoothing the hair from my face as I sobbed. Part of me wanted to run away, but Papà had threatened to disown me and I couldn't leave her. Any chance of continuing my training with Nonna would be gone if I left. They were the two anchor points in my life, my hope of a better future. I had little choice but to accept my engagement.

I wept until my tears were spent and the hot rage was replaced with hollow desolation.

I went to the schoolhouse the following afternoon to return the books Santoro had given me. Nobody could stop me from learning. I could now speak and write in formal Italian more fluently and that in itself motivated me to keep going. I'd devoured the information on modern Italian history, regional social history and geography and even the first part of Dante's *Divine Comedy, Inferno.* I kept a dictionary by my side to look up words I didn't understand, writing them down, along with their meanings, in a notebook that Mother Superior had given me.

While I was waiting for Santoro, I walked across to the map at the front of the classroom again and found Spain, where the civil war was underway. Santoro had explained the war to me but I didn't understand why the fascists were fighting against the traditionally Catholic republican government for control of the country. Here in Italy, Il Duce had remained on good terms with the Church. I decided that I'd follow what was written about the progress of the war in the local newspaper and when Vincenzo next wrote, I'd find where he was on the map in relation to the fighting.

I finally met Massimo after Mass one Sunday. He was a short and stocky man with a pleasant face, not exactly handsome, but not ugly either. He seemed nervous, rubbing his fingertips over each other. Noticing that should have made me feel slightly less resentful towards him, but all I could think about was that he would soon control my life – some nerves, a nice smile and a polite manner weren't going to change that fact.

'You're a maga, a healer?' he asked me as we stood with my parents and siblings in the piazza outside the church. The chatter of the congregation buzzed around us.

'That's right,' I said tightly. 'I work with my nonna, Mariana Palamara.'

He nodded, wiping his hands on his trousers. 'I've heard wonderful things about you and your work. You must have a special gift.'

I frowned, adjusting the edge of my headscarf. Compliments weren't going to make me like him either. 'Grazie. It's part of who I am and very important to me. I'd be lost without it.'

'Of course. I understand what you mean. I always wanted to become a priest but when my older brother died, I had to take over the family fishing business.'

'Oh, I'm sorry,' I said, taken aback at his honesty. Maybe he would understand my desire to continue studying.

He shook his head and smiled. 'No need. It was a long time ago and I love being out on the boats now. I want you to know that I respect what you do, helping people and caring for the community. Please don't feel that you have to stop working with your nonna once we're married. Unless you want to, of course.'

If it wasn't for my own incredulity, I would have laughed out loud. Papà was standing nearby talking to Mamma, and I noticed him go rigid, his eyes narrowing at Massimo's words.

'Really?' I studied his expression. I tried to find a hint of insincerity, but he seemed genuine. 'But why would you do that for me?'

'The work you do, helping people, is valuable. My oldest boy, Luigi, is studying at teacher's college in Reggio and I hope Franco will follow in his footsteps. Service to others is God's work . . . and I just want you to be happy.'

I nodded, stunned. 'How would I get back to Bruzzano each day?'

'I'll buy you a mule to take you to your nonna's and back every day.'

Faint with relief, I stared at him, not sure what to think. Perhaps Papà had chosen a man who would not crush my spirit after all.

Massimo smiled at my reaction. 'You bring comfort and joy to others when life is filled with hardship and pain. I wish my wife's life had been easier . . . Let me bring some comfort to you,' he said, as though it was the easiest thing in the world. But he had no idea that the idea of marrying someone not of my own choosing made me desperately unhappy.

The following week, Massimo came for dinner and took me walking through the village in the evening, my parents following behind. It was late January and the dead of winter but he only wore a jacket over his shirt and trousers. I supposed that he was used to the cold, out on the open sea every day. Thankfully most people were indoors playing cards and drinking wine and coffee. I still felt like I was being paraded like a prize cow, though.

'May I hold your hand?' he asked as we walked.

'Alright.'

He took my hand in his. It was thick and calloused, probably from years of dragging in fishing nets, and felt strange. I forced down a wave of panic.

'This feels unnatural for me too,' he whispered.

I glanced at him sharply but there was no anger, only compassion and sadness.

'My wife's hand was the only woman's hand I've held for twenty years. It's been two years since she died, along with our baby, and it still feels that I'm dishonouring her memory by even walking with you, although she'd tell me it was time to find happiness again.'

'I'm sorry about what happened to your wife.' Women died in childbirth all the time but it didn't make it any less painful. Often there was something a healer like Nonna could do, or a midwife, if they arrived at the woman's side early enough, but many times there was not.

'Grazie. She couldn't have any more children after a difficult delivery with our second son, Franco, and when she fell again so late in life, we thought it was a miracle. But it wasn't to be.'

'And do you think you will find happiness again?' I asked, pulling my coat tighter against the chill of the breeze. The streets were nearly empty, slivers of light spilling from the cracks in the doors and shuttered windows.

'I think that sometimes happiness can be found where you least expect it. I'm a lucky man to have been betrothed to such a beautiful and accomplished young woman as you. I'm sure that I can be happy with you. But I'm perhaps not the man you were hoping for.'

I blushed deep red and was thankful that it was too dark for Massimo to see. I didn't know how to respond, not wanting to lie to a man who was so obviously genuine and honest, so I said nothing.

After a moment, he nodded. 'I can promise you that I will be good to you. I know that your father wanted a husband who can give you a secure future and I can give you that, but I also want to give you more. I won't push you or rush you and I hope that over time we can get to know each other on a deeper level and make each other happy . . . maybe even find love.'

I started and looked up at him. 'Love?'

'It's what we all want, isn't it? But not many of us find it. I was fortunate to have found it once. Maybe I'll be lucky again with you.'

'Maybe,' I whispered, feeling sad that he'd ended up with me.

I didn't know what love was but I was sure that it didn't begin like this.

Massimo and I were married on Sunday, 28th February, 1937, a clear and bright winter's day,

'Are you ready?' asked Teresa gently as she tugged on my sleeve to smooth the fabric and ensure the dress sat right. It was a simple white satin floor-length dress with long sleeves. There were tiny pearl buttons at the wrist, a ruched waistline, round neckline and fluted skirt that showed off my figure.

Teresa had insisted on making my wedding dress, spending many long nights over needle and thread to have it finished in time. I had never wanted a white dress but Teresa had insisted. Massimo could afford it and all of the village would expect it of me.

'I'll make sure you have a beautiful dress,' she'd murmured. 'You'll be the most exquisite bride Bruzzano has ever seen.'

I remembered when Teresa was standing in my place, the night before I went to the monastery. 'One day you'll both be standing here in your own wedding dresses that I've made,' she'd said to me and Paola. I'd stared at her then, imagining what I'd look like in her dress for just a moment. My skin was fairer and I had green eyes and Mamma's wild, dark curls, but Teresa and I were similar in size. We were both petite, not as tall as Paola. Teresa constantly bemoaned that she should have been taller to do justice to the designs in Zia Francesca's fashion magazines but being small didn't bother me. I'd thought then that it was good to be quick and inconspicuous, able to get away with doing things that I shouldn't. But that didn't matter anymore.

Mamma and Teresa had sat me down to explain my wifely duties. I'd known something of what went on between a man and woman from watching the animals on our farm and conversations with Paola, but not everything.

'Massimo will expect you to lie with him on your wedding night,' Mamma had said gently. 'It will consummate your marriage, make it a sacred union in the eyes of God.'

I'd stared at them, aghast.

'Don't worry,' said Teresa, taking my hand in hers. 'Massimo seems like a kind and gentle man. The first time will hurt a little, but after that it will be better. You might even enjoy it.'

I'd frowned, trying to reconcile the grunts and groans that we'd heard coming from our parents' bedroom with the idea of enjoyment. Snatches of whispered conversations I'd heard between newly married women when I was younger flooded back. I remembered hushed voices and stifled sobs as they revealed that most husbands didn't consider the feelings of their bride on their wedding night and that consummation, more often than not, was an act to be endured. But I was most shocked to learn that love usually had nothing to do with it at all.

'But I don't love him,' I'd stammered. Marriage was supposed to be the pinnacle of a girl's life. My parents had married for love and I couldn't imagine sharing a bed with a man who was little more than a stranger and who I didn't love. 'If I have to marry, I want it to be for love.'

Mamma caressed my cheek. 'With time you will, God willing. And then you'll enjoy lying with your husband.'

'It was strange for us at first but Santoro and I are very much in love now,' said Teresa softly. 'It took a little time but—' she patted her growing belly affectionately, now six months pregnant, '—I enjoy our time together and our bond has only deepened with this child we've made. You have so much joy ahead of you.'

Tears had filled my eyes and I felt overwhelmed, suffocated by the expectation of the life ahead of me. Once children arrived, all my dreams would come to an end. But I'd swallowed the lump in my throat and the truth of how I really felt. There was no point upsetting them because there was nothing any of us could do.

Mamma and Teresa had enfolded me in their arms in silent support. If only I could run away – but it was too late for that.

Now here we were with Paola, in our old bedroom. My new home would be in Brancaleone, only about four miles away on the coast, but it felt like it was on the other side of the world.

'I'm ready,' I said. I took a deep breath to calm my nerves, refusing to think further than the next few minutes. Agata had written to say that although she couldn't be here, she'd pray for me on my wedding day. I wished that her prayers could bring me a miracle because I'd never be ready for this. And truth be told, it could have been much worse. The spectre of our wedding night hung over me but I reminded myself that Massimo seemed like a good man.

'Wait a moment,' said Paola, pushing another pin into my hair, coiled into a chignon. 'We don't want the veil to slip.' I was wearing Teresa's veil, edged with lace from Mamma's wedding veil.

'Now take off your shoes before you look in the mirror, or it's bad luck,' said Teresa.

I did as I was asked before she placed her dressmaker's mirror in front of me. I stared at my reflection. I almost didn't recognise myself.

'There, perfect,' Paola said. 'You look incredible.'

I grasped her hand. 'Who thought we would be here like this when we were last together in this room a year ago?' I whispered.

'So much has happened since then,' said Teresa, caressing the curve of her belly.

'If it wasn't for Vincenzo and you both, I'd be married too,' said Paola, shaking her head in disbelief. 'But I'll miss you, especially our conversations. It won't be the same.'

'Remember what we said then?' said Teresa, her eyes misty.

Paola nodded. 'We'll always be sisters.'

'I've never been more grateful for the two of you than I am now. I couldn't do this without you. I don't know that I'd have the strength,' I whispered, squeezing their hands.

'Of course you would,' said Paola, kissing me on the cheek.

'It will get easier,' said Teresa. 'Massimo's a good man but we'll be here for you when you find it too hard to bear on your own.'

'We'll always be here for each other,' repeated Paola. 'But now it's time to go.'

The wedding passed in a blur. I clearly remembered Massimo and his two sons, as tall as him, who stood by his side at the front of the church. But I barely remembered the vows, the blessing by Padre Giovanni, who had baptised me seventeen years earlier, the sugared almonds being thrown at us afterwards, the congratulations of family, friends and neighbours and the wedding meal with family back at home. Massimo's boys, Luigi and Franco, sat beside their father. They'd arrived the night before from Reggio where Franco also attended school, and would be staying with friends in Bruzzano for the night. Although they were polite and pleasant, our meeting must have been as strange for them as it was for me.

Before I knew it, I was in Massimo's truck, waving a tearful goodbye to my family before we pulled away into the darkness of evening on our journey to my new home.

'Are you tired?' asked Massimo. 'It was a long day.'

'A little,' I said, my belly squeezing with nervousness. The gold wedding band felt heavy and strange on my finger. I couldn't stop playing with it. The truth was that I was exhausted, not so much from the activity of the day as from the emotion. I couldn't tell him that I was terrified of what I knew I had to do later that night. Although Massimo had been a gracious groom, attentive and thoughtful, I couldn't imagine being intimate with him. I'd been numb through-out the ceremony, blocking out what I was about to do, but whenever reality brought me back to the surface I felt a stab of pain. Only during the meal did I have the comfort of my sisters, Mamma, Nonna and Zia Francesca.

I looked up to the dark sky filled with stars, the same stars Vincenzo would see in Spain, whatever horrors he was expe-riencing in the war. It gave me some comfort and strength to know that we were still connected, if only through viewing the same night sky. If he could deal with the nightmare of war, then I could cope with the ordeal ahead of me.

The moon cast a silvery glow across the Bruzzano River. Even in the darkness there was light and where there was light, there was hope.

'I hope you like the house,' said Massimo. 'It needs a woman's touch after my being alone all this time.'

'I'm sure it will be lovely,' I said automatically.

It was only a short drive, ten or fifteen minutes, and I longed to put my head down, close my eyes and sleep. Forget this day had ever happened, even for a little while.

Massimo grasped my hand. 'I mean it, Giulia. I want you to be happy there.'

I smiled weakly. None of this was Massimo's fault. 'I know. It might just take me some time to adjust to living in a new place.'

'Take all the time you need,' he said.

It occurred to me that he was nervous too. It seemed like he really wanted this to work but what if his words were just empty promises? Massimo was about Papà's age and was probably a traditionalist like him. It couldn't bear thinking that I may have exchanged one form of control for another.

'It's a shame it's late now,' Massimo said when we arrived at the house. 'The view over sea and coast is beautiful from here.' He took my bag and guided me to the front door. 'I'll show you around in the morning, when you're ready.'

I nodded, unable to speak as a wave of panic engulfed me, and stepped over the threshold. It was a modest cottage but furnished well, with a comfortable-looking lounge at one end of the room and a long dining table at the other, tiled floors throughout. It was bigger and more modern than our home in Bruzzano. I took a deep breath. Maybe living here wouldn't be so bad, if I could get through this night.

Massimo shyly showed me to the bedroom, placing my suitcase on the bed. 'I'll let you get changed in peace,' he said. 'I'll be in the next room if you need anything.'

'I can't get out of this dress on my own,' I said, suddenly embarrassed.

Massimo nodded. 'Let me help you then.'

I turned for him to undo the buttons on the back of my dress, feeling unnerved by the closeness of him. He lifted the loose hairs at the nape of my neck and placed his hands on my shoulders. I was surprised at the warmth that radiated from them. But as he began unbuttoning, I felt myself tense.

'There, all done,' he said, stepping back. I breathed a sigh of relief. He'd done nothing more than I'd asked.

'How did you manage them so quickly?' I asked in amazement as I turned to face him. I could feel the dress sitting precariously on my shoulders.

'Fishing nets require nimble fingers to repair,' he said, smiling, his face lighting up with pride – and something else. Was it humour? I was shocked to see that he almost looked handsome.

'Grazie. Could you help with the wrists too?' I asked, presenting my arms to him. 'Otherwise, I could be here all night.'

'Of course.'

We had never been this close before. His head was bent as he focused on the last buttons and I could look at him without his scrutiny. Although he wasn't what I found attractive, the look of concentration on his face was endearing. It was at odds with the rugged looks of a man who had spent the last twenty or more years at sea. His suit jacket strained across his back and the tops of his arms, and I could imagine the bulky torso underneath. His closeness and warmth were strangely comforting. I frowned in confusion, not sure I understood these mixed feelings at all.

Massimo took this moment to look up and quickly stepped away. 'I'll leave you to change,' he said.

'Grazie, Massimo,' I said awkwardly, holding my dress to my chest as it began to slip down my arms. I watched as he closed the door behind him, unsure what his expectations for this evening were. A horrible thought entered my mind. What if I fell pregnant from just this one night? I sank onto the edge of the bed, feeling dizzy and faint. I gasped for breath, the realisation that I was trapped hitting home.

The time had come to do what I must. But I didn't know if I could do it without kicking and screaming, without trying to push him away. All I could think was that with this one act, all my dreams could be shattered and my life would be over. Why hadn't I thought of talking to Nonna about ways of preventing pregnancy? Was that possible? If so, it was the only thing I could control. I dropped my head into my shaking hands, feeling wretched and afraid.

When Massimo returned, I was perched on the side of the bed wearing the fine linen nightdress that had been part of my trousseau. I felt vulnerable and exposed in the thin cloth, even though it covered me from neck to ankle.

'Do you need anything?' he asked as he removed his jacket and tie and placed them on the chair next to the dressing table with its own mirror.

I shook my head, staring at my hands clenched so tightly on my lap that they were white. My mouth had suddenly gone dry and my heart was pounding.

'Don't look so terrified,' he said softly. 'I won't force you to do anything you're not ready to do.'

My head shot up and I searched his face, desperate with hope. 'Really?' I managed to say, swallowing hard.

He sat beside me and nodded. 'There's plenty of time for that. When you're used to me and feeling comfortable, we'll take small steps in getting to know each other more intimately.'

I sagged with relief, not sure how I'd been blessed with such a kind and compassionate man, wondering briefly whether Papà had known Massimo would be good to me.

Massimo took my ice-cold hands in his. 'I'd rather wait until we can both enjoy the experience. I want you to be happy, Giulia.'

Tears filled my eyes. 'You mean it?'

'Of course.' He leaned across and kissed my forehead. 'It's been a long day and I know you're tired. Let's go to sleep. There's so much I want to show you tomorrow.'

I glanced at the bed anxiously.

'I'll sleep in the boys' room until you're ready to have me by your side,' Massimo said.

'Grazie,' I whispered. I took a deep shuddering breath and breathed it out slowly, sending a silent prayer of thanks to the Madonna.

9

I couldn't believe my luck in marrying such a kind man but I worried it was too good to be true: Papà had chosen Massimo to tame me and I waited for the day when he'd exert his control over my life. Massimo's sons had come to pay their respects and had returned to Reggio again, leaving Massimo and I on our own. Massimo showed me around and introduced me to the locals. Although officially part of the village of Brancaleone a couple of miles further inland in the hills, the hamlet supplied fish and seafood to the whole district and had a busy distribution and community hall, a small marketplace set back from the beach and a tiny church on the rise overlooking the marina. Massimo had explained that everyone was involved in the processing of fish, from the fishermen and boat crews to the women and children who sorted and cleaned the day's catch and readied it for delivery to the surrounding villages.

Massimo was true to his word and made no advances towards me in the weeks that followed. He bought the mule that he'd promised, a good-natured creature that I called Nero, for his black colouring. Nero took me to Bruzzano each day to continue my training with Nonna. She'd advised me on the options to prevent pregnancy and I'd begun taking the herbs in anticipation. I was still afraid of becoming a mother before I had established myself as a healer, but with the consideration Massimo showed me, I gradually grew closer to him.

While I studied with Nonna, I would sometimes take lunch with my parents, but I found it difficult to talk to Papà, kissing him coldly on the cheek and holding myself tightly. I was still furious, despite Massimo and I getting along so well. Unsurprisingly, Papà took credit for finding me such a thoughtful, kind-hearted husband but what did surprise me was that his attitude to me had changed. Now I was a married woman, I was finally respectable in his eyes. I slowly realised that he'd never understand how I felt. In the end, I relented and began to speak to him again. It was more to make Mamma happy and keep the peace than anything else. What was done was done.

Massimo was usually waiting when I got home, rested and clean, with no trace of fishy odours. He was so proud of his fishing fleet, which he'd built up from a single boat left by his father. He owned five vessels now, which he scrubbed clean every day after returning from the sea. It was usually dark when he left in the morning. He'd park his truck at the jetty, ready to transport the fish he caught to markets and restaurants along the coast. Deliveries would sometimes be done by lunchtime, other times later in the afternoon. He helped me in the kitchen, showing me the best way to cook the fresh fish on the woodfired stove. Often there were sardines, tuna and turbot, as well as squid, octopus and prawns. But my favourite was swordfish, its oily, meaty flesh falling apart in my mouth. It was especially good accompanied by a thick sauce of fresh tomatoes, with the saltiness of olives and anchovies, the sharpness of capers and sweetness of raisins adding bursts of flavour to the dish. Massimo always insisted on spoiling me with good cuts of lamb or pork too, as well as smooth wine from one of the well-regarded local vineyards. Over dinner, he would make it his mission to entertain me with exciting stories of adventure on the open sea. I was always fascinated by his tales, wide eyed with amazement and laughing uproariously. I found myself looking forward to our evenings together and the awkward partings before we'd retire to our separate rooms became a little more reluctant as we lingered longer.

There was something about Massimo that drew people to him. His brown eyes were honest and direct and his smile was warm. He had proven himself to be kind and gentle, not the autocrat my father had expected him to be. It was true that he was older, but it only meant that he was more patient with me than a younger man might have been. I still wasn't ready to take the next step, and I didn't feel the passion that Teresa told me she felt for Santoro. I wondered how long Massimo's patience would last.

The priest from Brancaleone came to our small chapel on Sundays and for the blessing of the fleet every spring. Massimo insisted that I accompany him to Mass rather than attend the early morning Mass like most wives so they could return home and prepare lunch. 'I regret not spending more time with the boys and their mother,' he'd told me. 'I was always so busy working and tired when I came home. I won't make the same mistake with you.'

Sometimes after Mass we'd walk along the beach to the jetty to inspect the morning's catch before returning to the house, where Massimo would pay his men. Sunday was the one day he refused to work, determined to spend the day with me at home or visiting my parents and Teresa and Santoro with their new baby, Nicolo, in Bruzzano.

One Sunday, Massimo and I were walking towards the jetty when I noticed fresh mounds in the sand above the high-tide mark.

'What's happened here?' I asked. 'It wasn't like this last week.'

'The loggerhead turtles come to lay their eggs at this time of the year,' he said.

I looked around the beach but it was empty. 'But where are the turtles?'

'They come at night, make their way up the beach and dig nests, then lay their eggs and return to the sea.'

'They leave their babies alone and defenceless?'

He nodded. 'They'll start hatching in about six to eight weeks and when the high tide is in, make their way to the water and swim away. They say that the females will return here when they're old enough to lay their own eggs.'

'That's amazing!' I said. Nature was a powerful force; each creature having the drive to behave in a certain way to ensure their survival. I thought briefly of the war in Spain and how I worried for my brother every day. Why didn't humans behave in a way that was self-preserving? Why did we have to kill one another in order to assert our dominance?

'Why don't I bring you down tonight? Perhaps we can picnic on the sand and watch the turtles come in and lay their eggs.'

'I'd like that very much,' I said, looping my arm through his.

As we walked along the jetty where the fishing boats were moored, there was a flurry of activity. Large fish the size of dolphins with dangerous-looking spikes lay on the deck of Massimo's felucca. It was the type of boat that had been used here for hundreds of years with a long mast, sails and six oars.

'Are they swordfish?' I asked.

'That's right,' he said, pleased I was taking an interest. 'They migrate into our waters during spring and summer. When the swordfish run in breeding pairs, rather than as solitary animals, they're easier to spear.'

'If we hit a female, which is larger,' said Aldo, one of Massimo's crew, climbing from the boat, 'the male usually stays with her until her fight is over. It's quite simple then to spear her mate. If we spear the male first, we have little hope of getting the female because she leaves the male and swims away.' He grinned at me mischievously. 'Just like a woman, I say. Fickle and difficult to please.'

'That's not true,' I said indignantly. I'd come to expect banter from Massimo's men, but this time it hit a nerve.

'I couldn't have a more faithful and loyal wife,' said Massimo, putting his arm around me. My belly gripped at his words, and I was determined to try harder with him.

I looked at the glistening silver bodies that had been swimming through the Ionian Sea only hours earlier. They were fresh, just the way the restaurants and buyers liked them. Seeing their corpses lying on the timber boat filled me with sadness.

'How do you catch them?' I asked.

'There's a man up on the mast who acts as lookout,' said Massimo, pointing, 'and one on the bow who's ready to throw the spear at the fish as we approach.'

'It's always a lively fight once we've hooked one,' said Mimmo, another of the crew. His hair was the same silver as the swordfish and I was sure that he'd worked with Massimo's father. 'They may be big but they're fast and agile and they often take us for a ride. It's long and exhausting work that needs deep concentration and strategy. Only the most skilled fishermen can fight the swordfish until it tires.'

'Isn't it dangerous?' I asked, intrigued and appalled at the same time.

'Not if we're careful,' said Massimo. 'Their spike is sharp but it's used to slash their prey when they hunt, not attack humans.'

I knew I'd never look at these fish in the same way again. They were magnificent, ferocious and wild, untamed and unpredictable as nature itself. They were never meant to be trapped.

'It's a contest between man and fish, just as it is between man and the sea,' said Mimmo. 'Some days the water is rough, making fishing difficult, especially when the storm season hits through autumn and winter, when the might of the sea can rise up against us and claim its due, like the wrath of Neptune.'

The old stories always held a grain of truth and I'd heard women of my nonna's generation tell stories about the devastating earthquake of 1908 and the wall of water that had inundated the coasts of Calabria and Sicily. But although tremors were common, earthquakes like that were rare occurrences, and there had been none for thirty years.

Later that afternoon, we set our basket of food and a blanket on the sand, built a fire and boiled seawater in a pot before Massimo showed me how easy it was to catch shellfish from the shore. The seafood was cooked in minutes, turning a vibrant orange colour. Wine, cheese, bread and fresh seafood on the beach was a perfect way to watch the sun go down behind the mountains.

'I've never had prawns and lobster cooked like this before,' I said, sighing with pleasure as I sucked the soft, smooth meat out of the last lobster claw. The salty sweetness was one of the best things I'd ever tasted.

'There's nothing better,' said Massimo, peeling a prawn. 'Freshly caught seafood straight into a pot of boiling seawater and eaten just like that.' He brought his fingers to his mouth and gestured with a kiss. 'Eccellente!'

I breathed in the tang of the fresh salt air and sipped the crisp wine Massimo had chosen, which went perfectly with the seafood and cut through the rich creaminess of ricotta and salty sharpness of the pecorino, both cheeses made by Paola. The fresh bread completed a simple but wonderful meal, soaking up the juices from the shellfish so there was nothing wasted.

'A perfect evening,' I said, gazing at the horizon. The sound of the waves lapping the shore was mesmerising. A full moon was rising, casting a glittering trail across the water.

'Look,' Massimo whispered, pointing down the beach. 'The first turtle.'

I watched it emerge from the water, cross the pebbles at the water's edge and make its way up the sand. The turtle was bigger than I'd thought, about double the size of a newborn lamb. The shell covering its body was patterned too. I wished I could see it in the sunlight to truly appreciate its beauty.

'Magnifico,' I whispered.

'That's nothing yet,' he replied. 'Wait until she begins to nest.'

As darkness fell and the moon rose higher in the sky, I watched the turtle reach an area where the vegetation met the sand. It flicked the dry sand away with its front flippers before digging with its back flippers. A light breeze sprang up and I shivered.

'Here, I'll keep you warm,' murmured Massimo.

I shuffled closer and he put his arm around me and covered me with the blanket. I rested my head on his shoulder as we continued to watch the turtle. It had finished making its nest and was completely still.

'She's laying her eggs,' said Massimo into my ear.

I squeezed his hand and he kissed my cheek in return. The turtle began to push sand over the nest with its flippers until its eggs were well hidden and we watched its silhouette as it began its slow journey back to the sea. In the water it was at home once more, fluid and graceful as the sea itself, disappearing from view.

Warm and drowsy in Massimo's arms, I watched as others came up the beach. 'That was wonderful,' I said sometime later. 'Thank you for bringing me.' I hugged him tight in gratitude, intoxicated by the night and moved by what I'd witnessed.

'It's a special thing and we're lucky to be able to see it. I'm glad you enjoyed it,' he said, gazing into my eyes. He was such a good man. I lifted my face to his and kissed his lips. They were warm and soft, the kiss light and gentle.

'Take me home,' I whispered.

Making love to Massimo was not what I expected. He started off slow, first caressing the skin on my neck, shoulders and arms. I was surprised to find I enjoyed his touch.

'Bellissima,' he whispered as he moved to my back.

I shivered with pleasure, as much at his words as his touch. He became bolder, his fingertips gliding across my breasts, my belly and my thighs, making me breathless. I'd never imagined a touch could arouse such exquisite sensation. But he wasn't finished, kissing and nibbling down the length of my body, the heat of his touch making my skin feel like it was erupting in flame. He returned to my breasts, grazing my nipples, gently sucking and teasing with his tongue. I gripped the sheets and gasped with the shock as a throbbing began between my legs and deep in my belly. Then his hand strayed lower and the room fell away. I held him tight, urging him closer as the excruciatingly pleasurable sensations grew. I felt like I would explode.

It was then that he nudged me with his manhood. I took a deep breath as he began to rock against me, the throbbing within me dissipating. Teresa had told me that it would hurt the first time, but it was only a sharp and sudden searing that lasted for a second before he slid home. Only then did he lose control and it was a matter of minutes before he groaned and shuddered on top of me.

'Are you alright?' I whispered, my hand on his damp head.

'I'm good,' he said. 'It's just been a long time.'

I nodded. So, this was normal.

'Am I squashing you?'

'No, not really.'

Massimo rolled off me onto his side and I felt the fluids gush from where we had been connected. He looked spent.

'Are you alright?' he asked. 'Did it hurt too much? I tried to be as gentle as I could.'

I kissed him lightly on the lips. 'I'm fine.' I smiled shyly. I wanted more of the kissing and touching. 'You were very gentle . . . it was nice.' I hadn't really known what to expect, but after the pleasurable sensations he'd aroused in me, I felt a little deflated somehow.

'It will be better next time,' he said. 'We'll learn about each other in this way too, just as we have in our everyday life.'

I nodded. Maybe it took time and practice for me to feel the exhilaration I had seen in Massimo's face towards the end.

He traced the line of my jaw with his finger. 'Tesoro mio! My sweetheart. You make me so happy, Giulia, and I hope that, with time, I'll also make you happy.'

My throat constricted and tears filled my eyes. I had never expected to feel anything for my new husband, but a wave of emotion was rising in me: gratitude that I had been so blessed with such a generous man. 'I'm lucky to have you, Massimo,' I said earnestly. 'I'm happier than I could ever have believed.' I reached up to kiss him on the lips. Massimo was my future.

The following months were better than I ever thought possible as I settled into my life with Massimo. He left early every morning, slipping quietly from our warm bed while it was still dark and starting the fire in the wood stove before putting on a pot of coffee. The aroma of freshly brewed coffee always brought me to the surface but Massimo would insist I stay in bed a little longer and kiss me gently before pulling the door closed. The deep roar of his truck engine as it rumbled down the street soon became vague background noise as sleep pulled me under until shafts of sunlight peeked through the curtains to wake me with the rising sun. After drinking the coffee Massimo had left me, I'd draw water from the well in the piazza for cooking and washing, do some housework around our cottage, then take Nero to Bruzzano.

My days with Nonna were only getting busier as my skills improved. Under Nonna's supervision, I was beginning to see my own patients at the clinic. After the morning session we'd have lunch, and then visit those who couldn't come to the clinic.

More often than not, we ended up having lunch or coffee with Mamma. She was always so happy whenever we went to see her, even though she'd begun looking after Teresa's little boy, Nicolo, who was a few months old now. Teresa had returned to dressmaking quite early but I knew that she and Santoro still secretly hoped to go to America one day.

I wondered if Papà knew about their dream as I watched him pack his pipe with tobacco one afternoon. I held Nicolo in my arms. He'd just fallen asleep and Nonna had gone to see whether Mamma wanted to put him in his bassinet.

'You're Massimo's responsibility now,' Papà said to me suddenly. 'If he lets you continue to work with your nonna, that's his decision. You've proved that you can behave and do the right thing, but you make sure she continues to keep her spells and potions away from us.' He nodded, his piece said, and lit the pipe. As though everything was now alright.

I took a deep breath. 'Papà, nothing's changed. Nonna only uses the old ways with those who believe in their effectiveness, just like our faith in the Madonna and the healing power of prayer.' I gazed at the sleeping baby, so peaceful and without a care in the world. I was surprised at how maternal I felt towards him, wanting to shield him from the troubles that were inevitably ahead of him. If only he didn't have to grow up.

He shook his head. 'No, I've seen the brevi and amulets she gives to people to ward off il malocchio. Don't you try to tell me different,' he said vehemently, pointing the pipe at me. Many of the villagers used the 'horned hand' and red coral amulets shaped into horns to ward off the 'evil eye', and brevi were small pouches usually filled with religious items, special stones or herbs, used for protection. These were ancient practices that had been used for centuries and harmed nobody.

'Alright, Papà, I understand,' I said, swallowing my irritation. Any further explanation would fall on deaf ears and if I pushed back, the gains I'd made with Papà would be lost.

But nothing was going to stop me from broadening my knowledge. I continued to visit Santoro at the schoolhouse once a fortnight to exchange the books he'd given me. We'd often sit for an hour or more as we discussed what I'd read or Santoro explained the background of whatever volume he was giving me. Although we talked about science, language and geography, history was his favourite subject.

'The book I've given you this week looks at the ancient civilisations of the Mediterranean,' he said. 'It's a book

I found in an old bookshop in Reggio while I was at teacher's college. I've never found another one like it.' He opened the worn leather cover reverently. 'What makes it so special is that the theories about some of the ancient civilisations and the migration of particular peoples have been supported by physical evidence – archaeological finds, manuscripts and inscriptions – to piece together plausible explanations. Take the ancient Philistines who lived in Palestine. They were constantly at war with the Israelites and the Bible tells us that they were originally from Egypt. But with new evidence, the modern theory suggests that they came from the region of the Aegean and ancient Greece.'

'Like the early Calabrese?' I asked, surprised.

'That's right,' he said, pleased. There was no doubting the passion he had for teaching, much like my passion for healing. He so enjoyed talking to someone who shared the joy of learning that often he'd have a pot of coffee waiting when I arrived and he'd push the pile of books waiting to be marked to one side. Sometimes I thought Santoro was wasted teaching at the local school; he should have been teaching at university. 'You see, all learning must be undertaken with a healthy dose of critical evaluation. Where has the information come from, is it from a reliable source, does it have a biased perspective?'

I was grateful for Santoro's time and insights. It was thought-provoking discussions such as these that made me question the context of anything I learnt. There was always more than one perspective to any given situation; a valuable lesson I tried to apply to life – even with Papà. But although I understood Papà's determination in finding us good marriages, it still made me quiver with anger. Like many others on the land, he worried about having enough for all of us. I knew this was Papà's way to ensure we had options, but there were other ways to ensure stability and happiness. Education was one of them and I wondered what I might have achieved if I'd been able to go to university. Perhaps I would have become a teacher like Santoro or maybe even a doctor.

After my busy days at the clinic, I looked forward to coming home to Massimo. We'd cook and talk about our day. Most nights he'd go to bed before me and I'd pack his lunch for the following day. I would read Santoro's books in the luxury of lamp light, write to Agata or read her letters about her life at the monastery. When he wasn't weary with exhaustion, Massimo would take my hand and lead me to bed. I had told him that I wasn't ready for a baby, that I wanted to finish my apprenticeship with Nonna before we considered a family. Even though contraception was against the Church's teachings, as well as Fascist policy, he agreed that I was only young and should take the herbs Nonna suggested. I felt safe, loved, respected and cared for. It was far more than I'd ever dared to hope for from a husband.

I spoke to Zia Francesca about my growing feelings for Massimo at the trattoria while helping her prepare for Mamma's surprise birthday celebration. We were planning a menu and working out what we needed. She told me that her marriage had been arranged to a much older man who owned the trattoria.

'Did you grow to love him?' I asked, pen poised over the list of ingredients I'd written.

'I did, over time . . . our daughter Sofia was born a few months before you and she was such a delight and joy to both of us, bringing us closer together—' Her eyes were shining with remembrance. 'But she died, not even a year old, from the Spanish Influenza brought back to the village by returning soldiers after the Great War.' I knew from Mamma how sad Zia was never to have any more children. Perhaps me being the same age Sofia would have been was why she and I were close. 'There was a distance between us after that. Neither of us could get past our grief. That's when Silvio came to work for us in the trattoria—'

'Don Silvio worked here?' I asked, amazed.

She shook away the sad memories and smiled. 'He did. He came to help us after Sofia's death.'

'How did he ever come to do what he does now and rise to such a powerful position?'

Zia counted the number of guests and added a couple of names. 'He was born into the "family", worked hard, proved his worth and when his father and uncles thought he was ready . . .' She shrugged. 'He works as an importer–exporter . . . but he's also capo locale, the boss of this 'Ndrangheta district.'

'He's a *boss*? I suppose I should have realised that if he's been going to the annual meetings at the monastery.'

'He's a powerful man, not a man to cross, but he's virtually family to me – and by extension you – and he'd go out of his way to help us any way he can.'

I thought about that for a moment. 'Did he ever marry?' I asked, the list in front of me forgotten.

She nodded. 'He's only a little older than me. He left the restaurant to join the family business and marry the wife his

123

father had picked for him, but Domenica passed away a few years ago from tuberculosis. He was devastated of course, but coming after the loss of their young son Gianni in a drowning accident some years earlier, well . . . he just buried himself in his work. I didn't see him for a time, and then sporadically, but since he turned up at the restaurant to bring you his gift, I've been seeing more of him.'

'But he's 'Ndrangheta,' I whispered. My parents had drummed into us to stay away from 'Ndrangheta and never speak about what they did. They were dangerous and unpredictable.

She nodded. 'I know, but Silvio's a good man. He can't help what family he comes from. And he and his men do lots of good for our community. They've contributed funds to the rebuilding of some of the ancient churches that have been condemned after being damaged in earthquakes, and to the resettlement of communities whose homes were washed away in the floods.'

'But they're involved in protection rackets and extortion!'

'It seems heavy handed at times, I'll agree, but it's a way of protecting local citizens from the corruption of the government officials and it oils the path of bureaucracy. The power of the locale can cut through red tape and ensure the ordinary people get what they need.' She shrugged. 'It's a double-edged sword. They're so deeply embedded in our society, there's nothing much we can do but accept their existence.'

I nodded. Zia Francesca's explanation made sense and Don Silvio and Don Giovanni had been nothing but kind as far as I knew. But I wasn't sure that people weren't hurt in the process.

What I was sure of however, was that life wasn't simple and straightforward and didn't always go the way we planned or expected. Zia Francesca and Don Silvio had made the most of the situations they had found themselves in and had taken comfort in each other, that much was clear. After everything I'd been through, I recognised the value of taking joy wherever we could. If we could find some distance from the anger, judgement and negative influences that threatened to overwhelm us, we might even be able to let go of our hurt and pain and accept the blessings that were under our very noses. I was trying to do just that with Papà and Massimo. Maybe I had to accept Zia's word that Don Silvio was a good man and look past his background. After everything she'd done for me, the least I could offer her was my love and support.

10

It was September when Nonna Mariana and I returned to the monastery for a week. Massimo insisted that I go, despite the big season his fleet was having. He was working so hard, but told me that he'd manage on his own as he had before and that Mimmo had invited him for meals if he wanted. All the same, I felt guilty for leaving him and couldn't help but make batches of biscotti and ensure there was enough bottled sauce, preserved vegetables and dried pasta before I left.

I couldn't believe it had been a year since I'd last been to the monastery. So much had happened since then and my life had changed more than I could have imagined. Fra Giacomo picked us up from the village and brought us up by cart and donkey, regaling us with stories of monastery life over the summer. But I wasn't sure how much Nonna heard, caught up in her own thoughts, craning her neck as we got closer to the heart of the mountains and grasping my hand with excitement when the monastery came into view. She hadn't been back for some time although she still wrote regularly to Mother Superior and Fra Fortunato.

When we arrived, we were ushered into Mother Superior's study.

Mother Superior rose to greet us, beaming from ear to ear. 'Mariana! Giulia!'

The two women embraced, laughing and crying. 'It's been too long,' Mother Superior whispered, holding Nonna's hands.

'The years got away from us,' said Nonna. 'It's so good to see you.'

'And you. We have so much to talk about. My dear Giulia,' said Mother Superior, kissing me on both cheeks. 'We've missed your smiling face around here.'

'It's wonderful to be back.'

'Congratulations on your nuptials. I'm very happy that you've been able to continue your training with Mariana. It would have been a terrible waste otherwise.' She leaned in towards me. 'Please tell me you've kept up with your studies.'

I nodded. 'My sister's husband gives me history books and I try to read the newspaper most days. Sometimes I even read out loud to Massimo.'

'Your husband doesn't mind?'

'No. I think he's proud that I'm trying to improve myself.'

'He's a rare man,' she said, nodding. Then she frowned, as a thought came to her. 'Have you heard the disturbing news about the Jewish people in Germany?'

I shook my head.

'Do you know much about the rise of Hitler and his Nazi government?'

I shook my head again.

'I'm not surprised.' She threw her hands up in exasperation. 'I've started listening to foreign radio because we get nothing substantial from our government broadcasts. Hitler is the German chancellor and his Nazi government is Fascist, like ours, but they've been persecuting their Jewish citizens for years. They have recently passed new laws that further target the Jewish people, forbidding them from marrying Germans and denying them citizenship. I wouldn't be surprised if we heard more disturbing reports,' Mother Superior said, shaking her head. 'I have a bad feeling about Hitler.'

Before I could comment, she strode over to her desk and patted the stack of books she had to one side. 'Don't let me forget to give you these before you leave.'

'Grazie, Mother Superior,' I said.

I left the two women to catch up and found Agata on her way to Mother Superior's study.

'You made it,' she said, grinning.

I hugged her tight. I'd missed her more than I realised. 'It seems like only yesterday since I was last here.'

'It's so good to see you. Come, I want to hear everything.'

'Agata, how are you?' I asked as we walked. 'How's your health?' She'd said nothing in her letters, but she looked healthy.

She smiled. 'I'm well, still in remission. Fra Fortunato's treatment has made all the difference, I think. And now that I'm his apprentice, I can take an active hand in my own wellbeing.' She took my hands in hers. 'And you? How's married life?'

As we stepped out into the garden, I glimpsed Fra Fortunato's greenhouse. I couldn't wait to see what he had planted in there.

'I'm ... fine.' I shrugged at Agata's look of surprise. 'It wasn't what I wanted but he's a good man.' I told her about the last six months.

'It sounds like you've found happiness,' said Agata softly.

'I think maybe I have. It's not the passionate romance I imagined when I was younger but Massimo's always thinking of ways to make me happy. He never complains about my work, when other wives stay at home to cook and clean and dote on their husbands. I could never have imagined saying this six months ago, but I'm lucky to have him.'

'It's one of the Lord's great mysteries,' agreed Agata. 'None of us knows the path we will travel but God.' She stopped and embraced me again. 'But I'm glad that your path has brought you here again. I've missed you.'

'And I've missed you,' I said, tears welling in my eyes.

Agata and I met Mother Superior and Nonna in Fra Fortunato's workroom. I smiled at the fond memories of the many hours crushing roots, preparing tinctures and learning the properties of herbs.

Fra Fortunato joined us, carrying a tray of coffee and biscotti. His solemn face lit up when he saw Nonna and me. 'I can't tell you how pleased I am this day has finally come,' he said, quickly placing the tray on the table. 'Mariana, it's so good to see you again.' He greeted Nonna with a kiss on both cheeks, squeezing her hands as though he was making sure she was real and wasn't going to slip away. Then he greeted me. 'Agata and I have missed your thoughtful insights,' he said, smiling. 'I can't wait to see how you've incorporated your lessons with me into your treatments and training with your nonna.'

'You did a fine job, Fortunato,' said Nonna softly. 'She's a wonderful diagnostician and practitioner and she's taught me a few new things too.'

'Ah, that's the real magic. I look forward to seeing what insights you have to share. Let's have a cup of coffee and catch up,' he said, gesturing to the table. 'We'll begin in earnest tomorrow. We have so much to discuss.'

Time flew while we studied with Fra Fortunato and before we knew it, it was time to go home. There was a flurry of activity around the monastery with all the preparations well underway for the festa. We were unable to stay and help Fra Fortunato and Agata, but our visit had been a great success. The men from the 'Ndrangheta arrived the day we were leaving; I saw them in the distance as the monks took their bags and showed them to their rooms while stalls and pavilions were being erected throughout the immaculate gardens.

'Our special guests,' said Fra Giacomo wryly as he hoisted our bags onto the cart.

'Did Don Giovanni and Don Silvio come today?' I asked.

'I believe they did,' he said.

'Will you give me ten minutes? I'd like to see them again.'

'I have all day,' he said, shrugging.

I spied Fra Fortunato with the men outside the monastery. I began walking towards him and when he looked up and saw me, he smiled and beckoned me over.

'Here she is,' said Fra Fortunato. 'Perfect timing. She and Signora Palamara are leaving shortly.'

'Buongiorno, Don Silvio and Don Giovanni,' I said, smiling. 'How lovely to see you both.'

'Buongiorno, signora,' said Don Giovanni. 'Congratulations on your marriage.'

I noticed that he'd lost a little weight but his round girth suggested that he hadn't entirely stopped eating the foods that he enjoyed.

'Grazie. I'm so very pleased to hear that you're doing well and thank you for your kind gift.'

He looked puzzled for a moment.

'The pen. I use it every day and think of you both.'

'It was nothing,' he said, but the cheeks of both men flushed with pleasure. He smiled and gestured to my mentor. 'I couldn't be in better hands and I've never felt so good since Fra Fortunato started looking after me.'

'He's the best,' I said.

'And you're walking in his footsteps, it seems,' said Don Silvio.

I laughed. 'Oh, I have a long way to go. But with his guidance, I hope to help those in need to the best of my ability.'

'Now then, we must go,' said Don Giovanni, 'before the others start without us and all the fabulous biscotti and cakes are gone.' He grinned mischievously.

'Until next time,' I said, smiling.

'It seems you've made yourself some friends,' said Fra Fortunato as the men walked into the monastery. 'With this work, you never know who you'll meet. It's a very important job to make people feel secure and safe at their most vulnerable. Not everybody understands that but it's always nice when it's appreciated.'

I wondered if he wanted to say more but Nonna, Mother Superior and Agata were walking across the courtyard towards us. It was time to say goodbye.

In the following months, Nonna and I were busier than ever tending to the needs of the district. Dottore Rosso, appointed by the government, had retired and his replacement hadn't yet been decided upon. Everything moved so slowly, especially in the south, where bureaucrats lined their own pockets whenever they could by granting favours to those who could pay. Sometimes inducements had to be given to get things done. Government appointments in the south were not desirable and it was difficult to persuade those from other regions to work here.

Massimo encouraged me to spend one afternoon a week at the marina, looking after the wellbeing of the fishing community. Massimo's own crew often came knocking on our door after dinner when they needed attention. At first it was nerve-racking, treating them on my own, but I'd always discuss my cases with Nonna and her reassurance gave me confidence. And the crew were always so thankful that soon I relaxed into my role. It wasn't long before they were calling me 'Mamma Giulia'. Friends and family in Brancaleone were coming to see me too and Massimo proudly told everyone that the marina had the best healer this side of the mountains. Even the wives and mothers of our crew accepted me into their fold, inviting me into their homes and teaching me how to crochet with silk.

But despite everything in my life going well, I couldn't always accept Papà's attitudes or keep them at arm's length, as much as I tried to ignore his strong opinions and pointed comments towards me. He still pretended that there had never been any disagreement between us now that I was happily married.

'See, you had nothing to worry about. I found you a good husband and made you a good match,' Papà said to me as I watched Massimo and Mamma through the window one afternoon. Massimo had come to pick me up after Nero had gone lame with a bruised hoof. He was walking around the vegetable patch bouncing Nicolo in his arms, who had woken while Mamma was picking radicchio, fennel and spinach.

I refused to acknowledge his comment, unable to believe he'd come out and said it. I'd expected it from him months ago, but had thought that by now, like me, he had finally been able to let our differences go. But I was wrong and the worst part was that I realised that I hadn't really let go either. I still hadn't forgiven Papà, even though Massimo was a good and kind husband.

'You should be thanking me,' he persisted. 'Your wild streak is gone and you're a respectable woman now.'

I turned slowly and raised my eyebrows in disbelief. 'Thank you? You think I should thank you?'

'Why not?' he said, indignant. 'Most women would be grateful to have a husband like Massimo.'

'You made me marry against my will, with no concern for my feelings or what I wanted for my life.' The desperation and fear I had felt back then rushed through me like it had been yesterday. I swallowed the lump in my throat and clasped my hands tight, to stop them from shaking.

'Baccalà, of course I considered your feelings,' said Papà, throwing his hands into the air in exasperation. 'I thought *only* about your welfare and your future. Your marriage brought back your honour and your family's honour. You've been able to continue your training, you don't have to struggle for money, you have only the best to eat and your husband doesn't drink or beat you. I know many who wish they were in your shoes.'

'But what if he'd been different?' I yelled, my restraint disappearing. 'You didn't know what he'd do, what he'd be like. You could have condemned me to a life where I would have been little more than a prisoner. There was no honour in what you did.'

Hurt flashed across Papà's face. 'You ungrateful girl! Do you really think I'd let you marry a man who would treat you badly? I was trying to do my best for you ... And I think I succeeded. Your life is blessed.'

I stared at him, as the truth of what he said sank in. My life was blessed, all that a parent could wish for their child, but he would also never understand why I found what he'd done so unacceptable. Tears spilled down my cheeks. 'Don't tell me you did this for me, Papà,' I whispered. I rushed from the room, past Massimo and Mamma, who were making their way inside, and buried my sobs in Nero's warm neck.

Life went on as it had for hundreds of years and we hoped that 1938 would be a better year, a year when Vincenzo would return from the Spanish war. Papà, Paola and Antonio, who had finished his schooling, worked the farm. Antonio had confided in me that all he wanted to do was follow in Vincenzo's footsteps and join the army. But Papà had pulled him out of school early to work on the farm. It was the first time I felt a connection to Antonio, who was struggling against Papà's wishes and expectations, just as I had.

With me by her side, Nonna could take on more business. Although I had learnt so much from Fra Fortunato, Nonna's experience taught me how to put my knowledge into practice. I was even able to suggest some herbal solutions when Nonna's traditional treatments weren't getting the results she wanted. Our collaboration made me see that I was on the right path. I loved my work, helping improve the lives of people in our community, and I learnt something new every day.

But no matter how busy I was, I always tried to make time to see Zia Francesca, either at the trattoria or her flat upstairs. I missed the time we used to share when I was working with her. I enjoyed her company and our conversations about anything and everything. But Don Silvio was also at the trattoria when I visited more often of late. I'd seen him at least half a dozen times since we'd visited the monastery, nearly six months earlier. But it was only when he first made lunch for me that I began to understand the depths of their relationship.

'I'm sure you've had a busy morning at the clinic,' he said when I knocked on Zia's door. 'Why don't you stay for lunch?'

I shook my head. 'I only came by to see Zia but if she's out, I'll see her another time.'

'She'll be back soon and she'll want lunch.' He smiled. 'Come on, stay. I make a good pasta aglio e olio, if I do say so myself. It was Domenica's favourite dish and Gianni loved it too, even with all the chilli I put in.'

I had work to finish at the clinic before the afternoon session, but the aroma of garlic and chilli frying in olive oil made my stomach grumble loudly and I relented.

'It smells so good,' I said, embarrassed. It had been a long time since breakfast.

Don Silvio laughed, moving the contents of the pan so they didn't stick. 'It's a simple dish but one of the best and I only make it for my family and for my friends . . .' He stared into the distance for a moment. 'And Francesca always says she wished she'd had a daughter like you,' he said softly.

'Zia and I have always been close.' I blinked away the tears that came with the compliment. Zia would have made a wonderful mother if Sofia had lived. 'She understands me. We're similar I suppose – strong-headed and we know what we want.'

Don Silvio laughed. 'You've got that right, but she's kind-hearted and generous too. She's a very special woman and I'd do anything to protect her and those she loves. Her happiness is my happiness.' He smiled, his eyes shining. 'And that means I'd protect you too. So, if ever you're in trouble or you need something, you can always come to me.'

'Grazie, Don Silvio.'

But all I could think was that he loved her and I felt sure that she loved him too, although she'd never talked about him in that way. I understood they had to remain discreet because they weren't married and because he was 'Ndrangheta. But although life had thrown them together under less than perfect circumstances, I was glad they had each other and seemed happy, just as Massimo and I were. Sometimes it took time to accept the blessings in front of us and even longer to declare them to others. And despite Don Silvio's confession, I decided to say nothing until Zia Francesca was ready to tell me herself.

Zia had given Papà a radio as a birthday gift, and after the success of his present, everyone crowding around, enjoying listening to his radio, Zia Francesca arranged to get one for Nonna too, so she could listen to music and the news whenever she wanted.

'Don't tell your father how I can get them at such a good price,' Zia whispered to me as we poured coffee out in the kitchen while Papà listened to the radio in the dining room. 'Don Silvio can get me whatever I ask for. Your father wouldn't approve if he knew.' I nodded and asked her to get me one too from the small amount I'd been able to save each week from my apprenticeship.

It was a novelty to hear news of the world outside of the village with a turn of the dial and I often listened to the radio with my parents after lunch – it was better than the stilted conversation between Papà and I. It was here that I learnt that Hitler had just successfully invaded Austria and our own leader Il Duce was becoming more aligned with him. The Soviets had sided with the Spanish government against Franco and his fascists aided by Germany and Italy, escalating the conflict in Spain.

Papà shook his head with worry every time he spoke about the threat of violence across Europe and Mamma would go pale, her eyes darting to the photograph on the cabinet of Vincenzo in his uniform. But none of us could stop ourselves from turning on the radio to learn more about the rising tensions across Europe, no matter how our worries grew.

11

The stirrings of discontent across Europe increased through the summer of 1938. Although I tried to follow the news by reading newspapers and Zia's magazines and listening to the radio, it was through Agata's letter that I really began to understand how dangerous things were getting. I'd told her that Vincenzo was still in Spain, in a war where neither side was taking control of the country.

The Church's influence will be under pressure if Franco's fascists win the Spanish war, Agata wrote. *Mother Superior says that the Church is at loggerheads with Il Duce over his friendship with Hitler, especially after his invasion of Austria and the Anschluss. The Pope refused to meet with Hitler when he visited Rome three months ago.*

I gasped in amazement. Snubbing one of the most powerful men in Europe and an ally of our leader was a big statement. Austria was a Catholic country, as was Republican Spain, and I could imagine Pope Pius XI's displeasure at our close ties to Hitler and his fascists, who openly dismissed the rights of Catholics across Europe.

Although Hitler promised to respect the Catholic Church in Germany, the Nazis have continued to persecute it, along with the Jewish people. The Jewish roots of the Old Testament and the Jewish beginnings of Jesus and his mother run contrary to Nazi doctrine. But Il Duce seems to be following in Hitler's footsteps . . . Mother Superior's learnt about a manifesto, soon to become law, persecuting Jewish Italians, from her contacts in the Vatican. The Church is furious with him as this manifesto suggests that the very roots of Catholicism are no longer acceptable.

I shook my head in disbelief, remembering my conversation with Mother Superior the year before. As someone from a region that felt isolated from the Italian union, its people ridiculed as backward, I felt able to identify with the Jewish people and the persecution they were experiencing. No human being deserved to be treated as second rate and inferior. I couldn't believe that Il Duce would copy the fanatical Nazis and succumb to such degrading laws.

Mother Superior's begun listening to a new BBC broadcast, Radio Londra it's called, to find out what's really going on across Europe and says she wouldn't be surprised if Hitler wants to take over countries like Czechoslovakia and Poland. He wants an empire, that's no secret. Il Duce will follow his lead, maybe expanding further into Africa or even Albania. She's worried for our future. But let's pray

*that common sense, rational behaviour and compassion
prevail.*

A dark cloud settled over me. If things developed as Agata
suggested, it would tear not just Italy, but the whole of Europe,
apart.

But it seemed that Mother Superior was right and, in
September, news that Hitler had taken part of Czechoslovakia
was broadcast over the radio and made headlines in the newspaper. Returning Santoro's books one afternoon, I looked
again at the map in the schoolroom, at Albania, to the east of
Italy, across the Adriatic Sea, to Czechoslovakia in the north,
surrounded by Austria and Poland, and all three bordering
Germany. It wasn't too hard to see where Hitler might go next.

'How can the leaders of Europe let this happen, after
Hitler's already taken Austria?' I asked Santoro.

He shook his head. 'I think they believe that by negotiating with him, they'll be able to keep the peace in Europe.'

I frowned. 'But it's not working, is it? Papà said that he's seen
rising aggression like this before, in the lead-up to the Great
War. He keeps muttering how Hitler's greed can't be allowed
to continue.'

'It's not as simple as that,' Santoro said with a sigh. 'The
different alliances between the European countries make
diplomacy a tricky art.'

'You mean our alliance with Germany?'

He nodded.

'There's hardly anything in the newspaper or on the news
about the terrible things the Nazis are doing. Aren't you
worried that we won't hear what's really going on until it's

too late and we're on the brink of war? Shouldn't we do something more? What about listening to the BBC's Radio Londra?'

Santoro stared at me a moment. 'Radio Londra's forbidden and there's a hefty fine and even imprisonment for any who are caught listening to it.' He sighed. 'We live in a Fascist state, Giulia. I'm as frustrated as you are about the limited information we're being fed by the government but we have to follow the rules. There's nothing we can do for now.' He handed me a book. 'Here, you wanted to learn more about the differences between the north and south. Read up about the circumstances leading to Italian unification and the reasons for the resistance of the Mezzogiorno to that process.'

I switched on Radio Londra, late one November evening, while Massimo slept in the next room. Although there were reports throughout the day, the safest broadcasts to listen to were late at night. I decided not to tell him about them, worried that he'd ask me to stop or – if I happened to get caught – that he'd be in trouble too. But this short report was the only way to get the truth.

I sat at the table, a blanket wrapped around me, drinking chamomile tea. A candle burned in one of the glass holders we'd received as a wedding present. Made to commemorate the Italian victory in Abyssinia, they reminded me of exotic places I'd never see, but most of all of Vincenzo and his stories. The introductory notes of what I learnt was Beethoven's Fifth Symphony came over the radio followed by the voice of 'Il Colonello Buonasera'.

I wasn't expecting the shocking news that the Nazis had moved against the Jewish people across Germany. I listened in horror to the reports that their synagogues, businesses and homes had been vandalised and destroyed, and hundreds had been arrested and imprisoned. I moved closer to the radio, my tea forgotten, unable to believe that the Jewish persecution could reach such terrible heights in Germany. I shuddered with disquiet. Hitler was trouble and I wondered how much further he'd be allowed to go before he was stopped.

Teresa was heavily pregnant with her second child when we gathered at the schoolmaster's house one Sunday a couple of weeks later. We were sitting around the woodfired stove in the kitchen, waiting for the pasta to cook for lunch. The men were in the nursery assembling the cradle and putting the set of drawers in place after sanding and waxing the furniture, ready for use once again.

'The only time I wake now is when this little one kicks me hard in the ribs and I realise I have to get up to go to the toilet before I burst,' she said contentedly. Nonna and I had treated her for her cramps and backache, common this late in pregnancy.

'It's a boy,' said Mamma. 'Your brothers did that to me towards the end, every time.' Her eyes were soft with nostalgia.

'I'd really like a girl this time,' said Teresa wistfully as she stirred the pasta. Paola was cutting the bread, still warm from the oven, before wrapping it in a tea towel. 'What about you, Giulia? I know you've needed time to get used to Massimo but you seem happy.'

I smiled. 'I am happy. Massimo's a good husband, thoughtful and considerate.'

'But?' said Paola, knowing me too well.

'Massimo and I agreed that we'd wait to have children until after I've finished my apprenticeship with Nonna.'

'It will soon be three years since you went to the monastery,' said Mamma softly. 'Surely Nonna will end your apprenticeship then.'

'Maybe. I think that I'd like a little one, especially after watching Teresa with Nicolo,' I said, putting my arm around Teresa and kissing her cheek. 'But we'll see. We have plenty of time.'

The men came out of the nursery and into the dining room, Nicolo on Massimo's shoulders. Papà slapped Massimo on the back. 'Mamma mia, thank God you're handy. We wouldn't have put it together without you,' he said.

Massimo grinned, his face flushing red with the praise. His eyes met mine and he smiled. I could see how happy he was and how much he enjoyed playing with little Nicolo. He'd been so patient and another child would give him so much joy. Perhaps it was time to think about stopping the herbs.

12

It was a cold morning in late January 1939. I heard Massimo get up in the pre-dawn darkness as usual. Anticipation tingled through my blood as I rested my hand against my belly. My monthly bleed was a few days late. Maybe, just maybe ...

'You're awake, tesoro mio,' said Massimo, his head peeking around the door. 'I just wanted an extra pair of wool socks. My feet were cold and wet yesterday.'

'I'll get them for you,' I said, rolling out of bed, opening the cupboard and reaching for the socks. The aroma of freshly brewed coffee enveloped me like the warmth of a cooking fire and I closed my eyes to breathe it in.

'Get back into bed and I'll bring you a cup,' he said, reading me like a book.

'No, I'll come and have breakfast with you,' I said, wrapping my arms around him and kissing his warm lips.

'It's too cold to be up,' he whispered, pulling me close. 'I'd rather spend the day right here by your side ... but unless we want the crew banging on our door, the best I can do is have breakfast with you in bed.' He sighed and took the socks from me. 'Thank you.' Then he kissed me gently as I began to shiver in my thin nightgown. 'Stay warm. I won't be long.'

I climbed back into bed. If I was pregnant, it would change our lives. But I wasn't worried about becoming a mother any longer. Massimo was devoted to me and he'd already promised to build me a clinic to begin my very own practice. I'd have plenty of help with the children from the wives and mothers of his fishing crew. I thought about baby Enrica, born just before Christmas, and the joy on Teresa's face as she gazed at her tiny, perfect daughter cradled in her arms. I imagined holding my own child, maybe only months from now, and a warm glow filled me.

Massimo brought in a tray of milk coffee and biscuits and settled on the bed next to me.

'How did I get so lucky?' I asked, clasping his callused hand in mine.

He shook his head. 'I'm the one who's lucky to have such a beautiful, clever young wife. I couldn't be prouder of you and everything you've achieved.' He brought my hand to his lips. 'I want to have a party in your honour when you've finished your apprenticeship. I know your father doesn't appreciate your many talents, but I do.'

I touched his bristled cheek, tears welling in my eyes. 'I couldn't be prouder to be your wife, you make me so happy. And maybe we'll have something else to celebrate then too.' I placed his hand over my belly. 'My courses are late.'

Massimo's eyes widened, his face alight with joy. I prayed to the Madonna that soon we'd become a family.

I was on my way home that afternoon, less than a mile from the marina, when Nero became skittish.

'Shh, Nero,' I said soothingly, patting his neck. I looked around but saw no danger; it was unusual to see wolves or wildcats this far from the mountain forests. Nero began to bray hysterically and I slid from his back before he could buck me off. I held his lead rope tightly in both hands.

'What is it, boy?' I asked, scanning the surrounding countryside from the crest of the hill. The mountains to the west were snow-capped, the foothills and fields in the valley were green from the winter rain. The sea to the east sparkled in the sunshine. Everything looked as it should. But then I realised how quiet it had become – even the birds had stopped chirping. The hairs on my arms stood on end and I knew that something was wrong. I pulled on Nero's rope to lead him down to the valley. Somehow that seemed to be the safest thing to do. But Nero refused to budge.

And then the ground beneath me began to shake. It seemed to go on forever. Rocks slipped and tumbled down the hill. The tremors I'd experienced had never lasted this long. I glanced desperately around but there was no shelter. The land was tilled and planted with wheat, but the fields were empty. Nobody was about. Thoughts flew swiftly through my mind, the knowledge I'd be safer down on the river flats taking precedence. I was at risk from landslides if I stayed on the hill.

Nero began to scream, the whites of his eyes stark against his black coat, and it took all the strength I had to tie him safely to a eucalypt tree nearby. I wrapped my arms around his neck, burying his head in my dress, as I tried to stop my own trembling to comfort the terrified beast. The face of a nearby hill fell away, rocks and soil, trees and bushes sliding to the valley below. I knew I had to get down to the river but I couldn't move.

Then, as suddenly as it had started, it stopped.

I breathed a sigh of relief. We were safe. 'It's alright now, Nero,' I murmured, stroking his flank with a shaking hand. I looked across the valley. The landslides had gouged fresh scars into the earth. Below me, roofs of farmhouses were missing terracotta tiles, and new cracks had formed in some of the walls. Brancaleone and Bruzzano were behind me, hidden behind the hills. I prayed that they had remained unscathed.

I squinted into the distance. From here I could see the marina, the cottages dotted along the shore, and I wondered if Massimo was still working on the boats. All I wanted was to be in his arms, safe and calmed by his presence.

'Let's go home, Nero,' I said when the donkey was finally calm enough to untie. 'We've had enough excitement for one day.'

I went to untie him, planning to lead him down into the valley rather than ride him, but something made me look out over the sea again. The water had receded, like in a king tide, but the distance was even further. The sandy shore that had been under water was now exposed, vulnerable as a fish on land. I stared, unable to comprehend what I was seeing. The church bells in Brancaleone began to toll from the hilltop in warning. I frowned in confusion, the jangling jarring my nerves.

Then on the horizon, I saw it. A massive wave rolled across the sea, gaining height as it raced towards land. An unearthly roar rushed across the valley. I stood rooted to the spot for what felt like forever, sure that I was standing at the gates of hell. Then I heard myself scream as the wave lifted fishing boats as if they were toys and approached the shore, the marina and our homes in its path.

'No!' I shrieked.

The fury of the wave hit the coast and a wall of water engulfed the marina and the homes along the shore, mine and Massimo's included, smashing everything. The water continued to rush inland, swamping the marketplace and pushing a fishing boat, broken from its moorings, towards the community hall like a bullet from a shotgun. I heard terrible sounds of rending before the red roof of the hall disappeared beneath the water. The wave reached its watery fingers towards the chapel on the rise but lost momentum and ebbed away slowly like a dying beast, leaving a splintered fishing boat against the ruined hall.

I stared, stunned, at the apocalyptic sight for a moment and then began to tremble violently. 'Massimo!' I screeched until my throat was raw. I had to get back to the marina. I had to get back to Massimo.

I forced poor Nero to carry me home against his better judgement, hitting his rump with a stick to make him run. I knew it was a bad thing to do but all my thoughts were consumed by Massimo.

The closer I got, the more I could see the damage that had been done. The boatsheds and jetty of the marina were gone and there was nothing left of the houses on the shore. My home was gone too, but that paled in comparison to my worry for Massimo. We could build again, as long as he was safe.

As we reached the edge of the flooding about a quarter of a mile from the sea, I slipped off Nero's back. His ears were pinned back with fear as the sound of screaming and wailing filled the air.

'Have you seen Massimo?' I asked one of the fishermen's wives as she came out of the tiny chapel.

She shook her head, looking fearfully towards the sea. 'We have to go to the hills before the water comes back. You can't stay here.' She turned at the sound of her name. She gasped and, sobbing with joy, ran towards her sister.

I scanned the horizon anxiously but the sea seemed calm. I tied Nero to a tree and continued on foot towards the marina. The pull of the knee-deep water as it receded made the journey treacherous and I had to concentrate on where I stepped. Odd pieces of furniture and timber were scattered across the marketplace and I spied bags of oranges, a bicycle and a child's doll. Friends and acquaintances, people I knew well, were screaming for their loved ones or rushing to cries for help beneath the debris of the damaged hall. I could only shudder at the boat that had been slammed against the building, praying that nobody was pinned there. Others were helping those too injured with gashes and bloody wounds to get up to the church. And there were those who did not move at all. I didn't know how many were hurt or had lost their lives but I couldn't stop to help, not yet. I had to find Massimo.

'Signora, stop!' called a voice. It was Aldo, one of Massimo's crewmen. 'It's too dangerous,' he said, hurrying towards me.

'Aldo, you're alright!' I said, hugging him and almost crying with relief. 'Have you seen Massimo?'

He shook his head. 'But the houses on the shore are gone,' he said gently. 'Yours, mine, all of them, smashed by the wave and everything dragged out to sea.'

I nodded. 'Your family?' I held my breath, dreading his answer. Nobody would have been able to survive that.

'Alive. They ran out of the house when the shaking started. My wife made every crew member's family come with her from their homes and the hall, up to the church for safety and sanctuary. Only Mimmo's mother, with her bad hips, wouldn't go. Her house is gone and so is she.'

I put my hand over my mouth in horror. Mimmo's mother had taught me how to crochet lace.

Aldo looked towards the sea nervously. 'Andiamo, let's go. It's not safe to stay here. Another wave could still hit.'

Fear filled me, like ice in my veins. I turned towards the sea, searching for the gathering wave on the horizon. Terror made me almost turn back towards the safety of the hills and Brancaleone but I wouldn't leave without Massimo.

'The men?' I whispered. I couldn't look away from a dead dog entangled in a length of sodden cloth, probably somebody's curtains.

'They'll be alright. Most went out to sea to make sure the boats were running properly after the work we did on them earlier and a few went to take fish to the villages inland. I was in the truck, on my way back from making deliveries up the coast, and I saw the wave coming in towards the marina.'

I frowned. 'But I saw the wave from the hills. How could they survive something like that?'

'They're safe enough out at sea.' He placed a hand on my shoulder. 'The real damage is when the wave hits the shallow sea bed and is forced onto the shore.' He gazed out over the marketplace and hall and his look of despair made my heart clutch. I prayed that Aldo was right and the rest of the fleet was returning home safely.

'Massimo's with them then?'

'Come, let's go back up to the church.' But I could see by the tightness around his mouth and eyes that he was holding something back and suddenly I was afraid.

'No,' I said, shrugging off his hand. 'Where was Massimo when the wave came? Was he still at the marina? Please, just tell me what you know.'

'My wife saw him there during the tremor when she sent everyone up to the church. He told her he'd stay to make some final adjustments on *La Focena*. It was the last boat. He wanted to take her out to test her when the rest of us arrived back from our deliveries.'

I stared at him, appalled, and he shrugged in apology.

'We've had worse tremors and he was safe on the boat . . . But nobody expected a tidal wave or for it to hit so quickly. We've all heard of these waves from our nonnos and we've experienced sea storms and cyclones but there's been nothing like this for generations.' His shoulders slumped with exhaustion. 'My wife said that by the time everyone was settled up at the church after the tremor had stopped, the wave had hit.'

I had to keep moving, find Massimo before the wave returned. Surely, he'd seen the sea recede and knew what it meant? He would have had time to get away.

'No Signora, it's not safe there,' Aldo protested as I climbed around a boat lying on its side. Its bulk hid the marina behind it and the sight that met me took my breath away. It was like a junkyard. Timber, rocks, dirt, cladding, twisted gates, a single shoe, a coffee pot were among the things washed up against the remaining sections of sea wall. I craned my neck to look further along the shore, up to where many of the fishermen's cottages once sat. Above sand littered with the same debris, there was nothing but a solitary gate post, incomplete timber frames and stone walls of homes stripped of their warmth, empty rooms staring with vacant eyes out to the sea. Our home was gone, everything that had been our life together lost.

I took a shuddering breath and turned my attention back to where the marina had been. Twisted metal jutted from the water, the smashed wreckage of timber boats still attached to their moorings, their shattered masts sticking out like giant toothpicks. Battered and broken boats snapped from their moorings lay along the shore like old sheep carcasses, their bones weathered with age. Among the destruction was one boat that I recognised and the blood drained from my face. It was *La Focena*.

I ran towards the water, my shoes and dress sodden as I clambered through the shallow water. I had to find him, I had to know.

'Mannaggia! It's too dangerous to go in there. The water will pull you out,' Aldo said roughly, coming after me. 'We have to go. Another wave could still come.'

I saw a body floating in the water and the breath caught in my throat.

Aldo swore behind me and then he grabbed me and held me tight. 'It's not him. It's not Massimo.'

The body in the water had straight black hair spread around them like a halo, not Massimo's tight curls. I drew a deep ragged breath.

'I have to find him!' I sobbed. 'Let me go.'

'No. We have to get you to the chapel and higher ground.'

'But he could be in there.' I struggled in his arms but he was too strong.

'He's not in there ... not now.' He held me tight as my legs gave way. 'Once the fleet's back, we'll all search for him, I promise you. But now you have to go.' He dragged me away from what was left of the marina. 'I'll take you to where it's warm and dry.'

Nobody knew if there was going to be another wave but it wasn't safe to stay close to the shore. Those who could left for the hills and Brancaleone. Aldo, his sister and Mimmo coordinated the evacuation and worked out who was missing. They insisted I go too, but I refused. It would take some time before people trapped under debris were freed and we'd know if Massimo had survived. I was out of my head with worry but the only way to stop myself from going crazy was to keep myself busy.

From what I'd seen from the hills, we were safe enough at the little church, and those who had serious injuries and couldn't yet be moved needed my help. A small group of women stayed behind, mostly wives, mothers and daughters of Massimo's crew, and we set up the tiny chapel as a make-shift hospital. There was everything from head knocks and cuts to deep wounds and broken bones. The most worrying of all, though, were those who were unconscious with no obvious injury.

Despite my deep shock and worry for Massimo, my body found stores of vigour I didn't know I had and energy surged through me as my training took over. Somehow, I was calm and focused, and together we kept the wounded quiet and warm, tending them as best we could with the limited supply of herbs in the baskets I'd tied to Nero's back. It wasn't enough, but we were all there was until Nonna arrived in Zia Francesca's car with Mamma, Paola and more supplies. Papà and Antonio and Santoro came in the cart and helped look for Massimo and the others who were missing. The risk of another wave seemed more remote as time passed and I sent a swift prayer to the Madonna for that blessing at least.

The fleet returned to the unfolding horror and joined the search for the missing while I worked with the other women well into the night as the last of the injured were pulled free from beneath debris. The rescue crews had recovered a dozen more people but a handful were still missing, Massimo included. The crushing disappointment nearly overwhelmed me. If I hadn't had my family by my side, I wouldn't have been able to go on. Instead, I focused on helping those I could. It was only when those too injured for our care could be transported safely to the nearest hospital in Reggio that I sent Mamma, Nonna, Zia and Paola home.

Finally, when I was too exhausted to do any more, I retired to a mattress on the floor of the chapel, and sleep descended swiftly and mercifully.

I woke with the sun shining through the windows, shocked to find Papà sitting next to me with a blanket around his shoulders and a hot drink in his hands. The events of the last day tumbled through my mind and reality returned like a red-hot poker through my heart.

'Buongiorno, did you sleep?' asked Papà, offering me the cup, as I sat up. His face was ashen, drawn with exhaustion. It was one thing for him to be involved in the search for Massimo but it felt strange for him to offer his support to me like this.

Still foggy headed, I nodded, hearing the murmur of quiet voices and the groans of those in pain. Massimo was still out there somewhere. I breathed in the coffee and sipped the strong, bitter brew in gratitude. It was going to be another long and difficult day. 'Did you?' I asked.

He shook his head. 'If only we'd had a few more daylight hours yesterday . . .'

'We'll find him today,' I said, like a mantra. I had to believe it.

Papà gazed at me, dark eyes unreadable and thick brows knitted in concern. 'I know you'll want to stay here today, but come home with me tonight. Let Mamma and me help you.'

'You want to help me?' I slid my hand over my belly.

Papà nodded.

'Then find Massimo. Bring him home to me.' My voice broke and I found it hard to breathe. I put the cup down on the floor, my eyes filling with tears.

'I'll do everything I can,' he said gently as he enfolded me in his arms. All the difficulty between us melted away. After the horror of the past day, any anger or resentment that I still harboured towards him seemed trivial. All that really mattered was that we were both alive and well.

I was thankful for his solid presence and rested my head on his chest for a moment, gathering his strength to me and finding the courage to do what I must.

The day passed in an exhausted blur, and when I wasn't tending to injured people, I was bucketing water from homes that still stood, picking up debris and finding tethered animals drowned in the deluge.

'Giulia!'

I turned listlessly at the sound of my name and was surprised to see Don Silvio. He kissed me on both cheeks and embraced me.

'I came as soon as I could get trucks, equipment and a team of men together to help with the search and rescue and the clean-up.'

I nodded. 'Massimo's missing.' I didn't have the energy to say any more.

He took my hands in his. 'Stay strong. We'll do everything to find him.'

Don Silvio and his men helped wherever they could: using tractors to lift heavy beams, twisted metal and ruined boats and to take away debris; employing motorised pumps to remove the water from the flooded streets and foreshore; assisting in the search for the missing. And as much as everyone was appreciative, many were still wary around them. But I was grateful for Don Silvio's presence and his efficient organisation of the recovery effort. If anyone could find Massimo, it was him.

However, as the sky turned violet, there was still no trace of those who remained missing and I heard whispers from the older women that it was unlikely they'd be found now. But worse still, people stopped talking, their mouths tight as clams, whenever they saw me nearby. The pity in their faces was almost too much to bear.

When I wasn't at the marina or Brancaleone, I was in Mamma's kitchen, stirring pots on the fire. The faint, un-realistic hope that somehow Massimo had survived and would walk into the village stayed with me as each day rolled into the next. It was the only thing I could cling to. I would wander the house aimlessly and often found myself patting Nero in the garden or at Nonna's, staring at the dried herbs hanging above her bench. Mamma, Nonna, Paola, Zia and even Teresa with baby Enrica in her arms, all fussed over me, making sure I ate and was never alone. I prayed to the Madonna to return my husband alive and well, while Mamma prayed over her rosary. The mantra 'we'll find him today' never left my mind. My pure strength of will had to count for some-thing. Papà was still out looking for him along with some of Massimo's crew and part of Don Silvio's team. Massimo had everything to live for if we were expecting a child.

As the third day came and went, I prayed harder than ever, my belief in a miracle overtaking all reason. Only lying in bed at night with Paola next to me did I finally allow myself to cry. Paola said nothing but put her arms around me and held me until I fell into an exhausted sleep.

Papà came into the kitchen on the fourth morning, removing his woollen cap and jumper. He'd been out early searching.

'What are you doing here, Andrea?' asked Mamma, stirring the thick sugo on the fire while I poured pasta into boiling water. We were making meals to take down to help feed those who remained at the marina.

'Leave that and sit down, Giulia,' Papà said softly, ignoring Mamma.

I looked into his face filled with weariness, pain and sorrow.

'No!' I shook my head, my hands trembling as Mamma took the sack of pasta from me.

Papà guided me to the kitchen table. 'Massimo's been found,' he said.

For a moment I thought that perhaps he had shown up in the village just as I'd prayed for, but Mamma's hands moved silently in the Sign of the Cross and I realised what Papà had said. He'd been found.

I stood from the small table, grabbing the edge as I swayed on my feet. 'Is he alive?'

A spasm of pain crossed Papà's face, grief etched deep into his features. Papà shook his head. 'I'm sorry, no.'

The room began to spin and I felt faint. Papà's strong arms were around me, guiding me back into the chair while Mamma pushed my head between my legs.

'Better?' she asked after a moment as I lifted my head.

Massimo was gone.

I nodded slowly and she took my hand and squeezed it. 'Where?' I whispered.

'His body washed up a few miles further along the shoreline. The sea currents brought him back,' said Papà softly, sinking into the chair beside me.

'The sea was his life,' I said, tears in my eyes. I remembered when we were getting to know one another, the fantastic stories he used to tell me of his adventures on the sea. I gazed into the cooking fire, the tongues of yellow and orange flames merging.

'We'll have to tell Luigi and Franco and discuss funeral arrangements,' said Papà. We'd sent word of the disaster to Massimo's sons in Reggio and they were staying with their mother's sister in Brancaleone. They'd now lost both their parents.

'I'll do it,' I said, but I could hardly move.

Massimo was a good man and didn't deserve this.

'He was happy with you, Giulia,' said Mamma, stroking my hair. 'It's more than many can say when they die, that they were truly happy.'

I nodded but a spike of pain pierced my heart. If only I'd agreed to have a family sooner.

It was 3 February, 1939, a wild and stormy day. A day I'd never forget. I woke to find blood on my nightdress and over the sheets of the bed. My monthly bleed had arrived. I'd never know if I'd been pregnant or not, but it didn't matter now. The last hope I'd held on to so tightly had slipped away and now there was nothing left to tie me to Massimo.

I had no time to cry or mourn this new loss. Paola helped me gather and wash the sheets before I put on the black dress Teresa had made for me, adding a black scarf over my hair, ready for church. It was nearly two years since I'd married Massimo and, although I was only nineteen, I was already a widow. With the weight of all my grief, I felt like an old woman.

Massimo's funeral was held in Brancaleone. His casket rested below the altar for those who wished to pay their respects to him, but it remained closed as the initial impact of the wave and three days in the water had made a mess of his body. I only hoped that he hadn't suffered. Aldo and the sailors had assured me that Massimo's death had been quick and described drowning as a peaceful release from life.

Massimo's sons, my father, Aldo, Mimmo and another close friend and crewmember carried the coffin out into the church-yard and to his final resting place. The wind was howling, pushing dark clouds across the sky, as though mourning with me. Although many of the women and men were openly crying, beating their chests and chanting laments, I'd been able to hold myself together, silent tears slipping down my cheeks. I was bolstered by Mamma, Paola, Teresa, Rosa, Zia Francesca, Antonio and Santoro standing wordlessly behind me, while Don Silvio waited respectfully and discreetly at the back of the crowd.

As my husband was slowly lowered into the ground, my resolve broke. I couldn't imagine him in this dark tomb forever. Mamma urged me forward to throw a handful of dirt over his coffin but all I wanted to do was run away and scream.

Eventually, I picked up a handful of black earth. 'Goodbye, Massimo,' I whispered with a shuddering breath. 'You were a good husband and you made me happier than I ever imagined. I'll never forget you.'

With a shaking hand, I did my duty, sprinkling dirt over the timber lid of my husband's coffin. It was then that the sobs I'd held back all day burst from me. I turned to the comfort of my family and my father held me in his arms as the shock of the last week finally took its toll.

13

The storms and bad weather continued and a few weeks later, Antonio became so unwell that he ended up in bed for a few days, a rare thing for an active boy of seventeen. While tucking another hot stone at his feet, I heard the front door open. I frowned in annoyance, as I wanted peace and quiet so Antonio could rest.

'We're not expecting anyone are we?' I asked, arranging the pillows behind him so he remained a little upright. Antonio shook his head and immediately regretted it as a coughing fit overcame him. It was a productive cough now. I handed him a handkerchief. 'I'll go and see who it is. I'll be back in a minute.'

I stepped from the boys' room and couldn't help the cry that erupted from my lips. 'Vincenzo! You're home!'

My eldest brother stood in full army uniform in the dining room, his bag still on his shoulder.

I flew into his arms. 'I can't believe you're finally here!'

'It's good to be home,' he whispered, hugging me tight. 'How are you? I heard about the tidal wave and Massimo's death. I'm so sorry you had to go through that.'

I drew back and sighed. 'Most days I wake up thinking that I'm at my place and in my bed and then I open my eyes and realise that I'm at Mamma's and it's Paola next to me, not Massimo ... I can hardly believe that it's happened.' Tears welled in my eyes.

'I'm glad you're back home with Mamma to look after you,' he said softly, pulling me to him once more. My family had gathered around me, given me the love and attention I needed, and Nonna had gently coaxed me back to doing a few hours in the clinic each day to keep my mind off my loss.

'I don't know what I would have done without her and Paola and even Papà.' Papà had been attentive, ensuring I had everything I needed, joining me in the kitchen as I made him and Paola coffee in the morning and insisting I stay at the table after lunch, asking me about my day and making small talk about the farm. But he seemed a bit lost, as though he didn't know what he could do to heal my pain.

I stepped out of Vincenzo's arms, smiling ruefully and wiping my eyes with the backs of my hands to take stock of my brother. He looked gaunt and somehow older. 'Are you well? Is the war over? Are you home for good?'

He dropped his bag to the floor. 'I'm well enough. Tired but no major injuries. Barcelona has fallen and it's only a matter of time before Franco declares victory.'

'Then it's over.'

'Officially, I'm only on leave. I thought Rosa and I might get married but after what you've been through—'

I shook my head. 'We could all do with some joy and Rosa will be so happy to finally be with you.' I squeezed his hands. 'Don't waste another minute without her.'

A few days after Vincenzo arrived, Papà received a letter.

'What is it, Andrea?' asked Mamma after Papà sat heavily at the table, his face the colour of ricotta. We were setting the table for dinner while Paola and Antonio were cleaning up after coming in from the farm. Vincenzo had just brought in wood for the fire.

'I've been called up.'

'What do you mean you've been called up?' asked Mamma sharply.

'My old regiment, the one I served in during the Great War, they want me back. They're taking veterans up to the age of forty-five . . .'

Mamma took the paper out of his unresisting hand. '"The First Bersaglieri Regiment has been re-established,"' she read. 'Whatever for?'

We knew from Papà that the Bersaglieri were renowned and respected mobile units of expert marksmen or sharp-shooters. Papà had been proud of his service in the Great War, of the stamina and endurance he'd needed as well as his marksmanship. He'd kept his skills sharp by going to the mountains every few weeks to hunt. Sometimes, when the weather was mild, he'd stay overnight and he usually came home with hares and sometimes a deer. We all learnt to shoot from Papà but none of us was ever as good as him.

'There's war coming,' said Vincenzo, placing the last log on the stack of timber.

'What are you talking about?' said Mamma crossly. 'The war's just finished.'

Vincenzo shook his head, his face bleak. 'No, Mamma. Hitler's only just getting started. Don't be surprised if Italy takes military action of its own. If Germany can invade whoever they want, why not us?'

'You're talking about further military conflict?' Papà shook his head in disbelief, taking the letter back from Mamma. 'How can you be so sure?'

'Because our regiment has also been recalled.'

'Oddio!' Mamma made the Sign of the Cross as Vincenzo pulled a letter from his pocket and opened it to show them.

'We're forming part of a new regiment, the 133rd Armoured Division Littorio, and we meet in a month to find out our duties.'

Mamma clutched the table to prevent herself from falling and I grabbed her arm, not sure if it was to hold her up or to guard against the dizziness that had come over me. After Massimo's loss and with Vincenzo finally home again, this news was a blow.

Vincenzo looked at me and shrugged an apology.

Papà nodded solemnly. 'If you're going too, conflict must be brewing. The Bersaglieris don't re-form for military exercises, but I'm sure that men like me are being recalled in case we're needed as reserves. We're too old to be frontline soldiers.'

But I wasn't so sure.

'When do you leave?' asked Mamma, sitting next to Papà. I knew she was trying to be strong, because she hadn't said a word about Vincenzo leaving again.

'Two weeks. We're garrisoned at Cosenza,' Papà said.

'Cosenza?' asked Mamma.

'It's about a third of the way from Reggio to Napoli,' said Vincenzo. Far away but still in Calabria.

'Two weeks,' she whispered, her eyes large.

Papà rested his hand on Mamma's shoulder. 'It will be alright, Gabriella. I'm sure I'll be home again in a couple of months, once I've passed the training.'

'It could have been worse,' said Vincenzo, joining us at the table. 'At least Papà can get home from time to time if he's required to stay longer. We'll be garrisoned somewhere probably near Torino.'

I stared at him, aghast. Torino was way to the north, near Italy's western border with France. Once they were garrisoned, there was little chance they could come home for any short period.

'Can't either of you find some way to get out of it?' Mamma asked desperately. I knew she was wondering how the family would cope and how we'd keep the farm running.

Vincenzo shook his head.

'What about you, Papà?' I asked.

He smiled sadly. 'I'm old but if they're calling veterans like me up, I doubt I'll be allowed to stay home, even if it is to only put us in the reserves.'

It wasn't uncommon for young men to dodge the draft, hiding in the mountains until they thought the authorities had forgotten about them. Others who could afford it merely paid them off and their names disappeared from the list. Papà was proud to serve his country and I knew he wouldn't shirk his duty. But what he'd avoided saying was plain enough: if they were calling up experienced men like my father, then a battle was looming. What none of us could know was whether it would be an Italian offensive like Abyssinia had been or in aid of the Nazis.

I shivered despite the warmth from the fire. I knew what it was to lose someone precious and the thought of anything happening to Papà or Vincenzo chilled me to the core. I could only imagine the fear that Mamma felt at the prospect of losing a husband and son. Then there was poor Rosa. 'What about your plans to marry Rosa?'

'We've talked about it and I wanted to speak to you all first. After Massimo, I was just waiting for the right time to tell you that I was leaving again . . .'

Mamma nodded, straightening her spine as she gathered her strength. 'Then you'd better tell Rosa that you're getting married before Papà leaves in two weeks,' she said firmly.

So Rosa and Vincenzo decided to marry two days before Papà had to leave. Because of Vincenzo's call-up, they received special dispensation to marry before the three weeks of marriage banns had been observed. Rosa hadn't taken the news of Vincenzo leaving well, but her anxieties were pushed aside by the busy preparations for the wedding. Vincenzo wasn't due to leave for another month, which meant they'd have two weeks of wedded bliss in the small apartment above the grocery shop that Rosa's parents owned.

Angelo and Stefano came to see Vincenzo after dinner in the lead-up to his wedding day.

'Mannaggia! Your last days as a single man,' said Angelo, grinning broadly as he came through the door and handing Vincenzo a bottle of wine. I finished clearing the table and put out fresh glasses.

Angelo and Stefano had changed in the two years since I'd seen them. Like Vincenzo, they were both dark from months in the sun, and lean and sinewy, like dried-out salami. Angelo's weathered face made him look much older than his twenty-four years, but the laugh lines around his eyes told me that the old jokester was still there. The hard planes of Stefano's face made him look gaunt and his expression was serious, as though he'd stopped laughing years ago. The boy who had pulled my hair to take the biscotti straight from the oven was gone. There was an intensity to his eyes that made me wonder what drove him now.

'It's time to settle down,' said Vincenzo, slapping Angelo on the back, 'time for the two of you to grow up and take on the responsibility of a wife and family.'

'Not us,' said Stefano, shaking his head emphatically. 'Too much to do to be tied down to one place.' He'd been a ladies' man like Angelo and my brother before they'd left for Abyssinia but I wasn't sure that was the reason he didn't want to settle here in the village. They'd seen so many exotic places in Africa, Spain and even Italy in the three years they'd been away. I remembered feeling the same way before Massimo, but then I'd never have experienced the unexpected happiness of a stable relationship with a man who gave me respect and supported my dreams.

'Who's going to be here for you when you come back home?' asked Vincenzo softly. 'After what we've seen, you know that family's everything and it's time for us to make our own.'

I slipped into the kitchen before they even realised I was there.

'Don't get all serious on us,' I heard Angelo say. 'Come on, loosen up and let's have some vino!'

The boys insisted that Paola and I join Papà in a game of scopa with them. Angelo and Stefano were shy with me at first, mumbling their apology for my loss, but soon the easiness returned. We'd known each other since we were children, after all. But all the same, I was surprised when Stefano began to ask me about the work I did with Nonna when we found ourselves alone at the table between games.

'When did you know you wanted to be a healer?' he asked, picking up a few spiced chickpeas from the bowl and popping them into his mouth.

I frowned, taken aback for a moment, not sure if he was serious. 'I've always known,' I said.

Stefano shook his head. 'I wish I'd been like you. I had no interest in knowing how a body worked before we went to war. The first time I saw what war could do to a man was when we marched past a lake lined with dead Abyssinian soldiers on our way to Addis Ababa. Our aircraft had attacked the area and it was whispered among our company that mustard gas was used. It was as though something had stirred within me and come to life. Now I can't think about doing anything but medicine and finding a way to help soldiers injured on the battlefield. It's a strange feeling.'

The images of men killed by poisoned gas made me sick to the stomach. But I appreciated Stefano's candour. I smiled in spite of myself. 'You're one of the lucky ones. Some people never find their passion. It doesn't always come to you straightaway, but what matters is that once you've found it, you never let it go. I didn't know how I would become a healer but I was determined to find a way.'

'I've been thinking that I could sit for the university test . . .'

'Then do it or you'll never be satisfied.' I put my hand on my chest. 'It's like a fire in your heart, a part of who you are.'

Stefano's eyes widened. 'That's right. That's exactly what it's like.' He frowned. 'But it's so different from anything my family have ever done so I want to make sure it's the right thing for me. Can you tell me a little about the sort of things you do?'

I told him briefly about the wide range of conditions that Nonna treated and the science behind the herbal treatments I'd learnt from Fra Fortunato and Mother Superior.

'Grazie, Topolina,' he whispered, as everyone returned to the table for another round of cards. I nodded, bemused by the fact that, after all these years, we actually had something in common.

Inevitably talk turned to the threat of war.

'If war comes, maybe it will be the thing that unites us,' said Vincenzo, placing a card on the table. 'Surely Europe's leaders won't take much more from Hitler.'

'Even Il Duce will have to do something,' said Angelo, slapping down his card in disgust.

'Il Duce thinks Italy's in a position of power after the win in Abyssinia, but he hasn't helped his own people here in Calabria. We're battling drought, flood, earthquakes and storms, and all he does is force quotas on farmers with fixed-price contracts that never seem to pay enough,' said Papà.

'You know, while I was away,' said Stefano, 'it became clear that although northern and southern Italians have different dialects and traditions, we're still the same people. We all worked together as a cohesive unit for the benefit of our regiment, no matter where we came from. If only Italians at home could see that working together would make a better Italy, one that would be beneficial for all.'

I noticed that Antonio was listening intently. He adored Vincenzo and his friends.

'I doubt that any alliance with Nazi Germany is going to help us in that,' said Papà. 'We'll be treated the same as we always have here in the Mezzogiorno.' He glanced at Antonio next to him, showing him his cards. 'Which one should I put down?' he whispered.

'Unless Il Duce is forced out,' said Vincenzo, pouring Papà and himself another glass of wine.

'Don't talk like that,' said Mamma, putting down her sewing, eyes wide with alarm. 'If anyone hears you say things like that against Il Duce, it will only bring trouble.' She stood up. 'I've had enough talk of war and policy for one night, enough of wine and loose tongues. I'm going to put on a pot of coffee.'

Vincenzo and Rosa's wedding was beautiful, despite the last-minute preparations. Family and close friends gathered to congratulate them and celebrate their happiness. Watching them in the church repeating their vows and seeing their faces alight with joy reminded me of my wedding day in the same church. Although I had been terrified, the look on Vincenzo's face as he gazed at his bride was just like the look on Massimo's when I'd told him that I might have been pregnant: promise. Despite the tears that filled my eyes I was incredibly happy for my brother and his new wife.

Papà spent the last days before his departure making sure everything was organised: that a price and a date had been negotiated for the shearing of the sheep in spring before the lambing; that the government contracts for the summer harvest of grain had been finalised; and that the bills had been paid. He spent long hours with Paola, Antonio and Mamma going over plans for the next few months. He didn't have anything to worry about though; Paola was more than capable.

We were all still shocked that he was leaving. The tearful goodbye from Teresa, and Nicolo, who adored his nonno, was enough to make Mamma and I cry. Teresa was a mess, sobbing as she farewelled Papà, before Paola returned the screaming Enrica to her arms and she had to calm herself for the sake of her child. Paola only hugged Papà tightly but I knew she'd miss him the most.

'Look after your mother,' Papà whispered as I embraced him. 'Make sure she doesn't take on too much on her own.'

I nodded, willing myself not to cry again, and kissed him on the cheek. If all went well, they'd be home on leave soon. I didn't know if I could contain my sadness and anxiety at his leaving. After the occupation of Czechoslovakia by Germany, the British prime minister, Chamberlain, had promised to come to Poland's aid, now almost surrounded by German friendly or occupied states. Vincenzo felt sure this would be enough to stop Hitler in his tracks – there was no war as yet.

'You won't have much time to miss me, Gabriella,' Papà said jokingly to Mamma, who pulled him close and kissed him with wet cheeks. 'I'll be back home soon.'

'You'd better, caro mio,' said Mamma. 'Or you'll be sleeping in the goat shed when you return.' Beneath the jokes was a deep love that had endured for nearly thirty years. In the years that followed their separation during the Great War, Papà had never left her for more than one or two nights. Until now.

Two weeks later it was Vincenzo's turn. Rosa was stronger than I thought she'd be, crying silently as she returned to the shop with her parents. Mamma was trembling as we went back into the house and I put my arm around her.

'Are you alright, Mamma?'

'I've just received a letter from your father. His regiment has been deployed and leaves soon. He's not sure exactly where but he thinks east, outside of Italy's borders. It can only mean one thing: there will be action. I'm afraid. He's not as young as he used to be.'

I shook my head in disbelief, thinking of Agata's letter. If Albania was the destination, as Mother Superior had suggested, then Il Duce had decided to invade a sovereign country.

We'd all hoped it wouldn't come to this. But as my sisters and I embraced Mamma and each other, I felt strong in our unity. No matter what happened, together we'd get through anything.

14

'Italy has been victorious in its occupation of our close neighbour, Albania,' said the radio announcer. I'd been listening to Radio Londra, anxious for any report of troop movements and military action, desperate to know anything that might relate to Papà and Vincenzo, but in the end the news was broadcast on Italian radio.

It was Easter Saturday, 8th April, 1939, four weeks after Papà had left. Mamma, Nonna, Paola and I stared at each other over the little braided dough shapes, each with a boiled egg nestled in the middle. We were making cuzzupe, sweet Easter cakes, for the following day.

'Armed demonstrations in Albania have affected negotiations for closer ties between our country and King Zog of Albania ... Italy needs Albania for military reasons and the decision was taken to occupy Albania, with troops landing on Albanian shores at dawn yesterday.

'The government buildings in the Albanian capital, Tirana, and all ports were captured and occupied by last night. Albania is now in Italian hands. The invasion was over within a day.'

'Your father was right,' said Mamma tightly.

'So quick,' said Nonna, shocked.

'Let's just hope that means that they had few casualties,' I said.

'I hope so,' said Mamma. 'But I won't know anything for sure until Andrea writes to me.'

'What will happen now?' whispered Paola. 'Will there be war because of this or will Papà come home?'

But only a week later, Vittorio Emanuele III, King of the Kingdom of Italy and Emperor of Ethiopia, was crowned King of Albania. It seemed that none of the European leaders was willing to take action against Germany or Italy. Perhaps war wouldn't come after all.

We managed as best we could. Some days, Mamma seemed lost without Papà, wandering the house aimlessly of an evening before bed. Other days she pushed herself past the point of exhaustion helping Paola on the farm and looking after Nicolo and Enrica. My days were busy, spent working at Nonna's clinic and visiting patients around the district. I helped on the farm whenever I could.

I also continued to work at Brancaleone and the marina, out of a room at the rebuilt hall. Don Silvio and his men were doing a good job, restoring the marina and its associated buildings, building cottages for the fishermen and helping the hamlet return to some sort of normalcy. It was painful for me to go to the marina each week, unable as I was to escape the memories of those terrible days. But the community still made me feel like I belonged. Fishermen would tell me stories about Massimo, pressing the best selection of fish on me to take home, while the women would bring me fresh zippoli, fruit and vegetables from the garden, as well as handmade linen to replace what I'd lost. I began to look forward to that one day every week as a connection to Massimo and to a very special and close-knit community.

Massimo had left me a third share of the fishing business and had written in his will that I could live in the cottage until I died or married again. But there was no cottage, only an empty plot of land now, and I couldn't think any further than the week in front of me. Aldo and Mimmo had agreed to run the business until Massimo's boys and I decided what to do.

Now it was the soft sounds of Mamma's weeping down the hall that woke me at night. She missed Papà desperately, spending her evenings with the rosary beads clicking between her fingers, whispering prayers for his safety. And although Papà and I parted on far better terms than we had been on while Massimo was alive, we'd never really spoken about the tension that had been between us. After the loss of Massimo, I knew that our differences just weren't worth fighting over.

We finally received a letter from Papà a few weeks later, which Mamma read out after dinner.

Dearest Gabriella,
We have been in Albania for the last month. The 1st Bersaglieri Regiment was part of a 100,000-strong invasion force. The Albanians had little hope and were quickly overrun.

*The country is rugged and mountainous, nothing unusual
to me, although some of the men have found travelling quickly
along the mountain passes a skill they've had to learn fast.*

Mamma paused and squinted, trying to read Papà's
writing. His spidery hand was often hard to read.

*While we were camped near an isolated mountain village,
five or six of the men came back leading a veiled woman on
a donkey. They'd been told that she was a famous beauty.
Maybe the villagers had sent her to keep their village safe and
maybe she had no choice but to go with the soldiers. All I know
is that the men were more than excited to see the beauty of
the woman under the veil. In front of all of us, they helped her
from the donkey and she was asked to remove her veil. She was
unwilling, very shy and not sure of what was going to happen.
I felt very sorry for her. A woman caught in the middle of a war
is often helpless and I didn't wish any harm to come to her.
But before I could say anything, she finally agreed to unveil.
Beneath the veil was a woman, and she might have been
a famous beauty once, but now she was an old woman with
tough, wrinkled skin.*

Peals of laughter erupted from Antonio.

'Is that funny?' asked Nonna, hitting the back of Antonio's
head.

'Hilarious,' said Antonio.

Nonna shot a look at Mamma but she only shrugged.
What could she do? Antonio had no real understanding of
what it was to be a woman at the mercy of a man. I'd seen

it more often than I wanted in the healing work Nonna and I did. There were many women with bruises all over their bodies, though they never attended the clinic for themselves, only their children. If I asked, they'd tell me that they'd fallen or accidentally banged themselves, but I knew the truth. The world was ruled by men, and women had very little power. I'd known that since I was a young girl.

'Go on, Mamma,' I said, shaking my head at Antonio.

The shock and horror on the faces of the men were so funny we couldn't stop laughing. The old woman thought it was a good trick and she smiled. She only had one tooth, and when the men stepped away, disgusted, she threw back her head and cackled like a witch. I could almost believe that she was a strega and had bewitched the men to believe that she was a beautiful young woman. But when none of the men claimed her for their own, she climbed back onto the donkey and turned its head for home.

'See?' said Nonna with a flash of reproach in her eyes. 'If you disrespect a woman, she'll find a way to make you pay, one way or another.'

My brother had the decency to look abashed, trying to contain his laughter. I also had to hide the smile behind my hand at the thought of the looks on those men's faces. At least the old woman had found a degree of power in her deception.

Mamma continued to read slowly.

The Albanians, it seems, have a lot in common with the Calabrese and I feel a kinship with these conquered people.

I thank God that I do not have to stay and watch their suffering. Our regiment is soon to pull out of Albania and we will return to our garrison at Cosenza. I'll let you know when I have leave to come home. I do not think it will be long and hopefully in time for the summer harvest.

Give my love to all.

Your loving husband,

Andrea.

'See, Mamma? He'll be home soon,' said Paola, darning Antonio's socks.

Mamma nodded and smiled, wiping her tears with the corner of her apron. I wondered how long Papà would be home for and if he would stay.

But a couple of weeks later, the front page of the newspaper reflected the news on Italian radio: Italy had signed an agreement with Germany, the Pact of Steel.

'It doesn't bode well for this country,' said Nonna, tossing the newspaper across the table. The alliance pledged continued support, friendship and trust between the two countries, but so far it seemed that Italy was doing all the supporting. What did other southern Italians think about this pact, if anything at all? Many were surviving hand to mouth, their sons and husbands off fighting Il Duce's wars. They were probably too busy to care about Rome's policies, especially when nothing seemed to affect them here, in this often forgotten and isolated part of Italy.

Nonna and I saw many women struggling to keep their small farms and businesses afloat. Many were up before dawn preparing food for the day ahead, washing clothes and cleaning the house before heading to the farm, often with a baby strapped to their back. At night, there was mending to do, spinning hemp to weave into cloth, as well as preserving food and balancing figures. More and more were unable to pay for what they needed in lire and Nonna and I had begun to take payment in produce or homemade goods. I wondered how long it would be until some were evicted from their farms and even their homes. Bureaucrats and male farmers tried to take advantage of the women running farms and the businesses, but Paola refused to take any nonsense. Government officials had tried to bully her with new quotas but, with Antonio's help, she'd warded them off. Not everyone had a male relative ready to support them, though.

'Surely Il Duce won't allow us to be dragged into any of Germany's problems?' said Mamma, cutting a piece of cheese. The three of us were having lunch before heading to the farm.

'Normally I'd agree with you,' said Nonna, 'but some of his decisions of late have been questionable.'

'He's done wonders for Italy,' said Mamma. 'Anyone will tell you how he's created more employment through the Great Depression, got rid of the Sicilian mafia, made Italy a great country again by adding Abyssinia and now Albania to our empire. Germany and Britain have empires, why not Italy?'

'Mamma Mia! Come on, Gabriella, you can't bury your head in the sand,' said Nonna, throwing her hands into the air. 'I know you're proud of Andrea and Vincenzo and you want their service to their country to mean something, but what about Calabria? He's done very little to help the people in the south.'

'Poverty hasn't changed and how can it, when even the local government officials are as corrupt as ever and line their own pockets with our hard-earned money?' I said, picking up the crumbs on my plate with my finger.

'I know,' said Mamma with a sigh. 'Now I'd just be happy to have you all back here, safe and well. I can't believe that Il Duce would allow us to follow Germany into war ... that would be unthinkable.' She put her head in her hands. 'I just want my family together again.'

I put my arms around her. 'We all do, Mamma. Let's hope that Il Duce knows what he's doing.' I glanced at Nonna, who looked grim. Wanting something to be a certain way didn't mean it would be like that. I knew that and so did Nonna. Everything I'd read and heard suggested that the aggression of Hitler and Il Duce had left Europe on a knife's edge. I wasn't sure what would happen next, but I doubted our Calabrese soldiers would be home any time soon.

I visited Zia Francesca with the news of Papà. I saw her regularly at her flat above the trattoria, looking through her magazines as we talked about life over a glass of vino.

'No matter what happens, your father will be fine. Don't forget, he's done this before,' Zia Francesca said, sipping her vino.

I nodded, feeling better for having confessed my fears to her. I picked up the magazine that was sitting on the table and flicked through the pages. 'It's beautiful. I've never seen illustrations in colour before,' I said in awe. It was a current edition, I noticed, June 1939.

'Silvio bought it for me. It's the first edition of *Tempo*, a new magazine from Milano and the first colour magazine in

Italy. I thought it might be good but I'm a bit tired of hearing the same old Fascist rhetoric. I'll have to wait until he brings a more recent edition of the American *Life* magazine.'

'He gets you American magazines?'

'There's a great demand for all things American, even though Il Duce believes that the American culture is decadent and the opposite of everything he's trying to do here in Italy, and yes, he gets me whatever I want.' She lit a cigarette and took a drag. 'Ahh, that's better,' she said. 'I know that almost everyone disapproves of me smoking but it's just what I need at the end of a long day.'

I nodded, noticing the cigarettes were American too. 'But how can you read the American magazines?'

'Silvio spent some time in America when he was younger and he's fluent in English. He's been trying to teach me but I'm not such a good student,' she said with a shrug. 'Somehow, I've learnt enough to read and understand the magazines.'

I wasn't really surprised that Don Silvio dealt in contraband and illegal goods but I was surprised that he spoke English and had spent time in America.

'Do you think I could look through one?' Although they were illegal, I was intrigued and hoped I could learn something just by looking at the pictures.

'I have an old one from early this year,' she said, grinning. 'You can look at it here with me but you mustn't tell anyone that you've seen it. You and I could be in terrible trouble, even arrested by the police.'

She disappeared into her bedroom.

'Here,' she said when she returned, dropping the magazine on top of the copy of *Tempo*. *Life* magazine had a photograph of a young boy in a strange hat on the cover. I opened the magazine with reverence. Inside was a colour illustration of a new American car and photographs of men shaving and young women in ballgowns.

'They're debutantes,' said Zia Francesca, sitting beside me. 'Young women, usually from wealthy families, who make their entrance into society at a special ball.'

I glanced at the plain black dress I was wearing, wondering what it would be like to wear such a glamorous gown. I had dressed in black every day since Massimo's death and would continue to do so until the first anniversary, when we held a memorial Mass. I hated black, it made me look sallow and pasty, but it was what was expected of me.

'Teresa would love to make these dresses,' I said softly. 'If only she had customers like that . . .' I kept turning the pages.

'That's an article about Winston Churchill, a prominent British politician, and his stance against Nazism.'

I stared at the page as she explained what the article said. I kept turning, shocked by pictures of women in scanty clothing for all the world to see. I stopped at the full-page photograph of a man wearing an animal skin cloak across his shoulders.

'I remember talking to Silvio about this one,' Zia said. 'The article's about the history and culture of Rumania's people and the threat of Hitler invading them for their wheat and oil fields.'

'Where's Rumania?'

'There's a map,' she said, turning the page. 'See here? It's next to Yugoslavia, which borders Albania, where your papà is, on its western side.'

I noticed that Rumania also bordered Czechoslovakia, part of which Hitler had already occupied.

'What about these people with their different hats?' I asked, turning my attention to another photograph.

'They represent all the different cultures and people who live in Rumania. They all live together in one country and speak one common language but as you can see, there's much variation between the individual cultures.'

I nodded, amazed by the variety of costume and the obvious poverty in some of the photographs. 'It's easy to forget that there's a whole world out there when we live here. How can we possibly understand what's happening in the rest of the world if we don't know anything about it?'

'I'm afraid we can't. But that's how our government wants us, to stay in the dark like potatoes and only learn whatever they feed to us.' She put her glass down on the table. 'Just keep in mind that everything you read or hear isn't always as things are. Il Duce likes to fashion news and information to his own advantage.'

'I know. I've been listening to the BBC's Radio Londra.'

She stared at me a moment. 'Please, be careful! The punishment for listening to foreign radio is harsh too: two months in prison and a one thousand lire fine. I hope you're taking precautions.'

I nodded. 'I know. I only ever listen while I'm alone at Nonna's and I've closed the clinic door or whenever I stay over and she's asleep late at night. I'd hate for anyone else to get into trouble.'

Zia touched my cheek. 'You're so much like me. Just keep your wits about you.'

*

Against the odds, Mamma's wish was granted: Papà and Vincenzo were home for the summer harvest. We all pitched in to help, even Santoro now that school was over for the summer, and Rosa when she wasn't at the shop. For the first time we really felt like a united family. Santoro still gave me books to read sporadically and I enjoyed sitting with him from time to time, discussing science, language or history. Vincenzo would paint pictures of the lakes and mountains near Torino in the north, telling us stories of life in the garrison.

Evenings were my favourite time, when we'd all sit around the table in the cool of the evening for dinner. Mamma, Nonna, Teresa, Rosa, Paola and I would congregate in the kitchen, talking and laughing as we prepared simple dishes vibrant with colour and bursting with flavour. The occasional addition of fresh fish to our meals always made me think of Massimo.

I had decided that I couldn't go back to living at the marina. Everything that reminded me of Massimo had been destroyed, all I had left was Nero, and my life was here, surrounded by my family and my work. I was earning my own income, so I gave the plot of land and my share of the fishing business to Luigi and Franco. I thought it would be kinder to leave the boys to start again and it felt good to be able to help set them up for their futures; their father's hard work would count for something and they'd be able to support their own families one day. They'd decided to come back from Reggio to run their father's fleet and, grateful for my gift, insisted on giving me a small percentage of the profits each month until I married again, because that's what their father would have wanted.

'Stefano has some good news,' said Vincenzo one evening when we congregated around the dining table to enjoy the zippoli, Italian donuts with anchovies, while they were still hot. It was just like old times, when Stefano and Angelo used to be almost permanent fixtures in our home.

'What is it?' asked Papà.

'Since I've come back from Abyssinia, I've been thinking about becoming a doctor. I've saved enough for university and I sat the entrance examination at the Messina university not long ago. Signora Lipari gave me a letter from the university while I was at the post office today.'

He caught my eye across the table and I smiled. Then he glanced at the expectant faces around the table.

'Allora!' said Mamma. 'Are you going to tell us?'

Stefano grinned, his face alight with excitement. 'I passed the examination and I've been given permission by my division to begin my studies at the start of the next academic year. I can continue until I've either been recalled or discharged from my regiment.'

'Congratulations, Stefano!' said Mamma against the cheering and shouting of the rest of us, kissing him on the cheek. 'Not just anyone can get into university and then study to be a doctor. Your parents must be so proud and we're all proud of you too.'

'Grazie,' said Stefano, his cheeks flushed with pleasure. 'My parents are happy. I'm the first one in my family to go to university.'

I looked at him with new-found respect and a little jealousy. I didn't know anyone else who had been to university. Luigi and Santoro had gone to college but university was much more difficult. It took real commitment, dedication and focus.

'At least you'll be better than Dottore Rosso was,' said Vincenzo.

'He couldn't be any worse,' added Angelo, elbowing Stefano in the ribs.

'That's enough, boys,' said Mamma.

'I thought you enjoyed being a soldier,' said Antonio with a frown.

Papà stood from the table and went to the kitchen, rummaging through the cupboard.

Stefano nodded. 'I do, but I think I can do more if I become a field doctor and help injured soldiers on the front line. I want to help restore lives, give men back to their families, give soldiers the chance to live a full and happy life.'

'That's a noble cause too,' I said softly. The intensity I'd seen in him was about making a difference. I understood that and the deep excitement of standing on the brink of making your dreams come true.

Papà poured liquorice liqueur into the glasses on the table and handed one to Stefano. 'Salute!' he said, raising his glass. 'Here's to your success and good fortune!'

We raised our glasses and drank to Stefano's success.

'You'll do us all proud,' said Paola, smiling.

Stefano nodded, misty eyed and touched by everyone's good wishes. 'How's the harvest going?' he asked as Mamma passed the dishes around the table. 'Paola, I hear you've been driving the new tractor.' Paola had persuaded Papà to lease modern machinery from the wealthy land owners in the district for the harvest season. The tractor made the process of gathering the wheat much faster and less labour intensive than using bullocks and ancient equipment.

'She drives it like she's been doing it forever,' said Papà, shaking his head in awe.

'Well, I've been doing it longer than anyone except perhaps for Papà,' she said, smiling.

'She's the only girl in the district who drives a tractor,' said Mamma proudly, handing the basket of fresh bread around the table.

'She's as good as any man,' said Antonio, cramming a forkful of eggplant parmigiana into his mouth. 'She runs the farm just like Papà would.'

'When all you men are away, somebody has to keep things running,' said Rosa, taking two slices of bread and giving one to Vincenzo.

'And an amazing job you all do too,' said Vincenzo, touching his wife's cheek and gazing into her eyes. 'Here's to our women,' he said, raising his glass. 'May we men be deserving of them and all they do for us.'

'Hear, hear,' said Papà, beaming with pride. 'May there be many more days like this, where we're all together, celebrating life.'

Papà was right. It didn't get much better than this. Even the threat of war seemed distant, and perhaps Papà and the boys could soon return to normal life.

'Alla famiglia,' we toasted, clinking glasses and smiling.

15

The joy at having our family together was shattered only a few weeks later on 3rd September 1939, when Britain and France declared war on Germany.

Nonna and I had arrived at the monastery just before the festa to help Fra Fortunato prepare his clinic and see patients. All the heaviness that rested on my shoulders had lifted now that I was back in the monastery gardens, breathing the fresh air and gazing at the forest-clad mountains once again. Everything seemed the same as always.

'I'm getting back to normal,' I said to Agata as we passed the ornate fountain, the centrepiece of the garden. 'It didn't feel right to stay at the marina. As much as I loved Massimo, it was time to start over. I'm so busy between working at Nonna's clinic and seeing my own patients at Brancaleone and the marina. I'm starting to stand on my own two feet and people are asking to see me, which is what I always wanted. But there was something about working in those hours after the tidal wave, treating those who had been injured or who had been pulled free from the debris. I felt somehow alive. Even though I was in deep shock and beside myself with worry for Massimo, all that fell away when I concentrated on helping people.'

'You like working in a crisis,' said Agata. 'And it sounds like you're good at it.'

'I don't know,' I said, sighing. 'I would never tell Nonna this, but the work has left me feeling a little bit unsettled – and unsatisfied.'

'I know what you mean. Sometimes I think about going back to the sanatorium to work. Although I love working with Fra Fortunato, I miss the constant stream of new people and the varied needs of each patient. Perhaps we're the same and we thrive on new challenges and constant change. Could you try working somewhere else, perhaps in one of the big cities like Reggio or Napoli?'

I thought of the American magazine I'd seen at Zia Francesca's. The stories about the world outside of Italy had reignited something in me that had been there since I was a girl. I wanted to learn, not just about Italy and our history, but about the world beyond our borders. Somehow the village had become smaller. 'Maybe one day,' I said, seeing Nonna talking with Mother Superior outside her study. Nonna was a remarkable woman, full of bristling energy, but lately her brisk walk had slowed and her back was beginning to bow. 'Nonna needs me at the clinic. She couldn't manage all the patients on her own. For now I want to focus on my skills and learning all I can from her.'

Then Mother Superior called us into her study at lunch-time to hear a Radio Londra broadcast and we sat in shock as the announcer translated the speech that the British Prime Minister Chamberlain had delivered minutes earlier.

'This morning the British Ambassador in Berlin handed the German Government a final note stating that, unless we heard from them by eleven o'clock that they were prepared at once to withdraw their troops from Poland, a state of war would exist between us. I have to tell you now that no such undertaking has been received, and that consequently this country is at war with Germany.'

Agata made the Sign of the Cross, pale with shock. 'What do you think Il Duce will do?'

I shook my head. A summer of hope, but now this. My heart fell as I realised the consequences of this news. If war came, Papà and Vincenzo could be on the front line.

'We will probably follow Germany into war,' said Mother Superior, turning off the radio with an impatient click, 'because of that ridiculous Pact of Steel.'

'But surely Il Duce never intended for us to go to war for Germany, especially this soon,' I interjected. 'We can't afford it after the campaigns in Abyssinia, Spain and Albania.'

She nodded. 'He's always made politically astute decisions in the past, especially in terms of Italy's economy, but ever since his friendship with Hitler . . .' She shrugged.

'War might not be on our doorstep yet but like you, I fear that it's coming,' Nonna said. 'At least the Vatican is independent and whatever decisions Il Duce makes, they won't drag the Church into siding with the Nazis. Italians will always be able to rely on the Church. Here, at least, life will go on as it always has and your community can continue its good work and care for the people of this area.'

I glanced at Agata and she nodded. It was time for us to visit the Blessed Virgin, the Madonna who had granted my wishes. This time my prayer was more urgent than ever. I would pray to her with everything I had to keep my family safe and whole, to bring us all back together again and to keep our beloved Italy from being dragged into a war that was not our own. I'd pray that Il Duce would remain true to this country and refuse to allow his alliance with the Nazis to send his people to hell on earth.

Don Silvio came into Nonna's clinic not long after with a young girl of about twelve by his side.

'Buongiorno, Don Silvio,' I said when I stepped out of the consultation room to see who was there. Nonna was visiting an elderly patient on the other side of the village. 'How lovely to see you. What brings you here?'

'My niece, Caterina,' he said, placing a hand on her head. 'She needs your help.'

'Of course, please come in,' I said, gesturing to the consultation room. 'How can I help?'

'Caterina's had terrible headaches for months now,' said Don Silvio once they were seated. 'She's seen various healers and doctors, but nothing's helped her. Can you take a look and see what you think?'

I tried not to frown. Persistent cases like this where a number of treatments had been tried were tricky to diagnose. 'I'd be happy to.'

I spoke at length to Caterina about the history of her headaches and while she talked, I watched as she fidgeted, twirling her hair around her finger, scratching at patches of dermatitis on her hands and moving her body restlessly on the chair.

'There are some biscuits out on the kitchen table,' I finally said to her. 'They're very good, my nonna made them. Go out and enjoy them while I make you up some herbs.' I smiled as she left the room.

'Is she always like that?' I asked Don Silvio.

'You mean never able to sit still?'

'Si.'

'She's just like my sister in so many ways, eager to work and a perfectionist. She always has to finish what she's started otherwise she gets upset and anxious, sometimes even irritable. And she's a terrible sleeper.'

I nodded, writing notes as he spoke.

'I see that you're still using the fountain pen,' he said softly.

I lifted my head and smiled. 'I love it. It writes so smoothly and feels perfectly balanced in my hand. I could never write with anything else now.'

'That's good,' he said. His eyes crinkled with pleasure before his brow furrowed with concern. 'But how are you managing?'

I shrugged. 'I'm managing. I have my work and my family . . .' I blinked furiously, horrified that I could still tear up so easily.

He placed his hand over mine, warm and reassuring. 'I remember how difficult those first months were.' A brief spasm of pain crossed his face and he smiled sadly. 'You and I both know the hardships of losing loved ones,' he said softly. 'It's never an easy road but time does dull the hurt and fills the voids in our hearts with new joys.' He patted my hand and looked around the room. 'It's a nice clinic you have here with your nonna, but I can imagine it would become a bit cramped when you're both busy. Have you ever thought of expanding?'

'Massimo was going to build me a clinic. But we have everything we need for now,' I said. 'And who knows? I might go to the city for a while to further my skills.' I felt a little shocked that I'd confided in him. It was the first time I'd said my dream out loud.

He nodded, looking thoughtful. I was sure he'd tuck that little piece of information into the back of his mind for future reference. At least he didn't tell me that I couldn't or that it was a stupid idea. 'Do you think you can help Caterina?'

'There are certainly a number of factors contributing to her headaches, but I think I can help. I'd like to try a mix of herbs for her to take and lavender oil to rub into her temples at night. From what you've told me, it doesn't sound like this has been tried.'

He sighed with relief. 'Grazie. Any help you can give her will be very much appreciated.'

I made up a mixture and gave it to Don Silvio. 'Let me know how she goes. I'd like to see her again in about six weeks.'

'Grazie, Giulia. Francesca told me I should have brought her here sooner but I'm very glad that we've come now,' he said, doffing his hat.

Although war had been declared, there seemed to be little military action by the British and French over the autumn and winter and life went on as normal for us as the year clicked over to 1940.

'There's hope up north that full-scale war could be averted,' I said one February afternoon while Papà and I were helping Paola make ricotta. Papà had just completed another roster manning the garrison at Cosenza and was back home for a few weeks. Since he'd been gone, Paola's skill as cheese-maker had improved even more, as she had the freedom to experiment with various techniques. She had orders piling up and if it continued this way, she'd have trouble filling the demand.

'With any luck, Italy might be kept out of the whole business,' said Papà, sprinkling salt into the whey and milk mixture simmering over the heat.

'Then you might be able to come home for good,' Paola said.

'Perhaps . . . But we can't live life waiting for what might be. I'd like to see you settled with a husband and family, although I do know that you can run the farm without me and that gives me great relief. You're now a better cheese-maker than I ever was and you can look after your mother if anything happens to me.'

Then he turned to me. 'You're out of mourning now. Nobody would think poorly of you if you began courting again.'

I stared at my father in disbelief. 'How can you say that after everything we've been through?'

He spread his hands. 'I'm not asking you to marry tomorrow, but I know some eligible suitors who would jump at the chance to court you or your sister.'

The familiar anger rushed through me as it did after his announcement of my engagement to Massimo. After the gentleness he'd shown following Massimo's death, I couldn't believe he was back to his old tricks. 'You what? You want to find me another husband?'

He stared at me a moment. 'You know I worry about you both and since I'm away so often with my regiment, if you both had good men to watch over you . . .'

'We're capable of looking after ourselves,' interrupted Paola firmly.

'But while Giulia works with your nonna —'

'This again?' I shouted, raising my arms in exasperation. 'I told you, Papà. I'm a well-respected healer in my own right. I don't need a husband to keep me safe or to keep me in line. Haven't I been through enough already? Haven't I proved myself to you?'

Papà shook his head and sighed. 'You're still young and I only want you to be happy.' He shrugged helplessly as he lined the colander with cheesecloth.

'I'm happy as I am. I have my work, I'm respected in the community and I'm home.' The truth was, as a widow, I had much more independence and I was fortunate to have financial security too. All my passion and drive were now channelled into healing. And another man might not be as understanding as Massimo had been.

'I know, but – mannaggia! I don't understand you girls,' Papà said, pinching his fingers together. 'You are lucky enough to do what you love, but let me tell you that life is always better when shared with someone special. Having your mother by my side means everything. And one day you'll want more than this. You'll want your own family. Children are the ultimate joy and I don't want either of you to miss out. Look how happy Teresa is, and now Rosa expecting her first.' He kissed each of us on the cheek. Mine was hot with indignation against his cool lips. 'Think about it,' he said softly.

I glanced at Paola, who shook her head. There was no point arguing. He really didn't understand. I gazed at the pot and the creamy white curds that were forming with resignation. 'Don't worry, Papà. I'll make my own decisions and I'll choose whatever's right for me,' I muttered with all the restraint I could muster.

By the time I visited Zia Francesca the following day, all I could talk about was Papà.

'Nothing's changed,' I said despairingly as she poured two glasses of vino. 'I can't believe that Papà's back to his old ways. After everything I went through with Massimo, I thought I'd done enough to earn his respect.' Tears of frustration trickled down my cheeks and I wiped them away savagely with the back of my hand. 'You've done alright without having to get married again.'

She took my hand and squeezed it, the look of sympathy on her face not reassuring at all. When all was said and done, I was back under my father's roof, and the thought that he could still decide my future terrified me.

'Si, but I was much older than you when my husband died. Your father's right, you still have your whole life ahead of you and if you want a family—'

I shook my head impatiently. 'Papà wants to tie me down again but I don't want to be stuck here forever.' I noticed the frown on her face but I was past caring what anyone thought.

'I want to see what's beyond Calabria and I know that if I settle here I'll never get to go.'

Zia Francesca sighed. 'I know what you mean. I didn't have that choice back then, I had the trattoria to run and starting again as a widowed woman in a new place wasn't something I was ready for. But if it hadn't been for this place, and I had my time over, maybe I'd have had the courage to travel to the northern cities and find work in one of the big restaurants there.'

'But you're happy here,' I said.

She nodded. 'I have the trattoria, all my family ... and Silvio.' She shrugged, as if in apology.

'No, Zia,' I said, suddenly feeling stronger. 'You have to stand up for what you want. You deserve happiness like anyone else and don't let anyone tell you that what you're doing isn't right.'

She took my hands in hers. 'We're the two black sheep, you and I. My arrangement suits me. So continue to do what feels right for you and if your father insists on telling you how to live your life, well, I'm sure you can go and live with Mariana or you can always come and live with me.'

'Grazie, Zia.'

She picked up her wine glass. 'Here's to strong women who know what they want.'

'And two black sheep,' I said. 'Salute!'

16

But all thoughts of the future were dashed when Il Duce's voice rang across the airwaves one afternoon in early summer, 10th June 1940.

'Men and women of Italy, of the empire and of the Kingdom of Albania. Hear! The declaration of war has already been handed over to the ambassadors of Great Britain and France. We embark on our campaign against the plutocratic and reactionary regimes in the West, which have always raised obstacles against our advance and have often threatened the very existence of the Italian population. And we will win; to finally give a long period of peace with justice to Italy, to Europe and to the world.'

Paola, Mamma and I stared at each other in shock. It had finally happened. Italy was at war.

'No!' Mamma cried. 'Not again.' Papà and Vincenzo were already with their regiments; they'd left a few weeks earlier. Vincenzo had found it difficult to leave Rosa and their new baby Pepe, only a month old.

I glanced at Paola, her face etched with fear as she stabbed the needle she was using to mend Antonio's shirt savagely into the fabric. 'It's alright, Mamma,' I said, rising from my seat and putting my arms around her. She clung to me, trembling, and all I could do was hold her tighter, pushing the rising panic within me down for her sake. 'They've all done this before. Hopefully they'll be back home with us again soon.'

It was still hard to believe that Germany had invaded France, who was fighting back, with the military might of Britain behind it. Now Italy would come to Germany's aid – four major European powers locked in battle. Like Mamma had said, a war just like the Great War. Despite my frustration with him, I wished that I'd hugged Papà and Vincenzo tighter and told them again how much I loved them.

'They'll write to us as soon as anything changes for them,' said Paola soothingly.

'Maybe they'll remain at their garrisons on standby,' I said, kissing Mamma on the cheek.

'I hope so,' she whispered, but the optimism on her face disappeared as quickly as it had come and I realised how much Mamma had aged. 'Turn the radio off. I've heard enough and there's work to be done.'

Papà sent word that his regiment was being headquartered in Napoli, further north and more than double the distance from home. Teresa was grateful for Santoro's mild deformity and relieved that he would never be called up.

'It's not too bad,' said Mamma, trying to be brave for all of us. 'Napoli is still a long way from the action and perhaps Papà can come home from time to time.'

Only days after war was declared, Italy joined Germany's fight against France and invaded its southeastern alpine border. Rosa came to show us a letter Vincenzo had sent, telling her that he was being deployed to France. We were all worried sick and tried to comfort her as best we could as we sat glued to the radio, desperate for any news of the French battle.

But the battle was over before we could get a sense of where Vincenzo might be. France had fallen to the Nazis.

Our first reaction was relief: Vincenzo was safe. We hugged Rosa as she sobbed, releasing her pent-up worry. I could feel how thin she was. She'd stopped eating when she'd received Vincenzo's letter despite Mamma's and Nonna's coaxing.

Then the repercussions of France's defeat hit me.

'I can't believe that France has fallen,' I whispered. 'Where will the Nazis stop?'

The might of Germany had overrun Belgium, Holland and Luxembourg in its campaign to take France and it had won. Mussolini announced this as a resounding success – our first major victory of the war – and the radio reports said the Italian people were excited by the prospect of a quick and triumphant war. Surely the only reason Il Duce was loyal to Hitler was so that he could continue his own expansion of the Italian Empire? But at what cost?

'It's madness,' said Nonna, shaking her head sadly, the sewing on her lap forgotten.

'At least the battle's over,' Rosa said. 'Vincenzo will be home again soon and maybe the war will be over.'

I doubted that Britain would back down after the occupation of its ally but I remained silent. I didn't want to upset them further.

To get my mind off the war I visited Zia Francesca on her evening off. When I arrived, Don Silvio was cooking dinner. The faint smell of boiled chickpeas was overlaid with the fruity scent of the olive oil and rosemary he was adding to the pan.

'Join us,' he said. 'We're having lagane e cicciari. Francesca usually makes it for me but I decided to make it for her. There's plenty here.'

'Yes, stay,' said Zia, her hand on my arm. 'It's always good to see you.'

I nodded. 'Can I help?'

'No, sit down and talk to me while Silvio cooks for us,' said Zia, smiling wickedly.

'That's right,' said Don Silvio. 'You both do enough the rest of the week. Enjoy this one night off.' He put the wooden spoon on the side of the pan. 'Here, let me open a bottle of wine. It's one I brought from Napoli, a white that will go nicely.'

'Bello!' said Zia with approval as she went to the cupboard to get glasses.

I sat at the table and picked up a recent edition of *Grazia*, a new women's magazine.

'Francesca tells me you prefer the American magazines, just like her,' said Don Silvio, opening the wine.

'Yes. They're so different to the Italian ones Il Duce allows us to read.'

He smiled, splashing some wine into the pan before filling the three glasses. 'I've been bringing them for Francesca for years, ever since I went to New York to live.'

'You were in New York? Is it as glamorous as people say?'

201

He laughed at the excitement on my face and in that moment, I glimpsed the boy he might have been: curious, enquiring and full of life. I wondered what he might have done if he'd been born to a different family, a family who could give him a good education.

'Si, I was, and yes, it was. It was amazing and frightening all at the same time. It's such a huge city, very different from growing up here in Calabria, and the opportunities are endless. I was sent there to learn the import and export business. But I didn't speak a word of English and had no choice but to learn quickly otherwise I would have lost any chance I had to take advantage of my good fortune.'

'I'd love to visit new places one day,' I said dreamily. I took a sip of wine. It was nothing like I'd tasted before, crisp but substantial, with a beautiful herbal scent. Massimo would have enjoyed it.

'Where would you go, Giulia?' asked Zia, sitting beside me.

'The big cities of the north, Roma and Milano to start with, anywhere as long as it isn't Calabria.' I was twenty-one years old now and I felt my life slipping through my fingers.

Zia nodded with sympathy.

'What's wrong with Calabria?' Don Silvio's eyebrows were raised in surprise but I could see he really wanted to understand.

I shrugged, embarrassed. 'Things have been the same here as they have been for hundreds of years. I see how different the north of Italy is from Zia's magazines and the books Santoro and Mother Superior give me. It has progressed and modernised and I want to be a part of that. Perhaps to work somewhere I feel more challenged and where I can learn something new to bring back to the clinic one day.'

Don Silvio nodded thoughtfully, stirring the pasta. 'I know your father wouldn't approve, but someone with your gifts should expand their horizons, if that's what you want to do. Besides, lots of women in the north live independent lives. As long as you know where you want to go and you have a job to go to, there shouldn't be any reason for you not to live your dream.'

'Part of me wishes I'd done that when I was younger,' said Zia softly.

I followed her gaze and caught the private moment between her and Don Silvio. I wondered about the opportunities that had passed her by, the decisions she'd made that had kept her here.

'Maybe it's something to think about,' I said, feeling lighter than I had for some time.

Nonna and I again travelled to the monastery just before the festa of the Madonna. People still made pilgrimages even in times of war. When we returned home, Vincenzo's letter was waiting. He was back in Torino, safe and well, along with Angelo and Stefano, who had been recalled to the regiment after the declaration of war.

Rosa read out the letter over coffee one September afternoon, while Mamma bounced Pepe on her knee.

We have left an occupying force in France but we can't treat the French harshly as we hear the Germans do. France is a beautiful country; the Alps are spectacular, the mountainsides covered with green pastures and wild flowers in the summer months.

The villages are quaint and full of character and the French people are stoic but friendly enough to us Italians. You would all love it, especially you, Giulia.

I smiled, trying to imagine the French countryside, equally jealous that Vincenzo had seen it with his own eyes and pleased that he'd thought to tell us about it.

For now, we are garrisoned in Torino and awaiting our new orders. I don't know what will happen. You may already know that the German air force, the Luftwaffe, has begun an aerial campaign against Britain, bombing British targets in the hopes of forcing an armistice. But in my opinion, attacking such a great power can only make this war worse.

Rosa put down the page and began to cry. Paola and Teresa crowded around her, comforting her. I'd been worried too, after hearing reports of the bombings in Britain on the radio. Il Duce declared his support for such action in newspaper articles and radio broadcasts, proclaiming that defeating the British and their colonies in North Africa, the Middle East and Gibraltar would allow Italy to become great by expanding its empire through the Mediterranean. I remembered photographs in Zia's magazines of the grand old buildings and the lush gardens on the edge of the large river in London. I could imagine what bombs would do to those beautiful places. But I couldn't understand how Il Duce could support such ruthless and brutal violence against ordinary people who had nothing to do with the war. But the British were fighting back, their bombers attacking the heart of German government, Berlin.

Local men were drafted into the army. Some disappeared into the mountains or, if they could afford to, became students to avoid conscription. Just like in the Great War, women, old men and children managed the day-to-day affairs of life in the south. Papà was able to return home for a week here and there, which soothed Mamma's nerves and brightened her spirits, but with the routine Paola, Mamma, Nonna and I had refined to manage the farm, family, the clinic – our lives – it almost felt like he was a visitor. He did all he could to help Paola manage the farm, and said nothing more to either of us about finding husbands, especially now that all the good men had been called up.

The time always passed quickly and he was soon on the bus again to Napoli for training and to man the garrison.

By autumn the government had introduced heavy rationing of essential foods like olive oil, butter, pasta, rice and flour. Our family was better off than many, but we feared that the prices for our produce would fall as a result of stockpiling.

It was no surprise when almost everyone attended our local festival of the Madonna to pray for the safety of our men and guidance in managing the farms. Paola, Antonio and I had squeezed through to the front of the crowd to watch the procession arrive at the small church that overlooked the sea, on the road between Bruzzano and our neighbouring village, Ferruzzano. Mamma and Nonna were further back, talking to some friends. Teresa had decided to stay home with Nicolo and Enrica as she was heavily pregnant once again. Rosa was keeping her company.

'Isn't that Stefano?' asked Antonio, pointing towards the men helping to carry the Madonna in front of the procession.

'Don't be ridiculous,' I said. 'He's in Torino with Vincenzo.'

'But I'm sure it's him,' he insisted.

'Where?' asked Paola as we squinted into the sun.

'See? Holding the handle of the caravan.'

The procession reached the crest of the hill and moved towards the entrance of the church. One of the men turned his head to scan the crowd for a brief moment, perhaps to look for his family, and his gaze came to rest on us. He smiled.

Paola waved. 'It *is* Stefano,' she said in surprise.

'I told you,' said Antonio smugly.

'What's he doing here?' I asked as the procession swept the Madonna away to be reunited with her twin behind the altar of the church. 'I wonder if Vincenzo's on leave too?'

After the Mass was over, we congregated around the long tables set up in the piazza for simple refreshments. Antonio went off to find some friends while Mamma, Nonna, Paola and I retired to the shade under the olive trees.

While refilling my drink at the table, I saw Stefano push his way through the press of people towards me.

'Mamma can't wait to talk to you,' I said when he made it. 'What are you doing home?'

'We've all been sent home temporarily until there's further need for us. I've come back a little early to start my second year of university but Vincenzo and Angelo should be back next week.'

'Mamma will be pleased,' I said. 'How have you been enjoying university?'

'It's been good, a lot to learn. But it's definitely what I want to do.' Stefano stood there looking uncomfortable for a moment.

I looked pointedly at him and raised an eyebrow in question. 'What's wrong?'

He smiled shyly, an unexpected smile. At twenty-six, he was self-assured, a soldier who carried himself with confidence. 'I was wondering if I could talk to you about herbal medicine and traditional healing before I return to university. We have a botanical garden there growing medicinal herbs and I'm interested in the way they work.'

'You really want to know?' I stared at him in surprise. I'd thought he'd want nothing to do with traditional healing, like most doctors.

'Yes. After all, what you do has been practised for hundreds of years.'

'Then why didn't you learn herbal medicine instead?'

'Because I've seen so many different injuries on the battlefield, shattered bones, gaping wounds, torn limbs, blood pumping from bodies and massive trauma – injuries that require surgery as well as medicine. These are men who have sacrificed so much for their country and I want to be able to put them back together, heal them so that they can resume some semblance of normal life.'

It was obvious his passion was consistent and consuming, like mine, and his calling as real as my own. 'Come to the clinic tomorrow if you're free,' I said.

'Grazie, I'll be there,' said Stefano, nodding eagerly before he turned away.

Stefano, true to his word, came to the clinic the following morning. He watched Nonna and me work, helped tidy up the workroom and even assisted us when he could see we needed it. I was surprised to find that he was a good help, quick thinking and easily made connections between what we'd tell him about a herb and its clinical application. He joined us for lunch in Nonna's kitchen where he asked us questions about techniques and herbal remedies, and I found myself enjoying this new role as tutor. I asked him questions in return, about what he'd been studying and how it related to illness and healing of the human body.

He stayed with us for the whole afternoon and our conversation continued as we cleaned up and closed the clinic. It was an eye-opening experience for the three of us, as we discovered that not only could we learn from each other, but also that we ultimately had the same goal. I couldn't wait to write to Agata to share my thoughts on what we'd learnt.

I invited Stefano home for dinner that evening where he regaled Antonio with stories of the beauty of the French countryside and the French people. I watched him talk with his hands, his face alight with passion. He was so different to the brash, cocky boy of a few years before. He was tall and lean, long limbed and broad shouldered, with curly hair that had lightened in the summer sun. He had brown eyes flecked with gold and a sensitive mouth framed by a heart-shaped face.

After dinner, Stefano joined us for the evening passeggiata. There were people sitting outside their homes drinking wine or coffee, enjoying the cooler evening air, as we took our customary walk through the village. It was a slow circuit, because we stopped so frequently to chat to our neighbours.

Stefano and I lagged behind, keen to continue our conversation about medicine. I wanted to learn more about modern medical practice and the science he was learning at university.

'Maybe I can bring you my textbooks to look through next time I visit,' he said. 'Everything's so much better explained in the books.'

'That would be wonderful,' I said, filled with excitement.

'It's the least I can do after what you and your nonna have given me today. I know it's only been one day, but already I can see how what you do should be the fundamentals of what doctors should learn.'

I shook my head. 'But you learn about the human body in great detail, about the effects of medicines and treatments that I'd love to know. It's so important to understanding how to heal a patient in the best way possible.'

'I see the potential of combining what we know, the modern with the ancient, the knowledge with the practical. Surely that's best for the patient?'

I stopped in the middle of the street, the soft sea breeze lifting the strands of hair around my face. The night air still held the heat of the day in it and without the cooling breeze, it would have been stifling. It was dark, but the lights from the houses spilled out onto the road, illuminating Stefano's earnest face. I could see how excited he was.

'Maybe you're right, but you still have another five years of study and who knows what you might learn? You might discover that modern medicine is better than what I do.'

He shook his head and grasped my arm. I nearly pulled away at the shock of his touch because it felt like a spark had passed between us.

'No, don't you see, it's not so much the knowledge as the attitude. Science can only explain so much but clinical application, seeing something work on a patient, time and time again, is just as valuable a tool. What you do has worked for hundreds of years. We might not always be able to explain why, but there will be a reason and if it helps to heal a patient and makes them feel better, it's just as valid a treatment as the scientifically explained option.'

I tried to focus on what he was saying, make sense of what I was feeling . . . There had been no spark. I was lonely, that was all.

I nodded slowly as the sense of his words came to me. 'But you want to be a surgeon. How can traditional medicine help you then?'

'Modern surgical techniques put a body back together. It's only part of the treatment. What about the care of the wound afterwards, relearning to use the part that's been injured and the shell shock and psychological problems that not only soldiers but ordinary people suffer from?'

'Maybe you'll have to come to the clinic again,' I said, with a smile.

'I'd like that,' he said softly.

'Keep up, you two,' called Antonio, running back to retrieve us.

210

17

'**T**his weather's crazy,' said Signora Lipari one morning at the clinic, shaking out her drenched coat before placing it over a chair just inside the front door. It was October and the autumn rains had set in. 'Not only is it costing the earth to buy what we need thanks to rationing, but now the weather has closed the roads again and we can't get anything. I've had enough.' She peeled off her sodden cardigan. 'The government officials must think we're stupid. I'm not going to do without so that we can feed the Germans. To top it off, we don't even have enough fuel to run the tractor and harvesting machinery because we're sending it to the war effort. Can you believe that?'

Amelia Lipari hadn't been the first person to complain about the way the government was treating farmers. From what I'd seen during my rounds, there seemed to be a rising wave of anti-war and anti-government resentment among the locals.

But other than rationing and requisitioning of our fuel and produce, the war still felt distant. Teresa had just had her third baby, Bruno. He was a beautiful boy and it was delightful to watch Nicolo, who was now three years old, and Enrica, not yet two, so enamoured with their baby brother. I was amazed at how Teresa was able to make them, still virtually babies themselves, feel special while tending to Bruno and running a household. I'd gained a new respect for her: she was a good mother, a wonderful dressmaker and a mighty woman. Vincenzo was home and helped Rosa at the shop and Paola on the farm when Papà returned to Napoli from time to time for his allotted rotations.

In November, however, the war suddenly seemed much closer when Napoli was bombed by the British, destroying its oil refineries. Papà's regiment was sent back to Albania and we learnt that they'd pushed on to invade Yugoslavia, then Greece. Papà felt so far away. I wondered if he'd ever make it back to us. At least Vincenzo was still home for Christmas.

Stefano came home for Christmas too and visited Nonna and I at the clinic. He thanked us for sharing our knowledge by organising a picnic in Bruzzano Vecchio, the old village, though Nonna decided to stay back to help Santoro with the small children to give Rosa, Teresa and Mamma an outing and a few hours to themselves.

'I thought of a trip to the beach at first,' he confided to me as we walked along the stone steps that led to the top of Rocca Armenia. 'But then I remembered you probably don't like the beach anymore and I didn't want to bring back difficult memories for you.'

I touched his arm briefly. 'It's alright, Stefano, but thank you for thinking of me. Besides, it's too windy along the coast and who likes getting sand in their clothes?'

He laughed. 'You're right, this has the best views of the district and it's the perfect time of year to see everything so green. It's my favourite place to come and think.'

We found a sheltered area surrounded by low crumbling walls and shrubby broom trees with unobstructed views all the way to the sparkling sea. I could see Mamma, Paola, Rosa and Teresa on the steps cut into the rocky outcrop and Vincenzo, Angelo and Antonio on the dirt path below us.

'Perfect,' I sighed.

We laid the blankets on the ground and began to unpack. The smell of freshly baked bread wafted from the basket, and the spicy salami, salty hard cheeses and creamy ricotta were the perfect accompaniments to the bread's crunchy crust and soft centre. The sharp homemade wine washed it all down afterwards, warming my stomach and leaving me feeling relaxed and alive. I'd also brought the delicate nacatole and rich fruity petrali biscuits we'd made for Christmas, the perfect finish to a simple but wonderful meal.

After lunch, we wandered around the ruins of the castle.

'Come, I want to show you something,' said Stefano, excitedly.

I followed him through the labyrinth of ruins to a small chamber that jutted over the side of the mountain. The gently undulating hills unfolded below us, the towering blue mountains in the distance.

'Beautiful,' I breathed. The heady, floral scent of bergamot filled the air from the orchards in the surrounding district.

The citrus grew well here and had become a new way for struggling farmers to make money by selling to the growing fragrance market.

We sat on the window ledge, our legs dangling over the side, and Stefano pulled out a couple of ripe oranges and a handful of almonds, peeling the orange with his pocket knife before separating the segments. He passed me one as we talked about our aspirations for the future.

'I realised the other day that I've never really thanked you,' he said.

'For what?' I bit into the orange, a burst of tart sweetness filling my mouth.

'For persuading me to follow my dream to go to university.' He reached across to wipe the juice that dribbled down my chin as if it was the most natural thing in the world. 'You inspired me.'

I felt a flush of heat rise to my face and shook my head with dismay. 'I'm no inspiration! Your purpose has always seemed so clear to you, but I'm not sure what mine is anymore.' I shrugged. 'All I know is that I want to go beyond the village and maybe, like you, even help those involved in the war.'

'But you're doing what you love right here,' said Stefano. 'Vincenzo told me that your reputation has grown across the district and you're so busy that you work all hours of the day. Surely that is your purpose?'

I nodded. 'I love what I do but there is so much more to learn.' I stared off into the distance, gazing at the green of the orchards that lined the hillsides below. A sudden thought crossed my mind. 'Before I went to the monastery, I wanted to join the Red Cross. It was a crazy idea but maybe there was something in it. After the tidal wave, I learnt that I work well in times of crisis and chaos. I felt alive and so focused.'

'I feel the same out on the battlefield,' he said softly. 'I'll never forget the first time I saw maimed soldiers in Abyssinia, many barely recognisable. Mostly there was nothing we could do but watch as they died. Those who could be saved with the butchery they called field surgery sometimes lingered for weeks with festering wounds. Others survived without arms or legs, feeling wretched and knowing that they'd be a burden to their families when they returned home.' He shuddered, as though imagining that fate for himself. 'But worst of all were the screams of fractured minds at night, men who were reliving the trauma. I vowed then that I'd one day help our soldiers.' He gazed into my face and frowned with concern. 'I hope to join a medical unit when I've studied longer and had more experience, but how will you go about it?'

I sighed. 'I haven't worked that out yet. Nonna needs me here for now. But I pray to the Madonna that when the time comes, I'll know how best to serve those who need me. Until then, I'll continue to help our community.'

'Maybe we can work together one day. Imagine how many people we could help with my medical knowledge and your healing skills,' said Stefano, his face alight.

'Maybe,' I whispered.

It seemed that the war would drag on for months. When I wasn't working, I listened to the radio. The early months of

1941 were bad for Italy. According to Radio Londra, not only had the assault against Greece come to a standstill, but the North African conflict against the British wasn't going so well either. Talking to Zia Francesca always helped. Sometimes, Don Silvio was there when I visited and I began to talk to him about my fears.

'I'm worried about Papà,' I told him. Papà continued to write to us from his regiment in Greece but never in any detail. 'There aren't enough Italian forces to maintain their position. All the back and forth fighting has got to be draining their resources and now with the British arriving to support the Greeks . . .'

'Don't forget that your father's a seasoned soldier,' Don Silvio said. 'He knows what he's doing.' He passed me a cup of coffee, the rich aroma of the dark brew already sparking me up. Coffee was beginning to become scarce but Don Silvio made sure Zia always had enough for the trattoria. Patrons would come from miles away just for a cup.

'I know,' I said, sighing. 'It's just that with all the uncertainty, not knowing where or how Papà is or when Vincenzo will leave again, I feel like I have to be strong to support Mamma and Rosa. And then there's the clinic and my patients in Brancaleone.'

'You still want to leave and work in the north?' he asked, sitting beside me.

I glanced at him, startled that he'd read my thoughts. 'I want to help victims of war, even if I can't think about going anywhere right now.' I glanced at him, afraid he'd tell me I was deluded, but he only put his hand over mine and smiled.

'Well, that's admirable work, Giulia. You'll know what to do when the time is right.'

I was glad to have him to confide in. It was like having a second father, one who didn't try to tell me what to do.

By the time the combined German and Italian forces prevailed in Greece in late April, and then in North Africa, I learnt that Addis Ababa, the capital of Abyssinia, had fallen to the British. War seemed to be all around us and I felt a shift in the community. It was the general opinion of the locals that Italy was involved in a war that wasn't ours. People began talking about our soldiers coming home to help on the land where they were needed.

Nevertheless, Vincenzo, Angelo and Stefano were ordered back to their regiment and sent with the invasion force into Yugoslavia. Rosa discovered that she was pregnant again after Vincenzo's departure, and I couldn't shake the bad feeling in the pit of my stomach.

Thankfully Papà returned to Italy only a couple of months later. Mamma cried when she read his letter telling us that he was safe and well and that his regiment had been assigned to the 8th army and the defence of southern Italy. He explained that protecting the south, even though the war was so far away, was a prudent but most likely unnecessary precaution. Paola and I sighed with relief to know that he was garrisoned in Napoli again. It was as though we could almost reach out and touch him.

Nonna and I had decided not to go to the monastery this year, thinking it was best to stay and support Mamma and Rosa with Papà and Vincenzo away.

In November, Rosa delivered a healthy baby boy, who she named Enzo, after his father. I whispered my own prayers that Vincenzo would return home soon to see his new son and that 1942 would be a better year.

But my prayers went unanswered. Vincenzo, Stefano and Angelo still had not returned when Stefano's mother passed away suddenly, early in the New Year. I expected to see Stefano sometime after the funeral, but he never came and I began to worry. Finally, Vincenzo wrote to say that he, Angelo and Stefano would be home from Yugoslavia in February and asked that Zia Francesca and I meet them with her car at the marina in Brancaleone, where the army truck was dropping them off. We didn't understand why they weren't travelling on the bus as usual, but I took the opportunity to go early and see who was at the marina.

'Aldo!' I called, waving to Massimo's old crew member at the end of the jetty.

He squinted back towards the shore. 'Giulia? Mimmo!' he shouted. 'Come here, it's Giulia.'

I embraced the men, kissing their cheeks affectionately. 'It's been a while since I've seen you,' I said. I looked around the marina, newly rebuilt but as busy as I had remembered it. The salty tang of the sea air reminded me so much of Massimo. 'How's business?'

'Good,' said Aldo. 'The boys have managed well.'

'They've had the best teachers,' I said softly. 'Are they here? I'd love to see them.'

'Luigi's still out on the boat,' said Mimmo, gesturing with his chin. 'He's been running the business while Franco's away at war.'

'Where has he gone?' I asked, even as my heart dropped with disappointment at missing them.

'He's somewhere on the Russian front,' said Aldo. 'The last letter wasn't good. Their uniform and boots aren't warm enough to cope with the freezing winter conditions there.' He threw his hands up in the air. 'I can't imagine somewhere that cold.'

'Let's hope he comes home soon,' I said.

We reminisced on old times while I waited for Vincenzo. I laughed at their stories, although they brought a shadow of sadness over my heart. I still missed Massimo.

Our conversation was interrupted by the rumbling of an army truck. I ran to Zia Francesca and we watched as the truck stopped and Vincenzo, Angelo and Stefano emerged. I was horrified to see that Stefano was on crutches. Vincenzo and Angelo helped him hobble across to where we waited by the car. Stefano was pale and drawn and so thin, with black smudges of exhaustion under his eyes. My heart leapt to my throat. What had happened to him?

'Come on, let's get you into the car and back home,' said Zia Francesca.

Stefano shook his head. 'No, I can't let my father see me like this. After what he's just been through, he'll only worry.' He looked down at his leg and then up at Vincenzo pleadingly.

'He wants you and Nonna to treat him before he goes home,' Vincenzo said.

'Alright,' I said. 'Get him into the car before he collapses.'

'What happened?' asked Zia Francesca, glancing into the rear-vision mirror at Stefano as we drove back to Bruzzano.

'He's been in hospital in Zara on the Dalmatian coast, with shrapnel wounds and a broken leg,' said Vincenzo. Stefano gasped with pain as we hit a pothole on the road. 'It happened during an attack by Yugoslav partisans.'

It wasn't until we arrived at the clinic and I removed Stefano's bandage that I realised how terrible the injury had been.

'It needs redressing,' I said softly.

'They couldn't get it to heal,' said Stefano, wincing as I probed the red and weeping wound on his thigh. 'The shrapnel sliced through my leg, hit the bone and fractured the femur.' He lay back, pale as the sheet on the bed. 'The bone seems straight. Has it set well?'

'We can examine it properly later, once you've had a rest,' I said hurriedly.

He shook his head. 'I'm fine. The truth is I couldn't wait to get back for you to look at it. You'll know exactly what the wound needs to repair. They reduced the fracture twice, once in the field hospital and then again in Zara after the plaster cast had disintegrated with the journey. I was lucky they cut off the first cast because the wound had become infected. I was in a second cast for a month but when it was removed the doctors discovered that the wound hadn't healed as well as they'd hoped.'

No wonder he hadn't been able to get home after his mother's death.

'I'm so sorry this happened to you – and about your mother.' I touched his forehead, which was damp with perspiration despite the cool day. 'Nonna and I will have you right in no time.'

I smiled reassuringly, but deep down I was worried. The wound looked bad enough, but red streaks were beginning to extend past the edges of the injury and if we didn't get the infection under control soon, he'd end up with blood poisoning.

Zia Francesca had taken Angelo home to Ferruzzano where he was going to tell Stefano's father what had happened. Stefano would stay at the clinic until he was well enough to come home. As much as Stefano didn't want his father to worry with the recent loss of his mother, if it was my child, packs of wolves wouldn't keep me away. Nonna and I would do everything we could to improve Stefano's condition before his father arrived.

I gave Stefano a tonic to help him sleep while Nonna and I decided what herbs would best help his wound. He only stirred when I gently placed a poultice of mashed garlic, fresh honey and calendula over his wound before bandaging the area with clean cloths. I glanced at Nonna, who gazed at him thoughtfully, her brow creased in a frown.

'If he improves during the next week, he'll be fine,' she whispered as I picked up the dish and we left him to sleep. 'Otherwise he might lose his leg.'

I nodded stiffly. 'I know.' I blinked the tears from my eyes. Stefano and Angelo had been almost like brothers for most of my life. But I felt more for him than that. Things had been different ever since he came back from Spain and we'd developed a friendship that had grown out of our mutual interest in healing.

Nonna squeezed my shoulder. 'He's a strong boy and he has a lot to live for.'

'I'm just glad that he's here and we can take care of him,' I said, my voice catching. It was such a shock to see him like this, worn down and vulnerable. 'He would never have had the constant care that he needed at the hospital.'

'Why don't you put some lavender by the bed so he has a restful sleep while I make us some lunch?' Nonna said, kissing my cheek.

The next few days were touch and go. Stefano's fever rose and the red streaks crept up his leg like a malevolent spider. His father, brother and sister came to see him. Stefano's sister and her family had moved in with their father and brother to keep them company and help look after the farm. They wanted Stefano home but it was impossible to move him. Instead, they came every day, worried that they'd lose him too, despite their faith in Nonna and me.

I stayed by his bedside, even through the night, as Stefano writhed in his sleep and called out in his delirium. His skin was hot to the touch and I wondered when we'd have to make the decision to take him on the long and painful journey to hospital to have his leg amputated or risk losing him to blood poisoning.

But with careful monitoring and under the eagle eye of Nonna when I was too exhausted to see clearly, Stefano began to improve and his fever finally broke.

When I came in to check on him one day, a week after he arrived, the bowl of minestrone was empty and the slices of bread and cheese gone.

'We were worried we might lose you,' I confided, slumping into the chair beside him.

'I'm not going anywhere,' he said, his eyes flashing with determination. Although the insidious streaks were subsiding, he was still too weak to do more than sit up in bed but at least he was lucid and impatient to get up and do something. He'd asked for his medical books, now on the bedside table, insistent that he keep learning until he was up and about.

'That's just as well,' I said, smiling. 'Otherwise, you'd give me a bad reputation.'

'We can't have that,' Stefano said with a grin before his expression became serious once more. He reached across and took my hand, bringing it to his lips and kissing it fervently.

My breath caught in my throat at the spark that flashed between us. It had been so long since I'd felt a man's touch. A feeling of warmth rushed through me and I couldn't disguise the blush that I knew was rising in my cheeks.

'Thank you from the bottom of my heart. I knew that placing my life in your hands was the best thing to do.'

He released my hand and I allowed it to hover for a second, gazing into his beautiful gold-flecked eyes. His brown hair reached his shoulders now, and was spread over the white pillow. I touched his pale cheek, the week-old stubble soft against my palm, before dropping my hand to my side.

'It was our pleasure,' I said. A torrent of emotions overwhelmed me. Had he only kissed my hand out of gratitude or was there something more? I stood abruptly. 'I have work to do. I'll check on you again later.'

Don Silvio came by to pick up more herbs for Caterina one afternoon while Stefano was recovering at Nonna's.

I'd seen Caterina a couple of times after her first appointment and she was calmer, sleeping better and her headaches had improved. Over coffee, Don Silvio asked Stefano about his time in Yugoslavia and was surprised to learn that he was studying to be a doctor.

'Although I'm in my third year, my studies have been interrupted because of my service and my clinical skills aren't as developed as they should be. I hope to join a medical unit to learn more about field medicine but it will be a long time before I have anywhere near the skills that Giulia has,' said Stefano, turning to smile at me. His wound had stopped discharging and was beginning to resolve. He was getting stronger by the day, able to sit at the table to join us for meals, and the dark circles under his eyes had all but vanished. 'I'm fascinated by what she and Signora Palamara can do to correctly diagnose and heal a patient so quickly and completely. It's because of them that I can still walk on my own two legs.'

Don Silvio nodded, sipping the coffee we reserved for special guests, obtained thanks to Paola's black-market dealings. 'You won't find any more talented healers than these two anywhere in Calabria,' he said proudly. 'Giulia has helped my niece when others couldn't. You're lucky to have them care for you so well.'

'I know how lucky I am,' Stefano said softly, 'and I don't know how I can ever repay them.'

'You don't have to repay us anything,' said Nonna gently. 'We've known you since you were a boy and it's thanks enough to see you get better and live your life.'

As Don Silvio was leaving, he stopped at the front door. 'I don't know if I have any right to say this to you, but you're almost family . . . just like a daughter to me.'

I frowned, puzzled and touched at the same time. 'What is it? You know you can say what's on your mind to me.'

Don Silvio nodded. 'You may not realise this but I think that young man feels more than gratitude for you.'

I drew back, embarrassed, my heart beating hard against my chest. 'Stefano?'

'He's in love with you. And perhaps you are in love with him?'

'Don't be ridiculous. I'm just helping him for Vincenzo's sake.'

'My dear Giulia, I know what you've been going through since the loss of your husband but you're still young enough to start again,' he said, taking my hands in his. 'You have to let go of your pain and leave the past behind you. You and Stefano have much in common and I see how close you are. You remind me of Francesca and me. Don't let time slip you by until the opportunity has gone. All I'm saying is that maybe it's time to move forward, to be happy again. You could do much worse than him.'

I stared at Don Silvio, speechless, as he lifted my hand to his lips.

'Buona notte. Thank you for the herbs,' he said as he stepped into the night.

Don Silvio's comments stayed with me even long after I had gone to bed. I considered my growing friendship with Stefano until it made my head ache. We had so much in common and my heart raced whenever our eyes met. I couldn't deny the jolt of connection when our hands touched.

18

I was walking home in the dark one day after visiting a patient on the edge of the village when I was startled by the sound of screaming. It was instinct that made me run towards the noise but I stopped dead in my tracks as I turned down an alleyway and saw a man being held down. Two men in caps were beating him while a heavily pregnant woman watched, her eyes wide with terror, a third man's hand over her mouth. I knew I shouldn't be there, so I retreated to the shadows, unable to look away.

'This is what happens when you don't follow the rules,' said one of the attackers. Blood poured from the victim's mouth as he was forced to his knees.

The woman tried to struggle free, ripping the hand from her mouth. 'He was only trying to feed us. He's been out of work and with the baby coming soon—'

'Your husband stole from the wrong people and now he must suffer the consequences.'

The punches continued, measured and methodical. The metal on the attackers' knuckles glinted in the dim light and my skin crawled with revulsion. The husband's cheek split open like a ripe peach, blood spurting down the damaged pulp of his face and his head lolled to his chest. I glanced around. There was nobody about, the doors of nearby homes firmly shut.

'He can't make enough to put food on our table,' the woman wailed, bending double in despair. 'Sheep and goats go missing all the time. Why target my husband?'

'The others will pay but this will teach your husband a lesson he'll never forget,' growled the man holding her. He nodded and the men released her husband, who collapsed to the ground like a ragdoll.

The woman stifled a scream. 'The 'Ndrangheta think that they're the law in this land but God watches you and He'll be the one to judge you for what you've done,' she spat.

The man backhanded her across the face and she fell heavily, grunting as she hit the ground.

'Giulia?'

I turned to the hoarse whisper so quickly I almost lost my balance.

It was one of Papà's friends, still in his farm clothes and obviously on his way home.

'What are you doing here?' he whispered.

My gaze darted back to the scene at the end of the alleyway.

'Come away,' he said urgently, taking me by the arm.

'But I have to help them.'

He shook his head emphatically. 'No. There's nothing you can do. You mustn't get involved. Come, I'll walk you home,' he said, gently but firmly guiding me back to the main street.

It was only then that I realised that I was shaking uncontrollably and my face was wet with tears. But what shook me to the core was the terrible truth I couldn't escape: this was the world Don Silvio was involved in.

I didn't sleep that night. When I finally closed my eyes, heavy with exhaustion, nightmares jolted me awake.

'Are you alright?' whispered Paola, turning over in bed.

'Just bad dreams. Go back to sleep.' The images wouldn't leave my mind: the bloody face; the senseless body falling to the ground; the pregnant woman looking on in terror.

I had always known that the 'Ndrangheta used violence to achieve their aims but Don Silvio seemed the very antithesis of this. I'd allowed the fact that he was the capo locale and what that meant to fade to the furthest recesses of my mind. Now I couldn't stop thinking about it. How could he condone such behaviour? How did he sleep at night, when he knew that ordinary people were being beaten on his behalf?

I was distracted all the following day. Even when Stefano came for his treatment late in the afternoon, I wasn't myself. He'd returned home to his father in Ferruzzano and although Nonna and I could have seen him there, Vincenzo insisted on borrowing Zia Francesca's car a few times a week to bring him back to the clinic. I noticed how Vincenzo's company boosted Stefano's spirits, talking together while Vincenzo helped him walk slowly through the village.

'What's wrong?' asked Stefano when I'd finished redressing his wound, which had finally closed.

I shook my head. 'It's nothing.'

He touched my hand and I felt the same thrill. 'Talk to me, Giulia. You'll find me a good listener.'

I searched his face, finding only hope, and realised that I wanted to trust him. 'Alright. Come to the kitchen and I'll make us some herbal tea.' Nonna was out, visiting Mamma.

When we were at the table with a cup of mint tea I told him about Don Silvio and the brutal assault I'd witnessed in the alleyway.

'It must have been awful, not being able to do anything to help them,' he said. 'Have you seen either of them since?'

I shook my head. 'They haven't come to the clinic and we haven't been called out. I haven't heard of any stillbirths either. I've kept an eye out but even with my home visits around the district I don't get to see everyone.'

'Perhaps they'll both be alright.' My hand rested on the table and he covered it with his own. His skin was warm from the teacup and I found comfort in it. 'The more important issue now is what are you going to do about Don Silvio? He's an important man in the 'Ndrangheta and the responsibility for what happens rests with him. At the very least, he knows what happened.'

I shrugged helplessly. 'He's only ever been kind and good to me. Somehow, he took it upon himself to be my patron of sorts all those years ago and now he's become a friend. I don't want to offend him.'

'I think part of your problem is that because of his bond with your zia, he considers you family and he wants to look out for you and protect you, like he does with her. But you have to distance yourself from him. It's the only way you'll be able to resolve this conflict you're feeling.'

'I know, but how?'

'Go see your zia and tell her what happened. She'll let Don Silvio know what you saw and how distressed you are. If he's the man of honour you say he is, he'll step away.'

I looked into Stefano's face, surprised by the ferocity I saw there. It was clear that Stefano wanted to protect me. Maybe Don Silvio was right and Stefano had feelings for me, just as I had growing feelings for him.

I went to visit Zia Francesca and told her what I'd witnessed.

She pulled me tight to her. 'I'm so sorry you had to see that.'

'How can Don Silvio be part of something so brutal?'

'He has no choice,' she said. 'He was born into that world. The only way he can leave it is through death. So, he does the best with what he's been given.'

'Please tell me you're not part of their world,' I whispered, tears sliding from the corners of my eyes.

'It's not that simple.'

I pulled away. 'What do you mean?'

She sighed and sat on the lounge. 'Silvio and I have been friends for a long time. My husband occasionally helped their family with the book-keeping.'

'But how can you continue to be friends with him, knowing what you know?'

'He's a good man who at times struggles with the requirements of his job. I have to separate the man and my friend from the work that he does.'

'So you pretend that none of that happens?'

'No, Giulia, I'm well aware of what goes on, but we can't change it, whether we agree with it or not. I can't walk away from Silvio, so I choose to deal with it in this way. It's

230

complicated, for him as much as for us, and he needs your friendship as much as he needs mine.'

I shook my head in frustration, needing time to process what Zia had told me. It would have been easier to walk away from our friendship, stay away from the 'Ndrangheta as my parents always advised, but now that I knew Don Silvio as a man, it wasn't that simple.

Stefano's leg wasn't healing as quickly as I'd hoped.

'Why don't you all go to the old baths in Motticella?' said Nonna.

'Near the ruins of the ancient monastery?'

She nodded. 'The mineral waters have a reputation for healing. It might do his leg good and he'll be able to move better in the warm water.'

Vincenzo arranged the outing and we brought Angelo, Paola, Antonio and Zia Francesca with us. Even though he was smitten with his two sons, Rosa insisted that Vincenzo join us and have some fun. It was wonderful that he had an extended leave. His unit was waiting until the rest of the division had assembled before they'd learn about their next posting. But we were determined to make the most of every day that he was home. We took Nero and the cart up to Motticella, a small hamlet on the flat of the hill two miles further inland from Bruzzano Vecchio. Some said that the town had been founded in the times of the Norman conquest and had Viking roots.

'I haven't been here in years,' I said to Stefano as we climbed into the rugged hills. Antonio was up front with Vincenzo and the rest of us rode the cart. Despite Vincenzo's careful driving, the jolting along the rough road made Stefano wince in pain. 'Zia Francesca brought Paola, Teresa and me here when we were small. Teresa told her that she didn't want to go into the water because it smelt terrible and the baths looked old. Do you remember, Zia and Paola?'

'We'd all had chicken pox,' said Paola. 'We couldn't stop scratching even when we were feeling better. But once we were in the warm water, even though it smelt a little like rotten eggs, the itching was soothed.'

'Mariana suggested that I bring back mud, which your mother rubbed onto your skin every day to stop you from scratching and soon the sores healed and left no scars,' said Zia Francesca. 'It was a long time ago.'

'I've heard my mother speak about the hot springs too. They used to go as a family every year to take the healing waters,' said Stefano with a wistful smile.

I squeezed his hand in sympathy without thinking. Even after weeks of touching him to treat him, I still felt the electricity between us.

Before long we were high in the hills, past the tiny township and the ruins of the ancient Basilian monastery. It was here that the Bruzzano River sprang out of the mountains and carved its way out to the sea and where the healing waters bubbled forth from the earth. I sensed it was a special place. No wonder a monastery had been built here. The monastery was long abandoned now, nothing more than crumbling rock amid long grass, bright yellow broom bushes and blackberry brambles tumbling over it.

We unhooked the cart and tethered Nero to the ancient gnarled oak tree that stood guard over the spring before walking slowly along the ridgeline and down to the chasm in the rocks where the hidden pool of water collected.

It was like we had entered another world. Warmth enveloped us before we even saw the steam rising from the water, protected on one side by a wall of stone, smooth from centuries of water washing over it. My brothers couldn't wait to strip down to their short pants and jumped into the water with glee. Zia Francesca, Paola and I stepped back to miss the splashing then Paola and Zia Francesca went behind a rock to change.

Stefano stared after the boys wistfully.

'See?' I said, pointing. 'The ancient monks carved steps and seats into the rock so they could bathe in comfort. You can get in more slowly there.'

'I don't want to be a hindrance to you,' he said quietly. 'You go and have some fun too; you deserve it after all the hard work you do. I'll get in when I'm ready.'

I shook my head. 'I came for you. It was Nonna's idea to help your rehabilitation, so we'll both get in at the steps and we'll do some movement with your leg in the water.'

'Alright. I'll do as I'm told but then you have to promise to have a little fun.' He held my gaze and the flecks of gold in his eyes sparkled like Nonna's amber ring in the sunlight. I felt myself blush.

'Let's see how hard you work first,' I murmured. 'Turn around while I get into the water and then you can join me on the step.'

Stefano did as he was bid, watching my brothers swim lazily across the water while I pulled off my dress and wrapped myself in an old bed sheet, which I discarded beside the pool as soon as I slipped gently into the water in my petticoat.

'Your turn,' I said once I was safely under the water.

I watched Stefano undress with the efficient movements of a soldier, yet there was nothing rough or brutal about him. The sight of him took my breath away. He was beautiful, with broad shoulders, a chiselled torso and long, elegant legs. His left side was marred by the livid red of newly formed skin over the site of his injury. The humid air had made the dark mass of his hair spring into riotous curls as I knew mine had also. I couldn't take my eyes off him. He was like Hercules, a ferocious, determined expression on his face as he stepped down into the water.

'Come on, Stefano,' called Antonio across the pool. 'Get over here.'

I shook my head clear of my ridiculous fantasy. 'No, he has work to do first.'

Stefano grinned. 'I'd better listen to the boss.'

I pushed him hard, using the water as resistance to strengthen his leg and the warmth and buoyancy to improve the movement of his knee. Paola in her petticoat and Zia Francesca in the sleeveless, legless swimming attire common throughout the north of Italy, but which would have been considered scandalous by those in the village, joined in with Antonio's game of catch the rock.

'Come on, Giulia, hasn't he had enough?' persisted Antonio.

'A few more movements, then he's all yours,' I said.

Stefano groaned. 'You're a slave driver,' he said, swimming back to me, kicking his bad leg more strongly now.

'It won't be long before you have good mobility and strength again,' I said, drawing his heel towards his buttock.

'I didn't think I'd even have partial use of this leg ever again,' he said, grimacing at the stretch. 'I have you and Nonna Mariana to thank for this miracle.'

'It's just good management and attention to detail,' I said. I was touched by Stefano's appreciation. We both knew that it could have ended in disaster. He'd told me about other men who'd had similar injuries and never been able to walk properly again. Others had endured an amputation in order to save their lives, but their lives were never the same.

'How can I ever thank you, Topolina?' he asked softly as I released his leg, his thigh muscles no longer tight. We were standing so close I could almost feel the length of him against me.

'There's no need. I only want to see you better and able to return to university.'

'Is that all?' he whispered, his lips close to my ear.

I could hardly breathe. The noise from the others on the far side of the pool faded away. 'What else would it be?'

'I don't know about you, Giulia, but sometimes I wish that my leg would take longer to heal so that I can spend more time with you . . .'

'You do?' I stared into his eyes and felt lost in them.

Emboldened, he reached out under the water and encircled my waist with his arm, pulling me to him. I slowly wrapped my arms around him, feeling myself soften against the hard planes of his body in the silky warm water.

'Oh, yes. I've never met anyone like you before . . .' He tucked a stray curl behind my ear, which only undid me further. 'I'd stay here with you forever.'

I felt his desire, the hard ridge against my belly, and knew that if the others weren't nearby, there'd be no turning back. He dipped his head and kissed me, gently at first but with an increasing passion that made me want to explode.

When he pulled away, I could only stare at him, my gaze travelling from his expressive eyes to his sensuous mouth. I touched my mouth in wonder. Kissing Massimo had never been like this.

I brushed his lips with a fingertip and smiled, then pushed myself away, swimming to the middle of the pool. I glanced at the others but nobody had noticed, except Zia Francesca, who raised her eyebrow.

'We've finished,' I called to my brothers. 'Stefano's all yours now.'

'Thank you for helping him,' said Vincenzo one evening not long after our trip to the springs. We were sitting in the kitchen, waiting for the pot of coffee to brew for Papà. He'd arrived home for a few days from his post in Napoli. We were fortunate that Paola could still supply us with coffee beans, but they were becoming scarcer. The weekly ration was often non-existent and barley or chicory were common substitutes. I often used dandelion too, but when Papà was home, Mamma made sure he had real coffee to drink. 'He said that the hot springs made a big difference and he feels more limber than before.'

'You know I'd do anything for you, Vincenzo,' I said. 'And I couldn't leave him like that even if he wasn't your friend.' I fiddled with the edge of the tablecloth. 'Do you think that the army will discharge him?'

Vincenzo took a long swallow of barley coffee before answering me. 'Only if he's not fit for any duties.'

'Stefano told me he has medical leave until he's assessed by the army doctors but that won't be for another couple of months.'

'We'll have to see what happens then, but he won't be joining us in North Africa. They'll most likely move him to another unit and if his leg's still playing up, place him in an administrative role.'

'North Africa?'

'We only just found out. With the Americans joining the war, they've decided to help the British try to push us out of Africa.'

'Have you told Rosa?' Rosa was fragile and we'd have to rally around her and give her extra support when Vincenzo left again.

He nodded, looking unhappy. 'She's begged me not to go and won't stop crying. I don't know what to do.'

I squeezed his hand. 'It's hard on her, especially with a small baby, and she worries about you. When are you leaving?'

'Some of the units in our division have already been sent to Tripoli and the rest of us follow in a few weeks.'

'You're going to Libya?'

'Yes, but I'm not sure for how long. We'll be sent wherever we're needed most. We need a decisive win to take North Africa. Up till now nobody's been the clear victor but with the Americans coming . . .'

I sighed, feeling heartsick. 'When will this war end?'

Vincenzo put his arm around me and kissed my cheek. 'Don't worry. We'll drive the British out of North Africa, return home and be loved and adored as heroes.' He grinned. 'Is Papà still insistent on you settling down with a family of your own?'

'Not lately. Maybe he's realised it's not worth the headache of fighting with me since he's barely home. And if he were to suggest another husband, it could be the thing that finally pushes me to leave this place.'

Vincenzo laughed. I'd told him about my dreams to work beyond the village.

'Why do you ask?' I said with a frown.

'What's going on between you and Stefano? He's been asking me a lot of questions about you.'

'I don't know what you're talking about.'

'Yes, you do. You've taken quite an interest in him too.' He sat back and looked meaningfully at me. 'Maybe it's because you're my sister, but he has the utmost respect for you and he enjoys talking to you.' He got up and poured a small cup from the coffee pot for each of us.

'But that doesn't mean anything. It could just be professional respect.' I didn't tell him about the kiss and the lingering glances we'd shared. I wasn't sure how I felt, what I wanted to do about him. About us.

'Whatever you say, but I know what I see and if you decide to do something about it, I can tell you that I'd approve.' He put up his hand as I went to interject. 'Stefano's a good man. After seeing what we've seen, I know how important it is to share a life with someone special, and to have children, to know that, through them, your memory will live on.'

I hugged him tight, my heart aching for what I knew he'd suffered during the war. 'Oh, Vincenzo.'

He kissed the top of my head and then tipped the contents of his cup into his mouth. 'Ah, that's good. You'd better drink yours while it's still hot and get a cup to Papà before I drink it all myself.'

By the time Vincenzo left for North Africa in March, Stefano was almost ready to depart for university in Messina and return to his studies. Stefano's departure weighed heavily on me as I checked his leg and reviewed his recovery. He was walking without crutches now, but still suffered after long periods of standing or walking. He was my last patient for the day and I'd closed the clinic, as Nonna was already at Mamma's.

'It's going well now,' I said, pulling his trouser leg down. 'Just keep doing what you're doing and the leg should strengthen further with time.'

'It's so much better than I imagined it would be and so much better than if I'd stayed in hospital.'

'You might have died,' I whispered, touching his cheek.

'But because of you, I didn't.' He caught my hand and kissed it. 'Can you imagine what a good team we'd make if we worked together? I could do the surgeries and you could do the aftercare.'

I nodded. 'At least I wouldn't have to say goodbye to you.'

'I won't be gone that long,' he said. 'I'll be back after the medical assessment.'

'I know.' I put the eucalyptus oil on the table. 'What do you think they'll do?'

'I'll be transferred to another unit—'

'What about a medical unit?' That's where he'd originally wanted to be. He'd most likely be involved in the running of a field hospital, close to the front line but not in harm's way. I didn't mention that knowing he was relatively safe would dampen my anxiety.

He nodded, looking thoughtful and even hopeful. 'If I can be useful in a medical unit, I could learn so much more about medicine on the battlefield.' He still held my hand and pulled me towards him. 'Will you miss me?'

'I'll miss our conversations about medicine, but it will do you good to be back at university.' I couldn't look at him. We hadn't spoken about what had happened at the mineral baths.

He looked at me with such intensity that I felt myself melt. 'Just our conversation?'

I shook my head. I leaned in to him without thinking and our lips touched. Stefano could definitely kiss, I decided, as I wrapped my arms around him and the kiss deepened.

The world slipped away, our hands sliding along each other's bodies, exploring the curves and savouring the sensations. At last he drew away, touching my cheek and clasping my hand as though he couldn't bear to be separated from me.

'I don't want you to go,' I whispered, clinging to him.

'I'll come back as often as I can,' he said, caressing my face. 'Because I can't imagine a single day without you.'

19

Thoughts of Stefano were never far from my mind. I knew my feelings had grown although I wasn't sure what that meant for me. Even when a difficult case demanded all my attention, thoughts of him were in the background, wondering what he'd do differently, how he'd be intrigued by a certain presentation. Memories of his touch would come flooding back at the most inopportune times.

One beautiful spring afternoon I was called to an outlying hamlet after a young boy spilt boiling water over himself. When I arrived, the boy was pale and crying, cradled in the lap of his twelve-year-old sister, while his mother was feeding a new baby at her breast.

'I didn't know what to do,' said the mother tearfully, trying to coax the fretful baby to take the nipple. 'I was boiling water for pasta and turned away for just a moment to pick up the baby. I heard a terrible scream and Giuseppe had knocked the water all over himself.'

'Where did it burn him?' I asked.

'On his back,' whispered the girl. 'Mamma called for me. I was outside feeding the pigs and she sent me to get the neighbour. Giuseppe was screaming louder than the baby.'

I turned to the little boy and crouched beside him. 'Hello, Giuseppe, my name's Giulia and I'm going to have a look at your back.'

'No,' he said, beginning to whimper. 'It hurts.'

'Do as the signora asks,' said his mother, rocking the baby as she paced the room. She looked exhausted and defeated. I wondered when she'd last had a good night's sleep.

I lifted the towel covering his back gently and stifled the gasp that rose to my lips. 'Did you put ink on it?' I asked. A big black stain was soaked through the boy's singlet and I couldn't see the burn at all. The ink had dried, sticking the cloth to the skin.

'My neighbour told me it was the best thing for burns,' said his mother. 'She used the ink from her fountain pen and applied it straightaway but it hasn't got any better since this morning and he hasn't stopped crying. That's why I sent for you.'

I nodded. 'I'm glad you did.' I wondered if Stefano knew that ink was a common folk remedy, whether he'd seen anything like this. I'd seen it used on minor burns, which healed without complication, but the problem was that nobody knew how it could react with a larger area of badly damaged skin.

'Isn't it the right thing?'

I glanced up at his mother, whose face was pinched with worry. She was fiddling with a small worn pouch, the brevi she carried with her to protect against injury, illness or witch-craft and evil spirits. Her lips moved in a prayer to invoke help for her son.

'Cold water is the best thing for burns,' I said, trying to look under the fabric as the boy squirmed in his sister's arms. The wound was large, about the size of my hand. I could see the edge of reddened skin and felt the blisters on one side, raised and hard under my touch. The other edge was flattened and damp, oozing fluid, which worried me. Part of the burn had been disturbed as the blistered skin was ripped away with the singlet. The burn was likely quite deep and now required extra care to prevent infection. 'Did someone try to take his singlet off already?' I asked.

'Papà tried to when he came in for lunch,' said the girl, 'but Giuseppe screamed so much that he left it alone.'

'Do you have cool, boiled water?' I asked.

The mother nodded and went to get some for me.

'We have to take his singlet off very carefully. Hold him still,' I said to the girl as I reached for my scissors. 'Now, Giuseppe, stay still and I'll try to be as gentle as I can.'

I cut delicately around the burn as the boy continued to whimper but, to his credit, he didn't move. Finally, the singlet was off, leaving a patch of black-stained cloth over the burn. Carefully, I dabbed the cloth with the water until inky liquid dribbled down his back and the cloth was ready to peel off.

'Don't move now,' I said sternly, using care to remove the cloth without taking the skin with it. 'Shh, we've nearly finished now,' I said, resting my hand on his shoulder and stopping for a moment as he grew restless. He settled again and I returned to the painstaking process. Eventually the cloth came free without damaging the ruined skin further. I brushed the little boy's hair from his eyes. 'You did very well, Giuseppe. Let's make you better now.'

Although olive oil was a common treatment for burns, I decided to apply linseed oil first to seal the wound, then calendula and St John's wort oil to his bandages to help with the wound management. I wanted no trouble with his recovery.

'Leave the bandage on and keep it clean and dry. I'll come back every day to check his wound,' I said to his mother when I was done. I handed her a bottle of tincture that included garlic, echinacea, rosehip, yarrow and chamomile for prevention of infection, promotion of wound healing and to help soothe and calm young Giuseppe. 'Make sure you give him this three times a day.'

'Grazie,' she said with a sigh. The woman reached for a parcel on the table. 'Please take this salami. It's a special recipe handed down through my family. I can't pay you today but I promise to pay you tomorrow.'

'Grazie,' I said with a smile. There were too many who were only just surviving but most were too proud to take something for nothing. 'This is more than enough. The main thing is that we get Giuseppe better.'

But despite my determined efforts to focus single-mindedly on my work, my thoughts would often drift to Stefano, leaving me feeling scattered. The conflict I felt between wanting to be with him and wanting to preserve my independence stopped me from sleeping and nearly drove me to tears. In the end, I confided in Zia Francesca and Don Silvio. He was at her flat when I went to see her. At first, I was uncomfortable, the attack I'd witnessed weeks earlier flooding back. How could I act the same around him now I'd seen the brutality of his world? But for Zia's sake I had to try.

'I've never felt like this before,' I said, sitting on the lounge chair at her flat. 'With Massimo it was different.'

'You're in love,' said Zia, kissing me on the cheek.

'That's what I told her when I saw them together.' I reluctantly took the glass of red wine Don Silvio handed me. For Zia, I reminded myself. 'Drink this. You'll feel better.' If Zia could see the same kind, generous man, then so could I.

'I knew when we went to the hot springs,' said Zia, sipping her wine.

'Alright, you two,' I said hotly. 'So, what do I do about it? The timing's all wrong.' I put the glass on the side table. 'I've worked so hard to do what I want and I still have so much I want to do. I don't want another man trying to run my life.'

'Why can't you have both? Love and the fulfillment of your dreams,' Don Silvio said.

'Tell Stefano what you want, Giulia,' said Zia. 'And listen to what he wants.'

'Sounds to me that you both want the same thing,' said Don Silvio. 'To heal the victims of war.'

I nodded, reaching for my glass and taking a big swallow of the wine.

'You can follow your passions and make your dreams come true together, you know,' said Zia softly. 'If you work together and support each other, you'll both get what you want, and you'll both be happy.' She reached for Don Silvio's hand. 'Learn from us. We once considered running away together but couldn't abandon our responsibilities.'

Don Silvio kissed her hand. 'I'll always regret not leaving my life behind and choosing Francesca. Those years we could have had together are lost to us. But I never wanted to involve her in the harsh and violent world I've had to endure every day. It was never the life I wanted but I couldn't walk away from it, as much as I wished to.' It occurred to me that Don Silvio was trapped, just as I had been when Papà arranged my marriage to Massimo. We both had made the best of our situations. I had been blessed with a good husband but Don Silvio would never be free of the shackles that tied him to the difficult life he led. His world was a fact of life and me pretending it didn't exist didn't do service to the sacrifices both he and Zia had made. Somehow, I had to reconcile the Don Silvio I knew with the stark reality of what he did.

'We were never happy until we found our way back to each other and were honest about what we wanted,' said Zia. 'We agreed that marriage wouldn't be right for us. Silvio was adamant that I didn't become a formal part of his family and therefore of the family business – and I have the trattoria here. We keep our relationship quiet and discreet. Very few people know, not even your father, Giulia.' I felt honoured that they trusted me to keep their secret.

'It's the best we can do and our arrangement works for us. We might not be conventional, and there are people who won't approve, but we're happy.'

Zia touched his cheek and they shared such a look of utter devotion that I wanted to cry with happiness for them. 'Love is a rare thing, Giulia. Do what's right for you and Stefano. Be happy.'

*

Stefano and I agreed to meet on a hot day in June at the old castle on Rocca Armenia where he'd arranged that family picnic an eternity ago. I couldn't believe how nervous I was as I climbed the steps to the castle: my heart was pounding and my hands were clammy. I couldn't stop wondering if his feelings ran as deep as mine. I'd not been able to think about much else but him over the last few months, drifting through my day-to-day life in a daze. It was getting harder to hide my secret smiles and I found it difficult to concentrate even on my work. As much as I had loved Massimo, I had never felt like this.

I glimpsed the back of Stefano's dark head between the stone walls as I made my way to the top of the rocky hill. The breath caught in my throat at the sight of him. After weeks of fantasising about him he was finally there, broad shouldered and feet planted firmly on the ground. A soldier's stance. I wondered how I'd gone so long without noticing how beautiful he was.

He must have heard my steps because he turned to me and smiled. 'Giulia!' he called, reaching out to take me into his arms.

'I've missed you.' I touched his smooth cheek. He'd shaved for me and was wearing his Sunday best. I found his effort endearing.

'I've been waiting for this moment for months,' he murmured, holding me in a tight embrace as he kissed me. All the pent-up frustration and desire we'd been feeling was clear in our kiss. It was passionate and explosive, leaving me in no doubt of his feelings for me.

We pulled away, breathless.

'How are you? How's your leg?' I asked awkwardly, trying to get my feelings under control. All I wanted was to feel his body against mine, skin on skin. There had been so many nights when I'd imagined what we'd do when we were finally alone again.

'Getting better all the time,' he said, flexing his knee, but his eyes never left mine. I quivered with anticipation. 'But my injury's been a godsend.'

'Why's that?'

'It's brought me to you, amore mio,' he said, lightly tracing the curve of my cheek.

I closed my eyes and leaned against him, resting my head on his broad chest.

'I've received my posting. I wanted you to be the first to know.'

I drew away, fear and anxiety taking over. But the look on his face was one of excitement, not dread. 'It's good?'

He nodded, grinning widely. 'I couldn't have asked for better. My leg's meant that I'm unfit for frontline fighting and I'm being transferred to the medical unit attached to the 26th Infantry Division Assietta. They're assigned to the defence of Sicily and are stationed in Caltanissetta in the middle of the island.'

'That's wonderful news! And it's what you've always wanted.' It was such a relief that he was stationed somewhere safer and closer to home. I couldn't bear the thought of worrying about him as well as Vincenzo and Papà.

'I can't believe my luck. It's almost too good to be true. I start there in July, after my end-of-year examinations, but there's not much to do so I've been given permission to begin my fourth year at university then return to the unit to improve my clinical skills and field training. And the best thing of all is that it means that I can still see you.' He picked me up and twirled me around and I laughed with joy.

Stefano took my hand and led me to a low rock wall, the perfect place to sit and look out over the valley below. 'I'd love for you to come to Messina sometime. It's a beautiful city and I think you'd like it.'

'I'd like that very much,' I said. 'Tell me more about it.'

He put his arm around me. 'It's an ancient city, a melting pot of so many different cultural influences. You can even see the fascinating mix of all the great Mediterranean and European empires that have ruled Sicily in the architecture.'

'How?' I asked, shifting against him to get more comfortable.

'The churches and cathedral are centuries old, and you can see the Arabic and Byzantine domes, the imposing Norman arches and pillars and the Baroque flourishes. Then there are the great libraries. You'd love all the medical and herbal books, the ancient texts . . .'

'I can't wait to go,' I said, hugging him with excitement.

'But it's the people who live in the city that I find the most interesting. The more I learn at university, the more I want to help the poorer people around the city. The only way many manage on the tiny rations is by tapping into the black market, but if they have no money or nothing to trade . . .' He shrugged helplessly. 'Some of us want to set up a clinic when we return to university to help those suffering from malnutrition and illnesses resulting from starvation.'

'That's what I love about you,' I whispered.

'You love me?'

I felt my face flood with heat. 'That's not . . . I mean . . . I've never felt this way before, not even with Massimo.' The love I'd had with Massimo was safe and warm, generous and kind, but with Stefano it felt uncontrollable and passionate; he thrilled me in a way I'd never imagined.

I looked into his steadfast, shining eyes and realised that what I felt for him was more than passion and desire: it was a deep and abiding love and a meeting of minds.

We were soul mates.

'I've never felt this way either,' he said softly. 'You're on my mind from the moment I wake until the time I fall asleep . . .'

'Really?'

He nodded and smiled shyly, taking my hand in his. 'I want us to be together. I know I can't be with you as much as I want but Messina's not far.' He brought my hand to his lips, and gazed at me earnestly. 'Let's start courting. We can tell our families about us.'

'You love me too?' I wanted to hear him say it. I wanted to be sure that I was doing the right thing.

'I do,' he whispered before gathering me in his arms.

I sighed at the touch of his lips on mine. There was no place I'd rather be than in his embrace.

'Then let's not waste another minute,' I murmured.

As the kiss deepened, I pressed myself against the hard planes of his torso and felt my body ignite. I pulled him to me, wanting him like I'd never wanted any man before, so different from when I was with Massimo. This was a need that was furious, unstoppable, unquenchable – beyond reason.

He broke away, his gold-flecked eyes never leaving mine. I touched his beloved face, scratchy with stubble and knew that I couldn't, I *wouldn't* stop now. I reached for his belt in silent answer to the questions his eyes asked and he lifted me onto his lap. All I wanted was for us to be joined, to be one. Nothing else mattered.

There was something in the idea of pledging our love in this ancient place, in the open air, with the land we knew so well spread out in front of us. We were declaring that we belonged to each other, no matter where we were in the world.

After all that had been taken away from us, we were asking for benediction from God and the land that we'd been born and raised in.

Stefano came to dinner that evening. He insisted on doing things the right way and wanted to ask my father's approval to court me. Papà was home and we didn't know when we'd next have the opportunity to talk face to face, so we decided to tell my parents after dinner. I didn't want to rush into marriage and Stefano agreed that some time for us to get to know each other better was a good idea before we announced an engagement. The truth was that I needed to be sure that we wanted the same things and that we could work as an equal partnership before we made our vows. Stefano knew how tense my relationship with Papà had been since my arranged marriage to Massimo and he didn't want to give my father any reason to cause me more pain.

'You may know that Giulia and I have become close since my injury,' said Stefano when we were alone with my parents at the table.

Papà nodded, taking a sip of his vino, as if to fortify himself. Suddenly I was worried that he wouldn't make this easy.

Stefano glanced at me and smiled reassuringly. 'I owe my recovery to her and in the process, I've discovered that we have so much in common. The truth is that we're in love and I want to ask for your blessing for us to begin courting.'

'That's wonderful news,' said Mamma, hugging me tight. 'Love is a precious gift and you're twice blessed, since God has granted you this gift again. I'm so glad that you're happy.'

'Thank you, Mamma,' I said, kissing her soft cheek.

Papà gazed at Stefano. 'I've known you since you were a child, Stefano. You've always been just like family.' He turned to me, his eyes misty. 'Is this what you want, Giulia?'

I stared at him, shocked. He'd never asked me what I wanted before. Emotion rushed through me, pride that he seemed to finally respect me and relief that I was free to make my own choices. 'It is, Papà,' I whispered. 'He makes me happy.'

'You deserve to be happy after what you've been through,' said Mamma, clasping my hand.

'She's a wonderful woman and a gifted healer,' Stefano said proudly.

I smiled at him, thinking of what we'd shared at the Rocca Armenia.

'Of course she'll have you,' said Papà, with an expansive wave of his arm, his face flushed with wine. 'You come from a good family, you're a hard worker and one day soon you're going to be a doctor. Then Giulia can settle down and have a family of her own and leave the proper healing to you.'

I nearly choked on my vino. Not sure I'd heard correctly, I glanced at Stefano. He looked as horrified as I felt. Just as I'd thought I'd earned Papà's respect, he'd shown his true feelings about who he thought I should be. At least Stefano had known him long enough to know what he was like. But I still felt the hot rage rush up my throat.

'What's wrong with the work I do?' I spat. 'I'll have you know that Stefano values my work and one day we want to work together.'

Papà shrugged. 'That's up to Stefano when you marry.'

Mamma squeezed my hand tightly and I saw that Stefano was looking at me, eyes wide with alarm. I took a deep breath. I remembered Zia Francesca's and Don Silvio's words. I couldn't spoil this moment for us.

'Do we have your blessing?' Stefano asked Papà quickly.

Papà nodded, smiling broadly. 'Yes, you know that I love you both and you're like a son to me, Stefano. Nothing could please me more than to welcome you formally into my family.' He put his arm around Stefano's shoulders. 'Of course I give you my blessing.' He raised his glass. 'Salute! To your future!'

'To your future,' echoed Mamma, her eyes filled with tears of joy.

I glanced at Stefano, our eyes locking. Finally, I was free.

20

Nonna and I resumed our trips to the monastery in September 1942. It was our best meeting yet, as we discussed Stefano's injury and how successful his recovery had been by combining the medical treatment he'd been given by the army and our herbal remedies. There was a real gap between the two types of treatments but like Stefano had said all along, if we could merge the best of both, the results could be incredible. I told Agata about my growing relationship with Stefano and how different it was from my relationship with Massimo. She was so excited for me and wished us nothing but happiness.

When we returned home, Don Silvio brought Caterina to the clinic for another appointment. Her headaches had become a thing of the past, but every now and then she required further treatment to keep all the hormones of puberty in balance and prevent her skin rashes from flaring up. When my examination was finished, Nonna took her to the kitchen to eat her favourite almond biscotti with some fresh milk.

'I was very happy to hear you worked things out with Stefano and that you're courting,' Don Silvio said when we were alone. He was looking tired and a little haggard but still as immaculately attired as ever in a tailored suit. 'How's he finding his new role in Caltanissetta?'

I put down my pen and closed Caterina's notes. 'He's doing well, thank you.'

'Has he been continuing his studies?'

'He's been able to take extended leave in Messina and is starting his fourth year of medicine.'

Don Silvio nodded. 'A friend of mine works at the university in Messina and tells me that Stefano is a fine student. He'll make a good doctor someday soon.'

I raised my eyebrows at him, suddenly suspicious. 'You didn't have anything to do with his assignment, did you?'

He evaded my gaze. 'I know how worried you were about your brother and father, and I wanted to give you every chance of happiness with him.'

'You did this for me?' Tears prickled the edges of my eyes. It would have taken a large amount of pull to place Stefano in the right regiment and to gain the agreement of the university to allow him flexible study periods.

'It was the least I could do. Francesca and I want to see you happy.'

I blinked back the tears and grasped his hand across the desk. 'Thank you, Don Silvio. You're a good friend. It means more than I can say.' I was grateful to have someone of his power and influence on our side but he was still 'Ndrangheta after all and I worried that this favour might come at a cost.

'My pleasure,' he said, patting my hand affectionately. 'We all help each other where we can.'

'Turn on the radio,' shouted Zia Francesca as she burst through the door one day not long after. 'The war's come to Italy!'

'What are you talking about?' I asked, hurrying to the small table against the wall where the radio sat next to Mamma's coffee cups. We were far from the Eastern Front in Russia, the campaigns in Africa and the Pacific war, where the Japanese had taken Singapore and even attacked Australia, so remote on the other side of the world.

'The Allies have started bombing Genova, Torino and Milano,' she said.

'Papà's regiment was sent to Piedmont in August,' I said, staring at her, horrified, before turning on the radio. Piedmont was only twelve miles from Torino.

Mamma, Nonna, Zia Francesca and I huddled around the radio, our eyes wide with alarm as we heard about the intensified Allied bombing campaign concentrated on the northern Italian cities where most of the manufacturing factories for the war industry were located. After that, we listened to the Vatican station every day, because it became the most reliable account of what was happening in Italy. Mamma barely slept, constantly worried that Papà was in danger of being bombed.

Many of the raids occurred without warning in daylight and Torino was hit again in October but sustained little damage compared to Genova and Milano. However, icons such as La Scala, the famous Milano opera house I'd always fantasised I'd one day visit, were already damaged by previous raids.

'I can't believe that the air-raid sirens sounded only when the enemy aircraft were over the city,' said Nonna, after another broadcast was over. 'They had only basic shelters to take cover in.'

'They don't have enough men to dig out those who are trapped and injured under collapsed buildings, let alone to retrieve those who have been killed,' said Mamma, pouring coffee into Nonna's cup with a shaking hand. We usually ate together at Mamma's house of an evening. Rosa and the boys joined us too, often staying overnight. We'd hear Rosa crying in bed and the dark smudges under her eyes were always present. 'I wonder if Andrea's regiment is involved in the rescue and clean-up process.' Mamma put the coffee pot down with a thud, closed her eyes for a moment and took a heaving breath. We hadn't heard from Papà since the bombing had begun.

'Those poor people had nowhere to go afterwards. Imagine that, no way to leave, nowhere to go and water, electricity and sewerage services disrupted,' said Paola, checking over the monthly farm accounts spread out across the table. Her cheeses were now being sold in bigger towns like Locri and Reggio, and she was negotiating successfully with buyers and merchants.

'The civil defence system isn't working as it should,' I said, glad to be finally off my feet. It had been a long day, first in the clinic and then visiting those who couldn't come in to the village.

'The people up north would have no idea how to survive without the city's infrastructure and services,' said Antonio, taking the papers Paola had looked over. 'They're not tough like us southerners.' Antonio was also very good with numbers and now looked after the farm finances, under Paola's supervision. He was finally happy here in Bruzzano and on the farm with Paola, his charisma and charm making him popular around the village with the old men and women and the girls alike. He reminded me so much of Vincenzo. But he was twenty now and although Mamma thought that he should settle down with a wife soon, he refused to court any of Mamma's choices. I understood his position. He wanted to choose for himself, just as Paola and I had wanted to. But I knew why Mamma was worried about securing his future: next year he'd be twenty-one and eligible to be drafted into the army. If the war wasn't over by then, there was no telling where he'd end up, perhaps even as far away as Russia, on the Eastern Front where Franco, Massimo's son, had been sent.

'I don't know how many of them will fare once they end up in the countryside,' said Mamma.

'What are you talking about?' asked Antonio, pulling the blackened shells of the roasted chestnuts out of the hot coals of the fireplace. I loved castagna season. It reminded me of my childhood: picking the glossy brown nuts with my siblings, trying to see who could collect the most and waiting for Papà to roast them in the fire that night then, with burning fingers, breaking the brittle shells from the soft kernel within. The burst of creamy deliciousness, warm on the tongue, was well worth waiting for.

'Don't you listen to the news?' asked Nonna.

'Il Duce has decreed that the northern cities like Milano should be evacuated to the surrounding countryside and villages,' said Mamma.

'To keep everyone safe and allow them to live a rural existence with fresh air and fresh produce,' said Nonna sardonically.

'But they have to stay with locals in their own homes, share what they have and those who still have their jobs have to commute back to the city each day to work,' I said.

'It's never going to work,' said Mamma. 'It's a recipe for disaster.'

'Imagine if they were sent here?' said Paola.

Antonio snorted with amusement or contempt; I wasn't sure. 'Most wouldn't last more than a week. But nobody's going to come here because nobody wants to bomb us. There's nothing here but mountains and sheep and we're too far from Rome and the north to be of any importance to anyone.' He passed the bowl of castagne across to me. I took a couple of nuts, dropping them quickly onto the table. They were still too hot to peel. 'Il Duce has finally lost it. This war was supposed to be over after France was defeated, now the British are bombing us when it's not even our war. It was a mistake to join Germany and he can't even protect our own people properly. Did you see him in the newspaper? He's round and fat . . . he looks beaten.'

'You do read the news,' said Nonna dryly, nodding in approval.

'Of course, Nonna,' said Antonio, grinning. She lifted a sceptical eyebrow at that. 'But I can't tell you all my secrets.'

Nobody else reacted to Antonio's controversial statement and I knew why. It was because we all agreed and we weren't alone.

The higher quotas of grain and produce we had to deliver to the government – without decent subsidies – to be stock-piled, meant we had a food shortage on our hands. Prices for the most basic supplies had skyrocketed so that even people in the cities with regular wages spent most of their money on what food they could get. People weren't going to work, instead spending their days finding food. But the lire wasn't worth what it once was, and we were worried that even a good income wouldn't be enough to survive. Nobody cared about our victory in Abyssinia or the empire Il Duce wanted to build anymore. All they thought about was survival and they blamed Mussolini for that.

With the tightening of quotas on agriculture and the shortages of food and coal, the black market flourished. Soon anyone with even a bit of common sense was trading on the black market, like Paola. 'Whatever we don't need, we'll sell,' she'd told us defiantly some months earlier. 'If the government wants to cripple us, we have to find another way to survive.'

'It's too dangerous,' Mamma had said, clutching at her arm.

'I'll have Antonio with me. And most of the other traders are women too.' She kissed Mamma's cheek. 'Don't worry. We'll be back within the day.' Black-marketeering was a lucrative business that Paola became quite proficient in and, aided by Antonio, she brought other local farms together to improve their buying and selling power and their ability to supply the village with what they needed. They took Benito and the loaded cart up into the mountains to trade on the black market at a secret location. The prices were always better than the set government prices and if there were things we didn't have, such as kerosene, fuel, or sewing needles and thread, Paola could usually find them there or learn where to obtain them from her contacts. She also helped Rosa and her parents source what they needed for their shop. Some days she travelled to Reggio to buy and sell, as did many other women from all over the district.

'May the Madonna watch over you,' my mother whispered every time, before hugging her and giving her blessing to the venture.

Some of the local government officials knew it was going on but turned a blind eye as long as they benefitted too, from either a monthly payment or gifts of items they were unable to source themselves.

Nobody in the family was surprised at Paola's quiet calm and steely determination to get things done. Papà had told her how proud he was of her efforts to bring in more money and keep the farm afloat, but it was Vincenzo's letter that she kept in her drawer next to her bed. Our eldest brother had always had faith in her abilities: *You're the family negotiator to be sure, as good as the best men in the business. You have a cool head, you're shrewd and you won't back down. Papà is so lucky to have you running the farm. Without you, we'd struggle. I hope they all appreciate how special you are.*

Tears had filled Paola's eyes when she'd read these words to me. I'd only squeezed her hand. She knew it was true. The five of us would never lie to each other, not about anything important. But Vincenzo's next words had me a little worried.

After arriving in Libya and carrying supplies to combat units near Tobruk, we joined the highly decorated military strategist General Rommel and his German Panzer units to chase the British 8th Army back to Egypt and out of North Africa. But the Americans have entered the battle here, providing fresh men and new supplies, and a boost of energy to the British forces. We stopped outside the railway depot at El Alamein on the Egyptian coast where both sides reached a stalemate. But we'll continue our push at El Alamein as soon as we have reinforcements. With General Rommel in command, we'll surely win the war in North Africa.

It's hot and dusty but us Calabrese cope better than the northerners. All the same, I wish I was home, to swim in the sea and hike in the cool of the mountains. It can't be much longer before it's all over and I'm back and you can teach us a thing or two about the black market. Kiss Pepe and Enzo for me and tell Rosa that I love her and I'll see her soon.

Although Vincenzo painted an optimistic picture for the sake of us at home, I could read between the lines that all was not going to plan.

According to Radio Londra and the Vatican radio, further Allied troops had landed along the North African coast and another battle had indeed begun at El Alamein. I stayed glued to the radio each night with Mamma, Rosa and Paola, even though the penalty for listening to foreign radio had increased to an impossibly steep fine and three years prison. Each of us was anxious for Vincenzo, but it was hard to know where his regiment was fighting or even how the Italian and German troops were progressing against the British. All we could do now was wait for his letters.

But more than anything I wanted Stefano by my side. I thought back to his latest letter.

My unit has started a clinic in Caltanissetta and the locals, much like our farming community at home, were beginning to trust us and come about their various ailments, but a few days ago we had an emergency and now it's all hands on deck. There's a phenomenon in this area where small clay craters and mud volcanos erupt with hot subterranean water when the pressure rises beneath the ground. The eruptions create fissures in the ground, destroying homes and buildings, trapping the occupants and causing terrible burns and injuries. We've set up a field hospital and, while we work helping the injured, the medics train me in various techniques and treatments. The rest of the time I'm helping manage patients until they're sent to one of the major hospitals for further treatment or sent back home.

I envied the work he was doing and imagined how much I could do in the chaos of a bombed city. Treating the wounded while there was still a threat of danger, without proper services, equipment and hospitals – I could do that. Then I looked at Nonna, Mamma and Paola. They all looked exhausted and I knew I couldn't leave them when they needed me most. The greatest responsibility of all rested on the shoulders of women. We were the ones who kept the family together, kept our farms and businesses running, put food on the table and made sure we all survived. But we couldn't do it without each other.

21

Stefano arrived home from Messina just as Mamma decreed it was time to kill the pig and make salami. I knew that it was partly to dispel the worry she carried for Vincenzo. We spent the next two days making salami and sausages.

'How does this compare to slicing into people?' Antonio asked Stefano cheekily, as we broke down the pig with large and very sharp cleavers.

'Not much difference,' said Stefano, smiling. 'Except most people are still alive when the doctors cut into them, so they have to be a little more careful than we are.'

'You've seen operations?' asked Nonna, using a fine filleting knife to remove the meat from the bones.

Stefano nodded, swinging the cleaver between the pig's ribs and vertebra, making a loud thump on the wooden chopping board. 'It's not much different from this to be honest. The surgeons are sometimes called glorified carpenters with their saws, chisels and hammers.'

Rosa shivered and went pale. She was thinner than ever and we were worried about her. Her fingernails were ragged, bitten to the quick, and Paola commented more than once that if a strong wind blew through the streets, it would pick her up or break her in two.

'Rosa, can you put the trotters into the cauldron?' asked Nonna, seeing her discomfort. Not everyone could handle such gruesome talk.

Rosa nodded and hurried away to where the large pot was already boiling and would soon contain all the off-cuts. We'd cook them for a few hours in salted water before eating them as they were or adding them to the ragú. Our salt ration was only small and never enough, but Paola was always able to bring home whatever we needed for the salami.

'Have you done any yourself?' asked Antonio.

Stefano nodded. 'But mainly we practise our surgical techniques and suturing on butchered pigs.'

The look of surprise on Antonio's face made me laugh. 'How else can they learn?' I asked him.

'I know,' he muttered. 'It's just strange, that's all.'

'Isn't it a bit early to be doing surgery on real patients?' asked Nonna, passing another fillet of meat to me. Teresa and I were chopping the meat finely and placing it in a large bowl, ready to mince in the meat grinder and season with salt, chilli and paprika before marinating in alcohol. Mamma was washing the intestine cases we'd use to stuff the minced meat mixture into long coils that would be tied tightly with twine. Only then could the salamis be hung up to dry and age and the sausages taken to the kitchen for cooking. It was a time-consuming process but well worth it. The salamis would last quite a few months and their rich, intense flavour packed a punch.

'Since this is wartime and I'm attached to a medical unit, we're being taught some basic frontline techniques to help the doctors and surgeons as much as possible. But—' Stefano caught my eye and I smiled, '—I've been involved in a small outreach clinic in Messina and as a result of that, I've done some procedures under supervision, like appendectomies, tonsillectomies and cholecystectomies, on people who wouldn't otherwise be able to have treatment.' He then explained what each of the procedures were.

'There should be more like you,' said Nonna. 'Have you seen many injuries with your unit?'

'Not really. Some sprained ankles, broken fingers and a few accidents with rifles: a couple of gunshot wounds from discharging weapons. Even though they healed quite well, I've thought about the treatment you and Giulia used on my leg. I'm sure it's more effective and provides a quicker, more complete healing of the tissue, although it's perhaps more time consuming.' He squeezed my shoulder. 'I've spoken to my superior officer about using your techniques with our men and in the new clinic for the locals in Caltanissetta. There's not much work for us and we may as well help the community as much as we can.'

'I knew you'd be a good doctor,' said Nonna, stretching out her back from standing so long.

Stefano and I met a few days later outside Bruzzano Vecchio. We walked through the enormous Baroque-styled triumphant arch on the eastern side of the village to the derelict stone buildings beyond. I tied Nero to a post and left him to graze in a field while we climbed the steps up to the old Carafa castle.

'I love that we keep coming back here,' I murmured as we reached the top. The view was lush once more after the autumn rains.

'It's our place,' said Stefano, pulling me to him. 'Whenever I'm here with you I feel the endless possibilities that the world has to offer.'

'I'm so proud of what you're doing.' I sighed.

'What's wrong?'

I'd been unsettled by the news of the battle at El Alamein and couldn't shake off the bad feeling I had. 'I'm worried about them over in North Africa. The battle's been going on forever and after what Vincenzo said about waiting for reinforcements, I wonder how they're managing.'

Stefano lightly traced the line of my vertebrae with his finger and I stretched like a cat, indulging in the pleasure of his touch. 'The battle's not over until it's won. Our men have heart and battles have been won with courage and fortitude against the odds. There's a chance that Rommel will turn things around.'

I turned in his arms and looked into his beloved face. 'I'm afraid for him,' I whispered. There had been reports on the radio that our forces had incurred heavy losses.

'It's alright to be afraid. We can't know anything until they send word, and it will be weeks yet until Rosa receives a letter.' He stared at the road below, where an old woman was walking, balancing a terracotta pot on her head. Once, all women carried water from the river on their heads like

268

this. 'I should have gone to North Africa with Vincenzo. If anything happens to him while I'm safe and happy here—'

I shook my head vigorously. 'No, don't do that. It wasn't your fault that you were injured. Vincenzo's so happy that we're finally together and soon you'll be back to normal with your leg.' I couldn't tell him that I was secretly pleased that Don Silvio had arranged for him to be transferred to his medical unit.

Stefano sighed, flexing his hip and knee. 'I don't know, Giulia. It's still giving way when I least expect it. Sometimes I really struggle during surgery. I expected to be better by now. What if my leg stops me doing what I want to do? What if I can't stand for long hours, if I can't run or walk long distances? What good am I then? Do you really want to be with an old cripple?'

'You're not an old cripple and you're getting better all the time,' I said, laughing, and rubbed the uneven surface of his thigh. Although I was sure that it would still improve, it was never going to be as it had been before the injury. 'It was a terrible injury and it's going to take time.'

'But what kind of man am I if I can't do normal things?'

'You're my man,' I whispered, kissing him on the cheek.

He shook his head. 'You can do better than me.'

'What are you talking about?'

'I mean it, Giulia. You don't need a cripple, or a soldier.'

I frowned and looked into his face. His serious expression worried me. I grasped him by the shoulder.

'What happens to you if I don't come back or – worse still – if I come back further maimed? I couldn't do that to you.'

'Don't be ridiculous,' I said. 'You're in Sicily, far from the action. Besides, we both know the risks and I'm proud of your war service and how you want to help injured soldiers.'

'Yes, we both know the risks and I won't burden you with that risk. You're better off without me.'

I stepped away and stared at him in horror. I could hardly breathe for the pain his words caused me. He was going to walk away. I'd thought he believed in equality, but here he was trying to tell me what he thought was best for me, just like my father.

The rage surged through me like a cascade of lava. 'I'm not a child who doesn't see the consequences of her actions!' I yelled. 'And I don't need you or my father to make my decisions for me. I've made my choice with my eyes wide open. I want to be by your side, whatever comes. But if you can't see that and you can't honour the choice I've made as your equal, then I'd rather be on my own. I won't be controlled by yet another man!'

He gazed at me with flat eyes. 'Then you'd better not waste another day with me,' he said.

My heart dropped like a stone. He hadn't even considered my opinion or what I wanted at all. The air around me had thickened and all I could hear was my ragged breath. I watched as my hand slapped his face, hard. 'I don't want to see you until you're ready to be my equal in life.'

He said nothing, just looked at me with regret.

I turned and ran down the steps of the old castle back to where Nero was waiting.

Stefano left to go back to Messina without saying goodbye. That was almost more hurtful than the words he'd said to me. Stefano's actions told me that he'd meant what he'd said and I didn't know how to feel. I couldn't believe that he'd really walk away from me because of his injury and his insecurity. I knew that his physical prowess was important to him as part of what made him a good soldier. Most Calabrese thought that being strong and able to provide for the family made a man, but Stefano wasn't most Calabrese. Or so I'd thought.

I'd proven myself to be strong, resilient and resourceful – most women were. But maybe I'd hoped for too much and all men were essentially the same, unable to restrain their desire to control the destinies of those they believed to be weaker: women.

I'd survived loss and allowed myself to find love again. Why couldn't Stefano see that we were stronger together? Why couldn't he see that I wanted him not for what he could provide but because I wanted to share my life with him, because I loved him?

I was bewildered and hurt but most of all I was furious. His decision may have come from a place of love, but I would not be told how to live my life by anyone.

But by the end of the first week of November my brooding over our future faded into the background. Italy's forces in North Africa had retreated back towards Libya, unable to win against the Allies. There were accounts on Radio Londra of the courageous and heroic fight put up by the Italians, which made my heart swell with pride, but they went on to report of large losses to both sides.

I sat, transfixed by horror, as the aftermath of one battle was described by a war correspondent: 'But the strong resistance by the Italians was quickly spent by the overwhelming advances of the Allied forces. The parched ground of the desert, usually empty as far as the eye could see, was now strewn with the carcasses of broken down and burnt-out Italian tanks and the sight of so many men lying dead on the battlefield was enough to make a grown man cry . . .'

'Madonna!' My heart felt like it had shrivelled into a tiny ball of ice and I could hardly breathe. Vincenzo's division was motorised, with a large number of tanks. But there was no way of knowing where he was or if he was alright. I couldn't help the wave of relief knowing that Stefano was safe in Sicily nor the guilt that followed hot on its heels. It could have been him in that battle too.

It was washing day not long after I'd heard that report, and after boiling the copper and helping Mamma wash, we stood behind the house hanging out the sheets. It was a good day for drying, a mild day for November, with a gentle breeze beginning to pick up. Rosa's boys played in the garden, Pepe, now three and a half, raced between the sheets, trying to hide from Enzo, who toddled after him. He had just turned two and now that he was faster on his feet and understood more, Pepe was starting to enjoy playing with him.

'Rosa, Gabriella!' called Nonna from the back door. We turned to see her walk quickly down the path towards us, past the vegetable and herb garden, her brows drawn into a frown.

'What is it, Mamma?' said my mother, dropping a sheet back into the basket.

Nonna lifted her hand and for the first time I noticed the paper she was holding. 'Signora Lipari's grandson, Roberto, just delivered a telegram,' she said grimly. 'It's for you, Rosa. Your mother told him you were here.'

Rosa turned as white as the sheet we'd been holding and she swayed on her feet. She clutched my arm. 'No!'

'Sit down, bella,' I said, guiding Rosa to the outdoor table, even though my own legs had turned to jelly. 'Do you want one of us to open it?'

Rosa looked at Nonna and the paper in her hand in terror and nodded. 'I can't do it!' she cried.

'Mamma, Mamma!' called Pepe. 'What's wrong, Mamma? Why are you crying?' He ran to Rosa from across the garden and grasped her skirts, his small face creased in fear. Enzo stumbled after his brother and began to wail. I scooped him up, hugging him tight.

'I'll do it,' Mamma said woodenly, taking the envelope from Nonna with a trembling hand.

'We don't know it's the worst,' said Nonna gently.

I stood there, rooted to the spot with fear, Enzo howling in my arms. So many messages could be contained in that note. We'd even heard that there had been accidental reporting of deceased soldiers from time to time, sometimes they were missing in action instead, but most telegrams seemed to be touched by the angel of death, bringing only heartbreak to the families.

Mamma carefully opened the envelope, slipping out the note within. She stared at the page for a moment, and the blood drained from her face, leaving it grey and haggard.

'"I regret to inform you",' she read, before taking a shuddering breath. Mamma swayed on her feet, her eyes wild, and she reached out to grab the sheet on the line as she fell to the ground, pulling the sheet down with her.

'Mamma!' I screamed. I put Enzo into Rosa's unresisting arms, rushed to Mamma's side and knelt beside her. She was clammy but breathing.

'She's alright,' I said to Nonna. 'She just fainted.' I desperately untangled her from the fabric, unnerved that she resembled a corpse wrapped in a burial sheet. 'Mamma,' I said urgently, shaking her by the shoulder as Nonna helped remove the sheet now smeared with dirt. Pepe and Enzo were screaming in the background.

Mamma opened her eyes and as she became aware of where she was, she let out a howl of grief. 'My boy, my beautiful boy!'

Nonna and I exchanged a look of horror then Nonna cradled Mamma in her arms. My mother's body was racked with sobs, the telegram loose in her hand. Rosa sat still as a statue.

I pulled the telegram free and braced myself for the words I knew I'd find.

The message was short and succinct. The words blurred and I started to shake as I read them out loud. '"I regret to inform you that your husband Sergeant Vincenzo Tallariti has been killed in action during the Battle of El Alamein in Egypt."'

I looked at Nonna helplessly. A spasm of pain crossed her face but she grasped my hand and held it tight, her eyes closing briefly to take in this terrible blow to our family.

Rosa let out a keening wail, frightening Pepe and Enzo, who screamed again in terror. I stumbled to her, picked up Pepe and hugged Rosa close as she sobbed, her babies in our arms.

'I'm so sorry, Rosa.'

As much as I couldn't believe that my strong, vibrant, loving brother was dead and I wanted to scream and shout to God that it wasn't fair, Nonna and I had to be the strong ones now.

22

My beloved brother was gone: that bright and promising life extinguished in an instant by enemy fire. To make matters worse, there was no body to say goodbye to, no body to bury. Vincenzo lay with his fallen comrades in the dusty sands of Egypt, far from his family and far from home. Paola and I cried in each other's arms after Teresa went home to her family. We comforted Pepe and Enzo, playing with them while Nonna watched over Mamma and Rosa, who had both settled a little after Nonna's herbal tonic.

Rosa and the boys and Teresa and her children came every day to visit. We were stronger together, united in our grief. Only Papà was missing. He'd been notified of our loss but was across the country in the border towns of France where his regiment had been dispatched to aid the occupation forces. It was a long journey back to Calabria to mourn a son he couldn't bury and nobody knew when he'd come home.

I couldn't imagine how he'd be hurting, broken by the loss of his oldest son and so far away from us all.

Despite our grief, life had to go on. The animals needed feeding, the ewes and cow needed milking and the farm needed tending. Nonna and I had the clinic and our patients to see. It was difficult to get out of bed in the morning . . . I was reminded so much of my grief over Massimo; it was the support of my family that got me through that time and now I knew I had to support them. Teresa, Paola, Nonna and I took turns with Mamma and Rosa, making sure neither of them was alone.

We weren't the only ones in mourning. So many of our local boys had been sent to fight in the African theatre of war and too many families in the area had received telegrams just like we had. We heard that Angelo had perished. At least he and Vincenzo had been together until the end. My thoughts flew to Stefano. Angelo was his cousin and I couldn't imagine his grief at losing his two best friends. I knew that he'd be torn between relief that he'd been spared and guilt for not having been with them in Africa. All I wanted was to hold him and grieve for our loss together.

Stefano wrote to me a couple of weeks later.

I know this is a difficult time for you and your family. I can't believe that Vincenzo and Angelo are gone. I should have been there with them and I'm heartbroken by their loss, as I know you are. We were always inseparable and I remember the days that we played football and terrorised the village. We thought we'd be together always, that we were invincible.

I'm not getting much sleep but it's those moments before I do that I dread the most, when I think of Vincenzo and Angelo,

*and when I wish you were by my side. Their loss has jolted me
to the core and has reminded me to hold on tight to the important things of life. I regret the harsh words I had with you and
the way I left you. You are what's most important to me.*

*I've had time to think about what you said and when
I come home, I want to talk to you about our future.*

*I've managed to get leave over Christmas, so I'll be back to
you soon. I want nothing more than to take you in my arms
and bring you some kind of comfort.*

I was overjoyed and relieved by Stefano's letter but we had
a lot to work out if we were going to be equal partners.

'What's wrong?' asked Paola as I helped her make soap
that afternoon. 'Keep stirring until it's smooth.'

I glanced down at the pot of pig's fat. 'I'm sorry,' I said,
frowning. 'I'm a bit distracted.'

'You don't say,' said Paola, carefully mixing the soda ash
into the water, watching it froth and the bubbles subside
before she added more. 'Are you going to tell me what's got
you so scattered?'

I nodded, stirring the rendered pig fat. It had to cool
before we could add the lye mixture. 'I've received a letter
from Stefano. He wants to talk about our future.'

'Isn't that a good thing?'

'I honestly don't know. Vincenzo and Angelo's deaths—'
I hiccoughed and Paola squeezed my hand, tears in her eyes,
'—they've really affected him. He's realised that none of that
matters anymore. But what if we can't resolve our differences?
Massimo and I had a relationship based on love and respect
and he was proud of my work, but maybe the companionship

he wanted from a second marriage is different from what Stefano expects? What if the freedom and independence I expect isn't what Stefano really wants at all? What if he actually wants me to be like Rosa or Teresa, happy to bear his children and support his dreams while forgetting my own?'

Paola sighed. 'Stefano's not like that. I've seen the two of you together and you have respect for each other as well as a deep love.'

I nodded. 'I do love him.'

'Don't waste time then. None of us knows what's ahead. I know Vincenzo would be cheering from up above if he thought that it was his death that brought the two of you together to begin a new life. When Stefano next comes home, just tell him. It's time to stop mucking around and get married. So many people dream of having what the two of you have. Life is too short – you know that's what Vincenzo would say.'

Listening to her, something fell into place. I wanted to marry Stefano. I was sure we would work out our differences and begin to build our life together.

The bombing of the airbase in Reggio by Allied planes in early December was all anyone could talk about. Reggio was only about forty miles away and for the first time, the war seemed very close to our village. Although Palermo on the northwest coast of Sicily had endured many air raids over the last couple of years and Napoli had been bombed too, it was the first time anywhere this far south in mainland Italy had been targeted. The question everyone wanted answered was: How long until Calabrese were thrust well and truly into the war?

We still hadn't heard from Papà and as it drew nearer to Christmas, Mamma insisted on continuing the traditional Christmas baking. We'd lost Vincenzo but it didn't change the fact that there were others who needed Mamma's help and love. She was determined to make Christmas special for the grandchildren, making almond biscuits, spiced susomelle biscuits and torrone, orange-scented nougat studded with nuts, with Rosa and Teresa, who was pregnant again, and due in April. We still had our own eggs, almonds, dried fruit and honey and, thanks to Paola, spare milled flour from the extra wheat kept from the government requisition. With her black-market dealings, we could even get a small quantity of sugar and spices. Stefano would arrive any day and although I couldn't wait to see him, I was worried about the conversation we needed to have.

It was a terrible afternoon. It looked like heavy rain was coming and the temperature was dropping quickly. I helped Paola by moving the sheep into the shed and the storm moved in swiftly just as I finished. As the rain pelted down, I sheltered with them, pressed against their woolly coats, their pitiful bleating growing louder as the wind howled outside. Then, against a flash of lightning, I noticed a figure in an old poncho in the doorway, giving me a fright.

'Come in out of the rain!' I called before realising who it was. 'Stefano!' A smile lit up my face in spite of my anxiety. He looked wonderful, even though he was soaking wet, his dark hair plastered to his face.

He pulled off the sodden poncho and hung it on a hook on the wall. 'Paola said I'd find you here.'

'Mamma mia! Why didn't you wait until the storm had passed and I'd come home?' I asked, pushing through the sheep to get to the door.

'She said it was best I see you first.' He frowned. 'Is everything alright, Giulia?'

I took a deep breath. Trust Paola to make me sort this issue out straight away.

I grabbed an old towel and handed it to him. 'You'd better dry off before you catch a cold,' I said. The tension between us was palpable. I knew this conversation had to be done but now that he was here, my heart was hammering. 'Come over here where it's warmer.'

I took his ice-cold hand and led him through the crush of trembling animals to the small platform stacked with bales of hay out of reach of the sheep at one side of the shed.

'Here, let me dry your hair.'

'No, stop, Giulia. Tell me what's wrong. Are you happy to see me?'

'Of course, I am. It's just that . . . when we last saw each other . . .'

'You're shaking.' He took my hands in his. 'I know that I had no right to speak to you the way I did, to try and decide what was right for you. But I only did it because I love you.'

'I know,' I said. 'You say you love me, but what do you want from me? Do you want a marriage where you decide what's best? Where I support your dreams and have your babies?'

He paled. 'No, how can you say that?' He dropped his head. 'I was afraid, Giulia, afraid that I wouldn't be enough for you, that I'd bring you hardship and pain. That's why I

281

pushed you away. But after losing Vincenzo and Angelo, I realised that I was being a coward and a fool.'

I cupped his cheek. 'You've never been a coward but I agree you were a fool.'

'I'm sorry, Giulia. I made a terrible mistake and I've hurt you.' Tears trickled down his face. 'Can you forgive me?'

'That depends, Stefano. Do you promise that we'll always make decisions together?' I never wanted my choices taken away from me again.

'That's what I want too, to share our lives completely.'

'What about children and my work?'

'That's what I admire about you. You're a wonderful healer and I'll support you in whatever you want to do. Your life and your work will never come second to mine. And children . . . well, I'd love them one day, but we'll decide to have them when we're both ready.'

I kissed the wetness from his face. 'Are you sure?'

'I've never been more sure of anything in my life.'

My shoulders slumped with relief as he traced the curve of my cheek lightly with his finger. He bent to kiss me and the feel of his lips on mine and his body pressed against me after weeks of anxiety were intoxicating.

'It's a rare opportunity, to be alone with you like this,' he whispered, sliding his hands under my coat and over my coarse linen dress. 'And it will be a while until the storm passes.'

'Then let's take our time,' I replied, holding his hands still. I stared at him a moment. His eyes never left my face, waiting to see what I was going to do next. The air between us was infused with an invisible spark that grew in intensity. I pushed the coat from his shoulders and helped it loose from his arms as it fell to the ground. His shirt clung to him, outlining his broad chest, and the breath caught in my throat. He was beautiful and I wanted him then and there but instead, I peeled the wet shirt from his body and set it on the hay to dry.

Stefano reached for me but I shook my head. 'No, not yet.'

I placed my hands on the warm skin of his chest, revelling in the feel of him, the springy dark hairs under my palm. My fingers trailed slowly down and I unbuttoned his trousers.

'Stop, Giulia,' he gasped. 'I haven't seen you for so long . . .'

But I found his arousal exciting and cupped him to see what would happen. Stefano groaned.

I reached for his lips, the long kiss deepening as it drew me into him, his musky scent, the soft feel of his lips, the warmth of his mouth. Every sense was heightened, my body attuned to his. I pulled him to me as I lay back on the sweet smelling hay.

'My turn,' he whispered into my ear, unbuttoning my dress and grazing my nipples with his hands. The exquisite tenderness nearly drove me wild. He bent his head over me, taking my nipple in his mouth as his hands caressed the sensitive skin of my inner thigh, making me shiver. I knew what was coming and couldn't wait for his touch, wrapping my fingers in his hair and arching up to meet him. His insistent kisses moved lower until I gasped with the shock of a new and intense sensation.

I surrendered. Our love making was furious, exhilarating and tender. It was the physical answer to the emotional commitment we'd just made. In that moment I knew that we were meant to be together.

'Vincenzo would never have forgiven me if I'd let you go,' he said, kissing my shoulder afterwards.

'I can't believe they're gone.' I clung to him, overcome with emotion.

'All I keep thinking is that it could have been me. But it wasn't and I'll always carry the burden of my guilt and my joy that I'm here with you, Topolina.' His strong arms cocooned me against the outside world of hurt and pain. His skin was warm, his heartbeat steady and the rhythmic rise and fall of his chest lulled me into a feeling of security. We understood that our time together was even more precious when only a twist of fate had preserved his life – this time.

I kissed him then gazed into his eyes. 'Let's get married. Vincenzo wouldn't have wanted us to wait.'

Stefano nodded, threading his fingers through my long hair. 'He'd want us to live and I've been only living a half-life without you. I promise to be everything you need. Let's do it soon, cara mia. Let's begin this next chapter of our lives, no matter what comes.'

I sighed with deep happiness despite the pain of our loss. 'As long as we're together, nothing else matters.'

A few days before Christmas, everyone was home except for Papà. Although Stefano and I wanted to share our joy, we'd decided to wait before we told the rest of the family our plans. It was still too soon after Vincenzo's death.

'Nicolo wants to stay up this year and come to midnight Mass,' said Teresa over lunch as she smoothed her eldest son's blond hair from his face. He was five years old and looked so much like Vincenzo that it hurt.

'He's a big boy now,' said Paola, smiling as she dunked bread into her minestrone and fed it to Enzo, who sat on her knee. Following Mass, we always met our friends and neighbours around the bonfire in the nearby piazza, rugged up in our coats against the winter wind blowing in from the sea, drinking wine and eating Christmas sweets.

'He can join us for pasta aglio e olio afterwards,' said Antonio.

'Can I really?' asked Nicolo, his face alight with excitement.

There was a noise at the door and Mamma's face paled. Since we'd received the telegram, every knock made her worry she'd receive bad news about Papà.

'I'll see who it is,' said Antonio, pushing his chair back.

But the door opened and Papà was standing in the doorway, drawn and haggard but relieved. 'I'm home,' he said, his voice breaking.

Then everyone was up from the table, embracing him, surrounding him with love and joy.

23

'**W**e're mourning your brother and you want to get married now?' Papà asked. He had been home for a week. His regiment had returned to Napoli and he'd requested leave over Christmas, to be with Mamma this first year without Vincenzo. My parents had become closer in their grief, sitting together every evening and talking into the night. Stefano and I had waited until after Christmas to announce our plans, but we wanted to end 1942 with some good news.

'Yes, Papà,' I said, clasping Stefano's hand. He was thin and still looked exhausted. 'I know it's so soon after Vincenzo . . . but if you and Mamma agree, and Rosa too, we don't want to wait. Life's too short and Vincenzo would be happy for us.'

He nodded. 'Life is short and this is wartime. I won't deny joy and happiness when there is grief and sadness all around us.'

Tears filled my eyes. Vincenzo's death had been a blow to Papà but it seemed to have softened him. I wondered if he was beginning to surrender, if only a little, the iron grip he'd tried to maintain over his family. Massimo's death and now Vincenzo's had shown him that he couldn't control everything and that life had to be enjoyed whenever the opportunity presented itself.

'Yes, get married,' he said, opening his arms in a gesture of welcome and generosity. 'We wish you both a long life of happiness and joy.'

'Congratulations,' said Mamma, hugging me tight.

We set the date for March 1943, when Stefano and Papà could next come home. I couldn't wait to reply to Agata's letter of condolences for Vincenzo with the good news of my wedding. But it wasn't until I was sitting at my desk after a morning at the clinic, that I had the chance to put into words what I'd been wanting to tell her.

Rosa didn't want us to wait. She's so happy for us, insisting that we don't waste any time. I love Stefano with all my heart and I know that Massimo would approve and be happy for me but I wanted to ask for his blessing all the same. It's been four years since his death. I went to his grave yesterday. I took him daffodils, as I do every year. He used to give me them around our anniversary, always searching for the first blooms because he knew how much they made me smile. They're a symbol of new life, you know. I sat and talked to him until the sun dropped behind the mountain and when I left, I felt lighter and I knew that he's alright with me moving on.

Tears fell onto the paper before I realised and I quickly blotted them. I wiped my face with a shaking hand and took a deep breath. It was time to write about my joy.

Mamma's organising a wedding meal with close friends and family. I know keeping busy is her way of dealing with the loss of Vincenzo. I've asked Luigi, Massimo's son, to the wedding, but Franco's still somewhere on the Eastern Front, covering the German retreat from Stalingrad. Aldo and Mimmo will be there too. Teresa wants to measure me for a new dress but I refuse to wear white again. I think something smart and practical this time.

I'm glad you've finally made your decision. I know how difficult it will be to leave the monastery but I think you're right. You can do so much more to help back at the sanatorium in Napoli, especially with the war going on.

I've been unsure what to do once I'm married. You know how I've wanted to do more for so long but never could find the right time to leave? Well, Nonna surprised me the other day by telling me that perhaps it's time for me to spread my wings, to challenge myself and learn new things, and if I decide to move to Messina once I'm married, she'll be fine and the clinic will always be here for me.

I'd love for you to be here for the wedding if you're not already travelling . . .

I felt so lucky to be supported by the women in my life. I would never have achieved all I had without them.

*

Too suddenly, the day I'd dreamt about had arrived. Mamma, Paola, Teresa and I were together in my bedroom, just as we had been six years earlier, and now Rosa was here too. I smiled, thinking of that time. I was only seventeen and I'd been so angry. So much had happened since then. I was twenty-three now, a widow and overjoyed to be marrying again. My mother and sisters were truly happy for me and I could hardly wait to be joined with the man I loved. Papà had made it home the night before, exhausted but happy, and he waited in the dining room with Antonio and small glasses of liquorice liqueur to celebrate before we left for the church.

'It fits perfectly,' said Paola, admiring the final product. I could see by Teresa's expression and the occasional nod as she smoothed the dark blue fabric, pulling it across my body, that she was pleased with the result. She'd made sure I'd look my best, no matter what I'd chosen and was determined that Stefano would too, finding him a double-breasted suit, which she altered for him.

'You look sophisticated,' said Rosa, smiling. I took her hand and squeezed it. I could only imagine how difficult this day would be for her, thinking, like me, of her own wedding.

I looked in the mirror and couldn't believe the difference from the girl who had stood here six years earlier. She was a frightened, angry, naïve girl in a fashionable gown but now I saw an older, wiser woman who had experienced life a little more, wearing an elegant but practical dress. Somehow, I felt more beautiful than I ever had.

'I love it, Teresa,' I whispered. 'It's exactly what I wanted.'

'Now you can put these on,' Teresa said, handing me my shoes. She was just as superstitious as Paola but her face flushed with pleasure at my delight as she rubbed her distended belly absently. She was eight months pregnant and the baby was kicking her endlessly. She'd been pregnant last time I'd got married too.

'This is the day you'll remember,' said Mamma softly, tucking the last strand of hair into the pins at the back of my head. 'This is the beginning of the rest of your life, a life you'll share with the man you love. You may think you couldn't love him any more than you do today, but the best is yet to come. Time will make your love richer and deeper than you can ever imagine.' She kissed my cheek then shared a look with Teresa, who smiled as she took Mamma's hand. 'But remember we are always here for you and that we will understand the ups and downs that inevitably follow. You're never alone, even when Stefano leaves for the army.'

We'd decided that I'd move to Messina in the summer when Stefano was on university break. I was excited to be beginning my new life, working and living in a big city. But I was nervous too, to be leaving the district, going far from my family, and I was worried about leaving Nonna to run the clinic on her own.

'I know.' With tears in my eyes, I grasped my mother's and Paola's hands. 'I could never have got through everything and arrived at this moment with Stefano without all of you. I love you and I'm so glad that you're here with me now to share my joy.'

'Come on, now,' said Mamma, wiping her tears away. 'Papà will be beside himself if we don't join him soon.'

The day was perfect in every way. Tears trickled down my cheeks as Stefano and I repeated our vows and we were proclaimed husband and wife before we shared our first kiss as a married couple. Memories of my wedding day with Massimo seemed to surround me, overlaid with the new memories we made that day, much like a new shawl over a well-worn dress. But it felt comforting too, as though Massimo was standing at my shoulder, giving me his support and blessing, wishing me happiness. Although I wasn't superstitious, I took Massimo's benevolent presence as a good sign and a positive start to my second marriage.

It was wonderful to have all our loved ones around us and our combined family sharing a meal. Only Vincenzo and Stefano's mother were missing, a large hole left in our lives and hearts that could not be filled. I saw my brother everywhere, in the smiles of my sisters, a gesture my mother made, a turn of phrase my father used and the mischievous expressions on Antonio's face. I knew that Vincenzo was watching from above with pride, just like Massimo.

After dinner, the music began to play, the piano accordion adjusting its lilting strains to the slow, sinuous movements as I led Stefano into the tarantella, the traditional Calabrese dance where the partners never touched. The tambourine joined in, accenting the tempo, and then the castanets heightened the tension between us as we gazed into each other's eyes across the space between us. It was the most erotic dance. Stefano was like a god, dark, curly hair and penetrating brown eyes in a perfectly symmetrical heart-shaped face. His jaw was set in determination, perhaps to not succumb to the desire to sweep me off my feet and disappear into the night with me. But his jaw was balanced by soft and sensual lips, lips I couldn't take my eyes off. He was straight and tall but light on his feet as we danced around each other, shoulders and arms almost skimming as we passed.

The tempo rose as my pace quickened and Stefano danced around me as I spun, the faces surrounding us a blur, the room a flashing kaleidoscope of colour and sound, until he was behind me, so close I could feel the warmth from his body before I spun away again. We ebbed and flowed in the ancient dance of courtship until my sisters and the other women joined me on the floor and I was swept away in the centre of their circular dance while the men watched. My eyes drifted to Stefano on the edge of the floor, clapping to the music, daring me to become more frantic and wild. I couldn't wait until nightfall.

That night Nonna went to stay with Mamma, giving Stefano and me the greatest gift of all: privacy and solitude.

'Come and I'll help you get out of your dress,' said Stefano. We were at the kitchen table, nibbling on a little bread, cheese and salami that Nonna had left out for us with a glass of red wine. Neither of us was really hungry but we couldn't disappoint her and so we talked about the day until the tension between us could no longer be ignored.

'I can manage,' I said, grinning, as I finished off my wine.

'I'm sure you can. You're quite an independent woman after all, but I guarantee it will be much more fun if I get involved.'

I felt myself melt at his words. 'If you insist,' I murmured.

'Oh, but I do.'

Stefano took my hand and led me to the spare bedroom. 'Turn around,' he said.

I did as he asked, refusing to think about the night Massimo had helped me out of my wedding dress. Stefano undid the buttons on the back of my bodice slowly, kissing my neck until he slid his hands across my bare shoulders, pushing the dress over my arms and allowing it to fall to the floor.

I turned to face him, taking in the intensity with which he gazed at me. 'Your turn,' I murmured, reaching for his braces, which I slid off his shoulders. I began to unbutton his shirt and he dipped his head to kiss me, taking me back to the passion we'd shared at the Rocca Armenia and in the shed. The memories only ignited me further and I pulled his shirt off and began to frantically unbutton his trousers.

'Not so fast,' groaned Stefano, grasping my hands. 'I want you to remember this night as special. I want to pay homage to every part of your body until you beg me for mercy.'

'But it is special! We can go slow next time.'

'No, amore mio, I want you to remember my touch while we're apart and know that you are mine as much as I am yours. I'm going to make the most of every moment I have with you until I have to leave.'

'I'd never forget anything about you,' I whispered. I wrapped my arms around him, breathing him in, and surrendered to his touch.

Our lovemaking was slow and tender, then fast and furious, but above all passionate. It was more than physical: it was a meeting of two hearts and a merging of two souls. There was no doubt in my mind that we belonged together. There was no similarity to the affectionate ritual that I had experienced with Massimo.

Morning came too soon. I couldn't bear not to be touching Stefano: holding his hand as we had coffee and biscuits for breakfast; straightening his collar as he dressed; hugging him tight before we left our sanctuary. As much as we loved time with the family, we couldn't wait until we were alone in our bed and could explore each other's bodies, learning more about what gave us pleasure and what brought us closer together.

The few days after our wedding were bliss, but reality arrived with a visit from Don Silvio.

'I was passing through and I wanted to congratulate you on your marriage.'

'Come in.' I led him through to Nonna's kitchen. Stefano and Nonna were out.

'This is for you and Stefano,' he said, handing me a beautifully wrapped box. 'I'm sorry I couldn't make it to the wedding. It was a business trip I couldn't put off.' He shrugged helplessly. 'Stefano's a very lucky man and I'm sure you'll be happy together.'

'Grazie. You were missed but it's so good to see you now.' Stefano hadn't wanted to invite Don Silvio, knowing who he was, but had finally agreed to make me happy. I could only imagine how hard it was for Zia not to have him by her side at family events. But I'd also missed Agata, who couldn't make it when Mother Superior had become ill with pneumonia. She'd return to Napoli when Mother Superior had made a full recovery.

I put the present on the table and he took my hands and squeezed them. 'How is your family managing? Such a terrible waste . . .' He shook his head.

I blinked the tears from my eyes as I gestured for him to sit down. 'We're all coping as best we can. It's still so hard to believe.'

He sighed as he sat heavily on the chair.

'Are you alright?'

He nodded. 'It's just been a long week. There's a lot going on.'

'Let me get you some coffee,' I said, moving to the cupboard.

'Will you be moving to Messina to be closer to your husband?'

'In the summer,' I said. 'But it means leaving Nonna and the clinic.'

'Giulia, I want to tell you something.'

I put the coffee pot down and looked at him. He seemed uneasy, the first time I'd ever seen him this way. 'What is it? Is everything alright?'

He nodded. 'I suggest you stay here. Besides, Stefano won't be in Sicily forever.'

I frowned and dropped into the seat beside him, the present and coffee forgotten. 'Why? What do you know?'

He met my gaze. 'A change is coming and when it does, he'll want to be on the right side.'

'The right side?' I echoed.

'There's a reason he was transferred to a unit in Sicily,' Don Silvio said slowly.

Don Silvio hadn't organised Stefano's transfer just for me. A cold ball formed in the pit of my stomach. I'd thought that I had everything. I was blissfully happy even with the tragedy that surrounded us, and now this?

'You want him to do something for you.'

'Not for me, for Italy.' He straightened in his chair. 'I'll speak plainly, Giulia. Italy isn't faring well in this war. Mussolini and his Fascist regime have taken us to the brink of destruction and we can't let it continue.'

'But what does Stefano have to do with this?'

'We have to choose our side. Stay with the Fascists and Germans or align ourselves with the Allies. I know I'd prefer the Americans. We have an affinity with them, especially here in the south.'

'But the Allies have bombed cities in the south, including Reggio. How can we align with those who are damaging our cities and hurting our citizens?'

'All the more reason to choose a side. Stefano can do nothing and prolong Italy's agony or he can help – by providing information. We need someone we can trust and you're like family to me.'

I stared at him a moment, uncomprehending, but then it came to me. I felt like I was in the middle of a horrible dream.

'You want him to be a spy?' My voice seemed to come from far away.

'No, not a spy. I dislike that word,' he said. 'He'd be a patriot. Helping to shake the shackles of Fascism and prevent further devastation to our country. Surely you both want that?'

I shook my head in disbelief and pulled my hand away. Everything began to fall into place. Don Silvio had done so much for Stefano, who was now well placed to help Don Silvio and his associates. I wondered how involved the 'Ndrangheta and their Sicilian cousins, the Mafia, were in this act of treason. They had no love of the Fascist government that had tried to root them out and render them powerless. But what was the risk to my husband?

'Although this is an urgent matter, it was a difficult decision for me. I only want to protect you both but what I'm asking of you will help guarantee a bright future for you and your family – for all of Italy. Stefano is well placed in Caltanisseta, he knows the district and the local communities . . . This work is crucial.' Don Silvio nodded in the silent space of my speechlessness. 'I just wanted to let you know before I talk to him.'

'No, I have to speak with him first,' I said, pushing my shock to one side. I felt like I'd been punched in the belly. 'It'll be better coming from me.'

I wasn't sure how Stefano would take this. He had no love for Don Silvio and didn't know that he'd arranged the transfer to Sicily. Although it benefitted us both, I knew that he'd be furious, just as I was now. I still couldn't believe that we'd been manipulated – *I'd* been manipulated. Don Silvio's betrayal was shocking. Despite the friendship between us, he was just another man trying to force his decisions on me.

Don Silvio looked at me quizzically then must have realised the issue was more complex than he'd thought. 'Of course, I understand. But don't take too long. We'll need him to acquire certain information on his return to Sicily.'

'What if he gets caught?'

'We'll deal with that.'

He saw the look of fear on my face and touched my arm, immediately withdrawing his hand when I flinched.

'Don't worry, Giulia, he'll be fine. You know that your happiness is important to me.'

'Does Zia Francesca know?' I asked coldly. I wanted to slap his face and scream.

He shook his head. 'It's better that she doesn't.'

I stood stiffly and walked to the door, ready to see him out.

I wished I'd told Stefano about Don Silvio's role in his transfer earlier but I'd been worried about what he might do and relieved that he was somewhere safe. Now it seemed that Don Silvio had an ulterior motive and I'd only got us into deeper trouble by keeping silent. I had to tell him the truth and that we had to do as Don Silvio asked, no matter the risk. It would be worse if he didn't do what the 'Ndrangheta wanted.

I felt myself slide into black nothingness. We were at the mercy of the 'Ndrangheta. I was going to lose my husband.

I was a quivering mess when I finally had the chance to speak to Stefano later that night as we lay in bed.

'Giulia! I know that he's been good to you but I can't get involved with a man like that,' he said, appalled.

'I know. I couldn't believe it,' I said. 'After all the time I've known him, he's never asked for anything from me, not like this.' I turned onto my side to face him, the gold flecks in his eyes sparkling in the light of the lantern as he gazed at me. What if I lost him because of my stupidity? 'I'm so sorry, Stefano, I've been so naïve. But how can we refuse him?' I was shaking.

He pulled me to him. 'It's alright, Giulia. It's not your fault. He's just taking advantage of our situation.' He kissed the top of my head. 'I don't know how I can help, but if it's military information, I can't pass that on to him or anyone else, no matter who they are.'

'He promised he wouldn't ask anything that puts you in danger. But I have to tell you this, Stefano.' I wiped the tears from my face and took a shuddering breath. 'He was the one who secured your position in Sicily and the agreement to allow you to continue your studies in Messina.'

He drew away from me as the blood drained from his face. 'He what? So now I'm obliged to him?'

'He did it for us – for me, because he could see how worried I was about you.' I shut my eyes for a moment, knowing I'd see anger and disappointment from Stefano, emotions I felt too. 'I thought he wanted to do something good but now I see that he had another motive. I didn't know anything about it until after you'd already started. We're being manipulated but I don't see a way out, except to do what he's asked.'

'Using his power to help us is one thing, and perhaps with time I could accept what he's done and even be grateful, but I don't want to be obliged to him.' Stefano shook his head, his fists clenched tightly by his sides. 'To ask for information, that's something entirely different and it's serious. I'd be a traitor and, if caught, I'd be court-martialled.'

'I'm so sorry, Stefano,' I whispered, touching his face. 'I never imagined anything like this would ever happen. I know Il Duce has so much to answer for but to work against our own fatherland is dangerous . . .'

He took my hand and kissed it, staring up at the ceiling with its peeling paint. 'You're right, it is dangerous, but maybe we can find a way to learn how we're really doing in the war and what America's up to. I have to be sure that what Don Silvio's asking is the right thing for Italy, for the preservation of our nation and survival of our people, not just for the advantage and glorification of the 'Ndrangheta. Most of all, I have to know that it's the right thing for us.'

'How can we do that?'

'Maybe I can find something out from my commander or . . .' he frowned as he thought aloud, 'if he wants me to do something soon, we could both reach out to our relatives and see what they've heard from family and friends in America. And perhaps I could even contact some of the local men we knew in Abyssinia who went on to work as civilians in some of the hospitals and ports in North Africa.'

'I could speak to some of my patients too.' I felt more positive now, talking it through with him. 'I agree, we have to know more before we can decide what to do.'

'We're in this together.'

My heart swelled with love and gratitude. We were equal partners and we could get through this.

'And as much as you're worried, we can't do anything tonight,' Stefano murmured, before taking me in his arms and making me forget everything but him.

24

Paola and Antonio appeared at the door, half-carrying Papà.

'What's happened?' I asked.

'He just collapsed while we were moving the sheep,' said Paola anxiously.

'He was groaning before that,' added Antonio.

'I'm not dead yet. I can still hear you,' Papà grumbled.

Mamma and I helped get him into bed. He tried to get more comfortable but immediately let out a large moan. His face was pale, sheened with sweat and his eyes were glassy with pain. It was April and he'd come back from Napoli suffering with back pain that wouldn't go away. But he'd refused to let me look at him. 'It will pass,' he'd said.

'Where does it hurt, Andrea? Is it your back?' Mamma asked urgently.

He nodded. 'My back and into my hips.'

'Has he hurt his back?' asked Paola, hovering over him.

'Of course I've hurt my back,' growled Papà. 'I just need a few days—'

'How did you hurt it?' I asked, gesturing to Paola and Mamma to carefully take his boots off.

Papà shrugged. 'I don't know,' he said impatiently. 'Now if you'd leave me alone.' He moved again to try to get comfortable and grunted with pain.

I put my hand on Papà's forehead. He was burning up. 'Does it hurt anywhere else?'

He shook his head and I frowned.

'That's not right. Remember you were groaning in pain when you pissed this morning and you said it was like pissing thorns?' said Antonio.

Papà nodded. 'That's right . . . it felt like thorns and drew blood like thorns too.'

I felt his back for any tenderness or swelling. 'Is it sore here?' I asked, my hand pressing under his ribs. He grunted and I sighed. I knew how to treat this. 'I think it's your kidney,' I said.

'Don't be ridiculous,' said Papà.

'You listen to her,' said Mamma, rising to her full height. 'She knows what she's talking about.'

'I'll be fine in a few days,' he said.

'No, you won't,' I said. 'You need treatment. It looks like an infection, which could become serious, even life threatening.'

'I've told you before and I'll tell you again: I won't have you or your nonna perform any witchcraft rituals in this house and certainly not on me!' Papà shouted.

'You don't have a choice, Andrea!' yelled Mamma, slapping the bed in frustration. 'You're too sick and you need help.'

'It's alright, Mamma,' said Antonio, putting his arm around her. 'I'll make sure he stays in bed and takes Giulia's medicine.'

'Don't worry,' I said. 'He'll take it when he gets sick enough.'

By that evening, even wrapped up warmly, Papà's fever hadn't broken. He was too ill to get out of bed and was writhing in pain. Nonna came to see him and agreed that we had to act. We gave him a preparation of poppy for his pain and began his treatment with kidney herbs: celery, juniper, cornsilk, equisetum and shepherd's purse, as well as garlic and echinacea for the infection.

He finally fell into an uneasy sleep when his pain had settled. Mamma and I stayed with him through the night and when dawn came, his fever broke and the shaking and sweating began.

'He'll be alright now,' I said to Mamma and she started crying.

'He's such a stubborn old goat,' she whispered, wiping the lank, greying hair from his pale face. 'He doesn't like anyone telling him what to do.'

I held her in my arms as she sobbed, tired as I was. I was the same, so it was no wonder that Papà and I clashed. He might be doing what we wanted now, but I wasn't sure he would when he was feeling better.

I went to the clinic and when I returned at lunch time, Papà was awake and sitting up in bed. Mamma had changed his clothes and sheets but now he was dry and clear eyed.

'How are you feeling?' I asked.

'Better,' he murmured.

Mamma was beside him, feeding him spoonfuls of fenu-greek tea with honey and lemon juice to help the body to heal.

'You had us worried for a while there,' I said.

'You could have died,' murmured Mamma, brushing the tears from her eyes. 'If it wasn't for Giulia and my mother . . .'

Papà took Mamma's hand and kissed it. 'I'm not going anywhere.'

'No, you're not,' she said, glaring at him. 'You're staying in bed until Giulia says you can get up and you're not going back to the regiment until she says you're healed.'

'You've still got a long way to go until you're better,' I said. 'Your fever's gone, but you have to keep taking your herbs so the body can heal.'

He nodded.

I kissed his cheek. 'Mamma will look after you and I'll come and check on you later.'

While Papà was convalescing, Stefano's letter arrived from Messina.

I ripped it open in the privacy of Nonna's kitchen.

My darling wife,
I write to tell you that I passed all my examinations at university . . .

It seemed like a letter from a proud student to his new wife, telling her about his daily activities at university, the medical and clinical studies that he thought she'd be interested in and of course about his undying love and how much he missed her. But deciphering the code we'd devised, I learnt that Stefano had heard from his contacts in Africa that there was increased US military activity in Tunisia, Algiers and French Morocco. American supplies were being sent to the ports in those countries and there was a whisper that the Allies were turning their eye to Italy when the war in North Africa was over. The feeling was that Italy was the weak underbelly of Europe and if the Allies could get a foothold in our country, they were better placed to fight and ultimately defeat the Nazis. The war was coming to Italy.

I let out the breath that I'd been holding.

I stared at the final line of his letter for what seemed like an eternity, the fear growing inside me: *It's time to do what was asked of me.*

I stood abruptly and threw the letter in the fire, as the reality of what Don Silvio had asked hit me full force. We'd stalled as long as we'd dared but whatever Stefano did now would help the Allies invade Italy. If we were going to side with them against our own country – it was treason. I had to talk to Stefano in person, make sure we discussed all the implications of this decision. It wasn't a hypothetical exercise any longer. He was in danger.

I'd been to Reggio only a few times in my life as a child, twice with Mamma when she was buying preserving jars and fabric for Teresa, and once with Papà when he was thinking of buying new sheep. While the bus bumped along the coast road on the two-hour journey, I thought of the day I'd tried to leave to join the Red Cross. So much had happened in the last seven years that I'd never thought possible.

I was travelling alone for the first time in my life and as we got closer to Reggio, my nervousness grew. I was worried about working out where to catch the bus to the wharf north of Reggio before it and the ferry departed. But once I'd arrived in the city, there was so much to see and take in that my anxiety disappeared. The long, straight streets were alive, crowds of people going about their daily business. I glimpsed the enticing views that I'd seen in Santoro's post-cards to Teresa when they were courting, the tall palm trees and magnificent gardens facing the sea and the ancient ruins of the Roman baths on the seafront. I wished I had time to explore the city, but I had to reach Stefano before he did anything.

As I stood on the deck of the ferry that would take me across to Messina, the breeze blowing through my newly cut hair, I felt a sense of freedom and exhilaration. I'd taken a step forward and acted on my own, not waiting for Stefano's next letter or for something to happen. I was in charge of my own destiny. As I watched the mountainous island draw closer and I glimpsed the imposing church perched on the hill above the city, I prayed to the Madonna that I'd find Stefano as easily as I'd made my way here.

The streets of Messina were just as Stefano described: old and new; red-tiled roofs and ancient stone buildings; the smell of fish and spices, orange and incense; the roaring sound of motorbikes overtaking the bus as we climbed the hills; and buildings everywhere.

I asked for directions to the university and decided to wait outside the medicine building for classes to finish.

After waiting for nearly an hour, I saw him. 'Stefano!'

He turned from his conversation with another student. 'Giulia! What are you doing here?'

Then I was in his arms, safe and overjoyed.

'Is everything alright? Are you by yourself?'

'It is now that I'm here with you.' I grinned, proud that I'd made it all the way here on my own. 'It's just me but I can't stay long.'

'Your hair? You've cut it.' He frowned as he tilted his head to view my hairstyle.

'Do you like it? I wanted a change, something more modern and easy to look after.' I felt light and free without the bulk of my thick, wavy hair and I only needed to pull a hairbrush through it and it was done.

'I do,' he said finally. 'It suits you. It shows off your delicate features.'

'Just as well,' I said, smiling. 'Because I love it and won't be growing it out anytime soon.'

He took me to the gardens he'd told me all about, the Pietro Castelli Botanical Gardens.

'What's brought you here?' he asked as we walked hand in hand. Palm trees dominated this part of the garden and although it was only late morning, the cool corridors of green were refreshing.

'Your letter. I received it yesterday and I thought I'd better come straight away.' I looked around us but the garden was virtually empty. 'It's too dangerous to do anything,' I whispered.

'I don't think we have a choice,' Stefano said. 'People have met with accidents or disappeared for refusing to do less.'

'But if what your contacts in Africa tell you is true, it sounds like the Americans are coming to Italy.' I stopped and grasped his arm. 'And that means that whatever you do is dangerous. I'm worried you'll get caught helping Don Silvio and the Americans. It could be a traitor's death.'

He gathered me in his arms. 'It's alright, Giulia. If they want to use me to pass on some kind of strategic intelligence, they won't want me caught. I still think I have to do it. If the Allies are coming, we don't stand a chance. Perhaps we'd be better off siding with them. It might keep all of us safe.'

'The lesser of two evils?' I whispered. 'Promise you'll tell me what they ask of you. If we think it's too risky, we'll find a way to decline.'

'I promise,' said Stefano, kissing me. 'Now, let's find somewhere private. It's been so long since I've seen you.'

I felt stronger and more settled when I came back home. Whatever Stefano faced, we'd decide how to face it together. I continued with my work at the clinic, around the district and at the marina and Brancaleone, so busy that I was worried I'd have to turn patients away soon. I didn't know how Nonna would have coped if I'd moved to Messina.

Papà was improving too. He was moving about, first around the house, and then the village, visiting Teresa and her new baby Emilio. He was also drinking the tea I'd instructed Mamma to give him to flush his kidneys and make sure he was well hydrated. Mamma was a tough nurse, insisting Papà do everything I'd asked, and for the first time in his life, he'd listened. That told me how sick he'd been and how afraid he was of ever being that unwell and incapacitated again.

'Any more pain in your back?' I asked one evening as we sat drinking chamomile tea.

'No, just a little tired when I've done too much.'

'You'll be back to normal soon and you can go back to your regiment. Just make sure you take your herbs and drink enough water.'

He shook his head. 'It's crazy. I've never felt so sick before. I didn't think I'd be able to hold Teresa's baby in my arms.'

'We were worried about you, Papà. If you'd told us sooner that you weren't well, I could've treated you sooner.' I felt his back and abdomen. There was no more tenderness. His forehead was cool and dry.

He scowled. 'I remember something about that night. Were you and your nonna chanting some witchy charms over me?'

I stared at him, incredulous. 'After all this time.'

'Don't be stupid, Andrea,' said Mamma crossly, putting her teacup down hard so it clinked against the saucer. 'We were all praying for you. Believe it or not, we didn't want you to die.'

He frowned. 'You were praying?'

'Yes! To the Madonna, you silly old fool!' said Mamma, exasperated.

'So, you didn't do any witchcraft?'

'No, Papà,' I said, shaking my head and sinking to my chair. 'I've been trying to tell you for years, we don't practise magic. What we do is use the power of belief, of faith, to help heal people. If someone believes that a certain ritual will help them heal, then we'll use it as long as it's harmless, much like we use religious icons, medals of the saints, statues of the Madonna and prayer.'

'So, you healed me. It's your skill with the herbs that does the healing?'

I nodded. Finally, he was beginning to understand. 'Just like Nonna,' I said gently.

Papà looked at Mamma and she nodded too. 'Giulia healed you and she might have even saved your life.'

Papà looked down at the table. 'I saw what you did when Stefano was injured. Many men died during the Great War with wounds like that. I knew you were skilled and talented but . . .' He took a deep breath and nodded as though finally acknowledging the truth of what I did. 'I didn't know it was my kidney. Your zia died from the same thing. I remember my mother talking about it, the fever, the pain, the blood in the urine. The strega did nothing except chant a few words over her, give her some potion that made her worse and an amulet for my mother to put under my sister's pillow.'

The breath caught in my throat at the emotion of his admission. Relief, happiness, disbelief and sadness fought within me. Getting to this point had taken so long and caused so much anguish between us. I wiped the tears that slipped down my cheeks with the back of my hands.

He looked at me, his dark eyes sorrowful and apologetic. 'If I'd seen some other quack, they might have missed it.'

'But your daughter's no quack,' said Mamma softly. 'She's one of the most respected healers in the district.'

'I know, but after what happened to my sister . . . I thought I was protecting you, keeping you safe. I see why your reputation is spreading far and wide. I'm very lucky to be under

your care. I'll never question your or your nonna's skill again.'
He reached across the table and squeezed my hand.

I understood his fear and concern and now realised that everything he'd ever done had been to try to protect me. Maybe now he understood that I could make good decisions and choices for myself.

25

The sound of planes thundering overhead was unnerving. Our family was eating dinner, and everybody was on edge, wondering if this was the night that bombs would fall on our village.

'We have to go!' Mamma cried.

It was May and Italy had lost the war in North Africa, like Stefano said we would. The Italian colonies were gone and the dream of the grand Italian Empire to rival Roma was nothing more than the fancy of a leader who had brought us misery and heartache. Vincenzo's and Angelo's deaths were for nothing.

'It's alright, Mamma,' I said, grasping her arm and trying to soothe her. 'We're not the target. The planes are headed for the airbases and ports. They want to hit military targets in the cities, not small villages.' The reports on Radio Vatican and Londra said Reggio had been bombed relentlessly. I was so sad that the beautiful city had been damaged so badly.

The Allied bombs came again and again, destroying military targets in Messina, Palermo, Napoli and Reggio but also hitting residential areas and homes. There had been many nights that we'd heard the throbbing rumble of military aircraft in the distance, making their way across the Mediterranean from Malta, to find their targets on the western side of the Aspromonte Mountains.

'No, we have to go.' Mamma's eyes were wild with fear. 'Can't you hear how close they are tonight?' Her face was lined from worry and lack of sleep and her dark hair had become almost fully grey. Ever since Vincenzo's death, she seemed smaller, as though a piece of her had gone with him, and her anxiety about the safety of her family had intensified, especially for Papà, who was back in Napoli with his regiment. Napoli had suffered multiple air raids but Papà's regiment and garrison was unscathed and he assured us that they were nowhere near the Allied targets situated at the port. We prayed every day for his safety. I sent my thanks to the Madonna that Stefano was with his unit in Caltanissetta in central Sicily and not in Messina, but he'd have to return soon for his examinations.

The drone of the Allied planes was so loud it seemed they were overhead. The horror on Mamma's face and the terror on Teresa's and Rosa's faces, their crying children clinging to them, convinced me.

We left everything as it was on the table and grabbed coats, blankets and Mamma's bags packed with precious items, before scrambling out the door. We ran through the streets with many other villagers. Bruzzano had no underground bunkers nor any proper air raid shelters, so people sheltered in the sheds on their farms and under trees on the edge of the village while others stood in the middle of fields.

'Are you alright, Nonna?' I asked, taking her arm. She'd fallen heavily a few weeks earlier while collecting horsetail at the edge of the river.

'I'll manage,' she said, hobbling on her still swollen knee. 'But it's your mother I worry about.'

I glanced at Mamma holding Teresa's children's hands as she walked briskly up the hill towards our farm and the shelter of our sheds.

Nonna shook her head. 'She'll make herself sick with worry and she's making everyone around her anxious too. Look at Teresa – she's lost her milk from worrying so much. Now she has to pass baby Emilio around to the breastfeeding women in the village just to keep him fed.' Between looking after four children and finding work, as people couldn't afford to buy new clothes, Teresa had developed mastitis. We'd done all we could to treat it but her milk supply had still dropped.

'But we're all worried about somebody,' I said softly. I'd barely sleep, desperate to turn on the radio and hear the latest news reports about the overnight raids and their destructive results, needing to know that Papà and Stefano were safe.

Nonna patted my hand. 'It's not easy. We just have to pray that neither the Germans nor the Allies have any interest in our part of the world and that we'll endure, despite this wretched war.'

'Il Duce has a lot to answer for,' said Signora Lipari, taking her bottle of herbs from me a week later at the clinic. 'Have you heard that he's gone to see Hitler? Now that North Africa's been won by the Allies, some say he's gone to beg for German troops to protect Italy, fearing that the Allies will target us next. Whoever would have imagined that we'd be bombed so relentlessly here in the south?'

My skin crawled at her words. Stefano had told me that Hitler had sent two German divisions to Sicily to aid in the defence of the island and I shuddered to think how that affected the risk he was taking. Stefano had sent word to Don Silvio that he was ready to do what he'd requested and it wasn't long before he was contacted by Don Silvio's associate in Messina. He'd been given instructions to provide information like distances between certain coastal inlets, between particular rivers that flowed south of Caltanissetta into the Mediterranean, and the positions of bridges and small villages in the south of Sicily. Most of the information, he explained when he'd next written to me, was easy to obtain, but the danger lay in getting it to his contact. He thought the value of such information was that it might spare the local communities, reduce destruction and lower casualties if the Allies decided to invade Sicily. If they understood the lay of the land, they'd be able to achieve a precise and smooth strike. I'd written back, agreeing that his information could help protect the local communities and although I wished we hadn't been forced into this position, agreed that he should go ahead. Maybe it was time to take a side.

I nodded and sighed. I still had notes to write, the clinic to tidy and elderly patients in the village to visit before heading back to Mamma's to help with dinner. At least today I didn't have to go out to the farm but soon it would be time to get ready for the harvest and the whole family's help would be needed. It was a blessing that the air raid on the village never came because I couldn't imagine how we'd cope with the consequences of that as well.

'Did you hear about the raid a couple of nights ago?' I asked. One of the orphanages in Reggio had been hit, and babies and their wet nurses had been killed, and many nuns too.

'Who hasn't?' she said. 'It's monstrous what they've done. It's one thing to kill soldiers fighting face to face but another to kill innocent civilians who have nothing at all to do with this war.'

'So many babies,' I muttered, suddenly drained. It was horrific to contemplate this indiscriminate face of war and I wasn't the only one who felt terror in my bones now that the Allies had turned their sights towards Italy. With what Stefano and I had found out, Sicily was the most likely target. What I didn't know was when they'd strike.

'I'd name that animal of your father's something else,' she said, before opening the front door.

'You mean Benito?' I asked.

'Nobody wants to be reminded of a leader who's become a beggar and betrayed the pride of the Italian people. He's dragged our country down – he's dragged us all down with him. If only we could get out of this wretched war. It's not like it was our war to start with.' She shook her head. 'He has to go. I'm not the only one who thinks this. Fascism has never worked here in the south. All we do is work harder for a govern-ment that has no thought for the people it was supposed to help. As long as we keep supplying grain, they don't care.'

She leaned towards me. 'My son thinks that perhaps it's time that the tables were turned and we looked after ourselves as an independent state as in the old days.'

'I agree that Il Duce can't stay in charge forever, especially with the losses we've had. People everywhere have had enough,' I said. Massimo's son Franco and other troops who had survived the German defeat in Stalingrad had returned home to tell horrific stories of suffering the Russian winter without suitable clothing, their fellow soldiers dying so far from home. There was discontent in the north too, with large-scale strikes in the factories, workers tired of the long hours and poor working conditions in the name of the war effort. Perhaps there was merit in what Don Silvio had asked Stefano to do. A splintered nation made us weak and vulnerable; this was the time for all Italians to come together before we were in danger of having no country at all.

She nodded. 'Before I forget, we've been getting some draft letters come through the post office. Isn't Antonio of age this year? I know what a help he is to Paola and Gabriella on the farm . . . Perhaps it's time he disappears to the mountains for a few weeks?'

A few days later I was at Zia Francesca's flat, looking through her new magazines while she explained the articles to me. Zia had gone downstairs to check on the slow-roasted goat she had in the oven for the following day's menu when there was a knock at the door. The rich meaty aromas wafted in as the door to the lounge opened.

'Giulia? Francesca said you were up here.'

I looked up, the smile frozen on my face. 'Don Silvio! I didn't know you were here tonight,' I said tersely. Although these days I made sure Don Silvio wasn't at Zia Francesca's when I visited, I always worried about running into him.

He sat on the lounge chair across from me with a sigh. 'I just arrived. I'm on my way to Reggio.'

'You obviously received word from Stefano,' I said, putting the magazine to one side.

'I did. Thank you.' He glanced at the door but sounds of clattering in the kitchen downstairs signalled that we had a few moments before Zia came back up. I couldn't believe that he hadn't told her about this – I'd thought they had such a close relationship. Zia and I shared so much but I didn't want to be the one to tell her and hurt her. She'd be furious that he'd involved us and that he hadn't told her himself. 'I know it can't have been easy for you, worrying about your husband, but he's doing a good thing. His information has proven useful and we deeply appreciate what he's doing.'

I took a deep breath as the sharp pain of his betrayal hit me in the chest yet again. I was trembling. 'I thought you were my friend. But you forced me to make a difficult choice and you put my husband in danger. He's done what you wanted. Is he safe now?'

He nodded. 'I'm sorry,' he said softly. 'This was a special situation and we needed someone we could trust like family. I promise never to put you in that position again.' He took my hands in his. 'You know you're like a daughter to me. You can come to me anytime you need something without obligation. For the sake of your zia and for the sake of our friendship, can you forgive me?'

'Alright,' I whispered reluctantly. For the sake of the friendship we'd had, I prayed Don Silvio would honour his word.

It would take a long time to truly forgive him, but maybe this was a start.

He got up then, opening cupboards in the kitchen, and came back with a bottle of wine and three glasses. 'Now, tell your husband to be alert over the next few weeks. The Allies are coming to liberate us from the Fascists and the Germans and when they arrive, they'll need all the help they can get to lift Italy back on her feet.'

I stared at him. 'You asked him to be a traitor to his own country.'

Don Silvio shook his head. 'No,' he said emphatically. 'He's a patriot. Because of the work of your husband and others like him, the Allies have a chance to swoop into Sicily with as few casualties as possible. Our men will be persuading Italian troops to lay down their arms and surrender or better still, to disappear. Italy's only hope of survival is with the Allies. Call it occupation or liberation, it amounts to the same thing: a second chance for Italy before her destruction is complete.'

'But Stefano will never desert.'

'Don't worry, we want him safe and well to help the Allied medics when the time comes. There'll be many battles to come against the Fascists and Nazis and we need all the talent to keep our soldiers out on the battlefield, ready to return to their families when this is all over. That's what he wants too, isn't it?'

Another thought occurred to me and I looked at him in horror. 'Antonio – he's nearly twenty-one, he'll be drafted soon.'

'My advice is to tell him not to go,' Don Silvio said, sipping his wine. 'He can hide in the mountains.'

'He'll be breaking the law. If he's caught, he'll go to prison.'

'Not likely. As long as he can stay away from the government officials for another month or two, he won't need to worry. If he feels like he wants to do his duty after that, he can make his own decision about joining the Allied campaign.'

'Join the Allies?'

The sound of footsteps on the stairs made Don Silvio glance at the door and lean forward. 'It's been arranged. When the Allies defeat our forces and those of the Germans on the island, Stefano – and your brother, for that matter – will be free to join the Allied forces,' he said quickly. I shook my head. This was a lot to take in. 'You should be proud of him,' he said with a smile.

He raised his glass as Zia came into the room. 'Salute! Here's to the future.'

My eyes were open to Don Silvio now. He would act in his own self-interest and so would I. If our paths aligned and we wanted the same thing, well and good.

'Salute,' I replied, finally raising my own glass. I would use him for my own purposes as he had used me.

It wasn't long after that Antonio received his draft letter, requesting him to present himself at the garrison in Reggio.

'I don't think he should go,' I said softly.

'But it's the law,' said Paola. 'He'll be arrested.'

'Not if he disappears. I know where he can stay safely hidden in the mountains,' I said, winding my fingers in my skirt anxiously, wondering how Mamma and Paola would take this. Our family had never shirked their duty.

'I never expected this from you, with Stefano in Sicily doing his duty,' said Paola, scathingly.

'Haven't we lost enough?' I couldn't tell her what I knew. Not yet.

'That's right, I'm not going,' said Antonio, smiling smugly at my unexpected support. 'What's the point? We're losing the war and I refuse to give Mamma and Papà any more heartache. Besides, with the continuous bombing, the chances of even leaving Reggio are slim. And I'd be of more use here at home with you, helping on the farm.'

Paola and I looked at each other in surprise. Neither of us imagined that Antonio didn't want to go. He'd always idolised Vincenzo and Stefano and their soldier's lives.

'How can you be if you're in hiding?' she asked in frustration.

Antonio raised an eyebrow in surprise. Paola was rarely cranky, but the strain on her from the government demands was showing. The food shortages across the nation had become critical. We couldn't always fill the quota of products that the government required, either because we didn't have the right farming equipment or because of the drought and flood seasons. When we did, we had to creatively store some away for our own use and lie to the officials otherwise we too would have no flour.

'It will only be for a few weeks,' he said gently. 'Then the officials will have forgotten about me and I'll be back to help you like I always have. The Fascists already have Papà and Stefano and our family have paid the ultimate price for a war that isn't even ours.'

'It's your duty, Antonio,' said Paola, standing firm. 'As much as I'd love for you to remain here.'

'I'm staying to protect you and this family,' he said.

'It's for the best, Paola,' I said.

She gazed into my eyes for a moment and then sighed. 'Alright,' she said. 'If it keeps him safe.'

I visited Stefano while he was sitting his end-of-year examinations at the Messina university. I had to discuss all that Don Silvio had told me and not even Mamma's fear and anxiety nor the threat of invasion was going to stop me. Mamma didn't know what was at stake for Stefano and me, but she did remember when Papà was away in the Great War and understood how much I wanted to see my husband. I promised her that I'd just go for one day and that I'd be careful. It was heartbreaking to travel through the streets of Messina and see how much had been damaged and destroyed by the months of bombings. Through the window of the bus, I saw families sheltering in the twisted ruins of homes and buildings and I wondered how many had been injured. I wanted to be somewhere like this, where I was really needed, where I could do some real good. I'd promised Mamma that I'd come home and I knew that my family needed me now, but one day soon, I'd go.

Stefano was surprised to see me waiting outside the examination hall when he'd finished his paper. The joy on his face made me wish I could surprise him more often.

He pulled me to him. 'Is everything alright?' he asked. 'It was dangerous for you to come.'

I nodded. 'I just had to see you. I found out something from Don Silvio.'

His face tightened. 'I'll take any excuse to see my wife,' he murmured, then kissed me as though there was nobody watching.

It was late when we finally spoke of Don Silvio, lying in bed with the blanket and sheets kicked off after passionate lovemaking, the lantern turned low. Stefano had taken me back to his room, both of us desperate for the feel of each other after weeks apart.

'How have you been managing, supplying the 'Ndrangheta with the information they want?' I asked softly. 'I've been worried about you.'

He sighed, running his hand lightly along my spine. 'It was simple at first, distances, positions of villages, information any local could give them, and so the risk was low. But then they asked for more sensitive information.'

'What did you do for them?'

'I gave them maps and photographs of the Sicilian coastline and detailed military positions. I felt like a traitor of the worst kind. But when I witnessed how the Germans treated Sicilian civilians and our troops and I remembered your words about having to take a side, I felt more sure that I was doing the right thing.'

'Oh, Stefano!' I rested my forehead against his. 'I'm so sorry that you've been put in this position. If it helps at all, Don Silvio called you a patriot. Maybe what you're doing really will help finish this war and put an end to the misery of too many Italians.'

'When I was asked for military details, I knew that the Allies were planning to come here. If the 'Ndrangheta and Mafia are helping the Allies to enter Sicily as a means of ending this war maybe it's what the Italian people need to come together and fight for our country.'

I nodded. 'If Don Silvio thinks you won't be here much longer, the invasion will be soon, but he assures me that you'll have a position with an Allied medical unit. I'm not sure where or when but as long as you stay safe until then . . .'

'But if I choose to work for the Allies, I have to be sure that it's the right thing.'

'This might be our chance to make a difference.'

To be on the side that could bring Italy hope, healing and unity was a powerful idea. Without these things, I feared that our country would never be the same again.

26

The Allies had landed in Sicily. It was horrifying that the war on the land had reached Italian soil and was so close to us in Calabria. At the same time, I was relieved that Don Silvio's information had been correct and that Stefano and I had not made a fatal decision. It was mid-July 1943 and the invasion of Sicily was all over the news. We were in the heart of the European war and whatever happened now, one thing was for certain: there would be more suffering for the Italian people.

Stefano was with his unit in the centre of the island when the first British and American forces landed in Licata on the southern coast. Even with the extra German troops flooding the island, most of Sicily had quickly been taken by the might of the Allied forces. Only Mount Etna and the northeast corner of Sicily remained under Italian and German control. But there was no news of Stefano and his division and for weeks, I spent half the night on my knees, praying for his safe return.

'He'll be alright,' said Papà. He was on leave again, a blessing with the constant air raids over Napoli.

'How can you be so sure?' I asked. Everyone had gone home or to bed except the two of us and Mamma. Antonio was still hiding in the mountains until the Allies had control of the south.

'He's with the medical unit, which will be behind the front lines. He'll remain with the field hospital and his duties there while others retrieve the wounded from the battlefield. The Allies have no need to kill medical personnel.'

I sank down beside him. 'Thank you, Papà.'

He put his arm around me and kissed the top of my head. 'You've been through enough. Do you know how proud I am of you?'

I shook my head, speechless.

'You were always a spirited child and I worried that it would get you into trouble. But I shouldn't have worried. You're strong, brave and principled, just like your mother and my sister. You're a very fine healer and Stefano is a good man, the perfect match for you. I see that you both want to help people and make this world a better place. I was wrong. I'm sorry. There should be more like you. If God's listening to my prayers, then He'll protect Stefano so he can finish his studies and the two of you can do God's work together, have your own family and live a full and happy life. That's all I want for you.'

'I know, Papà.' I wrapped my arms around him and kissed his scratchy cheek. To hear him say he was sorry and how proud he was of me meant the world. I'd never expected such words from him.

'It looks like I have strong women all around me. Our family wouldn't have survived this far without Paola's management of the farm, and the village has much to thank her for. And Teresa's a wonderful mother and dressmaker. Then there's your mother, who I love even more than the day we married. I'm a lucky man to have had her love all these years.'

'Andrea, Giulia! Come quickly!'

We jumped up and raced to the dining room, where Mamma was sitting listening to the radio.

'What is it, Gabriella?' asked Papà.

'Shh, sit down and listen,' she said, waving her hand at him. 'Something's happened in Roma.'

'What?' Papà sat beside her, his brows lowering as he listened intently to the radio announcer.

'Attention. Attention. His Majesty the King and Emperor has accepted the resignation from the office of the head of government, prime minister, and secretary of state, His Excellency il Cavaliere Benito Mussolini, and has named as head of government, prime minister, and secretary of state the marshal of Italy, Sir Pietro Badoglio.'

'The Fascist government has fallen,' I said, shaking my head in amazement. Finally, after twenty-one years in power, Mussolini was finished.

'Does this mean that the war is over?' asked Mamma, hope etched across her weary face.

Papà took her hand. 'I don't think so. But maybe it's an opportunity for the Italian government to negotiate with the Allies. This must be the beginning of the end. No Italians want to be aligned with the Nazis, none except Mussolini, and now he's gone.'

'The sooner it's over for us, the fewer mothers have to know the terrible loss of losing a son to this war.' Her shoulders slumped. 'Oh, Andrea, I'm so tired. I just want it to be over, and have you by my side with all our children and grandchildren around us.'

'I know, amore mio.' Papà lifted Mamma to her feet, tears in his eyes.

'You two go to bed,' I said. 'I'll finish up here.'

Mamma caressed my cheek before Papà led her to bed.

After visiting the post office every day hoping for news, I finally received a letter from Stefano in early August. I wanted to jump up and down for joy but instead, I traced the familiar handwriting on the envelope and pressed it against my heart before running back to Nonna's.

Cara mia,

I'm alive and well. Our division has had almost constant contact with the Allies since the early days of the invasion. We are now on the north coast, pushing towards Messina. With the number of casualties we've had, I've been busy in the field hospital. The Allies have almost overrun us and I think all we can hope for is to be evacuated back to Reggio before we're completely crushed. In their desperation, the Germans have been commandeering civilian vehicles at gunpoint, treating the locals with brutality and disregard. For weeks we've heard stories about the Germans taking locals' animals and food, occupying their homes, raping girls and women and beating or shooting dead anyone who objects or resists. I believe the

*stories because they treat us, their counterparts, with disdain
and contempt.*

*As a medic, I know that I'll be fine whatever happens, but
I worry for the men in our regiment. I'll find a way to contact
you when I know more . . .*

Stefano was alive and well! A heaving sob erupted from
my lips. The danger had not yet passed but soon, God willing,
he'd be with the Allies and safe.

'What does that man in Rome, Badoglio, think he's doing?'
asked Signora Lipari at the post office one morning. 'How
can we continue a war that nobody wants?' Prime Minister
Badoglio had announced to the nation that Italy's involvement in the war would continue, despite the end of the Fascist
government. In Bruzzano's piazza, the black Fascist flag was
pulled down and burned in protest. The Aquila, the eagle of
Rome, outside the local Fascist headquarters was defaced and
smashed and their representatives were chased out of town by
an angry mob.

'We can't simply tell our soldiers to lay down their weapons
and go home,' said Zia Francesca, shrugging helplessly. She
was collecting a parcel for the trattoria. 'We can't afford
to make an enemy of the Germans now. There are already too
many Nazi troops in Calabria for my liking, and more pouring
into Italy to help resist the Allies.'

'I know I'd rather be on the side of the Americans,' said
Signora Lipari, 'even if it means fighting those crazy Germans.
Most of us have relatives and friends in America and many of

them have written to say the same thing: that their president just wants to win this war and stop the Nazis. They have no problem with Italy.'

'We're damned if we do and damned if we don't,' I said glumly. No matter what connection we had to America, Reggio and Sicily were still being bombed by the Allies. From what Stefano had mentioned in his letter, it would be no better with the Germans. We'd either continue to have the Allies attack us or we'd have the Germans against us. Italy was in an impossible position.

'This was never an Italian war. Badoglio needs to listen to the people or he's no better than Mussolini,' insisted Signora Lipari.

'Time will tell what the government does, but life still goes on,' said Zia, nodding.

Papà had returned to Napoli, where his regiment awaited their orders. Now that the Allies' arrival seemed imminent, Antonio slipped back from his hideaway when he could to help Paola on the farm. In the mountains he had joined a group of disaffected young men who refused to fight in a foreign war and were ready to rebel against a government that was doing little to help its people. But the war was on our doorstep, whether we deserved it or not, and I couldn't help thinking that this was not the time for rebellion.

By mid-August, according to Radio Londra, the bulk of the Italian and German divisions had withdrawn to Calabria, and Sicily was under Allied occupation. I was proud that Stefano had contributed even in a small way to the Allied victory, but in the confusion of troop movements, I had no idea where he might be and the worry that he'd been discovered or wounded in those final days ate away at me so that I felt sick to the stomach.

One morning as I was collecting the yellow flowers of St John's wort from the fields before breakfast, I heard a dog barking in the distance. Straightening up and stretching, I surveyed the landscape. Coming towards me along the road was a squad of about ten soldiers. I squinted in the sunlight and felt sure they were not Italians: they weren't wearing the right uniform.

I picked up my skirts and ran back into the village. 'Soldiers are coming!' I yelled. I went to the church and banged on the door of the priest's residence. 'Padre, soldiers are coming,' I repeated through gasping breaths as he opened the door and stared at me in astonishment. 'They're just outside the village.'

'Are they Italian?' he asked.

I shook my head. 'No, but I don't know if they're Allies or Germans.'

He grunted. 'Either way, the people of this town won't view them kindly.' He thought for a moment. 'I'll ring the bell. It's the only way to warn people in time. Knock on as many doors as you can and tell people to stay inside. With any luck they're just passing through and won't trouble us at all.'

I nodded, dubious, but there was nothing else to do. I turned and began knocking on doors, encouraging others to help me warn the village as the bell started to toll. I made sure I warned Santoro and Teresa at the schoolmaster's house and Rosa at the general store before climbing a stone wall to see the soldiers' progress.

I could see helmets at the end of the road. 'May the Madonna protect us,' I breathed and sprinted to Nonna's, but she was already outside her house. 'Come on,' I said, pulling her by the arm. 'Let's go to Mamma's. Soldiers are coming.'

We ran with other villagers, some dragging pigs and sheep from their yards into their homes. I banged on Mamma's door and she opened it immediately.

'Quickly, come inside,' she said, slamming the door behind us and bolting it firmly.

We rushed to the shuttered windows and peered outside as men in uniform milled about the street.

'They're German,' whispered Nonna after we heard them speaking among themselves.

They were thin, haggard and dirty, desperate men and not at all like the tall, proud Germans we'd heard about. But desperate men were the most dangerous of all. I remembered what Stefano had written about the Nazis in Sicily and I shuddered. What did they want here?

'They're our allies,' said Paola.

'They might be but I'm not letting them in here,' said Mamma. 'I hope Antonio is safe in the mountains.'

We watched as they knocked on doors but nobody answered, our knuckles white against the shutters as we waited to see what they would do.

'I don't think they mean to harm us,' said Nonna. 'Otherwise, they would have already done it.'

'I'm not so sure,' I whispered, more afraid now than I had been during the air raids.

'I just wish they'd go away,' muttered Mamma.

The soldiers climbed over fences and walked into gardens, picking ripe tomatoes and anything else they could get their hands on. They broke branches as they roughly pulled fruit from the trees.

'The hide of them,' said Paola. 'They're stealing all we have! That produce has to last for months.' She started for the door and I pulled her back although I wanted more than anything to rush out and snatch the produce back.

'No, Paola, you can't go out there! We don't know what they might do. They could attack us or shoot anyone who tries to stop them. It's not worth the risk.'

A squealing pig was dragged from its pen, the soldier jubilant at his find. I was appalled by the theft in broad daylight but then I noticed how frail he was, his uniform hanging off him, and when I looked at the others on the street, I wondered how long since they'd eaten a decent meal. 'I think they're hungry,' I whispered in surprise.

'I don't care if they're hungry,' said Mamma, although she was trembling with fear. 'They can pay for what they're taking, like anybody else would.' Every theft was a blow to our community but nobody came out to confront the soldiers. Instead, we watched silently from our windows.

'Yes, but like Giulia pointed out, they still have guns on them,' said Paola.

'We'd rather go hungry than be shot or have our daughters raped,' said Nonna grimly.

Other soldiers followed his lead and chickens were taken from their coops along with the eggs and our milking cow.

'Not Bella,' cried Mamma. 'We've had her for so long. She's part of the family.'

'Shh, it's alright,' I whispered. 'Paola can find us another milking cow, can't you?'

'You know I will,' she said confidently, but I wondered how scarce livestock was going to be if Germans were scouring the countryside like this.

'Where do you think they're going?' asked Mamma, peering through the window.

'Away from here,' hissed Nonna.

'I think they're heading to Reggio and the west coast to stop the Allies when they cross to the mainland,' I said. 'But maybe they got separated from the rest of their unit, got lost in the mountains and ended up here.'

Suddenly one of the men kicked in a door across the street and four men followed him inside.

'Oddio!' said Mamma, her eyes wide with shock. We could only watch helplessly, not knowing what was happening inside the house of our neighbour, Signora Romeo. At least there were no young men or women there, just a wizened old lady.

The door opened and the men walked out again with bottles of olive oil, jars of olives, wheels of cheese and strings of dried mushrooms.

'We have to do something,' said Paola. 'If they raid every home like this, we'll have nothing left and we'll all starve—' But whatever else she was going to say was cut off by the little old lady stepping outside of her door and waving the men goodbye.

'She's done it to save the rest of us,' said Mamma slowly, moving her hands in the Sign of the Cross as the men disappeared down the street, carrying their finds and leading their stolen animals to the other end of town without touching another home.

'Thank God for Signora Romeo!' said Nonna.

'What about our sheep?' said Paola in consternation. 'Surely they have enough now.'

'I guess we'll have to wait and see,' I said.

'It could have been so much worse,' said Mamma, mopping her brow with her handkerchief.

After a while, when we'd seen no more soldiers, we felt game enough to go out onto the street. Signora Romeo greeted us.

'I have to thank you,' she said, as she shuffled towards us. 'Without your warning, I would have had my best products out for them to find.'

'Whatever happened?' asked Mamma.

'One spoke a little Italian and somehow I managed to get him to believe that my preserves and oil are the best in the village and everyone else's is poor quality.'

'Why would they believe that?' Paola asked.

'Because I told them I'm a strega and that I cursed every-one's olive oil this year, so mine would be the best. Then I waved around an old amulet I had and mumbled some words in front of them, telling them that bad things would happen to them if they took any more from the village.' She shrugged. 'I thought it was best if they were just gone. Asking them to put anything back was asking for trouble. I told them they could stay a little longer, that I'd enjoy the company of young men like themselves, but unfortunately they decided to leave.' She began to cackle uproariously, slapping her hand against her black skirt.

Mamma grasped her by the shoulders and kissed her downy cheeks. 'You could have been killed but you saved the village, you saved us all.'

'It was nothing,' she said, but she beamed with pleasure.

There was a knock on Nonna's door late one evening towards the end of August. I was staying with her and had made chamomile tea for us both before bed.

'I'll get it,' I called. I walked to the door. 'Who is it?' I asked.

'It's Roberto Lipari,' said the boy's voice.

I opened the door. 'Is everything alright? Is it your nonna?'

'Nonna's fine but someone delivered a message for you at the post office this evening. I was closing up and a man I've never seen before was waiting outside and asked if I could bring you this letter.' He handed the note to me. 'Nonna's waiting for me. I'd better get home.'

I glanced down at the letter and my heart started to thump. 'Thank you for bringing it so late, Roberto. Buona sera.'

I closed the door as if in a dream and opened the envelope with trembling hands. A single sheet of paper slipped out into my hand, signed by Don Silvio.

Dear Giulia,

I apologise for making contact with you this way but there was no time for me to come and see you. I'm on my way to Cassibile in Sicily and don't know when I'll be back your way. I've sent this letter with a trusted friend who will make sure it reaches you.

I wanted to let you know that I've had word of your husband. He has arrived in Calabria with the rest of his division, under the leadership of the 6th Army Commander Guzzoni and is safe and well. They wait with the Italian and German forces for the arrival of the Allies but they cannot prevail.

He has been a considerable help to us in supplying information and it will soon be time for him to make his position known. I've arranged for him to receive details of who he should report to to find a position within the medical corps. I would hate for him to be caught on the wrong side of this situation and go north to his divisional headquarters in Asti. A large number of German troops have been positioned in the north as well as south of Rome, on the pretext of helping defend against the Allies but in fact, we've recently learnt, ready to take control of our country the moment Badoglio surrenders to the Allies.

For your own safety, do not travel far in the next weeks. The news will be broadcast soon. When it happens, the battle for Italy will truly begin. It's time for us to all become patriots and aid our country in any way we can.

I know that you will keep this information to yourself. It would cause panic if any of this was known.

I sagged against the wall. At least I knew Stefano was safe and well, although I still had no idea when I might see him again. Don Silvio was right, the battle for Italy was just beginning.

27

We didn't have to wait long. On the evening of 8th September, while Mamma and I were shelling peas, Nonna was repairing Antonio's trousers with needle and thread, and Paola was going over the farm accounts, the soft music on the radio stopped suddenly and an announcer's voice sprang to life, introducing Prime Minister Badoglio.

'The Italian government, acknowledging the impossibility of continuing the unequal struggle against the overwhelming power of our opponents, and with the aim of sparing the nation further and more serious harm, has requested an armistice from General Eisenhower, commander-in-chief of the Anglo-American Allied forces. This request has been met. Consequently, all hostilities against Anglo-American forces by Italian forces, everywhere, must stop. Italian forces, however, will resist any attacks coming from any other source.'

I sighed. The calm before the storm was over.

'We're no longer at war with the Allies,' murmured Mamma. 'I can't believe it.' She looked stunned and relieved at the same time.

'But we can't act as a neutral country, be friends to both the Allies and Germans, when both occupy our country,' said Paola, frowning in confusion.

'But maybe now Andrea can come home and Antonio too,' said Mamma, hope blossoming across her face.

Nonna took off her glasses and rubbed her temples. 'Maybe, but I'm not sure that the Germans will allow us to leave this war peacefully. The Italian military and government have allowed more German divisions onto Italian soil since the Allied invasion of Sicily.'

'We're in the middle, fence-sitting,' said Paola, closing her books with a sigh.

'It looks like it,' I said. 'And until Italians choose a side and make a stand, the war will only be drawn out.'

The following day, Allied forces landed north of Calabria, where German forces had retreated to, and fighting began. There were radio reports of Italian troops disbanding and leaving their posts. For them, our surrender meant the war was over. Men who had been posted nearby had been trickling home, some as deserters in the face of the Allied arrival and others following the dissolution of their units. They were thin and haggard, exhausted and demoralised, blood oozing through their cracked, worn boots.

'We didn't come back home like this,' said the shocked old men sitting outside their houses, veterans of the Great War. 'We were straight, tall and proud.'

I'd heard nothing from Stefano and had no idea whether he was still with his division or whether he'd joined the British army when they reached the mainland. My worry for him was constant, like a bad tooth. All I could do, all any of us could do, was take each day as it came.

But almost immediately, the Nazis occupied Rome and the reality of our situation hit home: the Germans weren't going anywhere, determined to fight the Allies in our homeland. Napoli was now also occupied by the Germans and our fear for Papà intensified.

'Remember, Andrea's unit is carabinieri, military police performing local policing duties. They won't be targeted by the Germans provided they continue to keep local law and order,' said Zia Francesca. The trattoria was closed today and she had joined us for dinner after hearing about the situation in Napoli. Zia hadn't seen much of Don Silvio since the Allied landing, telling me he was busy working as an intermediary between the Americans and the Italian people. I could see how proud she was of him but also how much she missed him.

'But how can he do that when the Germans are imprisoning or killing civilians and troops?' asked Paola. 'I'd never have imagined that German soldiers would fire on a harmless crowd and burn the National Library.'

'How can the carabinieri stand by when the Nazis shoot dead any Italian troops crazy enough to stay in the city while they round up civilians to send to their labour camps?' asked Antonio indignantly. After encountering German units laying mines and booby-traps for the Allies in the mountains, he had managed to return home unscathed. It wasn't until Signora Lipari told us of her son's involvement that we heard how the band of young men had attacked a few Germans in the rearguard before melting into the mountain forests and disappearing from view. Mamma had been furious and screamed at Antonio until she was hoarse, before dissolving into tears and sobbing that she didn't want to lose another son. Since then, he'd been attentive to her, remaining in the village and helping Paola. But I knew that it would only be a matter of time before his anger at this war and the government would resurface through some sort of rebellion.

'Your father's a smart man. If he believes he can no longer do his job, he'll either be on his way home to you or he'll join the locals, who won't go down without a fight,' said Nonna. 'The Napolitani are just like us and they don't take kindly to being told what to do, especially by foreigners.'

'Papà won't turn away from a fight if he thinks an injustice has happened,' said Antonio, playing with the radio. Although the Allies were setting up their own radio stations, broadcasting was still chaotic and the most reliable sources remained Radio Londra or the Vatican radio. The whirring sound the radio made as he jumped from frequency to frequency was getting under my skin.

Suddenly we heard a voice loud and clear and stopped what we were doing. The Italian government, including Badoglio and the Royal family, had made it to Brindisi on Italy's heel and were safe from the Nazis. It was here that they intended to set up government under protection of the Allied forces. The government would continue as normal, despite German occupation of Rome and much of northern Italy. Pamphlets had been dropped across major cities to inform the Italian people of the wellbeing of its rulers and government.

But the news wasn't over. Mussolini had been rescued from a secret Italian prison by the Nazis and was now presumed to be in Munich, meeting with Hitler.

'How much more can happen?' asked Nonna, slumping into her chair.

'At least we have a functioning government,' I said. 'But I never thought we'd have to worry about Mussolini again.'

'There's trouble ahead,' said Antonio darkly. 'And it's going to drag all of us in.'

Antonio was right. A couple of weeks later, Mamma, Nonna and I were listening to the radio while cleaning the mushrooms we'd picked when the announcer's voice rang over the airwaves.

'Newsflash! Mussolini, recently rescued by the Nazis from his mountain prison in the Italian Alps, has been appointed head of the newly formed Italian Social Republic in Salò, northern Italy. In Mussolini's words, it is a return to the origins of Italian Fascism. The new National Republican Army is now recruiting men to the Fascist cause against the Italian government and monarchy ...'

'Mussolini's back?' I stared at Nonna and Mamma. 'How can this be?'

'Hitler and the Nazis,' said Nonna darkly, taking the mushrooms from my plate and cutting them into slices. 'They're intent on causing trouble.'

'Those men Mussolini's recruiting, they're Italians too, countrymen who will likely come face to face with our own troops one day.'

'Just when we thought that Italy could be saved from the Germans,' said Mamma, pushing the mushrooms in the frying pan around savagely. Their earthy aroma filled the room but all I could think about was how chaos had been unleashed.

The news report continued.

'In other news, the American 5th and the British 8th Armies are now joining up on their march north towards Napoli, where the situation is escalating, the Germans having officially assumed military control of the city. A state of siege has been declared, with reports of German troops threatening to kill anyone openly hostile to German occupation.'

'Napoli!' breathed Mamma, turning to us, wide eyed. 'Andrea's there.'

My thoughts turned to Agata. I wondered whether she'd made the journey from the monastery to the sanatorium before the arrival of the Allies.

It was hard to track the movements of Italian soldiers now that so many regiments had dispersed. Some men had been caught in the north and drafted into the Republican Army while others had joined the Allied forces.

'There is so little mail getting through. There's no way of knowing how Papà or Stefano are and I noticed how quiet Mamma was at dinner,' I said to Nonna one evening towards the end of September. I knew how worried she was about Papà.

'She hates being apart from him like this,' said Nonna, uncoiling her plaits from her head. 'After the Great War, she vowed never to be parted from him again. Although she was proud of your father for doing his duty for Italy, it was tough managing everything on her own.' She began to unplait her grey hair with nimble, but knobbly, fingers. 'You know that they have always been patriots, even then when it was uncommon. Many people in the south still believed we should be independent from the rest of Italy over fifty years after unification. But your parents always saw the benefits in a unified Italy, a brighter future for you children.'

'And now they've lost a son,' I said, pouring tea into our cups.

'Despite her loss, your mother is proud of Vincenzo. He was a leader among men, courageous and honourable to the end. He fought for the future of our country, so that the rest of us could one day live in peace.' She put her hand on my arm. 'Never forget that, Giulia. His sacrifice was for us. So, live the very best life you can live in honour of your brother.'

I sat down beside her. Tears trickled down my face. 'I miss him, Nonna. I can't imagine what Mamma's going through now that Papà's caught up in Napoli. I'm worried sick for Stefano, not knowing where he is or what he's doing, and I know that nobody can tell me anything about him but at least he's with the Allies. But I've been thinking, maybe there's a way of finding out where Papà is – Don Silvio. I'm sure he has his contacts, even in Napoli.'

'Anything we can find out will help your mother,' she said, patting my hand.

I smiled wryly. Nonna didn't know the half of what had happened but, if Don Silvio could help and there was no further obligation ... 'I'll go and see Zia Francesca in the morning. She'll know how to send word to him.' I kissed her on the cheek. 'I'll feel better if I try.'

Three days later, Roberto from the post office came into the clinic as I was tidying up. He had a letter delivered by the same anonymous man. I couldn't wait to see what news Don Silvio had managed to find about Papà. Sitting at the kitchen table,

I used the knife next to the bowl of fruit to slice open the top of the envelope. There were a couple of pages of tightly written script. Don Silvio's letters were usually brief. My heart began pounding as I read greedily.

I was able to learn of your father's whereabouts. He remained in Napoli after the German occupation with other members of his unit. From what I could ascertain, they were intent on protecting the locals from German brutality and were involved in clashes with German military. They succeeded in preventing many deaths of local citizens and freed those imprisoned and bound for deportation.

My heart filled with a warm glow. I couldn't wait to tell Mamma. I blinked away the tears of pride that blurred the next words.

You and your family should be immensely proud of the heroic actions of your father but I'm sorry to be the one to tell you that he and the other members of his unit were killed while protecting the city as the Germans left Napoli and retreated north, only a day before the first Allied forces arrived.

My brain froze. I read the words on the page again, but they remained the same. It couldn't be true.

In a state of shock, I read on. There had to be some explanation, some mistake.

With the chaos of the war, I felt it imperative to check the facts so as not to cause you any undue pain. But it is true.

345

Your father's identification tags were on his body when he and the other men were located. You'll be reassured to know that they have been taken to the nearby sanatorium and laid out by the nuns there. Your mother should receive a telegram once the official paperwork has been lodged.

Stefano travels with the British 8th Army to Napoli and I have sent word to him to go to the sanatorium when he arrives in the next day or so.

A sob of relief burst from my lips. Stefano was alive and well, and safe with the Allies.

I hope you don't think me presumptuous, but I have also left instructions that a member of your family will come to collect your father's body in the next few days. I'm sure you want to bring him home to bury him, especially when your brother is so far from home. Now that the fighting has moved north and the German army has retreated to the Volturno River, I can safely arrange transport to Napoli for members of your family, perhaps you and your mother. I'll notify Stefano so he can meet you at the sanatorium when you arrive. It's the least I can do for you at this time of grief. Please find the details on the following page.

My heart goes out to you and your family.

Don Silvio

I stared at the page for what seemed like an eternity, wishing the letter would somehow disappear and I'd wake up from a terrible dream. But the words on the page remained and even as they began to blur, I couldn't escape the truth. Papà was gone. I suddenly felt like a hollow shell.

I was sure of one thing though: the longer I sat here, the longer I could spare Mamma and the rest of the family this pain. I didn't know if I could face watching their hearts break just yet.

'Giulia, are you ready to go to your mother's?' called Nonna as she closed the front door behind her.

I stayed rooted to the spot, terrified of the moment when the world would begin turning again and I'd have to feel.

'Giulia,' called Nonna more urgently, her shoes clicking against the tiled floor as she came closer. 'What's wrong? Is everything alright?'

She came around the table. In one glance she took in my face and the letter in front of me and blanched. 'Cara mia,' she said before dropping beside me and enfolding me in her arms.

It was then that I cracked under the weight of my grief. My hard, emotionless exterior was gone and my molten interior gushed out like the lava from Mount Etna.

'Papà's dead,' I stuttered between shuddering sobs.

'Oh, Giulia,' whispered Nonna, hugging me tighter.

'How am I ever going to tell Mamma?'

She kissed me on the head. 'We'll do it together.'

As soon as we came into the kitchen, Mamma knew something was wrong. She put down the eggplant she was slicing and came to my side.

'Have you heard something about Stefano?'

I shook my head, tears again welling in my eyes. 'It's Papà.'

Her eyes widened and she covered her mouth so she didn't make a sound.

'Come, sit down, Gabriella,' said Nonna, guiding her to the chair.

347

'I dreamt about him a few days ago and I felt him close to me all the next day but I thought it was because of the dream . . .' Mamma looked from Nonna to me desperately, pleadingly.

I knelt beside my mother and took her hands in mine. 'I've had word from someone I trust who has connections everywhere. I asked him to find Papà and he's just written back. Papà was killed defending Napoli and its people from the Germans.'

Mamma drew a short, sharp breath and began to shake. 'Show me the letter,' she whispered. She was as white as the wall behind her.

I pulled the letter from my pocket and gave it to her, sitting on the chair beside her.

'He's a hero, Mamma,' I said when she'd finished reading.

'But now he's gone. I've lost him forever.'

'You should be proud of what he's done,' said Nonna. 'Andrea did what many others didn't. He stayed and protected those who couldn't protect themselves.'

Mamma stared unseeing at the letter on the table as tears slid down her face.

I squeezed her hand, unable to stop my own tears from falling.

28

Mamma and I went to Napoli to bring Papà home. We were picked up in a car sent by Don Silvio before dawn. The driver, Gino, was quiet and respectful of our loss. The sun rose above the horizon as we made our way into the mountains. It was hard to imagine that soldiers from two armies had travelled through these very mountains less than a month ago. The tranquillity of an eagle circling overhead and the display of vivid autumn colours among the tall pine trees were at odds with the wrenching loss and turmoil I was feeling. This was the furthest north I'd ever travelled, far away from home. I'd been dreaming about this moment all my life and now it was here, I was retrieving my father's body. It felt like a cruel and heartless joke.

'What's happened here?' asked Mamma, gazing out the window when we reached the western coast mid-morning.

'The Germans destroyed everything they could as they retreated,' said Gino. 'They laid land mines, blew up bridges and burnt villages and crops. Anyone who resisted them was shot and killed. There have been reprisal killings for actions against German soldiers.'

'This isn't war,' said Mamma, shaking her head. 'This is evil.'

'Once the Allies get to Roma, they have a good chance of ejecting the Germans and Mussolini's Fascist state,' said Gino confidently.

Mamma nodded, but held my hand tightly as we gazed silently out the window at the scarred landscape: burnt, blown up, excavated, the vegetation hacked and chopped down. Ditches had been dug across fields, mounds of dirt spewed across the ground where, Gino explained, mines had exploded. Crops were burnt and orchards and olive groves stripped and cut down so nothing could be harvested or salvaged. Only the bare blackened earth and the pale trunks were left. Charred remains of villages seemed hauntingly empty, fresh mounds of earth marking the graves of the fallen. It was like a scene out of Dante's *Inferno*. No – it was hell on earth.

It was a long drive, made longer by the many detours we had to make to navigate around partially destroyed roads. Surrounded by the evidence of war, Mamma and I sat in a stupor for most of the afternoon until we finally made our way into Napoli well after dark. At the checkpoint, the driver showed the Allied soldier our papers and we were allowed to enter the city. One of Don Silvio's sisters was taking us in for the night. It was too late to go to the mortuary.

We were stiff, sore and exhausted, and Antonella welcomed us with open arms, making us a hot tea while we sat in her kitchen. 'Thank goodness my brother sent me more wood,' she said. 'There's no firewood anywhere, unless it's taken from homes and buildings that have been destroyed in the air raids. There's no electricity or running water, I'm afraid, but we've been fortunate to have our water carted in. The Germans destroyed the aqueducts, the electricity stations and the sewers before they left.' She shrugged. 'We make do even though the air raids continue, this time from the Germans. We're lucky to still have a roof over our heads – thousands don't. The Allies promise to have the city up and running as soon as possible, though.'

'What happens to those who have lost their homes?' I asked, pulling my jacket closed. I was cold after a long day in the car, my nerves taut. Knowing what we'd have to do tomorrow reminded me of the terrible days after the loss of Massimo. And it only heightened my anxiety for Stefano as well as for Mamma, who seemed small and fragile as glass. I didn't know how I'd cope if it was Stefano who had died. The reality was that, as long as this war continued, there was a high chance that I would lose him too.

'So many people have been living in the tunnels, caves and catacombs under the city. Even the underground train stations and Roman aqueducts were originally used as air raid shelters but when people have nowhere else to go . . . We're survivors here in Napoli.'

But it was only in the light of day, when we were taken to the hospital to view Papà's body, that Mamma and I were truly able to understand the devastation of the city. Among glimpses of ancient Roman structures and stately build-ings, I saw homes gutted and buildings surrounded by piles of rubble, some with only a couple of walls still standing.

Metal posts and balcony railings were twisted, while the shattered windows stared out at the world like vacant eyes. Roads, pathways, parkland and gardens were churned as though a giant plough had bulldozed carelessly through the city, leaving gaping wounds in its wake. People wandered through the streets looking dazed, while skinny, barefoot children mobbed small patrols of Allied soldiers, no doubt looking for something to eat.

Zia's magazines had shown me a Napoli that was an ancient but glittering city, a place where exotic influences from around the world converged, but the Napoli I saw was crippled and destroyed, its soul ripped from its body. I wondered how the Allies, still pouring into the city, would ever get this once vibrant metropolis functioning again.

Once we arrived at the hospital, I was unable to focus on anything but what was in front of us. Mamma and I clung to each other as we were ushered into a room to view the body.

The nun pulled back the sheet to reveal my father's face.

'Amore mio,' whispered Mamma. She seemed to collapse in on herself, as if something within her had broken. She'd hoped beyond hope that Don Silvio was wrong, that it wasn't Papà at all. The truth was – so had I. We had already lost so much.

I put my arm around her but she shrugged off my embrace and shuffled towards Papà's body, caressing his waxen face with a trembling hand.

'Goodbye, tesoro mio. Until we meet again.' She bent over and kissed his lips gently, as if she didn't want to wake him from his sleep.

Papà looked peaceful, as though he was in deep slumber, but I wondered about his last moments. Did he know he was going to die without seeing his family again? Or did he hope that the angels were watching over him as they had every time that he'd been in danger? Perhaps he hadn't thought about that at all, instead focusing on protecting the vulnerable. The nun had said that he'd died instantly, shot in the heart, and that he would have barely felt a thing. I supposed it was some consolation, and there were many men who would say that this was the perfect way to die. My father was a hero, there was no doubt, and if he'd had a choice, knowing the outcome, he would protect those people all over again. But now he was gone and his body seemed an empty vessel.

'Oh, Papà,' I whispered. I wanted nothing more than to curl up in a ball and nurse my pain. All the time we'd wasted fighting with each other, and for what?

But regret would not bring my father back and my mother needed me now. I wiped my tears away and moved to Mamma's side, holding her tight until she was ready to leave.

Mamma and I were walking down the corridor afterwards when I heard someone call my name.

'Giulia?'

I turned. 'Agata! You're here,' I said with a half-sob. I embraced her, glad to see a familiar face, and introduced her to Mamma, who continued a little way down the corridor to wait for me.

'I heard from Stefano that you were coming today and I hoped to catch you. It's been so long since I've seen you,' said Agata. 'I'm so sorry about your father. It was so frightening with the Germans here but your father and the other soldiers who stayed were our saviours. Your father and his unit were the ones who protected us from the wrath of the Germans as they retreated. Without their efforts, we would have been slaughtered and this hospital burnt to the ground.'

I nodded. 'He was always noble, protecting those in his care.'

'It's good to see you, if only briefly. I know this is a difficult time. I'm here if you need anything. God willing, I'll see you again before you leave.' She dipped her head in farewell to Mamma, turned down another corridor and was gone.

'She's just like you,' said Mamma, lifting her hand to brush a stray hair from my face. 'Dedicated, committed and wanting to help those less fortunate. You're angels in this dark and broken world of ours.'

'Oh, Mamma, I would never have been any of those things without you and Papà.' I hugged her.

'Your husband is here,' she whispered close to my ear. 'Go.'

The breath caught in my throat as I glanced down the bare corridor. Stefano was in his army uniform and broke out into a huge smile at the sight of me. I had never been happier to see him.

I ran until I was in his arms. 'I'm so glad you're here. I can't believe he's gone.'

He kissed my face and mouth, wet with tears. 'I'm so sorry, cara mia,' he murmured. 'Are you alright? Your mother? How is she?'

'As well as can be expected,' I said, wiping my eyes. 'And you?'

'I'm shaken but alright.'

I looked into his eyes and saw his own grief. He'd known my father since he was a small boy.

'Let's get this paperwork over with,' he said, taking my hand. 'You've both been through enough.'

Afterwards, we walked to where Papà and his comrades had been cut down by the Germans.

'It was here,' said the nun who guided us. 'There were terrible clashes on the streets between Napolitani and Germans.'

We were standing on an ordinary city street but the rust-coloured bloodstains on the road told another story. I shivered with horror. This was where my father had died. He had been shot in the chest, his blood spilling onto the ground as he lay there dying.

'What happened?' asked Mamma, clutching my hand tightly.

'The Germans advanced on the hospital, shooting dead those within their reach, but your husband and his men came and began firing, killing all but a few Germans. Everyone in the Bersaglieri unit was killed and the German soldiers who remained had the good sense to flee. Your husband and the others were brought into the hospital to be laid out with dignity. They were true heroes and patriots. They saved the hospital and the vulnerable people in it.'

'Thank you,' whispered Mamma, her hand shaking as she blotted the tears from her eyes with one of Papà's handkerchiefs. She placed the flowers we'd gathered on the pavement and bent her head in prayer, or conversation – I wasn't sure.

When she lifted her head, she seemed lighter. She leaned on me heavily for a moment before we walked back to the car.

I finally had a chance to see Stefano alone later that evening. He picked me up from Antonella's and took me to a little park nearby. Sitting on a blanket on the grassy slope, we looked out over Napoli and the crescent-shaped shore beyond.

'How are you?' he asked as we unpacked the basket of food Antonella had packed for us: stuffed pitta bread, fresh green-skinned figs and wine. It had been a long day and my stomach ached with hunger. Stefano reached out for my hand resting on my lap and kissed it. His eyes drew me in and I wished we were back home, having this conversation in bed. I wanted to tell him everything while I lay in his arms, where he could console me with his kisses.

'Honestly I don't know . . . So much has happened in such a short time. I've missed you so much.'

'I've missed you too,' he said, squeezing my hand. 'There have been so many times I wished you were by my side to talk through things and help me make important decisions.'

'We have all night,' I said softly. 'We don't leave until tomorrow evening.'

'Then tell me everything,' he said, opening the bottle of red wine.

We talked about what had happened while we'd been apart as we drank wine and ate the bread filled with plump, earthy mushrooms, creamy ricotta and soft, roasted capsicum in olive oil. The meal was delicious and satisfying in its simplicity.

'Don Silvio did the right thing by me in the end,' said Stefano, wiping fig juice from his chin and sucking his fingers clean. 'After we crossed from Messina to Calabria, I was given the name of a British contact. With news of the armistice, I was free to offer my services to the British 8th Army, who were desperate for extra medical staff at the Reggio field hospital. I worked there until I was placed in a medical support unit as we moved north towards Napoli. It was dreadful, some of the things we saw . . .' His eyes clouded with pain. 'How can human beings treat each other in this way?'

I touched his arm in sympathy. 'I know. Mamma and I saw the aftermath as we drove up, and Gino, our driver, told us what had happened.'

'I wish you'd never had to make this trip, even though I've never been so happy to see you.'

'I'm glad I've seen the devastation. I understand what's happening to our country so much more now. And here in Napoli – it's a disaster.' I shook my head with sorrow. Perhaps it was time for me to have the courage to step away from what was safe and comfortable and do the work I was meant to do. 'There's so much to do and not enough people to alleviate the suffering of the Napolitani. How can they return to a normal life when the city's destroyed?'

'The Allies have already begun to restore essential services and infrastructure. Napoli's an important port for them and many units will remain here to direct further services to Allied military divisions as they advance towards Rome. They have a responsibility to our people and want to help civilians, especially here in Napoli, to return to as normal a life as possible.'

'As they should, after they've bombed half the city,' I said bitterly, taking another swallow of wine. 'What will you do now? Will you stay with the unit?'

'I'm awaiting reassignment. Hospital sites are already being investigated around the district and when the final Allied units assemble in the city in the next few days, medical teams will be sent to various hospitals, ready to receive patients and casualties from the surrounding district and the front line.'

'Look!' I whispered. The sun began to set behind the sea, the sky aflame with colour. Reflected in the azure waters of the bay was the dark peak of Vesuvius. The sight was magical and at odds with the destruction we'd seen.

'It's beautiful. I wish we could be here under different circumstances.' He pulled me towards him and put his arm around me as the breeze whipped up from the sea.

'Do you think you'll stay in Napoli?' I murmured.

He shrugged. 'I don't know. The surge of cholera and typhus in the city is being attributed to the poor sanitation but with teams in place to re-establish fresh, running water and sewerage disposal, we expect the rates to fall. Many of the Allied soldiers have succumbed to malaria, probably those who haven't taken their preventative medication. I know Agata's here but we could use your help too. The provision of medical supplies and drugs has been disrupted because of the skirmishes with the Germans. Agata was telling me that herbalists such as yourselves are being consulted here more and more to find ways to substitute medicines and find alternative methods of treatment for patients.' He smiled wistfully. 'I wish you could stay.'

'I don't want to leave you again,' I whispered. 'After what happened to Papà . . .'

'I don't want us to be apart either but I don't know where I'll be.'

'You're here for now. Let's make the most of the time we have.'

'Well, if you're finished, Topolina, I want to take you somewhere a little more private so I can kiss you without everyone watching.'

Mamma and I were on our way to the hospital the following afternoon to pick up Papà's body when an enormous explosion a couple of blocks in front of us shook the car, vibrating the ground like an earthquake. Gino hit the brakes immediately, and the car stopped in the middle of the road.

'Are you alright?' he asked, turning to us. His face was pale but he tried to remain composed.

Mamma and I nodded, our hands clasped tightly.

'What was that?' asked Mamma in a strangled voice.

I watched out the window as the plume of black smoke spread out from the site of the explosion, obscuring our view and blotting out the sun. It was like the apocalypse had come.

'A bomb. Probably left by the Germans,' he said. 'There have been a few explosions in buildings since they retreated, but nothing quite like this.'

'What building was that?' I asked.

'The central post office.'

We stared in shocked silence for a moment as the reality of the situation hit us.

'I have to go and see if I can help,' I said, wrenched from my daze by the sounds of people crying out in pain.

Mamma grasped my hand tighter. 'No, don't be ridiculous. It's not safe.'

'I promise I'll be careful.'

'No, Giulia! Don't go. I can't lose you too.'

I hugged my mother tight. 'I won't be long.'

'Your daughter is right,' said Gino. 'We should see if we can lend a hand. I've seen explosions like this before and I'll make sure she stays safe.'

Before Mamma could say any more, I pulled my hand free and opened the car door. 'Wait here, Mamma. We'll be back soon.'

'Cover your mouth and nose,' Gino said to me, 'and stay close behind me. Hold onto my jacket if it gets too dark to see.'

He handed me his handkerchief, which I tied around my head, and together we walked quickly down the street. My stomach was churning with trepidation and dread, appalled by the burning pieces of the building scattered across the road and pavement as we moved closer. Putting an arm in front of my face as we entered the hazy gloom, I realised that the cobbled street was littered with debris and the corner of the post office building was completely blown away. Windows in the surrounding buildings had been blown out and I felt the glass crunch under my feet.

I stopped at the sight of people lying on the street, some partially buried under rubble, others lying at odd angles where they had fallen following the blast. Sounds of moaning mingled with short sharp screams but from others there was nothing but silence. I stared at the carnage around me as a man whose foot had been blown away tried to get up. A woman nearby had been decapitated. Children, men and women, both civilians and military, were everywhere, motionless and crumpled like marionettes. I heard more shouting and through the gloom, I saw men in uniform beginning to take charge of the situation.

I was taken back to that terrible day of the tidal wave, the horror and loss surging within me like it was only yesterday. I wanted to run in the opposite direction but I remembered how it felt to help the victims of that disaster and I forced my feet forward.

A woman came towards us out of the smoke, her clothes and skin burnt and charred. 'Help me,' she murmured, her arms outstretched.

I rushed towards her, Gino following closely. 'Here,' I said, ripping off my coat and putting it around her as she stumbled into my arms. 'It's alright now. You're safe and we'll take care of you.'

Her dark eyes looked up at me imploringly. 'My daughter, she's only five ... I was holding her hand before the explosion ... we were walking past ...'

'Where did you fall after the blast?' I asked gently.

She looked around in confusion, her eyes glazed. I didn't think she knew how injured she really was. 'There,' she said, struggling to lift her arm as she pointed.

'Stay with her,' Gino said. 'I'll see if I can find her daughter.'

I nodded, guiding the woman to the pavement and helping her to sit before she collapsed as I kept one eye on Gino across the street. He looked through the rubble, then dropped to his knees and began digging through the debris with his hands, throwing pieces to one side. I held my breath, keeping the barely conscious woman upright, then I saw Gino scoop up a small child and carry her back across the street to us.

'Is this your daughter?' he asked anxiously.

The woman gazed at the child slumped in his arms, covered in blood and dust. She nodded, her eyes filling with tears. 'That's my Angela,' she said tremulously. 'Is she dead?'

Gino shook his head. 'She moved. That's how I saw her and then she called out to you.'

The woman took the child's limp hand. 'Angela, it's Mamma. You're safe now. It will be alright.'

I felt for the girl's pulse; it was weak and irregular.

'We have to get them to a hospital,' I whispered to Gino.

'I know. Let's get them to the car. We're better off taking them than staying here.'

Gino got us to the hospital via the back streets while Mamma and I cradled the woman and child in the back seat. I was worried that we would lose them both but they hung on until hospital staff took them for emergency treatment. We told the nurses what we had seen and by their grim faces, I knew that the next few hours would be touch and go for many of the victims.

'Will that woman and her child make it?' asked Mamma.

'It's too early to tell,' said the nurse. 'But you've given them the best chance possible by bringing them in so soon. I fear that there will be many casualties amid those who won't make it to hospital early enough. We're going to be swamped.'

'Come, signora,' said Gino slowly. 'They're waiting for us in the mortuary and we must be on the road before dark.'

We were going to drive through the cool night to get Papà home for his funeral and burial.

Agata was waiting for us afterwards. 'I can't stay but I just wanted to say goodbye and wish you a safe journey,' she said to us.

'Thank you, Sister Agata,' said Mamma. 'I hope we see you again in better circumstances.'

'One day this war will be over,' she said, smiling wistfully. 'Until then, we'll all do what we can.' She hugged me tight. 'I'm sorry you can't stay. I'd like nothing more than to work side by side with you, at least for a little while.'

It was then that everything seemed to fall into place. This was where I was meant to be. I could do so much good here. This was the time for me to spread my wings and continue my own journey.

'No,' I said, drawing away. 'I'm not going anywhere. I'm going to stay and help.' I turned to Mamma. 'I have to do this. It's where I can do most good.'

Mamma nodded, tears in her eyes. 'Nonna told me this day would come, that you'd outgrown the village.' She took my hands in hers. 'It's fitting that you're here, close to your father, helping those he tried to protect. You honour his memory and he'd be so proud of you.'

'But what about you?' I asked. Now that I'd made the decision, as much as I felt free and was excited for the future, I still worried about my mother. She'd just lost her husband and I knew she'd be anxious with me away.

'You've said goodbye to your father already and I have your brother and sisters at home to help and support me through this time. You don't need to be at the funeral. And there's Stefano to think about. You're only just married. If it means the two of you can spend more time together, I'm happy. A husband and wife shouldn't be apart.' She hastily dabbed the tears that were gathering at the corners of her eyes with Papà's handkerchief. I could only imagine how difficult it had been for her to say those words.

I threw my arms around her. 'Thank you, Mamma.'

'I always knew that somehow you'd make a difference and light up this world,' she said. 'I'm so proud of the woman you've become.'

29

When Stefano came to see me at Antonella's after the post office explosion to wish us a safe trip home, I explained that I was staying in Napoli.

'I know that you want to stay and help but your family needs you and it's not the safest place to be,' he said gently, taking my hands in his.

'You won't change my mind, Stefano. You know this is what I want to do.'

'But is this the right time? You're grieving.' His face was creased with concern, the amber flecks in his eyes luminous against the dark smudges of exhaustion.

'I'm still alive, while my father and brother are dead,' I said. 'I won't waste another minute. I'm supposed to be here, I can feel it in my bones.' I took a breath. 'It's time to broaden my horizons and expand my skills. I know I can achieve so much more here. And I won't leave you again. I won't.' I touched his cheek.

He pulled me to him. 'And I don't want you to go. As long as this is what you want, I'm the happiest man in the world to have you here with me.'

Agata got me work at the sanitorium and I was fortunate to get a room at the nurses' quarters after she put in a good word for me.

The hospital was large and modern and I worked with Agata, making and using herbal medicines to treat patients in conjunction with the doctors and nurses. Agata had paved the way with her knowledge and when it became known that I was also a student of Fra Fortunato, it didn't take long for the medical staff to accept me and respect my skills.

'I'm glad I'm here to help,' I told Agata one day in the dispensary. 'But when I look around me at all the destruction and misery . . . The Napolitani are barely surviving.' I shrugged, feeling a little helpless. I was doing what I'd yearned to do for years and although it was satisfying to be helping, was it enough?

Agata touched my arm. 'I know this place can be overwhelming at first but just remember that every life you help save, every person's recovery you aid, makes a difference to them and their family.'

I nodded and sighed. 'You're right. We can't heal everyone but we help as many as we can.'

Not even a week later, on 13th October, 1943, the Badoglio government finally declared war on Germany.

'Can you believe it?' Agata shook her head as she pounded dried herbs in the dispensary. 'How long has it taken?'

'I know. Italians have been siding with the Allies for weeks now, but at least there's no longer any confusion about what side they should be on,' I said.

'I suppose this allows the Italian army to formally join ranks with the Allies. I'd imagine that Stefano will be happy to be assigned to a specific unit but I know that you want him close for a little longer.'

I closed my eyes as I thought of how wonderful it would be for us to stay together in Napoli for a while. We'd hardly had any time together since being married. 'He's still a medical student but he's nearly qualified and I think he'll most likely continue to work at one of the hospitals here for a while. He's told me that the medical base of operations will be centred in Napoli at least until the Allies reach Roma.'

'I'm so pleased that you're finally happy.'

I nodded. 'I don't want to be parted from him again. Loss makes you realise what's most important.'

'Nobody knows what God has in store for us. We just have to make the most of every day.'

It was true. Life was a gift.

Within a few weeks, the Allies had set up medical facilities across the city and its outlying areas. The 300th General Hospital took up residency in one of the sanatorium buildings with the capacity for one thousand beds. The extra Allied support across the city made a difference to the morale of our Italian hospital staff and their patients; we all felt that Napoli's overwhelming medical problems finally had a chance to be overcome. As Agata had predicted, it wasn't long before I learnt to do what I could without overly worrying about all those I was unable to help outside of the hospital. I found I could work with more focus, clarity and purpose.

Stefano was placed in the 212th Division, an Italian auxiliary division assigned to the US 5th Army, and began working at a new hospital set up on the Mostra fairgrounds, overlooking the bay. He was living in the army barracks.

'We've set up in solid stone buildings and have water, electricity and sewerage facilities connected. There's even a good rail and road link to the port and the city,' he told me as we walked hand in hand through the large hillside park near the sanatorium. The view was magnificent from here, overlooking the sprawl below us, the sparkling blue waters of the Gulf of Napoli and across to the island of Capri. Mount Vesuvius sat benignly to our left. Napoli would have been a beautiful place if not for the war and the terrible scars that had been inflicted upon it. 'I've been promoted to captain and am working with an American surgical team – thanks to Don Silvio, I think. Although I'm only performing minor procedures at this stage, I'm observing larger surgeries and I hope that soon, as I prove myself, I'll be allowed to do more.'

'How long do you think you'll be there?' Luckily for me there was still plenty of work at the sanatorium to keep me busy, but I wondered if that would continue as Allied medical drugs and supplies became available once more. Agata had her specialised nursing skills and she had been a long-time staff member at the sanatorium, but I wasn't sure how long they would need me.

'It's hard to say, maybe until other hospitals are established closer to the front line, or maybe I'll be here the duration of the war. It's such a fluid situation.'

But the reality that we were very much still in a war zone hit with frightening precision the following evening. I'd cycled down to meet Stefano after his shift for a quick tour of the hospital and its facilities and it was dusk by the time he'd finished showing me around the fairground complex. Then the air raid siren sounded.

'Come on,' yelled Stefano, grasping my hand. 'We have to go to the bunker.'

Already we could hear the drone of Luftwaffe planes hurtling towards us. We ran, following the military and medical staff between the buildings. My heart was pounding in my chest and I wanted to scream with the visceral fear that was rising within me but besides the shouting of the air-raid marshals, guiding people to the shelters, everyone moved quietly. The air seemed to thicken and vibrate as the thrumming rushed towards us. I was sure that my innards had turned to water.

'Faster,' urged Stefano, looking up at the sky. I followed his gaze and saw the ominous dark spots against the violet, like a flock of menacing birds. I clutched his arm in terror as they materialised into bombers, sure I even saw the Nazi emblem on their tails.

The first bombs fell with an eerie whistling before we reached the shelter, shaking the ground violently. I screamed, disoriented, somehow transported to the earthquake in Brancaleone. My ears were ringing and I couldn't hear what Stefano was saying so I held his hand tighter and ran. Whistling signalled another round of bombs. This time they hit the fairground, the blast throwing me to the earth. I lay there stunned for a moment, my vision obscured by a veil of mist, and I panicked. A rush of energy filled my body and I jumped to my feet, glancing wildly about as I tried to get my bearings.

'Stefano!' I screamed. The acrid smell of smoke billowing through the air clung to my nostrils and I put my sleeve over my mouth and nose. I could make out vague shapes through the haze, and the shouting and crying seemed muted, as if I was suspended in time, distanced from the terrible reality. I followed the movement, stumbling through the fog, tripping over debris, hoping that it would bring me closer to Stefano, the shelter and safety.

Then hands clutched me.

'Giulia! Are you alright?'

'Stefano! I couldn't find you . . .' I hiccoughed.

'Come on. The shelter's just around the corner.'

Torchlight appeared through the gloom like a beacon of hope and, holding each other tight, we followed it to reach the safety of the bomb shelter.

'That was close!' whispered Stefano as the door closed behind us.

I blinked, blinded by the naked lights that hung from the ceiling as he led me past the press of people, many pale faced with shock, to a wooden bench. He pulled me to him then, put his arms around me and held me as I trembled.

'Are you alright?' he asked. His face was smudged with dirt. 'Are you hurt?'

I shook my head. 'Are you?' I touched his face, his arms and chest and legs. 'You're alright.' I sighed. 'I've never been in an air raid before—' The walls shuddered as another barrage hit, dirt and dust dislodging from the walls, doorway and roof. I grasped Stefano's hand, my eyes wide with fear. 'Are they getting closer?'

'I don't think so ... I think further away.' He touched my neck. 'You're bleeding.' He gazed at the blood on his fingers.

I put my hand to the side of my neck and frowned. The collar of my dress was wet.

'Let me see,' he said, using his doctor's voice.

I could feel the tension in his body and suddenly I was worried. He lifted my hair and wiped the blood with his handkerchief, feeling around the edge of the wound.

'Does it hurt?' he asked.

'No.'

'It's just a laceration, not too deep. Get Agata to put something on it when you get back to the hospital.'

Suddenly the horrible reality of our situation hit me. 'What would I have done if something had happened to you?'

He put his arm around me again, as if to protect me from all the ugliness of war. 'I can't predict what will happen to either of us,' he said softly, 'but we're safe for now. I know it's not the perfect life but we're making a difference and doing what we love. Every day I have with you, Topolina, is a gift.'

I cupped his cheek, touched by his honesty. 'If you can face the horrors of this war, then so can I. All I want is you by my side while we do what we can to bring healing to our ravaged land.'

30

Despite the best attempts of the Allies to bring the city to some kind of order, cases of typhus continued to soar. Napoli was in utter chaos. With so many homeless after the air raids, people had resorted to living in the ruins of buildings or crammed into the caves and caverns under the city. Without power, sanitation or fresh water, it was no wonder that infectious diseases like typhus were on the rise. The disease was carried by lice, which lived on clothing and bedding, so the Allies set up dusting stations across the city, trying to kill the lice and control the epidemic.

Agata and I were instructed in dusting people all over with DDT insecticide powder. She was asked to work within the hospital complex with other nurses while I was seconded to help local civilian doctors and nurses to man stations within the city.

'This is much easier than visiting the caves and cata-combs,' said one of the doctors I was working with as we walked towards a station set up outside a block of bombed-out buildings that many were still living in. 'It's dark and there's no ventilation and it stinks like sewerage and death, because people are dying of the disease and haven't been moved from those who are still healthy.'

An Allied truck lumbered past and pulled up in the piazza. Soldiers jumped out, ready to unload the supplies from the back. People appeared from buildings, doorways and alleyways and crowded around the truck. The soldiers yelled for them to remain calm but the crowd surged, pushing and shoving.

We stopped on the edge of the piazza, unable to get through. 'What are they doing?' I asked the doctor.

'The Allies bring regular supplies to the orphanage here: tins, flour, rice, chocolate. Often there are leftover packs and people are so desperate they'll fight to get anything they can.'

'I can't believe how bad things are here.'

The doctor nodded. 'People are hungry. The Germans destroyed crops and food stores as they moved through the district, air raids have damaged the city, supply ships haven't been able to dock and trains and roads from the north have been blocked. I can't begin to tell you how many patients I've seen with malnutrition, whose illnesses would improve or even disappear if they had an adequate diet. One woman told me that she and her friends stole tropical fish from the aquarium so they could eat.'

A few men and women edged closer and one of the soldiers stepped towards them menacingly, but I noticed young boys, street urchins, sneak around the side of the truck. One boy climbed over the edge and then an arm shot over the side, dropping tins, packets of cigarettes and chocolate bars to the boys below, before sliding back onto the ground and melting into the crowd.

'Did you see that? They're just children.'

The doctor shrugged. 'It happens all the time. It's survival. Many of them have lost their parents or been separated from them. Here they band together and form gangs that look after one another. Whatever they don't eat, they'll sell on the black market. The Allies' arrival has made Napoli one of the biggest supply ports in the world. Nothing much happens without the black market in Napoli and most of it is stolen military supplies. Cigarettes are common currency but even tyres and army vehicles are stolen and sold.'

'But who buys it all? Who can afford it?'

'Makeshift stalls are set up around the city all the time, selling army clothing, shoes, watches, ration packs, anything at all really, until the local or Allied military police shut them down. It's surprising how quickly the items sell.' He leaned towards me. 'But the big items move through the hands of army deserters, bandits, corrupt officials, desperate local workers employed by the Allies and of course the big dealers of organised crime, the Camorra. Nothing goes unnoticed by them.'

There was a shout from the crowd as a scuffle broke out.

'That's mine,' screamed a high-pitched voice. It was one of the boys. A large man was trying to take the tins out of his grasp and once the people around him realised what was going on, they joined the commotion, scrabbling for the food. Punches were thrown, men and women alike wrestling each other to the cobblestones. Children were in danger of being trampled on, all for a couple of tins of preserved food.

'Come on,' said the doctor, taking my arm. 'It's not safe here.'

'But what about those children?'

He shook his head. 'The soldiers will put an end to it.'

'How?'

'They'll either throw more rations into the crowd or just drive away. What else can they do? They're not like the Germans, who would have fired into the crowd to disperse them.'

I couldn't help but look behind at the screaming, fighting crowd as the doctor drew me along.

'I'm sorry but we have to go another way now.'

I frowned. 'Why are you sorry? You couldn't help what's going on here.'

'No – we have to pass the women by the wall.'

We turned the corner. Rows of women stood against the walls of the buildings lining the walkway. They looked like ordinary women. Then I noticed the small piles of tins beside them.

'What are they doing here?' I whispered.

The doctor urged me along. 'We have to go. We're already late.'

It was only as we began to walk past that I realised what was happening. A soldier, leaning against the wall with his trousers down, was thrusting furiously, the white of his buttocks flashing from beneath the khaki of his uniform. The woman beneath him stood still as a statue, her face blank. I raised my hand to my mouth in horror.

'They don't want your pity,' whispered the doctor as he walked faster. 'This might be morally reprehensible in normal times but they have more chance of receiving food this way than waiting for supply trucks to stop.'

I kept my eyes down and my own face blank as we walked, using all my willpower not to show my distress. At the end, as I looked behind me one last time, I shivered at the knowledge that it was only luck that kept our fates from being switched. The realisation slid through me like a cold, slithering snake, settling heavy in my belly.

'Scusa,' said a child's voice from the pavement.

I turned to find a boy of about ten plucking at the doctor's sleeve. Soulful brown eyes stared out plaintively from a filthy angular face beneath matted dark hair. Pitifully thin legs poked out of trousers that were too small for him. I wanted to scoop him up and take him home for a bath and a good meal.

'You want young, beautiful girl, not dry, old woman,' he said, gesturing to the women in the alleyway. 'My sister will make sweet music with you. She's thirteen, nice and young.'

'Go away,' said the doctor, pulling his arm free.

'You don't like girls? What about boys? I'll suck you off for a good price.'

'I said no.' The doctor reached into his pocket and pulled a few cigarettes from a packet. 'Here, take these and go and get yourself something to eat.'

The boy stared for a second, vulnerable almost, and then snatched the cigarettes. He pulled a postcard from his shirt pocket. 'I'm not a thief or a beggar.' He smiled and handed me the card. 'A fair exchange.'

'No, she doesn't want it,' said the doctor, but the boy was gone.

I stared down the street in confusion. The world I knew was upside down. Somehow there was honour and pride in the boy's transaction, despite the seedy and adult nature of it. But how could such concepts even be within the understanding of a child? Surely he didn't mean what he said?

'Give that to me,' the doctor said hurriedly.

I looked down at the card and gasped. I didn't think I was any prude but I'd never seen anything like it before. A picture of a man and woman, both naked, involved in an act of intimacy. But I couldn't look away.

The doctor plucked the postcard from my hand, screwed it up and shoved it into his pocket. 'I'm so very sorry that you had to witness such sordid dealings, but many Napolitani now have to make a living any way they can and with all the soldiers in the city, sex sells. Even children have learnt that they too can survive using this terrible trade.'

'What world have we stepped into where a child's survival comes before his safety?' I murmured. 'What has this war done to our children?'

'Welcome to Napoli,' said the doctor grimly. 'You've arrived in hell on earth.'

By February 1944, my time with Stefano in Napoli was over: he was reassigned to a hospital near Caserta, twenty-three miles north-west of Napoli and forty miles south of heavy fighting with the Germans.

'The patients from the battalion aid stations further north come to the hospitals in Caserta for additional treatment and surgeries but they need more medical staff,' said Stefano as we ate fish from a vendor on the pier. 'The casualty rate north of the Volturno River and along the Winter Line has been higher than expected.' The Winter Line was a series of German fortifications designed to prevent the Allies from reaching Roma. He shook his head in frustration. 'Any hopes we had of a quick victory with the liberation of Roma have gone. It's going to be a slow, hard slog through the mountain passes.'

'When do you have to go?'

'In a few days.' He caressed my cheek. 'I'll try to come back to see you in Napoli as often as I can.'

I stared out over the white-capped waves of the bay. 'I could come with you and help the partisans.' The partisans were Italian men from disbanded regiments or who had refused to be drafted. They had banded together to fight the Fascists, but had little support from the army and even less medical help. 'I can offer them the services of a healer.'

'But you have a job here that you love and where you're needed. I'll be in army barracks and we wouldn't be able to stay together.'

'Things have changed. The sanatorium has the support of the 300th General Hospital now. Agata doesn't need my help anymore and she always has her nursing if her herbal skills aren't required. What will I do? I have no qualifications the Allies would accept. They don't need herbs when they have a good supply of their medicines.'

Stefano nodded, his brows knitted in thought. 'That won't always be the case closer to the front line ...'

I dropped my piece of fish back onto the paper it had been wrapped in. 'Then it's settled. The partisans ... that's where I can make the most difference. I could look after their medical needs, extend my skills treating battle injuries. I'd be someone they can trust. Most will have only ever seen a healer and not a doctor. Perhaps you and I can even liaise if there's a case that requires medical drugs or surgical intervention.' I squeezed his hand with anticipation. 'We could work together like we always wanted.'

'I'll put you in touch with the commander of the partisan camp close to the new hospital I've been assigned to,' Stefano said, giving in to the avalanche of my excitement. 'If you're close by and I can see you every day, I'd feel a lot better about it. I'll also speak to the surgeons I work with – I'm sure they'll unofficially support anything I feel we need to do to help the partisans.' He wrapped his arms around me and kissed me heartily. 'This could actually work.'

My heart rose in my throat as the hope that we'd be able to stay together and finally work together flared. Everything seemed to fall into place. Here was the opportunity to become the healer I'd always dreamed of becoming. My first days at the monastery, my time working with Nonna, that terrible day of the tidal wave and the bombings in Napoli, all these experiences had led me to this point. It was my destiny and always had been.

31

I peered into the gloom as I did at every daybreak, trying to make out the shapes of the wounded as they were brought in from the battlefield. I'd been at the partisan camp near Caserta for a few weeks, but there had been no time to adjust to the horrors that came with every morning or the screams and moans of pain I was expected to soothe. None of that mattered because I was all they had and there was no choice but to pull on every last resource and bit of strength I had within me to do my very best for these soldiers.

The Allies' progress through the mountain passes was glacial, with back-and-forth clashes with the Germans. There was still snow on the ground and it was freezing, yet it seemed like the rain would never stop. If it continued, it would cause further trouble with mud and swollen rivers. The roads required continuous maintenance by the Allies but the knee-deep mud prevented vehicles travelling along the steep mountain passes. Stretcher bearers were employed to retrieve the wounded and bring them out of the battle zones, up and down steep and slippery slopes at night. Mules became the preferred method of transport for supplies, ammunition and the dead.

I heard a muffled shout, and the muleteers materialised through the mist, leading mules burdened with the dead and injured. It was my job to be there when the men returned, to see who could be saved and who was beyond any help at all.

'Quickly now,' I called urgently to the men in camp who came running to help. 'It's been a bad night. Let's get them onto stretchers.'

The morning passed in a blur as I assessed the incoming cases and prioritised the most urgent. Men screamed in agony as I peeled away clothes, blood from their wounds blending with layers of mud. I had to tend the bullet and shrapnel injuries that needed urgent surgery first, applying whatever first aid measures I could before sending a messenger for Stefano. I remained calm, steadily dealing with the patients in front of me. I had to stay focused to do my best to minimise the consequences for the patient, both physical and emotional.

'Mannaggia! Press here,' I said urgently to one of the partisan helpers. 'I have to tie the tourniquet tighter on his thigh.' The muddy man on the camp bed groaned as the blood soaked through the bandage on his leg and welled between my fingers. My assistant nodded and applied pressure to the wound while I moved the tourniquet a little higher and pulled it tight.

'That's better,' I said as the flow started to ebb. I cut the sodden bandage away and shivered at the torn flesh beneath.

The white bone showed through the skin and muscle. As far as I could tell, the bone hadn't shattered but fragments of shrapnel were buried in his leg. I hadn't yet got used to the terrible injuries or how humans could harm each other with such savagery, how a small piece of metal could inflict so much damage on a body. I didn't think I ever would. 'You'll need surgery,' I said softly, 'but first we have to stop the bleeding and prevent infection.'

The man stared at me, glassy eyed with pain, and I wasn't sure how much he'd heard or understood.

I patted his arm and smiled. 'Let's get you better.'

It was well into the afternoon before I had a chance to see those with less serious injuries, though 'less serious' was a matter of perspective, because even these injuries could become life threatening if left untreated. But at least I could take a breath, gather my thoughts and steel my resolve once more. And the sweet hit of energy from the American chocolate bars Stefano sent helped me to keep going when I was dead on my feet. This work took a lot more courage and strength to deal with than my work in Napoli.

'Trench foot is common in this weather,' I told a young partisan as he lay groaning on a stretcher. The condition could lead to gangrene; I'd seen it too many times during flood season, when villagers walked for days in wet shoes. The skin under the wet parts of his muddy clothing was white and wrinkled, and as I finished peeling off his wet socks, the overpowering smell of rotting tissue made me want to gag. I swallowed convulsively, willing myself to quell the urge to vomit. His feet were blue and mottled red in parts, with blisters and open sores on his toes and the bottoms of his feet.

'Can you help me?'

I nodded. 'Provided you do as I ask, I think you've got a good chance at recovery.'

'Anything, I'll do anything,' he said, grasping my arm.

'You have to change your socks every chance you get,' I said, pouring water into a foot bath. 'And you need new boots. You have to keep your feet as dry and warm as possible.'

'I thought I have to keep my feet dry,' said the man, looking perplexed as I placed his feet into the bucket.

'This is to clean your feet and help heal them,' I said soothingly. I was using herbs with antibiotic and antifungal qualities, some externally in the water and others to be taken as a tincture. 'I'll make up a bottle of herbs for you to take every day to help with healing and give you some eucalyptus oil to massage into your feet to keep infection at bay.'

'I'm glad I'm here even with my feet like this. It's nice to be warm and dry for a change,' he said, gesturing to the mountains beyond the partisan camp. Well hidden by the scrubby evergreen of the holm oak, acacia and strawberry trees, tents were scattered around the small opening of a large cave that gave the camp some protection from the weather. It was here that the leaders of the partisan group met, where meals were taken and those who were unwell or injured rested.

'I couldn't agree with you more,' I said, taking one foot out of the water and gently patting it dry.

'You don't understand. The Germans will do anything to prevent us from breaching the Winter Line. Their defences are layer upon layer: minefields, pastures of fire, trip wires, barbed wire, ambushes from defensive positions in hidden caves – it goes on and on. We even have to herd goats in front of us across mountain pastures and passes in case of land mines. It's slow going and not a pretty sight when they set one off, but better the goats than us.'

With the aid of the coded messages broadcast on Radio Londra, the partisans conducted smaller skirmishes around the German lines and even made reconnaissance trips through the Winter Line – the fortifications the Germans had built to stop the Allies reaching Roma – but their casualty rate was high.

'Let's hope the stalemate breaks soon and we're on our way to Roma,' I said, gently drying the other foot.

Antonio had arrived in the camp as I thought he might, with Signora Lipari's son. I was sure that Antonio believed that he was looking out for me but after losing Vincenzo and Papà, I felt it was my responsibility to look after him. I wrote to Mamma and Paola to tell them we were together and that I'd keep an eye on him.

I'd often have Stefano and Antonio over for dinner at the tiny cottage close to the station hospital in Piana di Caiazzo that I shared with the wife of one of the senior partisans and the Italian girlfriend of an Allied surgeon. It was rare to have time alone, especially over dinner, and I craved some normalcy with Stefano.

It was a miracle, then, to have the cottage to myself one night a couple of weeks after Antonio's arrival. Stefano had been able to swap shifts with another young medic to spend the night with me. We'd decided to have a belated anniversary dinner – we'd been married a year now.

It was the 21st March, 1944, and my two housemates and their men had gone to Napoli to view the eruption of Mount Vesuvius. The volcano had been smoking and rumbling for some time and had finally exploded, filling the air with ash and smoke. From what we'd heard from the Allies, villages nearby had been engulfed by lava flows while others were burning from flying embers. Even American aircraft based at the Pompeii airfield were damaged by the falling rock and ash.

'How are you finding things?' I asked, pouring wine. There was still wine to be found, but the quality was never guaranteed. At least it softened the frayed edges we were beginning to feel after weeks of fighting at an impasse.

'I'm so sick of the American rations,' Stefano said, gazing at the simple meal I'd made, 'they're stodgy, not like our food at all, but I'd even eat those just to have you here like this, all to myself.' With the long days we worked, we'd both adjusted to the American custom of a main meal at night. I found it hard to get used to, too heavy on the stomach before bed, but it was what we had to do. At least we weren't going hungry.

'Well, lucky I'm your wife now and I can look after you,' I said smiling back at him. 'And your new job?' Stefano had finally been included on the surgical team.

'It's exhausting and sometimes it's hard to keep track of all the patients, they seem to roll through like a factory conveyor belt. But I'm learning how we can best help many of these men. The Americans have come a long way with wound management since my injury.' He tapped his thigh.

The silver lining of this war was that it was pushing the boundaries of science and technology. New understanding of the way the body worked allowed advances in techniques and development of drugs like penicillin, which had revolutionised medical treatment. It was an exciting time to be a healer – I had so much knowledge at my fingertips. I was determined that when this was all over, I would pass on what I'd learnt to other healers like Nonna, Agata and Fra Fortunato. I was intrigued to see how using modern medicine with traditional healing could produce a better outcome.

Stefano nodded, swallowing his mouthful. 'It's as much about timing, from the assessment and first aid treatment of the injury, as it is about surgery. Everything has to happen within ten days.'

'Despite the terrible conditions,' I murmured, thinking of the muleteers and the stretcher bearers. They were the true heroes who allowed these injured soldiers a chance at survival and recovery. I made a mental note to ensure I cleaned wounds as best I could and used herbs that fought infection every time. 'Who would ever have thought that we'd be doing this? It's a blessing to be helping our soldiers.'

'It is,' said Stefano. 'We just have to beat these bloody Nazis now, so that I can take you home and we can do this every evening.'

I took his hand. 'Come on then, let's make the most of this night.'

The next couple of months were drawn out with periods of inactivity and lassitude interspersed with intense fighting, both for the Allies and partisans. It gave me time to write to everyone at home. Zia wrote to say that she only occasionally

saw Don Silvio now, but that she didn't mind, because she
knew he was away doing good for the people of Italy. But I
could read between the lines that she was heartbroken.
I wondered what had happened between them.

Paola also replied to my letter.

Nothing much has changed here at home. Everyone contin-
ues to struggle to make a living, although we've heard about
villages all over Calabria rising up against the government offi-
cials. They're sick of outsiders telling them what they can do.
They want more land and to rule themselves as they did in the
old days. It's funny, because I've been thinking for quite a while
about buying a plot on the river flats closer to the coast, when
we can afford it. I'd like to plant it with crops, probably wheat
as it pays the best. It should give us another reliable source of
income. As much as I'd like to demand the land for our use, I'll
do it the proper way and buy it so we have no problems when
the authorities decide to demand it back!

I'm glad that you're doing the work you love. We all miss
you here but we're proud that you're helping our brave men.
Remember to keep an eye on Antonio. Mamma says the rosary
daily now and prays that you both remain safe.

I missed Paola like an ache in my heart but it was Agata
I could confide in, who could best understand what I was
doing here.

The work is relentless, I wrote to her.

But I feel like I'm doing some good here. Antonio has come
to join the partisans but during the periods of fighting, my

anxiety grows. Every time Antonio leaves on a reconnaissance mission or a battle, I worry that it will be the last time I'll see him. I've developed a wheeze and cough, which Stefano blames on the constant wet and cold. He begs me to slow down but I know it's my fear. My breathing is always worse before Antonio leaves, or on the eve of a battle. The only relief I've found is the treatment you told me worked for you all those years ago, inhaling steam from under a tea-towel tent. Thankfully my symptoms always subside once I know that my brother has returned safely.

The first time Antonio had left to go on a mission I'd begged him to stay safe.

'I promised Mamma that I'd look after you out here. She couldn't take it if we lost you too, and neither could I.' Tears had welled in my eyes. I didn't want to face any more loss.

Antonio had cupped my face as though I was the younger one and brushed the tears away. 'Nothing's going to happen to me,' he said softly, his brown eyes clear and bright.

'Promise me. Promise on Vincenzo and Papà that you'll make it back safely.'

He had blinked with shock and nodded slowly, putting his hand over his heart. 'I promise on the souls of Vincenzo and Papà to stay safe and come back to you in one piece.'

Each time Antonio returned unscathed, I felt like a weight had been lifted from my shoulders. But then came the periods of waiting, dangerous times when morale fell terribly low and battle fatigue set in. While men played cards and tried to find ways to occupy their time between skirmishes, Antonio and I tried to lift spirits in the camp, organising sing-a-longs, talent quests and comedy sketches. Antonio's impression of Mussolini with his overblown rhetoric, bullish face and enormous paunch was uncanny. As for Hitler – I couldn't stop laughing. I discovered Antonio had a sharp wit and talent for humour. He reminded me so much of Vincenzo.

But the best time of all was when we'd reminisce on our childhood.

'Do you remember when you came back from the monastery and our neighbour Pietro blurted out that I'd ridden the ram across the field?' he said one afternoon as we sat around the campfire.

'Yes,' I said, nodding. 'Papà was furious.'

'Well, that wasn't the half of it. I'd arranged a race with the shepherd boy on the next farm, to see whose ram was faster. We raced and my ram won. But at the end of it, both rams were panting, their eyes bulging out of their heads, and I thought they were going to die.'

As he talked, his brown eyes expressive, his hands flashing quickly, a warm glow filled me. I was never close to him when we were children but now that we were grown up, I realised that we were a lot alike, passionate and wanting to live life fully and without apology, especially now that we'd lost so much. I was grateful for this gift of time with my brother, and the chance to get to know him better. The friendship that was developing between us brought me much comfort.

'I would have been in so much trouble, it doesn't bear thinking about! Papà would have belted me until I was black and blue. But, thank the Madonna, both rams came good and we were safe. For a whole week, the boy gave me the biscotti his mother had made for him as my prize and it was the best biscotti I ever had, knowing how close we'd both come to disaster.'

'You were lucky,' I said, laughing. 'The Madonna was definitely smiling on you.' I just prayed that she continued to smile on us all.

It was mid-May before the battle at Monte Cassino was won. Stefano arrived at the cottage by jeep early on the 18th while I was still checking supplies in readiness to receive more casualties at the partisan camp.

'What are you doing here?' I asked.

'The Germans have surrendered. The abbey is finally ours.'

'The battle's over?' I asked, looking at him properly. His shoulders were slumped with exhaustion but his face was alight with excitement.

He nodded. 'It's the breakthrough we were waiting for.'

'There'll be plenty of relieved commanders and generals out there,' I said, closing my bag.

'Surgeons too. The growing casualty list with no real advance in the Allied position was starting to get everyone down.'

I cupped his cheek, rough with stubble. 'I'd expect you to be celebrating with your unit or sleeping. You're dead on your feet.'

He shrugged. 'They need extra medical staff at the field hospital in Cassino. I'm going up now to lend a hand and I wondered if you wanted to come? Partisan units will be there and they would benefit from your immediate attention.'

I'd have men to tend to here but Antonio was at Cassino and it would be sometime before the injured men made it back to the camp. 'Alright. As long as you can get me back to camp afterwards. I have to know if Antonio is safe.'

Stefano nodded. 'I know. We can look for your brother while helping to bring the wounded down to the field hospital.'

I put my arm around him and kissed his cheek. 'Grazie, caro mio. I can't tell you how much this means to me.'

We drove through Cassino. It was a ghost town, rubble from destroyed buildings scattered through the streets. We'd been told that the locals now lived in caves dotted along through the hills.

Although I'd been told by many men about the battles, it was still a shock to transition from beautiful glades of trees to burned forest and shelled sections of mountainside as we approached the battleground. The slopes were scarred by craters punctuated with scraps of clothing, helmets and guns lying nearby. Piles of ammunition lay in fields ploughed by tanks whose silent guns pointed towards the monastery on top of the mountain. Companies of soldiers, either crying with joy or dazed with exhaustion and covered in mud and dirt so it was hard to see what uniform they wore, passed us on the road, while others lay where they had fallen. The stench of death permeated the air.

I put a shaky hand to my mouth. I couldn't believe my eyes when I noticed carpets of red poppies on the hillsides that remained. I wasn't sure whether to laugh or cry.

We enquired after Antonio's unit but it was chaotic and difficult to know where anyone was. We continued towards the monastery, guided by the white flag fluttering in the breeze above the great fortress now reduced to ruins.

The monastery was swarming with military personnel and war correspondents. We were directed to see a certain commander and Stefano and I walked through the grounds carefully, stepping around toppled walls and fractured ceilings, the magnificent frescos still evident on pieces of plaster. Sculptures lay smashed and broken on the ground, pages of books fluttered in the wind and artworks had been ripped and broken then scattered across the courtyard. This was an ancient place of learning but even the distinguished library was gone. The abbey would never be the same again. Like in Napoli, hundreds of years of history and culture had disappeared, never to be recovered.

'Careful,' Stefano barked, pulling me back as I was about to step around a fallen bell. He gestured next to the bell. 'An unexploded shell.'

I sucked in my breath and backed away.

'Here, take my hand and follow in my footsteps,' he murmured.

I nodded and clasped his hand for dear life.

The commander was in a long hallway lined with dressers. I'd seen drawers like this at my monastery, used for holding ceremonial and liturgical robes. 'Can I help you?' he asked with a frown.

As we walked closer, the smell of decay became over-powering and I gagged. It was then that I realised that some of the opened drawers were stuffed with corpses and for a moment I found it hard to breathe, wondering if these were the missing partisans, if Antonio was lying here.

The officer saw my horrified glance. 'The Germans had no chance to bury their dead during the fighting,' he said with regret. 'It was the best they could do.'

I nodded, taking short, sharp breaths but still transfixed by the gruesome find.

'What can I do for you?'

I heard Stefano talking but couldn't make sense of the words. I knew these makeshift caskets were meant as a kindness but all I could see was the lost dignity of a human life. Each of these men was somebody's son, father or brother. How could their families ever know about the grisly end these soldiers had met so far from home? They never could of course. I wondered briefly about Vincenzo far away in Africa and how his body had been treated but I pushed that thought away immediately. It was too painful to contemplate.

It wasn't until we were driving back down the mountain that I found my voice again. 'Have you heard anything?'

'Antonio's unit was never at the monastery. It was a Polish patrol who reached the abbey early this morning.'

I stared out the window, overwhelmed by the task of trying to find Antonio. He could be anywhere; he could be back at the camp for all I knew, which is where I should have been. But he could also be lying injured in a ditch. The vision of those bodies crammed into the drawers fuelled my search.

Stefano hit the brakes and stopped the jeep in the middle of the road. Columns of men continued to walk past us, unconcerned with our sudden halt. 'Is that him?' he asked, peering through the windscreen.

I followed his gaze, my eyes coming to rest on the back of a dark-haired head. 'Antonio?' I yelled.

The man kept walking.

I jumped out of the jeep and ran towards him. 'Antonio?'

The man turned this time. It was my brother and I ran straight into his arms, sobbing.

'Giulia! What are you doing here?'

'I came to find you but nobody knew where you were.'

He kissed my forehead. 'Of course not. Nobody was meant to know where we were. But I'm here now.'

'Are you alright?' I touched his face, arms and torso, relieved that he seemed unhurt.

'I'm fine. I told you not to worry about me.' He looked at the jeep and waved to Stefano. 'And all our men have made it back alive. There'll be some casualties but nothing you can't handle,' he said. 'Come on then, let's go and celebrate this hard-earned victory.'

32

Two and a half weeks later, in early June 1944, the first Allied troops entered Roma.

'It was incredible,' said Antonio when Stefano and I arrived. We were sitting on the steps by the Trevi Fountain and part of me couldn't believe that I was finally seeing the ancient city. 'It was like being a famous movie star. The crowds lined the streets as we entered the city, all dressed in their best church clothes. People were cheering and crying with joy, throwing kisses and flowers. Roma was ready to be liberated and we were hot property! It's such a shame that news of the Allied invasion of Normandy took the spotlight off our achievement, but I don't think that the locals minded too much. There were wild celebrations and parties and lots of grateful girls.'

It was easy to forget that the war was raging outside of Italy and across Europe. Although the Nazis had occupied Hungary, the Russians were pushing the Germans back on the Eastern Front while the Allies were heavily bombing cities in Germany. Surely now that Germany was fighting its war on three fronts it couldn't be long before it was defeated? Even in the Pacific, the war was turning against Japan after its invasion of India failed.

'Grateful girls?' I said, smiling.

'The women here are gorgeous, elegant, worldly and throwing themselves at us – bellissima! I've certainly learnt a thing or two since being here.'

'Be careful,' I said with a frown. 'Syphilis and sexual diseases were a real problem after the soldiers arrived in Napoli and I'm sure it will be the same here.'

Antonio nodded. 'Don't worry. I take care.' He peered into my face with concern. 'But you understand, don't you? This victory has cost so much. The months of fighting . . . sometimes you wished you were dead with the things you'd seen and done, things you can't forget. Everything comes down to base instinct, fighting to stay alive. A few hours of joy helps you to remember what living is like, because life is precious but fleeting.'

'I know,' I said sadly, gazing out across the mythological Tritons and their horses. I couldn't begrudge my brother his few moments of joy when he was going again into danger.

'Are you alright?' he asked, resting his hand on my shoulder. 'You look tired and you've lost weight.'

'It's just my cough,' I said, shrugging. 'I'll be able to look after myself better now.' I'd decided to stay in Roma as long as Stefano was working here. He'd been transferred to another surgical unit attached to the new 12th General Hospital. It was a promotion of sorts, as the general hospital was to be two thousand beds and the surgeries more varied. But only some of the partisans had travelled with the Allies to Roma, and it was time for me to look for work in the city. Stefano was worried about me, my wheeze turning into a persistent cough after working in damp conditions, so I'd agreed to take it a little slower for a short time.

I was proud of what I'd achieved, working as a healer and herbalist for the partisans and contributing to the successful journey north to Roma. But now I looked forward to the day when this war was over and Stefano and I could live together as husband and wife, and maybe even start a family of our own.

'What will you do now?' I asked Antonio, fiddling with the bottle of Coca-Cola I was drinking. It was a popular drink, brought in by the Americans, sweet and with the pick me up of a good cup of coffee.

'There are large numbers of partisans rising in the north, continuing the fight against the Germans and Mussolini's National Republican Army. Most are involved in disrupting the Fascists' preparations and activities against the Allies, and helping local civilians resistant to the Social Republic.'

'And you want to support them,' I said softly.

'I do,' he said. 'These men have been actively hunted, had their property confiscated and family hurt or killed because of their resistance. How can I not support them, men who've risked everything because of what they believe in?'

'What about here?'

He shook his head. 'Roma was left untouched by the Germans, who declared it an open city. What the Romani need is food, clothing and medical services. They need someone like you, not partisans inciting trouble. In fact, I think a girl

I've met, Angelina, will know where your herbal skills might be most useful here in the city.'

'Angelina?' I asked with a raised eyebrow. So perhaps there was someone special. 'When will you go?'

'As soon as can be arranged. There's a group of us willing to travel north towards Firenze and continue the fight.' Florence, as the Allies called it, still within the Fascist Italian Social Republic, had always been the cultural centre of the north, a city I had always dreamed of visiting.

I smiled wistfully and squeezed his hand, my belly clenching with worry.

'Promise me you'll be careful,' I whispered.

Antonio kissed my cheek. 'I always am.'

Not only did the lovely Angelina introduce me to her aunt, a Bridgettine nun who ran a clinic for those who couldn't afford medical services, but she also offered me a room in her apartment. I went to work at the nearby convent each day, where Sister Rosaria, glad of the help and expertise, would keep me busy tending to the poor of the local district. It reminded me of my time at the monastery. But to add to the strain on the city, refugees had begun pouring in from surrounding districts destroyed by the Germans, now that Roma was in Allied hands. Food, housing and employment was becoming scarce. I found the search for solutions to the social problems that accompanied those who presented to the clinic challenging, but the most rewarding of all.

The convent offered poor families simple meals, but it only solved part of the problem. Many children were pitifully thin, with hollow faces. Mothers, some unwell themselves, were often unable to afford to feed them enough and too many had to fend for themselves. If we could find a way for these children to attend school, then we could guarantee their wellbeing with meals, clothing, education and supervision for a big part of the day. In the end, we were able to provide places through the school the nuns ran.

Stefano and I met whenever we could for simple meals or sightseeing around Roma. The city was beginning to bloom again, coming out of its winter of oppression and, with the help of the Allies, resuming its place as the capital city of Italy. Badoglio had resigned and a new coalition government of anti-Fascist parties had been formed, with Bonomi of the Democratic Socialist Party becoming prime minister. Mussolini was still leader of the Fascists and supported by the Nazis, but democracy was returning to Italy and there was hope that, one day soon, our beloved country would once again become the vibrant, passionate and innovative nation it had always been known as.

'I never imagined standing somewhere as ancient as this,' I murmured to Stefano one day in August. We were at the Colosseum, the most famous landmark of ancient Roma. I remembered seeing pictures of it when I was at school. I was a long way from the small village of Bruzzano.

Stefano bent to kiss me. 'I'm glad that you're happy, Topolina.'

'I couldn't be happier. I'm in Roma, I'm here with you and I'm helping people. If only I knew that Antonio was safe and well.'

Stefano had heard from injured soldiers at the hospital that the partisans had driven the Germans and the fascist National Republican Army from Firenze before the Allied troops had even arrived. It was heartbreaking that Italians were now fighting Italians. I had no doubt that Antonio had been part of that push but where he was now, I didn't know. I was still staying with Angelina and with Sister Rosaria making sure I took care of myself, my cough was slowly improving. But every time I thought of Antonio, my anxiety soared. And now I was experiencing dizziness and nausea as well. I couldn't sleep from worry.

'I'm sure you'll receive a letter from him soon, or at least Angelina will.'

'I know he wants to do something useful.'

'If anything, he should be safer now,' Stefano said, putting his arm around me. 'It looks like those in charge are taking the partisans more seriously, as a real force in helping defeat the Germans and ending this war. They'll likely receive Allied support and supplies. But I'll see what I can find out about Antonio.'

'Anything will ease my mind,' I said, smiling.

'Happy wife, happy life, they say.'

'Well, I'd better show my appreciation,' I said softly, drawing him towards an alcove among the labyrinth of tunnels, walls and walkways. I just hoped we wouldn't get lost.

Angelina was just as worried as me that we hadn't heard from Antonio. We listened to Radio Londra together, trying to decipher the crazy messages that the announcer read out: 'the hen has laid an egg . . . the cow doesn't give milk . . . the major with the beard . . .' But they never made sense and we were no closer to learning anything about Antonio.

'I've got a letter,' she said, bursting through the door one evening. Her eyes were shining and her face was alight with excitement. 'It's from Antonio.'

I was in the kitchen making us a light meal of fried sardines like we had at home. I put the fish to one side, wiped my hands on my apron and sat with her at the little table. I was just as overjoyed as she was to finally have word.

Her hands trembled as she opened the envelope and pulled out the sheets of paper.

My dearest Angelina,

I'm sorry it's taken so long to write to you. I know that you and Giulia will be waiting for news, but this is the first chance I've had. You'll be pleased to know that I'm safe and well and causing maximum disruption around the German lines.

As you know the aim of our mission was to distract the Germans, making it easier for the Allies to expel them from Firenze, but I never imagined that we'd actually play a part in forcing them from the city. It was an incredible moment! But best of all is the work we've been doing in aiding the escape of Jewish Italians from Mussolini's Social Republic back to Roma . . .

'Your brother's an avenging angel,' Angelina whispered, her eyes wide with amazement. 'I wish I could have been there with him. I hope our men and the Allied soldiers cut down every last one of them. Those filthy Nazis deserve everything that's coming. Retribution must be ours, even though it will never bring my family back.'

Dread coiled through my belly at her words. 'What happened to your family?'

'I lost them all, months ago – my entire family, while I was visiting Zia Rosaria at the convent. When I returned home to our small farm in the Lazio countryside, they'd been slaughtered. All because they supported partisans in their community and hid their Jewish neighbours from the Nazi round ups.'

I stared at her in shock. I couldn't believe she was still standing, let alone functioning, after what she'd endured.

'I'm so sorry . . .' I grasped her hand. 'They died defending what they believe in, defending our homeland, just as my father and brother did. All we can do is honour their memory and carry on their fighting spirit.'

She nodded. 'That's why I have to help Antonio with the Jews he's sending to Roma.' She lifted a shaking hand to wipe the tears from her cheeks. 'You must be so proud of him.'

'I am, and I know that our father would be proud too.'

'The reports of massacres in the north are disturbing,' said Stefano one afternoon in September as he flicked through the newspaper Angelina had left on the kitchen table while I boiled water for tea. I'd been feeling unwell for weeks now and it was time to tell Stefano, but I didn't know how he'd take it. 'The Nazis kill anyone who resists them or is even suspected of being against them, but murdering entire families in reprisal . . .' He shook his head in disbelief. 'That's pure evil.'

The Allies had continued to push north but the Germans and fascist National Republic Army were causing havoc through Tuscany and Umbria and into Emilia-Romagna as they retreated, making the Allies fight tooth and nail every step of the way. Roads were destroyed, electricity and telegraph lines pulled down and cut, and fields of crops burned.

'Don't tell Angelina about that,' I said, pouring water over the fresh mint leaves at the bottom of the pot.

'Of course not,' he said, putting the newspaper down as I brought the pot to the table with a plate of biscotti.

'I'm glad we're alone,' I said, sitting across from him. 'There's something I want to talk to you about.' I nibbled on a dry biscotti to settle my queasy stomach. I was nervous about what I was about to tell him and the nausea didn't help.

'What is it? Is everything alright, Topolina?'

I gazed at him a moment, unwilling to say the words, because when I did, it would change everything.

'You haven't been able to get rid of that cough and I know you haven't been sleeping well and you look so tired . . . Is something wrong?' He took my hands in his. 'Tell me, Giulia, are you unwell? Please tell me it's not tuberculosis.'

I shook my head. 'No, it's not tuberculosis and I'm not unwell – not really. It's just that—' I swallowed convulsively and then blurted it out before I could find a way to delay any longer: 'I'm pregnant.'

Stefano took a moment to register what I'd said. 'You're pregnant?' His gold-flecked eyes gazed into my face with such love that my worries about how it would change our lives almost washed away.

I nodded. 'I ran out of my herbs and by the time I was able to replace them, I suspected that I was already pregnant.'

He squeezed my hands and brought them to his lips. 'Cara mia, I've been waiting for this moment for so long.' His face was suffused with joy.

'But the war.'

'Many others have had babies during the war, I suppose we'll manage too.'

'But we don't have a place of our own, a home for us as a family.'

Stefano went pale. 'Of course. Do you want to go back home to your family?'

I shook my head. 'No. I'm staying here.'

'I don't know how long this war will drag on for. Do you really think it's a good idea?'

'I don't care. I'm not leaving your side.' I took a breath, trying to be calm and reasonable. 'Do you think you'll remain here until the end of the war?'

He looked thoughtful for a moment. 'The 12th General is one of the biggest military hospitals in Roma. We're swamped with casualties from Southern France and the north, so I expect that, yes, I'll be here until the war's over.'

I nodded. 'Good. We're safe here until then. I'm not due until May – surely it will be over and we'll be home by then? But I'm not going anywhere without you.' I stared at him, daring him to challenge me.

He let his breath out with an audible sigh. 'You could continue to stay with Angelina until we can return home and if, by some remote chance, it looks like you'll have the baby in Roma, we can find somewhere small for you and the baby afterwards.' He rose from his chair and pulled me to my feet, hugging me tight, then kissed me. 'I can't wait to be a father.'

I'd waited so long for this to happen, afraid of what it might do to my life, how it might limit my freedom and independence but now that it was here, I was overjoyed, wondering why I had been so fearful. Now I couldn't wait to meet this little bundle of joy, the ultimate expression of the love between Stefano and me.

I woke to the sound of insistent knocking on the front door early one November morning. Angelina had come in late the night before and was a sound sleeper, so I dragged myself from my bed, shivering as my feet hit the cold floor, and pulled on my dressing gown and slippers. It was a lot cooler here compared to home and my body hadn't yet acclimatised. At least my morning sickness had finally settled and I didn't have to race off to the toilet to be sick.

I fumbled with the door lock, then suddenly I was in my brother's embrace. 'You're back,' I murmured. 'We weren't expecting you.'

'And I wasn't expecting to be here,' he said, grinning. He glanced at Angelina's room.

'She came in late,' I said.

Antonio nodded. 'Let her sleep. How about a cup of tea while you tell me how you've been?' He looked pointedly at my middle. I was three and a half months, not showing as yet. I'd written to him and Mamma, telling them of my news and although Angelina also knew, I'd decided not to tell Sister

Rosaria just yet. I wasn't sure what her response would be; I loved my work and wanted to continue for as long as I felt I could. I believed I was making a real difference in the lives of the community. Between the clinic and the convent, we were gaining the trust of the local families, a big step forward in solving the complex social problems they faced.

It was only when we sat down with our tea that Antonio told me what had been happening.

'It's terrible.' He passed a hand through his black hair, his expression dark. 'The Germans are hanging on, taking every advantage they can against the local people, using them as leverage against the growing partisan movement and ensuring that Italians fight each other.' He shook his head and sighed. 'To think that we ever revered Mussolini . . . Our country's fighting for its very survival, embroiled in a civil war that should never have happened.'

'But why are you here?'

'The Allies have come to a grinding halt on the Gothic Line, between Firenze and Bologna. It's been a hard slog through the mountains and the men are exhausted.' He paused, staring into space. 'We're so close to pushing the Germans out of Italy but the Allied generals have decided to winter on the line. The partisans were told to go home until the spring offensive.'

'What?' I looked at him, incredulous, my teacup halfway to my mouth.

'There'll be no activity over winter.'

'But why?'

'All we can think of is that the Allies want to keep as many German divisions tied up on the Italian front as they can so they have a better chance on the Western Front. With France now liberated, the Allied forces poised near the German border and the Soviets pushing the Eastern Front through Poland and liberating Yugoslavia and Belgrade, it's only a matter of time before they invade Germany and march on Berlin itself.'

I thought briefly of Papà, Vincenzo and Stefano and what they went through to take Yugoslavia for the Germans and now we wanted Germany ejected. The whole war had been crazy. I wondered how many men, women and children had been affected by the decisions of power-wielding men who thought little of the consequences for ordinary people.

I was furious. 'So we're meant to be the sacrificial lamb? How many men will die holding the Germans in battle here in Italy? What about our liberation? Italians are fighting each other so that the Allies can strike a blow to the heart of Germany! Our war could have been over soon and people could return to their lives. How much longer will this go on for?'

Antonio stared at me, speechless. 'I'm sorry. I know you want a normal life with Stefano and the baby.'

'No, I'm sorry.' I was mortified at losing control. 'I'm a bit emotional these days. I know you can't know what's ahead. But I am very grateful that you're back, safe and well.' I glanced at Angelina's room. 'And I know that someone else will be too.'

He smiled and patted my hand. 'It will be alright. The end is in sight. Soon I'll get to be a doting uncle and watch you be a wonderful mother.'

I nodded, trying to hide my crushing disappointment as I realised that my baby would be born in Roma and it would be some time before we'd live together with Stefano as a family. Our plans for the future might need adjustment but we'd find a way to manage in Messina while he finished university.

I'd barely had time to process Antonio's news when I was faced with another turn of events.

Stefano asked me to meet him outside the hospital one afternoon after I'd finished work.

'Is everything alright?' I asked as we sat at a table in the hospital cafeteria during Stefano's break. 'What couldn't wait until tomorrow?' The smell of hot coffee, even the instant coffee the Americans drank, made my mouth water. I hadn't had coffee for months and I sipped the black liquid, not sure what to expect. It was weak and bitter but better than roasted acorns or chicory.

'I wanted to tell you as soon as I found out. I tried everything but it was no good.' He shook his head.

'What are you talking about?' I was tired and wanted to get back to Angelina's flat to put my feet up.

'Most of the military hospitals in Roma are being relocated. The 12th General is being moved north to Livorno. It's fifty-five miles to the west of Firenze, closer to the front line, and it has a port. It's easier to access from all battlefronts than Roma.' He grasped my hand. 'I'm so sorry. I asked for a transfer to stay here but I have to go with the 12th.'

'When do you leave?' I stared him in the eye, refusing to become emotional. I'd just started to come to terms with staying in Roma for the birth, now this.

'In a week.'

'I'm coming with you.'

He shook his head with regret. 'You can't. It's too danger-ous for you that close to the front. I'd never forgive myself if anything happened to you or the baby.'

I pulled my hand out of his. 'You're leaving me here in Roma, pregnant with your child?' I hissed across the table. 'There's no way you'll have enough time to come all that way to see me. How far is it anyway?'

'Over two hundred miles. You're right, I won't be able to see much of you. Antonio will be here for a time but then he'll be north again . . .' He looked decidedly uncomfortable and a chill of disquiet crawled up my spine. 'I think it's best for you to go home to Bruzzano.'

I glared at him. 'You what?'

'It's the safest thing to do, Topolina.'

'Don't you Topolina me!' I said. 'You'd bundle me off home to sit quietly as your obedient wife until I have your child and you return home fulfilled and satisfied after this war is done with you! No! I'm not going.'

'I can't work properly knowing you're in danger.'

'I'll be fine,' I said with a wave of my hand. 'You know I will. You've seen me with the partisans—'

'No.' His mouth was set into a firm and stubborn line. 'Your mother's been through enough. Don't put her through any more worrying about you up here.'

I jerked back in shock. 'You're using my mother as an excuse? How could you?'

He slammed the table with his fist, making me jump. 'Mannaggia, Giulia! I'm right – there is no choice.'

I could see the fear-fuelled fury in his face. I knew he was worried but I'd proven that I could look after myself and make my own choices. I remembered what Paola had told me years ago about remaining calm and I took a deep breath, trying to be reasonable with him.

'Can't we just talk about it? I thought we agreed to be equal partners in this marriage, to make decisions together.'

'There's nothing to talk about.'

'Oddio! You're not even giving me a chance.' I stared at him, incredulous. I couldn't believe this was happening.

'I don't want you to be alone when you have this baby. You have your family there and all the support you need.'

'But not you,' I said. I felt like I'd just been slapped across the face.

'You know I don't want it to be this way,' he murmured, 'but I won't be swayed. We have no choice.'

'There's always a choice, Stefano,' I said, rising from the table. I stared at him, grasping the chair so he wouldn't see my hands shaking. I could go to Livorno anyway or even stay here in Roma. 'You want to take my choice away from me but I'm telling you that you won't stop me doing what I think is right for me and for our child.'

I refused to look behind me as I left the cafeteria, trembling with shock. I knew what was best for me and I was going to stay.

But my plan to remain in Roma was thrown into disarray when I received a letter from Nonna a few days later.

Your mother has fallen ill with a terrible fever. I've been treating her but she's slow to respond. I've tried all the usual herbs and treatments but I'm at a loss to explain why she's not improving.

I'm worried that perhaps she's losing her will to live after your father's death.

Tears filled my eyes and fear gripped my heart. Mamma had always been the strongest one in the family, the one who kept us all together. I couldn't believe she was so unwell or that she would give up hope. I felt sure that, between us, Nonna and I could find a way to make her better. But the timing couldn't be worse. I'd just decided to make my life here in Roma, regardless of what Stefano thought was best. I wanted to prove that I was capable enough to make my own way, with or without my husband's support. And if I went home now, there was no way I'd make my way north again before the baby was born. Stefano and I would be separated by an entire country just when we should be together as a family.

But Mamma was ill and needed me.

33

ntonio and I stood outside the house we'd grown up in. I didn't think I'd be back home so soon. We'd done so much in the time that we'd been away, even though it had only been just over a year. I took a deep breath and opened the door.

Paola, Rosa and Teresa looked up from the table in surprise. Rosa screamed, scaring little Enzo and Emilio, who both started to cry.

'You're home!' Teresa scooped up Emilio, her face alight with joy. She rushed to embrace us both, tears running down her face, Paola close behind. Soon Antonio and I were surrounded by our sisters, the two nephews on their hips. Surrounded by love.

'You made it back so quickly,' whispered Paola, hugging me tight. 'We thought you'd be longer.'

'We got lucky,' I said.

Antonio had insisted on accompanying me home; there was no way he was going to stay in Roma with Mamma so ill. I'd thought of asking Don Silvio for help arranging transport but I decided against it. It just didn't feel right. Although I was still furious with Stefano, I'd told him about Mamma. He couldn't travel with us but arranged transport to Napoli in an army truck and from there Agata organised a ride to Reggio with a hospital transport and then the coast bus brought us home.

I squeezed Paola tight. It was so good to see her again. 'How's Mamma?'

Paola shook her head, her eyes clouded with worry. 'Not good.'

'But we're all together again,' said Rosa, wiping her wet face. She kissed Antonio on the cheek and passed Enzo to him. 'He hasn't seen his zio for so long.'

Teresa took my hand and Antonio's free hand. 'Come and see Mamma and Nonna.'

Hugging my mother's thin frame, I realised how happy I was to be back.

'I'm here now, Mamma,' I whispered. 'Antonio too.' It was a shock to see her. She was pale, thin and gaunt. She was so weak she could barely stand, but at least she was up, not in bed, burning up with the fever like I'd feared. Or worse: on her deathbed.

'Everyone's home now and I can hold you all close to me. I've never been so happy,' she said.

'And you can see your new grandchild when they're born,' I reminded her. Now we were home and another grandchild was on the way, I hoped Mamma would have renewed purpose and the strength and fighting spirit that was central to all our lives would return to her once more.

She nodded. 'So much to live for.'

'Then we have to get you well again.' I kissed her on the cheek.

Nonna and I did all we could to get Mamma better. Her fever was intermittent, debilitating each time, so we had to almost start again with building her back up, but finally there was no more fever, although she was still weak. We tried new herbal treatments and got Teresa and Rosa to bring the children to see her. We took her to the hot springs at Motticella and cooked tasty dishes to tantalise her. Nonna was relieved to have me by her side, just as I was pleased to be working and living with her again. She seemed more stooped and hunched now and her hair was almost completely silver. But I still saw the strength of will in her green eyes and I knew that, together, we'd find a way to heal Mamma.

It was wonderful to be around my sisters and Rosa again. Teresa was dressmaking when she could and Rosa, still mourning the loss of Vincenzo, continued to work at the store. Paola had bought the plot of land she'd told me about, along the river flat between Bruzzano and the marina, and was growing wheat there, but her best source of income was from her cheeses, which were some of the most sought after in Calabria. She had continued her work on the black market and was a leader in the local farming community. Now that Zia Francesca wasn't working every day at the trattoria as fewer people could afford to eat there, we saw much more of her. Papà's death had affected her; she was almost as grey as Mamma now and there was a sadness in her eyes whenever she came to visit, but it had brought her and Mamma closer. Just like Mamma, she was on her own now; she hadn't seen Don Silvio for some months but I hadn't pressed her for the reason for their separation.

Between caring for Mamma and working back at the clinic, I didn't have time to think about my life in Roma and the people I missed there. And I refused to dwell on how Stefano had insisted on making a major decision for me.

There were rumours of the new government wanting to conscript young men to fight in the north, so Antonio went back into hiding.

'It's the Allies behind this and no southerners are going to be told what to do by foreigners anymore,' said Signora Lipari. It was almost Christmas and I was at the post office picking up the mail. I hoped that I'd receive a letter from Stefano, apologising for what he'd done.

'But Antonio and your son were both fighting for the partisans. Why would conscription to the army worry them now?'

'It's about choice. They chose to go to the partisans and they chose to come home. Those who have chosen to stay and protect their farms and families, to produce food for our community and region, have been made to feel as though they're enemies of this country, unpatriotic. But—' she leaned towards me, '—people are not happy with a government that refuses to look after all its citizens, not just those in the north. There are protests right across the south, and even talk about Sicily becoming an independent state once again. Other regions will follow.'

I nodded. 'I just want my brother home for Christmas.'

Signora Lipari frowned. 'Of course. Your family has lost so much and you must be missing your husband.' She patted my hand as she gave me the mail. 'How far are you into your pregnancy? Five months?'

I nodded, checking the mail. My heart dropped when I saw there was nothing from Stefano.

'You're on your feet all day at the clinic and looking after your mother. I'm glad she's feeling much better now. But make sure you get enough rest. The baby can take it out of you.'

I murmured my thanks and walked away. I'd thought coming home would be peaceful but it looked like the age-old issue of Southern separatism was raising its head once more and only discord and trouble would come of it. Although I understood it and even agreed with the principle, I also knew what was happening in the north, what those further up the peninsula had endured, what Italians all over were doing to eject the Germans from our land. How could anyone here really understand when they hadn't seen or been part of the conflict, terror and atrocities that bloomed around the progression of the war through Italy?

As 1945 dawned, Mamma continued to improve. She was walking about, doing a bit of cooking again, occasionally watching over Teresa's and Rosa's children and getting stronger. Antonio slipped home every now and then to see her, and Zia Francesca was helping her about the house. I hoped that, with time, Mamma would get back to her old self. I missed Stefano, but I was finding it hard to forgive him for what he'd done. His decision had felt like a betrayal, yet the longer we were apart, the more I just wanted him with me.

I cried with relief when I finally received a letter from him. I walked to the edge of the river and sat on the bank, glad that it was a cold, grey day and nobody was around. I wanted privacy and peace.

Tesoro mio Giulia,

The postal service has finally been restored and I've only just received your letter. I'm so relieved that you got home safely and that your mother is improving. She's in the best hands with you and your nonna and from what you've told me, I'm sure you'll have her back to normal before too long. I can only imagine how happy everyone is to have you and Antonio home. I hope you are feeling well and that the pregnancy is progressing without a problem. I can only imagine how quickly the baby's growing, and your belly too.

Work has been as busy as ever and I'm learning new skills every day. But although the casualties continue to pour in, sometimes I remember to look out over the spectacular view of the coast and the sparkling Ligurian Sea. It always reminds me of you and how much I miss you.

I stifled a sob. I should have been there with him. We should be together as a family.

It's so difficult knowing that you're so far away at the other end of Italy, but I feel consoled that at least you're with your family. I'm so sorry about how we left things. But Livorno is nothing more than a ruined city. So much has been bombed – buildings, industry, shipyards, the port, railways and transport routes. It hasn't stopped the Germans from setting explosives in public buildings, much like they did in Napoli, and the carnage continues.

I wish I'd done things differently, talked to you about my relocation, rather than telling you what I thought was best for you and the baby. But I can't tell you the relief I feel that you are far from the war, far from the evil of the Nazis.

Soon this war will be over and I'll make my way home to you as quick as I can. I can't wait to hold you in my arms and show you how truly sorry I am.

Buon Natale, cara mia. I wish I was there to celebrate Christmas with you and your family.

Sending all my love to you. Tell our baby that I love them.

Your loving husband,

Stefano

'Oh, Stefano!' I whispered. 'Why couldn't you have trusted me? We would have found a solution together.' I rested my hand over my belly. The hardest thing for me to swallow was that no matter what I had decided, I would have ended up back here anyway for Mamma. Our argument seemed so pointless now.

I looked at the water rushing over the smooth stones, feeling terribly sad and alone. These waters had come from high in the mountains where I'd once sat praying next to a waterfall. I closed my eyes, trying to regain the sense of calm I'd felt then. *Madonna, please look after him and keep him safe.*

When I opened my eyes, I felt somewhat stronger and knew that I wasn't powerless. I would continue to make my own decisions – and live with the consequences of my own choices.

'How are you?' asked Mamma one afternoon in February as we sat with the nettle and rosehip tea I'd made. I'd come up from the clinic before beginning my rounds of the village to check on her and was pleased to see her clear-eyed and moving around the kitchen as she used to.

'I'm feeling well,' I said, rubbing my protruding belly. 'Baby kicks me a lot at night so it takes a while to find a comfortable position, but other than that I have plenty of energy and I can still do everything I want. Here,' I said, taking her hand, 'feel how this little one kicks.'

Her eyes widened as the baby flexed and pushed out hard against my belly. 'Mamma mia! He's strong.'

I grinned.

'But how are you really?'

'A bit tired,' I admitted. It had been a long day and I was glad to sit for a while.

'I'm worried about you. You have to look after yourself too,' she said softly. 'You're nothing but skin and bones.'

'Don't worry, Mamma, I will. We just need to get you back to normal.'

'I know you've been working hard, especially since we went to Napoli, and I can't thank you enough for coming home and working with Nonna to nurse me back to health. I don't know what might have happened otherwise.' Tears filled her eyes and I had to swallow the lump in my throat.

I don't know what we would've done if we'd lost her. 'I'm so proud of all you've achieved, becoming a healer, educating yourself, and taking your skills to help the unfortunate people in Napoli and Roma and the men on the battleground. I know how much it meant to you ... working in those conditions and dealing with such terrible injuries and difficult problems takes a certain strength that you've always had.'

'I just love it, Mamma, and I love working with Nonna too but it's different in the city. The truth is that I miss it, the urgency and quick thinking, finding solutions to complex problems, moving from one patient to the next.' I missed the people and places I'd left behind, but most of all, I missed Stefano.

Mamma nodded. 'But you have to look after yourself now, make sure you get enough rest and don't work yourself to the bone. This baby needs you to give it the best start in life that you can and that begins in pregnancy. And you'll need your strength and determination during this time, and after, when you become a new mother. But I know that you'll be a wonderful mother. Your baby's lucky to have you,' she said softly. 'Just promise me that you'll cut back on the hours you're working.'

I nodded, blinking away the tears. 'If I'm half the mother you are, I'll be proud,' I whispered, hugging her tight. I wouldn't be the woman I'd become without her.

Antonio had decided to stay, as the battle between southern farmers and the local establishment had taken on a new ferocity. But I often saw him with a faraway look in his eyes when he thought that nobody was watching, and I wondered if he was happy with his decision.

One evening in early March we were talking about the day Stefano and I arrived in Roma. 'You miss her, don't you?' I said. I was round and cumbersome as I plonked myself down on the chair beside him, sighing as I took the weight off my aching feet. I only had about eight weeks to go but although I'd promised Mamma I'd look after myself, I'd refused to completely give up my work and worked shorter days instead. Nonna took Roberto Lipari, who showed an interest and aptitude for healing, on her visits across the district as an extra set of strong hands while Antonio helped Paola on the farm. I'd resigned myself to the fact that this child would be born before the war was over, before Stefano could get home.

'I think about Angelina every day, much like you do Stefano, but like you two, we both have other responsibilities.'

I closed my eyes for a moment as pangs of loneliness shot through me. I missed Stefano more than anything, the touch of his hands on my skin, the feel of him against me. Although he'd apologised in his way, all I could do was reply that I was well and update him on Mamma's condition. He'd written again, telling me about his work and how much he missed me but I hadn't written back yet. I was still upset and I didn't know what I wanted to write.

'She loves you, Antonio, and I know that you love her.'

'But she doesn't need me, not right now. There are people who need me here.'

I took his hand in mine. 'I'm worried about you.'

'Don't be. I'm fighting for the rights of those who can't fight for themselves. Caulonia has declared itself a republic, and other towns and districts are thinking of doing the same. It's time for the little man to stand up against oppression. If the government in Roma can't protect all its citizens and cater for the needs of the most vulnerable and disenfranchised, then it's time for the south to govern itself.'

'Just be careful.'

'I always am,' he said, smiling fondly.

34

One Sunday afternoon, I was sitting with Zia Francesca, looking through some magazines over a cup of tea.

'Did Don Silvio send these to you?' I asked.

'No,' she said brusquely. 'I told him not to bother.' It had become easier to get American magazines now that we were under Allied occupation and American soldiers were stationed in the big cities of the south. It was no longer forbidden to have American magazines and it was liberating to have the freedom to read whatever I wanted.

'What happened between you two?' I asked, looking quickly towards Mamma's bedroom, but she was still resting with the door closed.

Zia took a deep breath and sighed. 'He finally told me what he did to you and to Stefano,' she said.

'I'm sorry, Zia. I couldn't tell you.' I shrugged, not knowing where to even start. I still had mixed feelings about the difficult position Don Silvio had put Stefano and me in, even with everything he'd done to help and protect me.

She touched my cheek. 'I know he put you in an impossible situation and I'm sorry for that. But he didn't understand why I was so upset.'

'He betrayed you too,' I said softly.

She nodded. 'I couldn't have a man I couldn't trust around me so I ended it.'

'But you've loved each other for so long.'

She smiled sadly. 'We have, but he's changed. The work he does finally became part of who he is. And now he's risen even further within the 'Ndrangheta after his role in aiding the Allies.'

'I'm so sorry.'

She dropped the magazine to the table. 'Have you heard from Stefano lately?' she asked.

I shook my head. 'Not since last month and I haven't replied yet.' The bedroom door opened and I heard Mamma in the kitchen, looking for her favourite teacup.

'I know things weren't good between you when you left Roma, but I know how much you love him – and you have a baby on the way,' she said.

Mamma joined us at the table. I smiled and clasped her hand. 'Did you have a good rest?'

'Si, grazie,' she said, filling her cup, the fragrant scent of liquorice rising from the steam. 'Now what's this about Stefano? You know he had no choice,' she said, taking a bite of an almond biscotti and wiping the crumbs from the table into her hand impatiently. 'It's war and he's doing his duty.'

The pain and hurt returned to me like it had been yester-day. 'But he promised that we'd be partners and we needed to make this decision together. He took away my choice. How can I trust him after this?' Even talking about it made my anger flare, hot and bright.

'Mamma mia! He didn't take anything from you!' Mamma shook her head in exasperation. 'You're stronger than that. You've always done exactly what you wanted, ever since Massimo's death. Now you both have to do your duty, and your duty is to your unborn child. You know you're better off here, safe, well and among family who love you.'

I stared at my mother, the truth of her words sinking in.

Zia nodded. 'He was afraid for you. He was holding your life and that of his unborn child in his hands and he did what he could in that moment. This is wartime, Giulia, and nothing can be predicted. He made a mistake and he's apolo-gised. You'll be making a mistake too if you believe you can't trust him.'

I nodded. She knew what losing trust was about.

'You've always been impetuous,' Mamma said, cupping my cheek with her hand, warm from holding the teacup. 'Stefano knows it and still loves you for it. He's no doubt feeling the same hurt and disappointment you're feeling. Of course he'd rather be with you, living together as a family, but you have to let these feelings go. They'll stop you from finding the peace and happiness you crave.'

'Don't let something like this come between you,' said Zia. 'Find your way back to him.'

I dropped my head in mortification, a grown woman admonished by her mother and aunt. But they were right.

I was not powerless as I had been as a child under my father's roof. Stefano could make his choices but I also could make mine. I missed Stefano more and more and I just wanted him safe and well and back home with me. I knew the decision to leave Roma hadn't really been in his hands. It was my choice now to forgive him or to let our separation become a wedge between us.

'Since the attacks against the Germans have started again in the north and the Allies are marching through Germany, it won't be long before the Nazis fall and this war will be over,' said Mamma. 'Then Stefano will be back and you can start your new life as a family.'

I stared at her, dumbfounded, and she raised an eyebrow in response.

'Do you think you're the only one who follows the news?' Zia nodded and smiled. She'd known. 'Between the newspapers and the radio, I had to know exactly where you and Antonio were and what danger was coming your way. It was the only way to tell if you were safe.' She put her arm around me and kissed me on the cheek. 'Now promise me you'll write to Stefano soon.'

I did write to Stefano, filled with remorse. Our second anniversary had just passed. A year ago we were in the little cottage near Caserta, eating pasta and talking about our dreams while Vesuvius spewed. Now I was home, pregnant and feeling very alone without him.

Amore mio,
Happy anniversary! I write to you with a heart full of love and forgiveness. With the gift of time, I've come to understand

that you had to go to Livorno and why you were so insist-
ent that I come home. But you also have to understand how
hurt, angry and betrayed your words made me. You promised
that we'd always make decisions together. I only want us to be
a family.

All I could do now was wait for him to come home
to me.

By April, the Soviets and the British and American forces were
closing in from the east and west and the spring offensive on
the Gothic Line had well and truly begun, the Allies pushing
north and fighting for Bologna. Many people I'd spoken to
felt that the war was essentially over, especially since Roma
had been liberated. It was only a matter of course for the Allies
to push the Germans back over the Alps and into Switzerland
or Austria, or so they believed. But Antonio and I knew the
battle would be slow and intense and many Italians would
suffer or die in the process.

'I've heard on the radio that Bologna's finally been taken
by the Allies,' I said to Antonio one day in late April, 'and
the partisans have liberated cities in the far north of Italy:
Torino, Parma and Milano. You must be proud of them.
I know I am. It won't be long before the north will be free of
the Germans and maybe then life can return to some kind
of normalcy. I can hardly believe that the end of the war is
within touching distance.'

'Then Stefano will be home with you and the baby,' he
said softly.

I was overjoyed when I received a letter not long after that conversation, only to find that it was from Agata. She'd written to make sure Stefano was alright after hearing about the blasts that had occurred in Livorno after the Germans had left explosive devices in the public buildings. I immediately thought of the post office in Napoli and quailed. Even with Antonio assuring me that they would have sent a telegram if the hospital had been targeted or if Stefano was injured, I couldn't help turning the possibility over in my mind until it almost drove me mad. I wrote another frantic letter to Stefano and waited in no-man's land as our baby grew bigger. What Mamma had told me about needing strength became truer than ever. I had to be strong for our child and for myself. I continued to work through my growing worry, forcing the fear from my mind.

Only days later, Antonio came into the kitchen, kissing Mamma while she was cooking and spinning her around.

'What's got into you?' she asked, laughing breathlessly.

'Mussolini's been captured by partisans after fleeing Milano and he's been executed. He's dead! Finito!'

I dropped the broad beans I was shelling onto the table.

Mamma stared at Antonio. 'That bastardo's dead?'

Antonio nodded. 'He and his mistress have been hung up in Milano's Piazzale Loreto for all the world to see.'

I gasped at the horrific image but hope flared bright in my chest. It wouldn't be long before the war was over and Stefano could come home. I still hadn't heard from him. Guilt at the way we'd left each other weighed heavily on my mind. If he hadn't received my letter and something had happened to him, I'd never forgive myself.

'Allora, he deserves to be humiliated after everything he's done,' Mamma said. 'He betrayed Italy, consorting with that Nazi. Too many good people are dead because of him. Maybe they'll do the same to that madman in Germany when the Allies reach Berlin.'

'It's good news,' I said, smiling. 'I hope that it's the beginning of more good things to come.' Maybe this child would be born in a more peaceful world.

But the protests and riots in the south against oppression and injustice by the local and Italian governments had become more violent during the final days of the war. Teresa's husband Santoro came in the following evening, holding up a pale and bleeding Antonio.

'Oddio!' whispered Mamma, eyes wide with fear. 'What's happened?'

'He was set upon during one of the land protests,' said Santoro.

'Lie him down on a bed,' I said urgently. After the months of worrying about him with the partisans, Antonio had been hurt here, at home.

'Quickly, get some towels,' said Nonna to Paola.

Antonio was barely conscious, his skin as white as the sheets he lay on. 'He's bleeding from a cut on his head,' I said, blotting the wetness from his scalp and searching for the laceration. 'There.' I parted his hair to reveal a deep gash on the back of his head and a lump the size of an egg.

Mamma gasped with horror.

'It's alright. We can sew that up.'

Nonna nodded. 'The main worry is the bump on his head.' She turned to Santoro. 'Fetch me some cold water and, Paola, collect my herbal kit from the workroom. Everything we need for now will be in there.'

'Will he make a full recovery?' Mamma was almost as pale as Antonio.

'He's in the right hands, Gabriella,' said Nonna. 'Sit with him while Giulia and I get organised.'

Mamma dragged a chair next to the bed and held Antonio's motionless hand. I glanced at Nonna and she shrugged. It was too early to tell when he was going to regain full consciousness.

We cut and shaved the hair around the ragged laceration and because my eyesight was the best, I leaned over and stitched Antonio's wound neatly while Nonna made a poultice and mixed up an ointment for his wound.

My belly was tight and pain shot through my back as I straightened up. I ground my teeth together to prevent the groan in my throat from escaping. 'Do you know what happened?' I asked Santoro.

'One of my friends came to find me and told me that the protest had got out of control. When I arrived outside the town hall, protesters who had lost their legitimate requests were clashing with carabinieri and the vigilantes the local Fascists usually hire to do their dirty work. People who were only voicing their discontent were punched and beaten and threatened with guns. I saw Antonio on the ground, being repeatedly punched and then kicked in the head.'

Mamma began to sob. 'My poor boy, my poor, beautiful boy.'

It was while we were sitting in the kitchen with a cup of tea, waiting for signs of improvement from Antonio, that we heard the announcement on the radio.

'This is a newsflash! German radio has just reported that Hitler is dead. I repeat – German radio has just reported that Hitler is dead.'

'Hitler's dead?' said Paola in disbelief.

'Now Germany can end this madness and sue for peace,' said Nonna.

I squirmed in the chair, my back still aching. 'Finally, that lunatic is gone. It will be over soon,' I said flatly. It was hard for us to feel joyful with our worry for Antonio overshadowing everything else.

That night I had a restless sleep, tossing and turning, worried about Antonio and trying to get comfortable with the constant ache in my back. I was dull and listless the following morning and still the pain in my back refused to abate. Nonna and I took it in turns to check on Antonio while the other stayed at the clinic. He was conscious but groggy and in pain, not just from the blows to the head, but from the cracked and broken ribs that he'd sustained. He wasn't out of the woods yet.

By lunchtime my back pain had intensified and I was only able to pick at a bit of bread and cheese at Mamma's.

'Why don't I make you some tea to help ease your back?' said Nonna.

I nodded. 'I feel like I need to move around. I'll boil the water.' I stood and the sudden tightness across my belly took my breath away.

'Are you alright, Giulia?' asked Nonna, brows knitted with concern.

'I think it's starting . . .' A thrill of excitement and fear coursed through me.

Nonna put her hand on my belly as the contraction eased and nodded. 'Your baby's ready to come soon.'

I gazed at her, not sure how to feel. I'd seen many women in labour and each dealt with the experience in different ways. I was worried I wouldn't cope with the pain, worried something would go wrong.

Nonna put her hand on my shoulder. 'Forza, Giulia. Be strong, you can do this.' She kissed my cheek. 'Let's make you that tea.'

Nonna insisted that I remain with Mamma for the rest of the day. I was determined to help around the kitchen, preparing dinner, checking on Antonio, all while my contractions grew stronger and closer together. I didn't want to think about what came next. What if I gave birth to this baby and Stefano never came home? How could I raise this child without their father?

'Come on,' said Mamma as another contraction gripped my belly, bending me double. 'You have to keep moving. It will help the baby come.'

'How much longer?' I whispered. I swung between impatience and dread.

'Your waters have to break before the birth can really start,' said Mamma gently.

'I know.'

It was hours later, while Mamma and I were looking in on Antonio, who was sleeping fitfully, that I felt a wetness on my legs. I reached down and drew a trembling hand away, fearful of finding blood, only to find a clear, sweet-smelling liquid.

'Finally,' said Mamma. 'Now we can get down to business.'

By evening I was in full labour and Mamma called the district midwife who often attended first births.

'It's taking a long time,' I heard Paola whisper anxiously. It was the early hours of the morning and I was on Mamma's bed, the midwife making me pace the floor before allowing me to rest from time to time. The pain was unrelenting. I was exhausted, and a small part of me was scared that I wouldn't be able to do this.

'It's normal, especially for a first birth,' the midwife said. 'Your sister Teresa always has long labours.'

'How much longer, do you think?' murmured Mamma.

'Another few hours perhaps . . . it's hard to know,' said the midwife.

'Another few hours!' I groaned as another contraction began to build.

'Shh,' said Paola, wiping my forehead with a cool cloth. 'You're doing well.'

'Where's Stefano? He should be here. I want my husband!' I sobbed, gasping for breath as all my energy shifted to the vice-like grip around my belly. Nothing would have kept him from the birth of his child or from sending news if he couldn't be here. I was terribly afraid that something had happened to him, that he might be dead.

'Come on, up,' said the midwife in a businesslike manner. 'Walk around some more. The baby needs to move down before you can begin pushing.'

The night went on like this and all my focus shrank to the room I was in and the fire in my body. I knew there was a rhythm and I had to allow my body to do what it knew how to do, but I was terrified.

It was dawn when the urge to push finally overcame me. Paola and Mamma supported my arms as the midwife helped me into a squat. Screams rent the silence of the house as I pushed with all my might. I felt that I would split in two.

'One more,' encouraged the midwife. 'You're nearly there. I can see the head.'

I shook my head. 'I can't.'

'Yes, you can. Here, reach down and touch your baby's head.' She took my hand and guided it to the bulge between my legs. My fingers met wet silkiness against a curved hardness.

My eyes widened in amazement. 'The blessed Madonna,' I whispered.

'Now, two more pushes and you can hold your baby in your arms,' said the midwife.

I nodded, vaguely noticing the shafts of sunlight across the floor, and pushed with everything I had as my baby made its way into the world.

'You have a baby girl,' said the midwife, allowing me to sit for a moment. She handed me the slippery bundle still attached to me by the umbilical cord. I held her close to me, almost instinctively, shocked that I was suddenly a mother. The awareness that I had no idea what to do flooded through me.

The baby rootled about and found my nipple without my help.

'That will help the placenta come,' said the midwife with satisfaction. She touched my arm. 'Don't worry, you'll soon get the hang of it. You and your baby know what to do and you have the women of your family to help you when you feel unsure.'

I nodded mutely, awed by the tiny creature in my arms, my daughter. 'I promise you that I'll always support you, whatever you want to do in your life, and I'll be here for you, no matter what,' I whispered to her. Just as my mother had always been there for me.

It was afternoon when I awoke feeling refreshed. I was disoriented for a moment, unsure of where I was, but the soreness between my legs and aching through my thighs reminded me that I was now a mother. I was in Mamma's bed and turned to look for my baby, but she wasn't in the room with me. I sat up slowly, listening to the reassuringly familiar sounds of the house, and my anxiety ebbed. I could even hear the soft voices of Antonio and Nonna speaking from his bedroom, with music from Antonio's radio in the background.

I got out of bed gingerly, surprised I didn't feel worse. In fact, I felt rather empowered and almost like I could do it again. I shook my head with amazement at the ridiculous thought and, tying the dressing gown around my distended and flabby belly, I made my way out to the dining room.

'There you are,' said Mamma with a smile. She was tidying up after lunch and had put on a pot of coffee. The wonderful aroma of the dark brew made me sigh with pleasure. 'We wanted to let you sleep for a while. You were exhausted. Sit down and I'll get you something to eat.'

My baby girl was in the bassinette on the table, swaddled tightly and sleeping peacefully.

'Turn on the radio, Gabriella,' said Nonna excitedly as she made her way into the room, smiling as she saw me. She kissed me quickly on the cheek. Mamma switched on the radio and Nonna turned up the volume before she sat beside me. An announcer's voice blared across the airwaves.

'The war's over in Italy,' I whispered, hardly daring to believe it was true. It was 2nd May, 1945.

Nonna nodded, smiling broadly. 'The Germans have signed an unconditional surrender at Caserta and their troops have laid down their arms.'

'We made it, we survived.'

I glanced at my sleeping girl and then back to the joyful faces of my mother and grandmother. And then a tear slipped down my cheek. Papà and Vincenzo had paid the ultimate sacrifice for us and for Italy, but we'd prevailed – Italy released from oppression. I would name my daughter to honour their sacrifice, in their quest to bring freedom to Italy.

'I think I'll call my daughter Carla Vittoria.'

'Beautiful,' whispered Mamma, tears in her eyes.

'Her names are perfect. Born on the day of freedom and victory,' said Nonna.

I nodded, tears of joy and hope rolling down my cheeks. We'd been through so much but we'd endured. 'Now Stefano can come home and we can be a family.'

35

Victory Day in Europe came on 8th May, with Germany's surrender to the Allied forces. Amid the wild celebrations, the land protests took on an even darker tone. In Sicily, carabinieri fired into crowds of protesters, killing and injuring many, and the power of the mafia began to grow once more. Closer to home in Cosenza, protesters demonstrating against their ejection from unoccupied land clashed with soldiers sent in to dismantle the republic in Caulonia. All through the Mezzogiorno, insurrection was quashed. Terrorism, oppression and sabotage were not new to us in the south but now they were being used by the old Fascist establishment and large traditional landowners, along with intimidation and threats, to ensure that the voices of small farmers remained unheard. Although he was still recovering, I knew that Antonio was still agitating behind the scenes.

I wrote to Stefano at the hospital to tell him of the birth of our daughter. I cried while writing the letter, the ink smudging as I blotted the teardrops from the page. Baby Carla was thriving, having no shortage of those to love and look after her. I felt nurtured and supported by my family, but I missed Stefano. What had become of him? As much as I tried to believe he was safe and finding his way home to me, I couldn't ignore the looks of concern from those around me.

One afternoon in late June, Zia Francesca and I decided to visit Paola at the new plot and see her wheat crop, which was close to harvesting. It was a beautiful day, the fresh scent of lemons soft on the gentle sea breeze. I stopped at the top of the rise with Carla in my arms. Paola waved from the river flat below, a field of gold behind her, and made her way towards us.

'Any news about Stefano?' asked Zia softly.

I drew in a sharp breath and all my calm serenity fled. It had been three months since I'd heard from him and although I still believed it was because of the chaos of the final days of war, I was consumed by fear. I shook my head, tears in my eyes.

'I could reach out to Don Silvio and ask for his help in finding him. He'd do it for us, for old time's sake.'

'No.' I grasped her hand and squeezed it in thanks. 'I wouldn't do that to you. And I don't want to ask him for another favour. We're even now.'

'What will you do, then?'

'Stefano will come home to me. I'm sure of it.'

'You made it,' said Paola, smiling broadly as she arrived at the top of the rise where we waited. 'What do you think?' She stood beside us as we looked over the thick, golden crop of wheat, waving in the breeze: Paola's crop.

'It should be a good harvest,' I said. She was a successful woman in a man's world and I was so proud of all she had achieved. I hoped that one day my daughter would stay true to herself, just like Nonna, Zia, Paola and I had.

She nodded, beaming with pride. 'Come and have a closer look.'

Even with the distractions of everyday life, not knowing where Stefano was had become a constant ache in my heart. Only the demands of a small baby kept me sane. Carla took all my attention and was the focus of almost every waking moment. But between her night feeds, I would sink into a deep, dreamless sleep, making the most of the few hours' rest before her cries would wake me again. And so, I was surprised to find myself dreaming that night.

I was on the farm, sitting on the hillside overlooking Bruzzano and the river, with the azure sea beyond. I should have been relaxed but I was anxious and nervous. I was looking after the sheep for Vincenzo but was I waiting for Stefano to appear on the road below. Papà and Vincenzo walked towards me, pushing the sheep along to the fresh green grass nearby. Papà passed me some bread and a bottle of wine. The touch of his hand was warm and I could smell the tobacco from his pipe on his coat. He and Vincenzo sat and we talked and ate, like we had no cares in the world. Then Vincenzo pointed to the road below and I saw a figure walking along it. My heart pounded in my chest, hoping it was Stefano, but as he got closer, I realised that it was Massimo. 'He's watching over him,' said Vincenzo. 'Stop worrying,' said Papà. 'Everything will work out well . . . your greatest work has just begun.' Suddenly Carla was in my arms and Papà and Vincenzo touched her tiny face in blessing.

I woke to my daughter's cries but, somehow, I felt calm and rested. I sent a silent prayer of thanks to Massimo, who I felt sure was watching over Stefano as he made his way home to me. I wished with all my heart that I could have spent a few more minutes with Papà and Vincenzo, but I knew that they were with me always.

I recognised the handwriting as soon as Signora Lipari handed the letter to me. It took all my will not to rush away and tear open the envelope immediately. It was only in the privacy of my bedroom that I carefully pulled out the sheet of paper.

16th July, 1945.
Mia cara moglie, My darling wife.
How wonderful that we have a healthy baby girl! Carla Vittoria is a beautiful and fitting name for her. Our daughter will always be free to live the life she wants and in an Italy free from war. I'm so sorry that I wasn't able to be there for you through the pregnancy and at the birth. But you are my brave, strong, fierce wife and I always knew that you'd manage with your family around you. I wish I was with you now to kiss our baby daughter and to hold you in my arms and tell you how much I love you. I've never wanted anything so much in all my life than to be with you both.

I pray you receive this letter because it seems that you haven't received some of mine. I've read and reread each of yours and I'm so desperately sorry that we left each other the way we did. I regret the way I told you about Livorno and

I understand why you were so furious with me. I promised you that we would make every decision together and I know how capable you are of looking after yourself, but I never imagined how terrified I would be at the thought of you and our child in such danger. I should have talked it through with you.

I'm glad that you've forgiven me. I've thought of little else but you and our baby through these months of endless hardship and sorrow. The casualties never stopped coming through the doors and the surgeries were constant, day in and day out. Of course, there were many who died on the table and those were our most difficult days.

The hospital has only just become decommissioned, the remaining patients sent on to hospitals closer to their homes. I've managed to get a lift back to Roma with members of my surgical team. I was grateful to be with Allied soldiers, as violence has erupted in the north, locals and partisans taking vengeance on any remaining Fascists or those supporting the Social Republic and Germans. The truth is I can't wait to get home. I'll send this letter before I finish things up with the army and then I'll be on my way. Angelina and Sister Rosaria send their love and congratulations too. They both miss you.

You are my everything and I can't wait to begin our life together properly. I've arranged my journey home. I'm taking the train from Roma to Napoli and then will find my way from there. I'll be with you soon.

All my love,

Your husband,

Stefano.

I pressed the letter against my heart and began to cry tears of relief and joy. He was coming home.

Not long after, Teresa, Paola, Rosa and I were walking through the piazza after Mass, the children racing ahead to get to the fountain. It had been a special Mass in thanks of the end of the war, to give thanks for our victory and to pray for our men still making their way home; men like Stefano. I was overjoyed that he was safe and coming home but I still didn't know when.

The morning was already stifling. Mamma, Zia Francesca and Nonna lagged behind in the cool of the shade, chatting to the women in headscarfs, too many wearing black, who milled outside the church while Antonio and Santoro stopped to talk to Signora Lipari's son.

'I can't believe that the war is finally over,' said Teresa, shielding her eyes against the sun as she watched Nicolo, Enrica, Bruno and Pepe run across the cobblestones. She held little Emilio's hand firmly as he tried to pull away to join his siblings and cousin, while Enzo remained by Rosa's side.

'I never thought it was going to end,' said Rosa. 'How many men were lost?' She stifled the sob that rose to her lips and Enzo's arms went around her.

'It's alright, Mamma,' he whispered. He was a sensitive child, only two years old when his father had died.

'I'm fine,' said Rosa quickly, kissing the top of his head.

My heart squeezed with anguish for their loss and my arms tightened around Carla, praying that she would never have to grow up without her father.

'Come on, Enzo, let's go to the fountain with the others,' said Paola, taking the four-year-old's hand. 'It's time to cool down and have some fun.'

Teresa put her arm around Rosa and squeezed her shoulder in quiet sympathy. There was nothing any of us could say to bring Vincenzo back. But Emilio took that moment to wriggle free from Teresa's grasp and run towards the children.

'Nicolo!' Teresa called to her oldest, now eight years old. 'Wait for Emilio.'

Nicolo stopped and turned his dark head towards us as Emilio's chubby legs pumped as fast as they could to reach his beloved brother. We watched, each of us holding our breath that he wouldn't fall, until he was holding Nicolo's hand and they were walking together across the uneven cobblestones to join Paola and the other children at the fountain. Shrieks of joy and laughter filled the air as Paola and the children splashed in the shallow water.

'We have to pray that something like this never happens again,' I said, kissing Carla's forehead and smoothing her mass of dark hair. Our children were precious, I understood that even more now. And we had to ensure that their future was bright, in a place free from war and conflict, a place where they could grow up in peace and would never have to go to war.

All Carla and I needed now was for Stefano to come home, so that our lives could be whole once more.

Every day I waited for Stefano to return, my eyes darting to shifting shadows and unexpected movements, straining to hear the familiar footfall of my husband. But life had to go on and with Carla now a few months old, I returned to the clinic for a handful of hours each day.

I was helping Nonna in the dispensary while little Carla was sleeping when the front door opened.

'Giulia?'

I'd know that voice anywhere. I dropped the pestle into the mortar and rushed from the room. A silhouette stood in the doorway.

'Oddio! You're really here,' I said as I launched myself into Stefano's arms. He was home – haggard, thin and dirty from the road, but he was happy, healthy and mine.

36

I stared at the envelope on my lap. It was addressed to me, the familiar script making my heart wrench with longing, but the stamps with the former British King's head that lined the right-hand corner still seemed strange and out of place. I squeezed my eyes shut for just a moment and took a deep breath to calm my nerves but still my hands shook as I opened the letter nestled inside.

My dearest Giulia,
I've made the decision to stay. I've saved enough money for you and the children to join me and I don't want to be without you any longer.

My hand flew to my mouth and I sagged into the chair, glad I'd chosen the privacy of my bedroom to read this long-awaited letter. Carla, Luisa, Francesco and Luca were with Paola on the farm and I had a few precious moments to myself between the end of the morning clinic and lunch at Mamma's. Nonna had finally retired and now lived with Paola and Mamma while the children and I lived in Nonna's house.

> *You know it's for the best. We've tried everything else, but at the end of the day we both want our children, our family, to have a good life. Without the money I send home each month, you wouldn't be able to manage. We want a brighter future for them, a future where they don't have to struggle to put food in their mouths and warm clothes on their backs . . .*

Life in Calabria had changed little since the war. Making a living on the land was harder than ever and poverty was still rife. Calabria had suffered terrible natural disasters, crippling drought and destructive floods, and the south had plunged even further into economic decline, hardship and destitution. Villages damaged by the floods were abandoned and slowly rebuilt on the coast, including Brancaleone, now located at the marina. Our farm had been no different. Despite Paola's best efforts to modernise and diversify her crops and produce, we couldn't escape the droughts and floods. So many, like Antonio, had left for the opportunities of the northern cities where there was work and regular wages, and others had emigrated to countries on the other side of the world, including America, Canada and Australia. Teresa, Santoro and their five children were among them.

Zia Francesca still ran her trattoria and Rosa remained at the grocery store and lived in the flat above with her two boys. Don Silvio had passed away from a heart attack not long after the end of the war and while I was saddened by the news, choosing to remember his kindness, Zia Francesca had been inconsolable.

Nonna had been training Roberto Lipari, and he worked as my assistant now and we hoped that soon he'd go to Fra Fortunato to complete his studies. But over the years my work had been drying up. A new doctor from Roma had been assigned to the district and it was hard to compete with penicillin. Still, Nonna and I had visited the monastery almost every year.

Mamma helped Rosa with the boys and looked after my children when I was working in the clinic. Antonio worked as a merchant, living between Roma and Reggio, selling and distributing regional products, such as our olives and olive oil, our cheeses and salami. He worked with Paola to develop her cheeses and other produce, believing that the unique Calabrese food could become a star of Italy, and even become some of our best exports, sought after around the world. He and Angelina had married and he'd become deeply involved in politics, agitating for social and economic change in Italy. He kept assuring me that things were improving in the south, but still nothing had really changed.

I thought of the days after the war when Stefano had returned. They'd been filled with hope and joy – it was a time of new beginnings, or so we thought. We hadn't been able to afford for Stefano to return to university to complete his studies or even to move to Messina like we'd planned and, with a new baby, he'd had no desire to be parted from us again. So we'd stayed and he'd helped Paola on the farm, learning the art of cheesemaking. It was wonderful for Carla to grow up around her family and after everything we'd all been through, staying seemed the best thing to do.

But with the withdrawal of the Allied forces from Italian shores, the true extent of Italy's failing economy and growing inflation had become apparent. Sponsored by America, the Marshall Plan gave economic aid to Italy. I'd seen the posters – 'You too, can be like us' – but I doubted Italians would ever have the lifestyle of Americans, especially here in Calabria.

I took a deep breath to steady myself as I thought through the implications of leaving. Teresa and her family were settled and happy in America. They'd been there nearly four years now and I still missed her so much. Saying goodbye had been the most painful thing, and I didn't know if I could do it to my mother and sister all over again.

'How many memories are in this room?' Teresa had whispered on our last night together, lying on her old bed with Rosa. She'd come to say goodbye to her childhood home and Paola, Rosa and I had joined her before she left for Messina and the boat to America.

Lying next to Paola as I had so many nights through my childhood and youth, I stared up at the ceiling, its paint cracked and peeling. I rubbed my tummy absently, the tiny kicks under my hand reassuring, and made a mental note to tell Stefano that it was time to repaint the house.

'We've been through just about every emotion in this room,' I murmured. 'Joy, elation, desperation, sadness, grief . . . but we've been through it together and I know that I'd never have been able to cope without you all by my side.'

We lay there silently for a time before Paola said, 'What about before your wedding, Teresa? The night before Giulia went to the monastery. You tried on your wedding dress and we looked through your trousseau. You looked like an angel. And then we snuck out into the dining room and ate sugared almonds.'

'Sometimes I wish, if only for a moment, that I'd had your courage to stand up and do something different with my life, maybe work up north in one of the fashion houses, before I married and had children,' said Teresa. 'And your bravery, Paola, to defy Papà and stay here to do what you love.'

Paola and I shared a look. She looked as shocked as I felt. I'd spent all these years believing that marriage and life in the village was what Teresa had wanted. 'But you are strong and brave too, taking this step of going to America to give your family a better life,' I said to her. 'I can't imagine doing what you're doing.'

'Sometimes I wonder how I could leave you all, leave this town and Calabria,' she said, tears welling in her eyes. 'It's all I've ever known, but then I think of the children and their future, I think of the strength that each of you have and I know that I can be strong too, that I can take that leap of faith into an unknown future.'

'You're all women who've always known what you've wanted,' said Rosa. 'I admire that. I feel that Pepe and Enzo are the only things that anchor me now. I am lost without your brother and, although I've had a few proposals, I can't imagine marrying again.'

'There are definite benefits to being a widow,' I murmured.

'I know,' said Rosa sadly. 'I look at Zia Francesca and how happy she is with the trattoria, doing what she loves. And even Nonna Mariana, working the clinic all these years. I hope to be like that someday, but I'm not sure that I have their strength to do it on my own.'

'You're never alone, Rosa,' said Paola, turning onto her side to look across to the other bed. 'You'll always have us, no matter where we are. We're sisters, and sisters stick together.'

The four of us hugged and cried, as if it were the last time we'd ever be like this. Perhaps it would be.

Then the floods came: the worst in living memory, displacing whole towns and villages, leaving thousands homeless and crippling the region. The floods began like any other year, heavy autumn rains drenching the eastern side of the Aspromonte, flowing into streams and rivers that swelled and rushed towards the Ionian Sea. It was 1951 and I'd not long had our third child, Francesco. We were receiving twice our usual rainfall for October and it was too wet to go anywhere so the clinic was closed while Stefano was helping Paola move the sheep to shelter. The children and I watched the Bruzzano River from our kitchen window as it became swollen. I wondered how other towns and villages along the larger rivers that began high in the mountains were faring.

'I've tried everything, but we won't make enough money to support all of us,' said Stefano one night after the flood waters receded, following a meagre dinner of watery stew. He ran a hand through his hair. The farm had to support Mamma, Paola, Nonna and us and the three children. We'd lost the wheat and hadn't been able to sow a new crop; there'd be no harvest the following year. If we didn't have wheat, we couldn't mill flour, bake bread or make pasta. The surplus had always been sold for a reasonable price, which helped keep the farm running and maintained and paid an income to Paola and Mamma as well as Stefano. The olives, clementines and bergamot were all damaged and we had barely enough feed for the sheep.

'The agriculture sector's in ruins in Calabria. I'll have to leave to find work elsewhere, but not Reggio or Messina, there'll be no work there, especially after this.'

I knew he was serious. Stefano didn't say things lightly and I could see by his slumped shoulders how hard it was for him to accept we had little choice if he was to provide for his family.

I sighed and nodded, sitting heavily beside him. 'I wondered if the day would come when we'd leave Bruzzano. Maybe this is the push we needed. We always dreamed of living and working in a big city. I know you haven't been really happy here and you're not able to fulfil your potential. I'm not seeing as many patients as I once was and I think it's only going to get worse. It's hard to compete with modern medicine and the new drugs.' I paused, gathering my thoughts. 'We could move north to Roma with Antonio and Angelina or to Milano, where we both could get good paying jobs. Then we could save enough for you to finish university and resume your career in medicine. We could still get back to see your father and Mamma and Nonna from time to time. None of them are getting any younger.'

'If we went north, we'd never be able to give the children the childhood we want for them, the childhood we had, with plenty of space and freedom to roam and explore.' He grasped my hand, warm and reassuring. 'What if we followed your sister to the United States or . . . what if we went somewhere like Australia?'

'Australia?' I repeated, shocked.

Stefano nodded. 'I've stayed in touch with a couple of the medics from Australia that I worked with during the war. I always found their stories of home intriguing. Apparently, Australia is looking for migrants. There's plenty of work, the climate is similar to here and, with their wide-open spaces, land is cheap and easy to buy.'

'Don't be ridiculous,' I said faintly, feeling sick to my stomach. We couldn't leave Italy. This was our home; we'd fought so hard for our country and the dream of a better life for our children.

'My friends have urged us to come. We'd be able to save money more quickly and be in a better position for me to finally finish my degree while still giving the children the life we want for them. It makes sense.'

I was stunned. Teresa had told us how difficult it was to go to America with the restricted quotas for Italian immigrants. They'd been on the list for so long before they'd received a visa.

'What choice do we have?' The look of anguish on his face nearly broke my heart.

I nodded. He was right and our own family came first. 'Amore mio, I want to see you happy, with the chance to reach your full potential. Medicine's as much a part of you as healing is a part of me. I could never imagine not practising. And it's time you did what you love too.' I took a deep breath to steel myself. If Teresa could do this, then so could I.

'If Australia's as good as you say, it could give us the life we've dreamed of. Who knows, perhaps I can study further and one day we'll open up that clinic where we can work together.'

'It will be good for us, I know it,' Stefano whispered. He cupped the back of my head, pulling me towards him as he kissed me deeply.

But he'd come home crestfallen from Reggio not long after. Assisted passage to Australia was only available to young single men, not to families. We'd have to pay for our passage and there was no way we could afford for all of us to go. Luckily, Stefano was able to get a sponsor in Australia, one of his father's relatives, who had lived in Sydney for the last twenty years. And there was a job as well, in the Postmaster General's Department. He was told that he could finish his studies in Australia too.

'What if you go on your own and take the job?' I'd asked. 'See what you think of Australia and, if you believe we'd be better off there, we'll save as much money as we can between us until we can afford for me and the children to join you. Maybe then you can go to university, finish medicine and become a doctor.'

He raised his head, his forehead furrowed with denial. 'No,' he said emphatically, shaking his head. 'No, it's out of the question.'

I rested my hand over his. 'Stefano, our situation's not likely to change for some time. The longer we leave it, the harder it will be to get ahead. This is an opportunity for a better future for all of us, and I think we have to take it. If it's not what we hope for, you can come back home and we'll look at other options.'

'Mannaggia! I won't leave you again,' he said, his voice ragged.

'I don't think we have much choice,' I whispered.

'I made you a promise . . .'

'I won't say I'll like being apart, but you'll be doing it for us, for our future.' Tears filled my eyes. I couldn't believe I was telling him to go, but I'd learnt to be strong. And although I knew how hard it would be on my own with the children, we'd manage.

He stared at me, refusal and disbelief turning into realisation. 'You really want to do this?'

'I think we have to.' It was the hardest thing I had ever said but I'd known in my heart that it was right.

Being separated from you and from the children has been more difficult than I ever imagined and yet, I'd do it all again because this is a country where we can be happy and the children can thrive. We have a future in Australia. Although my studies haven't been recognised and I haven't yet been able to afford to go back to university to begin my medical degree again, I've saved enough money to buy a plot of land, ten acres on the outskirts of Sydney. It's enough to build a house on with a clinic for you, a vegetable garden that will provide us with an extra income and lots of room for the children to run around. If you agree, I'll go ahead and buy it and make sure the house is ready for when you and the children arrive. I know how much you'll miss your family so when we've saved more, we can bring your mother and Nonna Mariana out to visit us and, if they want, to stay.

Please say you'll come soon, Topolina. I can't wait to be with you and the children any longer. Being apart from you breaks my heart. I want to begin a new life with you by my side. Whatever we encounter, we'll be together.

I put the letter down. I'd prayed to the Madonna to bring my husband home. I'd hoped that we'd find a way to stay in Italy but I knew in my heart that this day would come. Stefano and I were always destined to leave Bruzzano, I just hadn't thought it would be to a place so far away. I remembered Papà's words from my dream. My greatest work was to give my children the best future I could. Australia was our future. It was exciting and I couldn't wait to be reunited with Stefano but I would always carry a sadness and longing for my homeland, for Calabria and its rugged mountains and hills and the sparkling waters of the Ionian Sea.

'When do you leave?' asked Agata as we walked with Mother Superior along the path between the Stations of the Cross. It was a beautiful summer's day, the vibrant green of the forest softening the sharp angles of the Aspromonte as the mountain peaks rose into the air and jutted against the vivid blue sky.

'In about a month.' Little Luca would be nearly a year old when his father would see him for the first time; I'd fallen pregnant just before Stefano had left.

'We'll miss you,' Mother Superior said, squeezing my hand.

I stopped and gazed into her face. She was old now and we both knew that this would be the last time we'd ever see each other. I blinked the tears away. 'And I'll miss you too. You've given me so much over the years and I can never thank you enough for that.' I gazed at the mountains that had seen thousands come and go, watched the stories of the pilgrims unfold over the years and had witnessed the depths of human emotion within this most sacred of sanctuaries. I thought about my own journey from the naïve young girl, a daughter of Calabria, to the woman of Italy I'd become. 'I wouldn't have achieved everything I've done without your wisdom and guidance.'

'Oh, Giulia, you've always had a passion for life, a thirst for knowledge and the strength of will to reach for your dreams. You only needed to know how to harness your talents and recognise the strength within you.'

'I don't feel so strong now. How can I leave all of this behind? Calabria's my home, it's in my blood . . .' The herb garden blurred with the beech and oak trees as my tears finally fell.

Agata hugged me tight and I felt her tremble too.

'You're stronger than you know. Ask the Madonna for guidance and help,' she said through her tears.

I nodded. The Madonna had granted me my heart's desire. I was a herbalist and healer like my nonna, I was married to a man I loved and we had four beautiful and healthy children. I'd forged my own path through life, despite the expectations of a traditional community, and I was respected for the choices I'd made. Now it was time for a new chapter, to create a new path for myself and my children.

'The Madonna understands,' I said, feeling resolute once more. 'Women will do anything for their children, make the most impossible decisions and endure terrible heartache for their wellbeing. I know we'll have a better life in Australia and it's the right thing for our family, but Calabria and those who have shaped me to become the woman I now am will always remain in my heart.'

Waving goodbye to Mamma, Nonna, Paola, Rosa, Zia Francesca and the boys as the *Sydney* pulled away from the dock in Messina was the hardest thing I'd ever had to do. Tears filled my eyes as I tried to imprint their faces on my mind. Carla, Luisa and Francesco hopped from foot to foot as they waved impatiently. They were excited and couldn't wait to explore the boat. They didn't understand that it would be a long time before we saw any of our family again. A sob exploded from my throat. I'd never imagined leaving my homeland, but as I hugged Luca tight and inhaled his sweet baby smell, it felt like I was cutting the cord between mother and newborn child.

It was only when my family became small, indistinguishable figures in the distance that I pulled the photo from my pocket with a trembling hand. I gazed at Stefano beaming with pride and excitement, standing on the block of land he'd bought, eucalyptus trees in the background. This was the future, our future.

I pressed his beloved face to my lips and turned towards the horizon, where I knew Stefano and Australia waited and where our new life would begin.

Author's note

A few years ago, I discovered an old black and white photo I'd never seen before on my father's fridge, of a young man in military uniform. He looked so much like my father it was uncanny and I knew it had to be my grandfather. I was surprised to see him in uniform as I'd been told that he was exempt from serving during World War Two. When I asked my father about it, he dropped this intriguing nugget of information: that his father had fought in the Royal Italian Army in the Italian wars with Abyssinia (Ethiopia) and Albania prior to World War Two. I had never imagined that my Nonno, a quiet and reserved man, had done anything quite so exotic as going to Africa or had fought in wars prior to WW2. It sparked my imagination and I began to wonder what his life as a young man had been like. How leaving his small village and the farm he ran in the very south of Italy to fight in foreign countries may have changed his perspective of the world. Maybe it had given him the courage to leave for Australia many years later, to find a better life for his family. I suddenly realised that there was so much more to him that I hadn't known. Sadly, both my grandparents passed away before I was old enough to think to ask them about their lives.

My love of family stories has been with me since I can remember. On my mother's side I have the big stories from my German grandmother and her meticulously kept documentation, photos and mementoes. But on my father's side I have only a few photos and the small snippets of stories, a series of moments which explain what life must have been like in Italy around the war years, much like a series of snapshots. When I was young, I found it hard to communicate with both my grandparents as neither spoke English well. But it was in the small things that they showed how much they cared. The snippets of story come from my father and his sister, but also from my own memories of stories my uncle told when I was young and in my memories of my grandparents.

My Nonno was a wonderful cheesemaker, a skill he perfected while on the farm in Italy, and always made the best ricotta. Some of my favourite childhood memories are of eating his creamy, soft, fresh ricotta drizzled with honey straight from the honeycomb. It was better than any dessert. He and Nonna kept a market garden on their ten acres on the outskirts of Sydney and I remember picking crisp young cucumbers straight from the stalk in the summer, along the long rows of vegetables. They were the most crunchy, beautiful cucumbers I've ever eaten. And the big red tomatoes hidden amongst the foliage, ready to be picked and sold on the side of the road, had the most heady fragrance. There was never any question about the sensational flavour that would burst into your mouth the moment you bit into them.

I'd heard the story that my Nonna had remained in Italy for a few years with her four remaining children, managing the farm, until my Nonno saved enough money for them to join him and my two uncles in Australia. I always wondered how she managed on her own, what a strong and resourceful woman she must have been. She was the one who brought the family together, she was the heart of the family, cooking for hours on a Sunday, when all the family visited. The food was always plentiful, aunts gathering around the stove, and I remember the mouth-watering pasta dishes, the fried zippoli, both sardine and plain, crostoli dusted with icing sugar that disappeared as quickly as they were fried, the variety of soups, vegetable dishes, salads and the rice pudding and fresh homemade bread. It was a delight for the senses as much as a feast for the stomach.

My childhood memories of my Nonna are sadly few. But I remember she had this wonderful old Singer sewing machine with the foot pedal and I knew she could sew almost anything you could imagine. The smell of the first pot of coffee on the stove of a morning shortly after dawn always woke me whenever I stayed over. I'd sometimes sit with her on the back verandah as she brushed her long, wavy, salt and pepper hair, watched her braid it with nimble fingers and wind the plaits over the top of her head, before walking with her down the back to milk the cow. My father told me that people often came to see her to seek help for minor ailments; babies with colic, adults with headaches among many other things. She used old folk remedies and he told me that she performed cupping, where a candle or flame is placed under a glass and when extinguished the glass is put on someone's back, creating suction to help with their respiratory or other complaint. She also cured people of the 'evil eye'. Somehow all this didn't surprise me and I wondered if in the recesses of my childhood memories, I'd seen her tend to people who needed her help. I used to play a game with my sister and younger cousins when we were at our grandparents' place where we had to gather herbs from the 'wilds' around us (weeds and grasses), to treat pretend injuries and to cook for our dinner. Many years later this crystallised into a love for herbal medicine and already a physiotherapist, I completed my herbal medicine diploma. This was all, of course, the inspiration for Giulia's and Nonna Mariana's characters. My nonna had limited schooling and was illiterate although very good with numbers and evidently incredibly intelligent. She regularly travelled across Sydney to see her newly married daughter, using two buses and two trains without any English. Like Giulia, I always wonder what she might have done if she'd had the opportunities to study further.

Much of *Daughter of Calabria* is fictional, a figment of my imagination, but my family stories weave through the fabric of the novel, as I've tried to paint a picture of what life might have been like for the people in the remote villages and farming communities of southern Calabria in and around the war years, just like my grandparents. I was fascinated to explore how they lived, how they might have viewed the various wars, Mussolini's Fascist regime, World War Two, the Allied invasion and the terrible split between north and south, as well as their views on life, the society they lived in and the world around them. I visited Bruzzano with my family, many years ago when I was thirteen and I still have wonderful memories of that time; the fabulous food, learning the language and the sense of lightness from the unhurried rhythm of life the locals lived. I'm sure you've heard the saying 'work to live, not live to work'. I planned to visit last year to touch base with family members, get more of a feel for the family stories as well as more information and to find the places that touched my soul, places I knew I had to write about. Sadly, COVID hit and all my plans went out the window. I was lucky enough to turn to my father and aunt who had been the previous year, and their stories of the people, places and food as well as the gorgeous photos gave me the initial start for my story. Researching on the internet, reading books on Mussolini's regime and documentaries on television helped me to blend my family stories, sense of place and the huge historical events that provided the background for my story, until *Daughter of Calabria* began to take shape.

I was fascinated to learn how much Calabria was affected by its geology. Surrounded by the edge of a tectonic plate, with a major fault-line running through Calabria, and within close proximity of two active volcanoes, it's a region that lives with the constant threat of earthquakes. The largest and most well known are the earthquakes of 1905 and 1908, measuring up to 7.9 on the Richter scale. The 1908 quake triggered a tsunami that destroyed much of the coast of Calabria and Sicily, damaging the cities of Reggio and Messina. I wanted to use this constant uncertainty in the story and fashioned the earthquake and tidal wave which killed Massimo after this historic event. The terrible floods of 1951 are real and were another common occurrence in southern Italy, followed by the 1953 floods. Both destroyed ancient villages and began a new wave of migration to northern Italy and overseas countries such as Australia, the United States and Canada.

I love that I've been able to honour my family through the small touches in my story. My grandparents did live in a small village on the tip of the toe of Italy during the Fascist and war years. They had a farm, one plot in the hills, one closer to the coast, and my grandfather was a cheesemaker. They did come to Australia separately, my grandfather first in 1951, followed by the two oldest sons and then my grandmother and the other four children came in 1954, followed by my oldest aunt and her family.

One of my aunts loves the farm and always wanted to create her livelihood from the farm, just like Paola. Another aunt was a fabulous dressmaker like Teresa and many of the first names I've used are in fact family names. One of my family members was the little boy who had the terrible burns on his back after an accident with boiling water on the stove, and when his mother had mastitis during the war, he was breastfed by one of the other women in the village. My father remembers his mother telling him about how afraid she was when the Allied planes flew overhead and how German soldiers came through their village just the once, lost and desperate for food. My oldest uncle's name was Santoro although we called him Santo, and he was a school teacher in Bruzzano, having studied at teacher's college in Reggio. I had to weave him and his love of history into the story. I remember as a child, listening to his stories of ancient history and of the Philistines who he joked about with me, trying to confuse me with my teacher called

Sister Philippine. He loved sharing his knowledge with others. When he was young, he wanted to become a doctor but his family couldn't afford to send him to university in Messina, Sicily. He was envious of one of his best friends who did make it to university and did medicine. My father was the first in his family to go to university, here in Australia. He did medicine and became a doctor. I had to put this passion and yearning for learning and the desire to help others that my uncle and father have, that my grandmother had and my daughter and I have too, into Giulia's and Stefano's characters.

But one of the greatest joys of looking into my father's family story has been reconnecting with family members and family friends who I haven't seen in some time. They all added to the rich fabric of my family story and to the story of *Daughter of Calabria*. They reminded me of the incredible Italian food I've had over the years, often simple but bursting with flavour, the large family gatherings, the huge celebrations, birthdays, christenings, confirmations, weddings, the love of dancing, the hypnotic music and dance of the tarantella that I've watched my aunts and uncles perform, the energy and carefree nature, women bonded together over the stove and the preparation of food, family playing cards, and the laughter and joy. I've reconnected with the best tasting pasta and sauce in the world, fresh garden salads, slow-cooked meats and meatballs, fresh bread from the bread oven and to top it off, my aunt's famous gnocchi and sauce. Pillowy, light and soft with just enough substance. And I've watched and been involved in the traditional process of salami making. It still amazes me how relatively simple and few ingredients can transform into one of the biggest flavour punches of Italian,

Calabrian cuisine. Most of all it's their generosity of spirit, the kindness of heart and big welcome of open arms that reminds me how lucky I am to have the rich culture, the lively passion and deep love of my Italian family.

I know I've only just scratched the surface of what Calabria and its people are all about. There's so much more to delve into: the wild landscapes, the vibrant and passionate people, the ancient and tumultuous history, the mixing pot of cultures that has become quintessentially Calabrese. I've discovered that I'm drawn to this part of the world and I can't wait to one day return to Calabria to trace my family roots, to explore what makes me feel connected to this place and perhaps bring further family stories to life.

Acknowledgements

This journey towards *Daughter of Calabria* would never have happened without my father, Domenic Martino. It was his story of his father, my grandfather, fighting with the Royal Italian Army in Abyssinia and Albania in the years before World War Two that started it all. It's been a joy to listen as my father shared his knowledge of his family, Calabria, the Italian culture and language, and the stories he heard from his parents and older siblings. This has just been the beginning of my learning about my Italian heritage and family and I look forward to continuing this journey of discovery with him. I hope this story makes him proud.

I couldn't have done this without everyone at Simon and Schuster Australia. Thank you for yet again bringing my story out into the world. I'm forever grateful for all the support and hard work in making *Daughter of Calabria* the beautiful novel it's become. From the magnificent cover with its distinct Mediterranean feel, to the sculpted, polished story and the dedicated sales and marketing programme, I couldn't be prouder of *Daughter of Calabria*. My particular thanks go to Managing Director, Dan Ruffino for his continued support and belief in me. To Commercial Publisher, Cassandra Di Bello, for her enthusiasm, encouragement and her calm and patient influence along the way and all her hard work and dedication in bringing this project together so beautifully. To Marketing and Publicity Manager Kirstin Corcoran for her effortless management of the marketing and publishing campaign and for making me feel supported every step of the way. A special thanks goes to Christa Moffitt for the gorgeous cover design, and to the Sales team who worked tirelessly to put *Daughter of Calabria* out into the world, so that I could share my story with you all. To editors extraordinaire – Kylie Mason and my mentor and friend Roberta Ivers, their insights and advice have always been what I've needed to elevate my stories to become something special. My thanks to you both for working on *Daughter of Calabria*.

To the family members and family friends I've reconnected with in the quest to learn more about my family and life in Calabria. A special thank you to my aunt, Maria Dodaro and family friends Sam and Frances Catanzariti for their generosity and kindness. I enjoyed every moment of my conversations with them and appreciated their patience as I learnt more about family stories, as I repeated recipes to make sure I got them right, asked endless questions and learnt how to make salami. Their delight at me including my children in this learning process, so that we can all hold on to and pass down family stories and cultural traditions, and ensuring that their heritage is never forgotten, is much appreciated. They've helped me understand the true essence of the Calabrian culture and way of life and have brought colour, life and authenticity to my story.

To my wonderful readers. Thank you for your ongoing support. It's been a joy and privilege to share my stories with you. I appreciate all the messages from you. Knowing that you've enjoyed my stories and that they've touched you in some way, means everything to me. Writing is a solitary task and a writer is nothing without their audience. I feel honoured that many of you have shared your own stories with me, some quite similar to my own. There's something special in the connection with you all and I feel very grateful for that. A particular thank you goes to Marcus Woehrle for sharing his amazing family stories with me. They helped especially in putting together the background information around the time the Allies invaded Sicily and Giulia's Ethiopian candlesticks come from his stories of his Nonna. Thank you too to Ingrid Burggraf for her stories of her father's dealings with the Allies in Italy during WW2. They helped me get a sense of the feeling between the Allies, Italians and the prisoners of war.

I couldn't have written this book in such a tight timeframe without the support, belief, nurturing and love of my family. Despite not always being able to see each other in person during the pandemic, their interest in whatever stage I was at in the writing process whenever we spoke, kept me buoyant and helped me to push on. Their encouragement when I had a mountain of work ahead of me, their patience when I worked through a problem in the story with them or explained historical background enthusiastically and their cheering when I'd made the next deadline, made all the difference. My children and husband continue to be my greatest supporters and it makes my heart swell with pride when they talk to others about my books or join me in reconnecting with family and friends, making salami and listening to stories about Calabria. I feel so blessed that my kids want to know about their heritage and that my husband does it all for me.

Working from home has been challenging for everyone since the pandemic hit and there was a time last year when all five of us were studying and working fulltime under one roof. Even now with my husband and daughter still home much more than before, we've had to adjust to the new working from home dynamics but I'm so thankful for the space, quiet and consideration they've given me to write each day. The extra help with school drop offs and pick ups, hot coffee on my desk each morning and lunch prepared for me most days have been an absolute luxury. I'm not sure I'll ever be able to go back to working in a silent house on my own! It's been a bit like being in a cocoon while writing *Daughter of Calabria* – safe, nurtured, focused on the writing and surrounded by those I love most in all the world. Italians have such a strong sense of family and the lives of most Calabrians revolve around their families. Writing this story has reminded me how important family is to me and I'm blessed to have my family safe, well and so close and my immediate family still under one roof. I know I'll treasure that for as long as I can.

Reading group questions

1. What do you think Giulia's life would have been like when she came to Australia?

2. How does the dynamic between siblings, Giulia with her two sisters and two brothers affect their view of the world? How does it affect their own lives?

3. How do Andrea's expectations and the traditional community they live in affect Giulia's behaviour and decisions? How do you think you'd cope in her shoes?

4. How do the women in Giulia's life help her become the woman that she is?

5. How does the relationship between Giulia and her father change over time?

6. Do you think that Giulia loved Massimo despite being forced into an arranged marriage? What do you think the benefits of an arranged marriage might be?

7. What are the differences between Giulia's relationships with Massimo and with Stefano? If Giulia had a choice, who do you think she should choose?

8. How did the war shape Giulia's attitudes and her future?

9. What do you think the particular challenges would have been in the relationship/marriage between Giulia and Stefano?

10. What are your family stories about life in Australia? Did your family immigrate after World War Two? How did they adjust to life here?

About the author

Tania Blanchard writes historical fiction inspired by her family history. She grew up listening to her grandparents' fascinating tales of life during World War Two and migrating to Australia. Coming from a family with rich cultural heritage, stories have always been in her blood. Her first novel, *The Girl from Munich*, was a runaway bestseller and shortlisted for the ABIA Best New Writer Award. Tania lives in Sydney with her husband and three children where she can often be found in the kitchen, cooking up a storm for her family, including her two cheeky dogs who think they're human too.

To find out more, sign up to Tania's newsletter at
www.taniablanchard.com.au
or follow her at:
www.facebook.com/TaniaBlanchardAuthor
www.instagram.com/taniablanchardauthor